Blackfoot

The Two Monarchies Sequence

Book Two

W.R. Gingell

Blackfoot

By W.R. Gingell

Cover by Seedlings Design Studio

With thanks to God; who brought me out, piece by piece, from
my own castle of confusion and dread.

ONE

Annabel was quite sure she remembered being born. Peter said that was rubbish, but Peter was always inclined to think that no one was quite as special or clever as he was. Annabel remembered the worried faces bent over her in her mother's arms, and the long, clever, brown face that came later, when all the others had gone. The clever brown one tied a sparkling rattle to a thread around her wrist and went away, and after that the rest of the faces looked less worried. They wouldn't let her take the rattle off, even when she cried for hours on end. By the time she was two, Annabel was used to the tug of thread about her wrist and the tinkling of the rattle when she moved. The only time it was silent was when she held it under the water in the bath.

When she was old enough to know the faces around her as Father, Mother, and Cookie, Annabel was allowed out into the garden to walk, her tiny silver rattle tinkling at her wrist. It was understood that this was a Great Privilege, and that Annabel was Not To Wander Off.

Annabel didn't mean to wander off. The thread around

her wrist had seen one too many baths and was brittle and tenuous. Cookie had looked at it that morning and declared that it would have to be changed that afternoon, which made Annabel sigh. It was always such a business, changing the thread. Father had to be there to carefully snip it with with silver scissors, and Mother had to be there to thread the new one through the eyelet at the end of the rattle. Cookie stood by the chair each time to hold Annabel's wrist with one pudgy hand, and the rattle with the other. It was the only time that Annabel saw the worry come back into her parent's faces.

The thread was woolly and loose when she was let into the garden. Annabel spun the rattle between her fingers without thinking about it, and the sound of bells followed her as she walked, so familiar that she no longer heard it. It wasn't until she was at the decorative fountain that a queer kind of silence fell on her ears and she realised with a nasty lurch of her stomach that the thread was gone.

Annabel gave a small squeak of dismay and pressed two plump fists to her mouth. She was never sure what was supposed to happen if the rattle came off, but it had been implied that its loss would lead to Terrible Things. She made a frantic dash back the way she had come, her eyes scanning the ground for the silver gleam that would give it away.

She wasn't quite sure when she noticed the difference. It could have been when she tumbled over a ragged clump of grass (Father made sure the lawn was scythed every third day), or it could have been the sudden, horrible chill in the air (home was always warm), and the smell of something unfamiliar in the air. Annabel picked herself up carefully, a tear trembling at the edge of her left eye, and as carefully stood still until the tear went away. Then she looked around her. The sky was darker than it had been, and Annabel, who hadn't yet begun to learn about the cycles of the triad, was confused. Why did the suns look so odd in the sky? Had she fallen asleep? Had the afternoon passed to dusk while she was sleeping? Was she, perhaps, like the Sleeping Princess?

No, she decided. She had been awake the whole time. That meant magic. Annabel trotted onward, her brown eyes studious and her chubby cheeks pinked by the chill, until she found that she was stuck. She couldn't see what she was stuck in and the ground was just ground, so she decided that was magic, too.

Annabel was still stuck in the enchantment when a witch came along to prod and her and chuckle gleefully.

"Oho, you're a fine specimen!" said the witch. "What a fine fish for my net!"

"Not a fish," said Annabel, biting her lower lip. Tears were threatening again– proper tears, this time, and she didn't at all like the looks of the witch.

"No, but you're a tasty little trifle just the same," said the witch. "Who would have thought that Old Grenna would pull such a plump little morsel! How have you escaped the clutches of every wizard this side of the Ice Wall?"

This didn't make sense to Annabel, so she said again, cautiously: "Not a fish."

"No, dearie," said the witch. "Not a fish. Certainly not a fish. Come along with you: it's bread-and-butter time."

"And that was it," said Annabel, plopping herself down on a half-block of marble. She and Peter had sneaked away to the old Ruins, the skeleton of a grand castle that had been their playground since the day they first met there. "That's all I remember."

"Yes," said Peter, "But that's just a dream, Ann. You know it didn't really happen that way."

Annabel looked at him without blinking, her chin perched on her plump fists.

"But it didn't, Ann! It couldn't have! If you had a cook and gardeners, that would have to mean that your parents were nobles, at the very least!"

"I don't know about that," said Annabel, "but I remember. They're not just dreams."

"You've been with Old Grenna for as long as I can remember. You were sitting in on her spells when you were four. People don't remember things that long ago."

"I know Old Grenna isn't my mother," Annabel said positively.

"Anyone with a lick of sense knows *that*," said Peter. "She's a thin old stick and you're as fat as butter. Goodness knows which cradle she pinched you from. I just said you've been with her for as long as I can remember."

Another time, Annabel would have asked why his remembrance was any more to be trusted than hers, but it was a pleasant, sunny, and not-too-cold day, and it was too much effort. Besides, Peter had brought sweets and hadn't yet shared. Instead, she said: "What are you working on, anyway?"

"One of the tickerboxes has started cannibalising the others," said Peter. He had the little black box on its back with its jointed legs stiff and curved above it. There was a tiny hatch open on its stomach, which Peter was prodding at doubtfully with an equally tiny screwdriver. Annabel could just see moving clockwork in layers, *tick tick tick*ing away as he worked at it. "I wouldn't mind, only I want to know *why*. I didn't program it to do that. I think it's building something from the pieces."

"What things?"

Peter shrugged and hunched his shoulders over his work. "Something different. Extra parts for itself. I don't know what." There was an irritated line between his straight brows that Annabel perfectly understood. Peter didn't like not understanding things. He liked to think that he knew everything. "Ann, tell your cat to leave my cog pieces alone!"

"He's not my cat," said Annabel, but she scooped Blackfoot up anyway. He bit her nose gently and let her pat his head.

"I don't understand what you see in that cat," grumbled Peter.

"That's because he scratches you."

"Did you notice that another one's turned up?"

"Yes," said Annabel. She'd seen the second cat yesterday, a small ginger thing slinking around the edges of the Ruins. Blackfoot had arrived first, five years ago, and sat scratching at her shutters each night until she finally gave up and let him in. Annabel was entirely disinterested in cats, but it wasn't long before Blackfoot was sleeping on her pillow by sheer force of personality.

"Well, stop attracting them. One's bad enough."

She tickled Blackfoot's ears. "Maybe it's an invasion."

"You can't call two cats an invasion," said Peter, always willing for an argument. "Pass the magnifier."

Annabel went back to Grenna's cottage by the long way that afternoon, Blackfoot trotting along behind her. In theory, she disliked any path that made her walk further than she had to, but Grenna had sent her out that morning in search of lillypilly berries and water from the old well, which meant that there was magic happening that afternoon. And magic meant that Annabel would be sitting for hours, stiff and crosslegged, on cold, hard flagstones. Grenna would draw chalk lines on the stones around her, mix ingredients, and mumble. Then the magic would start up, but Annabel never quite knew when, so it was always safer to keep her hands tightly folded in her lap. She only knew when it was over because Grenna told her so, smudging out lines and dismissing her irritably to her room. By then, Annabel would be exhausted. She sometimes hoped this meant that she had done magic along with Grenna, but none of the spells she tried by herself had ever worked, and Annabel had come to think of herself as merely one more of Grenna's ingredients.

Annabel arrived at the cottage as the triad was making long, late afternoon shadows from the hedgerows. The lillypilly berries were in her apron pocket, slightly squashed, and a tiny, leather-covered glass flask sloshed with water from the old well. Annabel had collected them before she met Peter in the Old Ruins, and they were rather the worse for wear.

She stopped at the gate while Blackfoot leapt lightly through the bars, and then quite deliberately rubbed a handful of dirt across the side of her face. Blackfoot stopped and sat on his haunches, staring accusingly as Annabel pulled a handful of hair from her plait and let it flop messily on her shoulder.

"Oh, shut up!" she told him crossly, wiping the last of the dirt on the front of her pinafore. It was faded, but it had been clean this morning. She carefully slumped her shoulders, hunching them forward and frowning at the dirt until she felt the familiar look of blank stupidity settle across her face. Then Annabel opened the gate and plodded up the path and into the cottage.

Grenna pinioned her with a glare as the door opened. "Home at last, are you? I suppose the well got up and walked away?"

Annabel blinked once, slowly and heavily. "No," she said. "It's still there."

Grenna gave vent to her own particular inarticulate crow of annoyance and snatched the bottle of water from Annabel's outstretched hand.

"I fell down," said Annabel sorrowfully, into the silence. "I hurt myself."

"Where are the berries, idiot child! Curse me sideways for having the kindness to nurture an imbecile!"

"Here they are," Annabel said, plopping two handfuls of battered and juicy lillypilly berries onto the table. "They're not squashed."

"Not squashed! The juice streaming from them and she says they're not squashed! *Don't* lick your fingers, stupid child! We've work to do and I won't have you dreaming away while you should be concentrating."

"What work?"

"Never you mind, nosy niggle. Wash your face and change into your flannels."

"It's *hot*," said Annabel. "Flannels are hot. Ow!"

"Get away and change before I clip the other ear!"

Annabel shuffled toward her room, one hand clasping her red ear. Flannels meant big magic, and she regretted coming home at all. She could have slept on the heather in the back hills if she'd stayed away: Grenna would only have stomped around the house for a while and cursed her for an imbecile.

When Annabel entered the workroom, hot and uncomfortable in her flannels, Grenna was busy drawing chalk circles. In the centre of one of those circles was a sleek, smoky grey cat. It was so sleek and smooth, in fact, that it wasn't until Annabel got closer that she understood how very big it was. Sitting on its haunches as it was, its head was just above knee-level.

"There's a cat," she said, not troubling to hide her surprise.

"A very special cat," said Grenna, her face shiny with satisfaction. She turned back to her work and added curtly: "Don't smudge the lines, or I'll wallop you from here to the turnpike. Sit down."

Annabel obediently sat down and waited. Much to her perverse delight, when Grenna turned around again it was to huff in annoyance: "Don't sit there, you stupid lump! Sit in the circle!"

"You said sit down," Annabel said mournfully, climbing heavily to her feet. Sometimes the stupidity could be a kind of game. "I sat down."

"Did you change out of your cotton underthings?"

Annabel said: "Yes," and sat gloomily in the centre of the circle. Her flannel underthings were particularly itchy, but under the grey cat's blue gaze she didn't quite dare to scratch. There was a reason that Grenna didn't work magic around cotton, but Annabel didn't really understand it and was always resentful of the discomfort of flannel.

"Stop fidgeting!"

Annabel stopped fidgeting, but the cool amusement in the grey cat's eyes made her say: "Are you going to use the cat?"

Grenna gave a high, crowing: "Ha! *Use* him! Use *him*! I should be so addled!"

A tight little ball of fear clenched in Annabel's stomach, and she thought that the amusement in the grey cat's eyes deepened. She settled herself more solidly on the floor, sinking into herself until she was looking out on the room with bland, stupid cow eyes, and readied herself for a long wait.

Blackfoot was curled up on her pillow when Annabel, weary and sore, returned to her room. She closed the door behind her and propped herself against it, rubbing her hands across her face to rid herself of the tiredness and stupidity and lingering nastiness.

Blackfoot sat up, managing to stretch in an entirely sarcastic manner, and regarded her with slit eyes. *Well, it was quite the exhibition today,* he said.

It was always a bit of a surprise to hear Blackfoot speak. Annabel blamed Peter: he was so insistent that Blackfoot didn't—*couldn't*—speak, that it was hard to persevere against his determined disbelief. It didn't help that Blackfoot's voice wasn't an audible one: it made Annabel feel, somewhat uncomfortably, that it was quite possible she was merely mad.

"Mind your own business," she told him. It was easy to be rude when she was half certain that his voice wasn't real. Besides, Blackfoot was almost invariably sarcastic, and, real or not, could always be said to deserve a rude remark or two.

It is my business, said Blackfoot, leaping to the floor. *It's embarrassing to have a human who pretends to be imbecilic.*

"If Grenna knew I'm not an idiot I wouldn't be able to spend so much time in the ruins with Peter."

*Not to mention having to work **much** harder,* mocked Blackfoot.

"She tells me things she wouldn't tell me otherwise," said Annabel. "It's safer like this. I can get away from some of the bigger magic when she thinks I'm out drooling in the forest. Anyway, I'm not your human. *I* didn't ask you to stay. *I* didn't want you sleeping on my bed– *or* eating half my dinner!"

You could do with a little less dinner in any case, said Blackfoot, but he twined himself around her ankles and purred anyway.

"I'm sure no one else has voices in their head that insult them," said Annabel gloomily.

Don't start that again. I told you, I'm not a voice in your head. I'm–

"I know, I know," grumbled Annabel. "You're using the enhancement field to amplify and project a meta-stream of conscience–"

–consciousness!

"Yes. That. I don't understand it." Annabel thought about that, and added darkly: "Peter would."

Peter is a cocksure little ragamuffin, said Blackfoot.

"Yes," said Annabel again. "Only he is very clever."

Hmf, said Blackfoot. *Fishing for compliments, are we?*

"No," Annabel yawned. "I've always been the stupid one. I know that."

Oh, go to bed, said Blackfoot. He vanished into the inky shadows beneath the bed, but when she had changed into her cotton nightie and climbed beneath the covers he appeared again, startling Annabel by springing noiselessly from the shadows to her pillow.

"I'm allergic," she told him, half-heartedly shoving him off the pillow. Blackfoot, a slithery whisp of shadow himself, merely flowed around her shoving and curled back up on the pillow. Annabel huffed, turned her ear to his furry warmth, and went to sleep.

By the next day there were twenty or so more cats at the ruins. Annabel saw them when she climbed into the crumbling courtyard, each stalking the others with the greatest of dignity. Blackfoot hissed at them with his ears flattened and said something beneath his breath that Annabel didn't catch.

She said: "Don't be rude," anyway, and then: "Why are they all coming here? And where's the one from last night?"

Blackfoot hissed again, his ears back. *You didn't say anything about a cat last night.*

"You were too busy being sarcastic," said Annabel.

"Still talking to the cat, I see," said Peter's voice. He must have been right behind her, because he leapt from the huge outer stones as Annabel turned her head.

"There's more of them," she said, ignoring the remark.

"I noticed," said Peter. "Keep them away from my tickerboxes."

"They're not *mine!*" Annabel protested. "I can't stop them from doing whatever they want to do!"

Peter gave the half-shrug that conceded a point. "Oh well, I'll think of something."

"Did you bring it?"

"Of course I did. Here: it's proper quality stock."

Annabel caught the carelessly tossed book with reverent fingers and caressed the blank pages. "It's perfect! Tell your mother I'll send her a portrait for payment just as soon as I can make the ink and find another pen."

"I'm not sitting still for a portrait," said Peter ungratefully. "She's got piles of paper and books at home, what else could she do with them but give 'em away?"

"Well, I think it's lovely to have a paper merchant for a stepfather," Annabel said enviously. "All that wonderful paper, and ink you don't have to mix! I'd never stop drawing."

"You never stop drawing anyway. What are you meant to be doing today?"

"Nothing. Grenna said I was getting in her way."

"You might as well come to lunch, then," said Peter, shrugging off his coat. His shirtsleeves were already stained with greasy brown marks and there were spots of the same on his suspenders.

"Thanks," Annabel said, not at all perturbed by the backhanded invitation. Grenna had her back on a diet of bread and water, claiming that Annabel was eating her out of house and home. Peter's Mother, on the other hand, was free with cheese, apples, and pastries, and was round enough not to care if Annabel was more than a little bit round too.

Annabel settled herself on a convenient slab of stone with her new book and searched for the nub of pencil that was always tucked away in her front pinafore pocket. She preferred drawing with pen and ink, but when neither were to be had, her tiny pencil was nearly as good. It had the added advantage of not leaving her face and hands ink-stained at the end of the day. It also had the advantage of a tiny eraser at the other end, a luxury to which Annabel didn't otherwise have access.

Annabel amused herself with sketching different angles of Peter's face, content to sit cross-legged on her stone while he amused himself with his tickerboxes. She didn't understand them, anyway.

*You don't **try** to understand them,* said Blackfoot. He was sitting on her shoulder, his whiskers tickling her ear. He always liked to watch her draw. *You like to think you're stupid.*

"I am," said Annabel equably, shading the cracks between flagstones.

"You are what?" said Peter, shooting her a sharp look. "You know, if you keep talking to yourself you'll soon be as mad as a pair of wet gnau in a hole."

"I was talking to Blackfoot."

"Got a lot to say this morning, hasn't he?"

"He's always got a lot to say," said Annabel, with a private smile for Blackfoot. He hissed, but not at her: over Peter's shoulder, three more cats were springing lightly into the ruins. "Did you figure out what your tickerbox was up to?"

"Oh, that's actually very interesting!" said Peter, immediately losing interest in Blackfoot. Blackfoot made a rude noise somewhere around Annabel's ear, though she wasn't sure if it was aloud or not. "It was cannibalising the others, just like I thought, and it was building itself a secondary engine."

"Oh. What for?"

"The main engine was getting overheated with the speed of the rotor shaft–"

"I don't know what that means."

"Speed and movement cause heat– don't do your cow eyes at me, Ann! The simple explanation is that the tickerbox was getting too hot, so it made itself a cooling engine with the rotor shaft and a few blades from another tickerbox."

"Should it be able to do that?"

"Of course not. It's not magic, it's clockwork. It can't think."

Piffle, said Blackfoot. *He may think it's just clockwork, but he's got so much magic dripping off him that he couldn't stop it influencing the clockwork if he tried. Not to mention the enhancement field– you're not listening to me, are you, Nan?*

"Blackfoot says you're wrong," said Annabel, applying herself to a profile view of Peter.

"If the cat thinks it can do better, it's welcome to try," retorted Peter.

Annabel drew in the annoyed crinkle in his brow.

You said one of the cats was at the house last night, Blackfoot said to her. *What was Grenna doing?*

"Don't know. Something big, though."

How was the spell performed? Was it laid out, item-based, or free-form?

"She laid out the spell," said Annabel, sketching another view of Peter with one of his brows up and his head cocked to hear better, his eyes still stubbornly on his tickerbox. "But the laying out looked like it was for item-based spells, only instead of items in the circles it was me and the cat."

"That doesn't make sense," said Peter, plucking at a wire strung tightly through his tickerbox. "The spell wouldn't work. It's meant to flow from the ignition point and through each of the components to its conclusion. You're not a spell *or* an item. The flow would stop at you."

You should have told me this last night, said Blackfoot.

"What's the cat saying now?"

"He's saying I should have told him this last night," said Annabel. The odd quality to Blackfoot's voice was setting off uneasy flutterings in her stomach. It almost sounded as though he was *afraid*. "Wait, I thought you didn't believe Blackfoot speaks to me."

"I don't," said Peter, hunching his shoulders over the tickerbox again. "I just find your psychosis interesting: you're having conversations with yourself. Why would you have told the cat about the spell last night?"

Annabel shrugged one plump shoulder. "Don't know."

Things are happening a lot more quickly than I expected, said Blackfoot. Annabel thought he was talking more to himself than her. *I should have taken you away the minute the first one turned up.*

"Taken me *away*?" said Annabel blankly. "Why should I go away? And do you mean the cats?"

They're not cats.

"What's it saying?"

"He says the cats aren't cats."

"Wrong again," said Peter.

"Don't be smug," Annabel told him.

He's right and wrong, Blackfoot said broodingly. *They **are*** *cats. They just weren't **always** cats. And some of them are less cat than others.*

Annabel thought about it, and came to a surprising conclusion. "Like you, you mean?"

Blackfoot bit her ear. *That's not important. What's important is that you don't go back to Grenna tonight.*

"I have to go home tonight!" protested Annabel. "Where would I sleep? What would I *eat*?"

Peter gave a rude snort of laughter, and she threw a handful of pebbles at him.

"Blackfoot says I shouldn't go home tonight."

"Oh, if that's all, you can use one of our guest rooms. Mum likes having you around: says you're restful company and you eat everything put in front of you."

"I bet you said something rude when she said that," said Annabel.

"*And* she clouted me for it," said Peter cheerfully. "All right, if your psychosis is telling you that something's up, you'll probably be safer at our place: Grenna gets up to some nasty bits of magic."

"Well, we'd better go soon," Annabel said, with a doubtful look at the positive stream of cats that had begun to flow into the ruins. "We'll be swimming in cats if we stay here much longer."

Two

Annabel woke some time in the wee hours of the morning, grumbling and unsettled in her borrowed bed, to find a cold patch on her pillow where Blackfoot should be. She sat up groggily, pawing hair out of her eyes, and automatically patted the mattress around her for him. "Blackfoot?"

There was not a whisper of movement to the shadows. A sharp prickle of unease woke her properly, bringing with it the realisation that for the first time in many years, she couldn't hear Blackfoot anywhere at the edges of her mind. Annabel kicked her legs free of the sheets and slid down onto the rug beside her bed. She knew Blackfoot wasn't in the room but she lit a candle and searched anyway, working her way across the room until she was sitting on the low window-seat, hot and bothered and confused. He'd never spent a night away from her pillow since she'd met him.

Annabel frowned into the bruising of purple and cobalt morning and picked at fragments of wood on the windowsill. It wasn't until she'd absentmindedly picked three or four curls of wood from the sill that she realised they were shavings that had been carved out from two sets of three deep gouges. They were evenly spaced, surprisingly deep, and only ended when the sill did, as if something (or some *cat*, though Annabel, with a sinking feeling) had been dragged through the window against its will. What had happened while she slept?

Something—some magic—had been performed that dragged Blackfoot away and out of the window.

Grenna, thought Annabel, hot and sticky with fear. Once, she'd stayed out to avoid one of Grenna's bigger pieces of magic. Grenna had sent out a Compel spell that weighed on her slowly through the night and at last woke her, forcing her home from her snug little hole in the castle ruins. Annabel gave a little gulping sniffle and realised that she was leaning precariously far out of the window– almost as if her body was trying to climb out without her knowledge.

"No!" squeaked Annabel, scrabbling away from the window seat. "No! Not again!"

But her feet were already edging for the window again, slow and reluctant and inevitable. She dashed for the door, pulling at the Compel spell just long enough to tumble into the hall, which mercifully ran in the right direction and didn't make it achingly difficult to walk.

Moonlight and shadow played on the walls through arched windows as Annabel hurried down the hall. Peter's room was just two doors down, convenient and unlocked, and didn't pull her far enough out of the proscribed route to drag at her. Annabel hurried across the room and bounced onto his bed, prompting a groan and a few choice words that would have made his mother box his ears if she'd heard them.

"Get off, Ann! Why are you so fat? And what are you doing on my bed?"

"Grenna's got a Compel on me," said Annabel, all in one breath. "And Blackfoot got dragged through the window and I think that was her too."

"What do you want me to do?"

"Can you get rid of the Compel?"

Peter sat up, fumbling for his glasses, and set a softly glowing ball of light spinning above the bed with a snap of his fingers. Annabel waited, fidgeting with impatience and worry as he studied her, and with one foot trying to make its way back to the floor, at last said: "Well? Can you?"

"Sorry, Ann. She's got a bit of you that she's using– hair or something. You'll have to go back. Want me to come with you?"

Yes, said Annabel's cowardly thoughts. Out loud, she said: "No. Grenna probably just wants me to go out and get some things for her. Once I get back the spell will stop pulling at me, anyway. Maybe I'll sleep in the garden instead."

Despite that, Annabel was even more nervous once she was out in the cool air. There was a distinct feeling of menace to the early morning, and a crawling feeling between the blades of her shoulders that tried to convince her that someone was watching her. Worse, she still couldn't sense even the faintest hint of Blackfoot at the edges of her mind. Was he *dead*? Annabel's feet began to move faster of their own accord, momentarily freeing her from the pull of the Compel spell, and she felt the tightness of fear stretching the skin of her face tight against the chill of the morning.

Annabel was sweating by the time she reached the lane to Grenna's cottage, despite the cold morning air. She stopped short in the rutted lane, her breath short and burning in the back of her throat, and stared.

There were cats *everywhere*. They lined the fence, straggling along it in clumps and couples; they perched on the roof of the cottage, peering at Annabel as she faltered on the path; and more disconcerting still, stared at her from the windows of Grenna's workroom. Annabel huffed out a rather shaky breath and came to the conclusion that if all the cats were here, then Blackfoot must be too, even if she still couldn't hear him. That made her feel better, and she was able to push through the gate and into the house without more than a brief thought of running back up the path to Peter's house and leaving Blackfoot to his fate. All the same, she made sure she eased the door open and shut without a sound, and when she went to her bedroom she changed into her flannels. Annabel didn't know *exactly* why Grenna made her wear flannels for magic, but Grenna's magic was plant-based and it stood to reason that cotton clothes could muddle her magic. It had occurred to Annabel, some time before she climbed into the scratchy wool flannels, that Grenna might find it easier to find her if she wore her cotton everyday clothes.

When she was flanneled and hot and uncomfortable, Annabel slipped back out of her room and went quietly in search of Grenna and the grey cat. She had a feeling that whatever Grenna was up to, and whatever had drawn Blackfoot and all the other cats here to the cottage, that grey cat would be in on it.

She found them in Grenna's work-room, the door open to allow a sprawling spell of chalk and braided cotton rope to trail away into the garden. From that door also issued Grenna's voice, dry and cracked, and higher than usual. Who was she speaking with? More importantly, why was her voice so different? It gave Annabel the nasty feeling that Grenna was actually frightened of whoever it was she was talking to. She hesitated at the bottom of the stairs, clutching at the cuffs of her flannels without the courage to take the last few steps that would bring her level with the door of Grenna's workroom.

Then, right at the outer edge of her mind, there was the faintest tickle of Blackfoot's voice.

Nan?

A warmth of reassurance blossomed in Annabel's chest. Blackfoot *was* here! She nudged forward, trying to avoid the worst of the creaky floorboards, and followed the trailing spell out towards the back garden. She held her breath as she passed the open work-room door, and through the gap she saw a brief flash of reflection in the window opposite the door. Grenna, her stick-like legs protruding below the hem of a flannel night-gown, was scratching nervously at her arms while the pale shadow of a large grey cat stalked around her.

Annabel darted for the door before either of them could notice her, hurrying out into the back yard with an uneasy crawling feeling at the back of her neck. Was that the same cat that Grenna had put in the spell with her? More importantly, why should Grenna be scared of a *cat*? Annabel shivered and scrunched her bare toes in the grass. Nothing made sense, and she was beginning to be even more frightened than Grenna's magic usually made her feel. The back yard wasn't much better than the front yard or the house, either: it was all cats out there as well. The only difference was that these ones were caught in parts of the spell, each sitting in a coil of pale rope that curled out from the main track of the spell. And as Annabel dithered, looking for Blackfoot in the darkness and confusion of cats, another cat slipped through the doorway and stalked across the grass to sit in one of the empty coils. She didn't bother to try and count the coils, but she had the feeling that they would match pretty closely with the amount of cats.

"A parliament-full," Annabel murmured, remembering

what Peter had said when the cats first arrived. Where was Blackfoot? Was he caught in one of the coils as well? She moved further into the garden, skirting carefully around the curls of the spell, her eyes searching the shadows and scrubby bushes for any sign of Blackfoot's inky black form.

"They'll put him in the middle of it," she said aloud, hunching her shoulders against the cold of morning and the even more pervasive cold of fear. Blackfoot was a special cat—was probably, if she thought about it, actually *more* than a cat. Grenna and the other cat that was more than a cat knew that, and they would have put him in one of the more important parts of the spell. Annabel couldn't do magic, but she had come to know a little bit about it after her years with Grenna. Like Annabel herself, Blackfoot was an important commodity, and his placement in the spell would be central. She turned away from the outer, curling edges that were more and more swiftly filling with cats, and carefully tiptoed through the blank spots in the spell, edging toward the middle of the spell piece that sprawled in the back garden.

Annabel found him in the centre of the main whorl of pale rope, just behind the well, stalking to and fro with his tail lashing.

Nan! There was a mixture of relief and irritation in Blackfoot's voice. *How did you get away from her Compel?*

"Didn't," said Annabel, shivering with relief. She crouched beside him, making very certain that she was still in a blank part of the spell, and that her flannels didn't go over that pale rope by so much as a single fold. "She lays them for the house, not for her. I only had to come back here. What's happening?"

This time the irritation was most prominent. *Why didn't you tell me it's your birthday today?*

"It isn't. Is it? I don't know. Grenna never told me when it was. What has my birthday got to do with anything, anyway?"

*Nothing, if it wasn't that it's this one, or that **he's** here, or that we're all here together. We have to get you to the Castle.*

"That's the first place she'll look for me," Annabel said, tugging nervously at her flannel sleeves. "She knows I go there with Peter."

That doesn't matter.

"What do you mean, it doesn't matter?" said Annabel crossly. She had forced herself to come out here and rescue Blackfoot despite her fear, and he was repaying that loyalty with impatience and reticence. "If you're going to be all morbid and mysterious, I'm going to leave you here."

Stop sulking, said Blackfoot, ruthlessly practical. *You need to get me out of this circle.*

Annabel propped her chin on her chubby fists and very deliberately let herself settle into a plump, stupid blob of slack-faced girl. As rebellion went, it was usually remarkably successful.

Don't do that, Nan, Blackfoot said. *There's no time to play stupid.*

Annabel stared at him with glassy eyes, her face expressionless.

Nan.

Annabel blinked, slowly and heavily, and became even more glassy-eyed.

*Nan, **please.***

"Oh, all *right*," said Annabel, shaking off her stupidity. "You shouldn't be so superior if you're only going to back down. Why can't you say please first?"

Blackfoot's tail twitched. *Habit, most likely. You'll need to be quick, Nan. If I'm still in here when they begin the spell there won't be enough of me left to know the difference between hello and please.*

"I don't think they can start it without me, anyway," said Annabel, looking around the garden. She needed something that would break the circle enough to get Blackfoot safely out. "Bother! I used to have salt out here somewhere."

They can't, said Blackfoot, *but I also can't help you from in here, and I rather think Grenna will be looking for you very soon. Use a twig if you must. I can make that work.*

Annabel took a few steps across the grass and snatched at a twig from one of the bushes, but instead of snapping away easily in her fingers it cut across them, as stiff and sharp as glass twigs. "Ow!" she said in surprise, and tried again, this time more carefully.

What's wrong?

"Nothing," said Annabel, wiping away a trace of blood on her flannels. "There's something funny about the bush. I'll get a twig from the hedge."

The garden was awfully still as she passed through the shadows to the hedge; which was odd, because there was a breeze tickling at her hair and her cheeks. And yet, not a leaf or twig stirred in the darkness. And when Annabel grasped a leafy twig from the hedge and tried to break it off as before, it cut into her fingers once again.

She tried again, this time wrapping the skirt of her flannel nightie around her fingers to avoid being cut, and found the twigs as obdurate as ever. With a slight uncertainty to her voice, Annabel said: "None of them will come off, Blackfoot."

Ah, said Blackfoot. He sounded quite calm, and even unsurprised.

Annabel looked at him accusingly. "What's going on? Did you know this was going to happen?"

Not exactly, Blackfoot said. *But I know how painstakingly precise he is.*

"He? I thought it was Grenna? Who is *he*? You said *he* before, as well."

I misspoke. She'll have made sure nothing around here can move.

Annabel left the question for a more convenient time, and said instead: "You mean she expected me to try and rescue you?"

Not exactly. She's frozen anything that could possibly fall or be knocked into the spell: it's a good idea for an outdoor spell that involves animals. If a falling twig breaks one piece of it by letting a cat escape at the wrong time, the whole thing could shatter.

"What's it *for*, though? What's so important about one or two cats?"

Blackfoot's tail lashed. *Find something else. What have you got in your pocket?*

"Don't know," said Annabel. There was only one pocket on her flannel nightie, but it was a big one because Grenna quite often left her in spells for hours on end and it was useful to have a few things on hand. "Food and paper and my pencil, probably."

She felt around in her pocket, and Blackfoot, suddenly sharp and prickly in her mind, said, *Pencil? You have your pencil?*

"Oh," said Annabel, pulling out her pencil with a wondering look. "It's wood."

Put it down, quickly, Blackfoot said. *Something in the house is stirring.*

Annabel put her tiny stub of pencil carefully on the curving edge of the circle that kept Blackfoot prisoner, and for a moment it teetered between his side and hers, too small to balance easily. Then it began to grow, though Annabel didn't think it took up any more room than it had taken up before, and before long there was a bridge for Blackfoot to cross between his side and hers.

Annabel, her mouth open in surprise, watched Blackfoot pad uneasily across the pencil-bridge, his tail lashing in discomfort. The fur on his back was ridged and stiff, which worried her: anything that worried Blackfoot was a Very Bad Thing Indeed. Still, why was he so uncomfortable with his own magic? She had seen him do magic before, but she'd never seen him so little at ease with it.

When he was safely across, he gave the smallest hop toward her, his back legs twitching a kick that was as nervous as it was quick. As he padded a swift, shadowy circle around her, Annabel reached out for the bridge in fascination and found herself holding her pencil once again. She put it back in her pocket, and heard Blackfoot say harshly: *Quick! Throw one of the other cats in. That one: the black one.*

"All right," said Annabel, very carefully dropping the other black cat into the circle that had once held Blackfoot. "But what about me? They'll see me as soon as they get out here!"

I'm sorry," said Blackfoot, and for a very cold moment, Annabel didn't quite understand.

When she did, she said, with a small wobble to her voice: "Blackfoot?"

I'm sorry, he said again. *They're going to catch you and put you in the spell. I can't help that. But without me in there they won't be able to do it properly and it shouldn't hurt you.*

"They wouldn't have been able to finish it without me, either," said Annabel. She was shivering: not with betrayal, because she knew Blackfoot; but with fear, because she *knew* Blackfoot. He was going to make her do something that she didn't want to do– something difficult or unpleasant that was entirely unavoidable. Peter was always forcing her to do things that she didn't want to do—or wasn't brave enough to do— and Blackfoot had caught the habit from him. The only difference, as far as Annabel could tell, was that Peter quite often had an ulterior, entirely self-motivated reason for pushing her into difficult situations. Blackfoot never did so unless he thought it was necessary, or unless it was something that would help her.

No, but they could do a storage working to keep all this power they're trying to harvest. Then I wouldn't be around to help by the time they caught you.

Annabel hugged shivery arms tight against her soft belly, her pencil gripped tightly in her left hand. "What are they harvesting?"

Souls, said Blackfoot, with terrifying calmness. *And magic.*

"Cats– cats don't have souls," said Annabel, trying very hard not to cry.

These ones once did, Blackfoot said. His back was to her, his cat-gaze scanning the hedge that blocked off the lane, gauging the leap he would need to make. There was probably magic there, too, but Annabel couldn't see that. *Call them futures, then. He's stealing futures.*

He leaped as he spoke, a stretching bound that had him dancing lightly on the top of the hedge a moment later. Annabel, who desperately didn't want to be left alone to the two shadows that were growing in the doorway of the cottage, hissed: "What about the others? Shouldn't we try to save them, too?"

Blackfoot's eyes glowed in the rustling shadows of the hedge. *It's too late for them*, he said. *They were lost as soon as she did the first working.*

He was gone the next moment. Annabel gave a subdued

sniffle and hid herself in a soft, quivering heap beneath the shadow of the hedge, but they found her at once, the big grey cat unerringly shimmering through the early morning fog and straight toward her.

"Get up," said Grenna, hauling at Annabel's arm. Annabel, quite used to this sort of fight, made herself as floppy and heavy as possible and simply tucked her head into her arms when Grenna passed onto the next stage of this particular game, which was to kick Annabel until she got up of her own volition.

Above her head and between kicks, she heard Grenna say to the grey cat: "I'm *trying*, your worship!" It scared her to think that the grey cat could be anything like Blackfoot, and she tugged herself tighter in desperation.

Nan, get up, said Blackfoot's voice.

Don't want to, thought Annabel, in a haze of panic. She knew he couldn't hear her, but she couldn't help answering him anyway. *Don't want to.*

Nan, she'll hurt you.

It hurts now! wailed Annabel in her thoughts. *I don't want to!*

But in the end it didn't matter whether or not she wanted to, because Grenna dragged her inch by inch toward the sinister, sprawling spell, gasping excuses to the grey cat all the while. Annabel, quivering and sniffling, was shoved into a larger coil of rope than the cats were confined in, and was miserable but unsurprised to find that once in, she couldn't get out. She huddled at the outer edge of it in spite of that, as far away from the grey cat as she could manage. It looked back at her with a cool sort of amusement, and it took quite a while to realise that she could still hear Blackfoot's voice in her mind, and that he had, from the sounds of it, been talking to her all along.

When she was thinking coherently enough to understand him again, he had fallen back on the old expedient of repeating: *Nan. Nan. Listen to me. Nan. Nan. NAN. Pay attention!*

Annabel gave one last sniffle and wrapped her arms around her knees. Blackfoot's voice said, with a gust of relief: *That's better. Good girl. This spell is a complicated one, so it's going to take a while. You need to listen to me very carefully, because it's also going to be a bit unpleasant. Can you do that? Sit down on the grass and wipe your nose if you can.*

Annabel plopped back on her rump in the grass and wiped her nose with the front of her flannels. Grenna glared at her and muttered beneath her breath, prompting Annabel to duck away reflexively, but didn't hit her. Instead, she picked her way through the intricate curls of the spell with a spryness that belied her crooked appearance, and eventually came to a stop somewhere in the centre of the spell, in a position diagonal from Annabel that formed a triangle with the coil that should have held Blackfoot. Annabel looked at her in some surprise. Was Grenna part of the spell too, then?

"It's ready, your worship," said Grenna to the grey cat. The grey cat seemed to give a brief nod, and then stole softly through the coils of rope to the very centre of the spell until it was between Grenna, Annabel, and the other black cat.

It's about to start, said Blackfoot. *You won't notice anything at first, but soon the cats will start to die: the outer ones first and then the ones closer in. It should be quiet, but if they start wailing just block your ears and close your eyes.*

Annabel felt her chin wobble again. Grenna didn't often do magic requiring death, but it always made her feel sick and dirty on the inside. She knew perfectly well there was nothing she could do about it, but that only made her feel even sicker, as if there was something that she *should* be able to do about it.

Grenna, her shiny eyes coming to bear on Annabel, said sharply: "We'll have none of your blubbering, thank you, miss! Just you put your fat face into your nightie again!"

Close your eyes, said Blackfoot's voice. *Just close your eyes and listen to me.*

Annabel closed her eyes, but instead of listening to Blackfoot, she listened to the alien silence of the yard. The wind teased her face but didn't stir through the greenery, and the only sounds were those of the cats mewling in their circles of rope, and the wheezing of Grenna as she tried to catch her breath after finding her place.

At first the mewling and hissing was a constant babble behind Grenna's wheezing. It wasn't until the hissing stopped completely that Annabel realised how very loud the mewling had become. Now it wasn't so much mewling as it was yowling, loud and wailing. Annabel opened her eyes without meaning to. The cats at the outer edge of the spell were writhing in their circles, teeth bared to the morning air. She turned her eyes away from them at once and caught sight of Grenna, her head thrown back with every sign of enjoyment, a blissful smile spread across her broad face. Grenna always had the same expression when she was engaged in death magic: Annabel thought, shivering, that Grenna must be able to feel all the magic flowing through the spell. Death magic spells were some of the few occasions when Annabel was glad she couldn't feel or see magic. The idea of enjoying that feeling was frightening.

It wasn't long before the cats in the spell around her began to scream. Even the grey cat in the centre of the triangle was yowling now, its smoky grey body rippling like mist and expanding as the cats around the edges of the spell shrieked.

Annabel's face ached from her eyes and all the way down

her throat, tears painful to hold but too frightened to come out. She tucked her face into her flannelled knees and covered her ears with her palms, the thunder of her heartbeat taking over the muffled screaming of cats. And faintly, in the back of her mind, Blackfoot's voice said: *It's all right, Nan. Keep your ears covered, that's a good girl. It'll all be over soon.*

I want it to be over **now**, thought Annabel piteously, pressing her hands more tightly against her ears. *Make it stop, Blackfoot!*

There was a patchwork of spotted black and white behind her eyelids where she had pressed her eyes too tightly into her kneecaps, but Annabel couldn't seem to stop doing it in spite of that. Her arms were aching, so she shifted her hands to give them some relief, and in the gap between covered and uncovered ears she heard someone groaning. It was a deep, gasping groan that sounded male, but that was silly because the only people in the garden were Annabel and Grenna. Annabel lifted her head cautiously from her knees, and through the blurry speckle of white and black she saw that the big grey cat was no longer a cat. It was a huge, vague, misshapen mound of shadow that writhed and bulged, groaned and grew.

Annabel whimpered, and became aware that Blackfoot was speaking to her again.

Nan? Nan! Get your feet under you. When I tell you to run, **run**. *You'll only a have a moment before Mordion is able to stand, and Grenna won't take long to notice, either. Don't try to go through the gate: it won't open for you. Go through the back door of the cottage and straight out the front.*

Shivering, Annabel took her hands away from her ears and pushed herself up from the grass. She immediately wished she hadn't: most of the cats were silent and still now, but the ones that were still wailing had risen in pitch and wildness until all of it blended into one scream that was underpinned by the shadow's—Mordion's—increasingly human groans. She covered her ears again as quickly as she could, her toes curling in the dewy grass and the dew-wet patch on the seat of her flannels making a coldness behind her. Grenna was still smiling blindly at the lightening sky, her head tipped back and her shoulders slumped, but in the centre of the triangle, the grey cat had become a man entirely.

As Annabel watched, he began to stir: not as he had earlier, all misshapen bulges and edges, but with deliberation and purpose.

Now! said Blackfoot. *Run, now!*

Mordion turned his head and looked at her, and Annabel froze, losing a precious second in the shock of it. Then Blackfoot howled: *Run, Nan!* and somehow she *was* running– heavily, frantically, her bare feet catching in rope and grass as she dashed across the spell. Her feet cleared the single step and stang painfully against the threshold; and behind her, she heard Mordion's voice grate: *"I'll. Kill. Him."*

Annabel's feet caught against each other and she plunged to the floor in a painful heap, palms and knees first. She scrambled to her feet again, looking behind her fearfully to where Mordion, rising shakily on one knee, a menacing shadow with real edges.

"Stay," said the shadow, its voice deep and rough. "Stay, or I'll go up to that house on the hill and kill him."

Nan! Where are you?

"I'll kill him," said the shadow again, but Annabel knew in a bright flash of relief that if he could have killed anyone—could have done *anything* magically—he would already have stopped her that way. Blackfoot was right: they hadn't been able to do the spell correctly. She turned and ran, meeting a snarling ball of rigid fur and teeth at the front door, then she and Blackfoot were pelting down the lane while Blackfoot's voice ordered: *To the Castle. You need to get into the Castle before he gets to you.*

Annabel would have liked to asked him *why* the castle ruins, but she was already gasping for air, too heavy and clumsy to run as long as she had been running, and she didn't have the breath to spare. So she simply concentrated on running, and in the back of her mind she heard Blackfoot's worried voice wondering in jumbled thoughts and ideas, why Mordion hadn't yet followed them into the lane.

Annabel stopped at the fork that branched off to both the ruins and Peter's house, but when she took a step along the lane that went up toward Peter's house, Blackfoot was there, snarling and spitting.

The Castle.

"But Peter!"

Send the message box. That's all we have time for. If he catches you…if he catches you–

"If he catches Peter, he'll kill him!"

*He can't kill anyone with as little magic as he's been able to gather. Nan, **please**.*

Annabel hesitated a moment longer, then fished for the message box with a shaking hand. The message box was one of Peter's tickerboxes: if you spoke into the one at the bottom of the hill, another tickerbox in Peter's room would parrot back what you'd said. It worked in reverse, but not always, and not very well. Annabel, sick with fear, pressed the button on the box and said: "Peter? Peter, can you hear me?"

There was a long, horrible silence, and then the tickerbox's impersonal, emotionless voice said: "Wot?"

"Peter!" said Annabel frantically. "That grey cat isn't a cat anymore and he said he's going to kill you!"

"Wot," said the emotionless little voice again. And then: "Ann...something happen?"

Tell him to get to the Castle as quickly as he can, said Blackfoot, whipping back and forth at her feet. *Nan, we have to go. Mordion's doing something back at the cottage: I can feel a **lot** of magic gathering.*

"Blackfoot says you have to come to the ruins as quickly as you can," said Annabel. "He says it's the only safe place."

"...perfectly safe...my own–" said the tickerbox, and abruptly stopped. When it started up again, it was to say with terrifying calmness: "...they're in my room...Ann, run...Mum... not going without her...Mum–" Then it gave vent to a long, protracted beep, and exploded.

Annabel shrieked and ducked her head into her arms, but something flew past her cheek so hotly and sharply that she didn't realise it had cut her until she felt the blood running down her cheek.

He's coming, said Blackfoot, and bit Annabel's leg. *Nan, he's **coming**. You can't do anything for Peter. I'm sorry.*

Annabel wiped her cheek with her shoulder and scrambled away down the path that led to the ruins. She couldn't sense the magic that Blackfoot obviously could, but she could hear it now: the sound of steady, deliberate footsteps further down the lane. Whatever Mordion had done, it had made him feel confident enough not to chase her. That idea frightened Annabel enough to make her break into a painful, floppy trot, and then into an outright run.

She was groaning for breath when she reached the first, outer ring of the ruins, and there she stopped, despite Blackfoot's urging. Annabel didn't know exactly why she'd stopped until it occurred to her that she wasn't just listening for those horribly steady footsteps from the lane: she was listening for Peter's careless passage through the woods on the hill.

Blackfoot, with very little patience left in his voice, said: ***Nan, get into the castle now!***

"Why?" she panted, her eyes caught by a dark, frantic movement at the top of the hill just below the shadow that was Peter's house. "What's so important about getting to the ruins? If he's got more magic now, he'll catch me wherever I go."

He can't catch you if you go into the Castle, said Blackfoot. He was back to pacing furiously at her feet, his tail lashing. *Once you're in, it'll seal itself up and won't open again until quite a lot of predetermined factors are met.*

"That's Peter," said Annabel, wrapping her quivering arms around her quivering middle and pointing with her chin at the tiny movement on the hill. "I can see him running down the hill toward the woods. If it's going to seal up, I can't go in yet."

There was a muddle of hastily suppressed bad words at the back of Annabel's mind where Blackfoot's voice always popped up. *Nan–*

"I'm not going until he gets here," Annabel said, settling into an immovable, quivering blob on one of the fallen wall stones. "I can't even see Mordion. Maybe– maybe he doesn't know which way we went."

He knows, said Blackfoot, as the rapidly-growing form of Peter disappeared into the woods. *He's not in any hurry. He thinks he has the upper hand.*

Sure enough, Annabel heard the measured tread of Mordion's footsteps down the lane just a few minutes later. She stood again, setting one foot on the broken wall of the ruins, the other digging into the grass with white toes. Above the hedge she could just see the top of Mordion's head as it drew closer: in a minute or two he would be able to see them.

She looked around wildly at the hill again. "Where's Peter? He should be here by now."

Don't know, said Blackfoot tersely. *Get into the Castle.*

"You said it'll seal up," said Annabel, hovering with one foot on the outer wall stones and the other on grass.

*It **will** seal up*, said Blackfoot, his tail lashing. *That's the idea. I can't protect you in this form.*

"Yes, but who'll protect Peter?"

I'm sorry.

"Mordion will *kill* him!"

I'm sorry, Nan.

Annabel, her voice quivering with fear, said again: "I'm not going until Peter's here."

Her eyes scanned the bottom line of trees for a sight of Peter, while her neck prickled to the deliberate sound of Mordion's tread up the lane. Annabel's foot wriggled a little further onto the stone, her weight shifting just slightly, and then Blackfoot's voice said: *There! At the tree-line!*

Annabel caught a breath. It was Peter, tearing along the lower slope of the hill toward the ruins as if death itself pursued him– and maybe it did, thought Annabel, gazing open-mouthed in dismay at the vast, rolling cloud of *something* that sped in his wake. He was throwing handfuls of something else over his shoulder as he ran, and with each handful the cloud gained ground until at last he was bolting in earnest toward Annabel and Blackfoot, his eyes wide and fixed, his mouth open to gasp for each breath.

"Run, Peter!" shrieked Annabel. Her weight was all on the foot that rested on the stone, her other foot raised on tiptoe in preparation.

He's not going to make it, Nan, said Blackfoot, leaping to the rock beside her foot as if to urge her on. *You need to get in there **now**!*

"You don't know Peter," said Annabel, her fingernails digging into her palms. "He raced the fastest boy in the village just to prove he could beat him. He doesn't even *care* about running, but he makes sure that he's the best at everything and he's *not going to die.*"

Peter stumbled at the meeting of the hill with the flat grassland of the ruins, and Annabel watched with her heart in her throat, hearing in her heartbeat Mordion's footsteps as they rounded the last bend of the lane. Then Peter was there, his eyes as wide as Annabel's and his feet flying. Annabel wasn't quite sure whether she grabbed Peter or whether Peter grabbed her. Certainly *someone* grabbed the other one, and there was an impact that sent them both flying for one terrifying moment that stretched out until it was both longer and shorter than was possible, then they hit the mossy flagstones of the castle courtyard.

THREE

Someone was wheezing, and that someone was likely to be herself, Annabel knew, because she could also hear Peter groaning and Blackfoot simultaneously hissing aloud and swearing inside her head.

"You can't say that!" she said, when she could speak again.

There was utter silence before Blackfoot's voice said: *Oh, could you hear that?*

"Peter could probably hear it," Annabel said crankily. She still hadn't quite got her breath back and everything felt as though it had been shaken loose inside.

"Ow!" said Peter, just as irritably. "Ann, you're *on* my *leg*! Stop talking to your cat and move!"

"Well, you're on my hand!"

"Why didn't you just get out of the way!"

"Couldn't," said Annabel, her face growing hot and tight.

Peter, sitting up with another groan, caught sight of her face and winced. "Don't start crying, Ann."

"I'm not crying."

Nan, what's wrong? Are you hurt?

"Are, too," muttered Peter, looking away. "Oh, for pity's sake, Ann, I just asked why you didn't get out of the way!"

"*Couldn't,*" sobbed Annabel. "Blackfoot said the ruins would seal up as soon as I went in and I *couldn't–*"

"All right, all right, all right," said Peter, sitting down beside her again. He was rather paler than he had been. "I'm sorry, Ann."

*Nan, **are you hurt**?*

Annabel, hopelessly lost in her sobs, choked out: "I'm not hurt. Peter is...just...a *pig.*"

"All right, I'm a pig," agreed Peter, putting his arm around her. "I'm *sorry*, Ann."

"I know!" wailed Annabel. "But I can't s– stop now!"

He patted her shoulder. "Shut up, then," he said. "We'll talk later. Right now I want to know who put all *that* around the ruins, anyway."

It was quite some time later that Annabel stopped crying. It was always the same way when she began to cry: it took a lot to get her to the point of actually crying, but once she'd begun, she couldn't stop until she wasn't able to cry any more. When at last Annabel was hiccoughing at uneven intervals instead of bawling continually, Blackfoot began to stir in her lap, butting his head against her chin. He had slithered into her lap when she didn't respond to his mental questions any longer, and now he said: *Nan, can you hear me?*

"Of course I can hear you," said Annabel. "When haven't I?"

Then stop ignoring me. We haven't got time to sit and cry.

"What do you mean?" Annabel said, with a sharp stab of fear.

At the same time, Peter asked curiously: "Where'd that magic storm go, anyway? Did the barrier around the ruins stop it, or is it still there?"

Dissipated, said Blackfoot shortly. *It was Grenna's: there wasn't much of it and it's used up now. It'll take Mordion a little while to find another source.*

"That was Grenna's magic?" said Annabel, wiping her grubby cheeks with the backs of her hands.

"Thought it was familiar," Peter said, in satisfaction. "It was just that the spell was put together differently. It was *savage*, Ann. Grenna did that?"

"That's what Blackfoot said. Peter, is your mother all right?"

"She's fine," he said, the satisfaction vanishing from his face. "It only wanted me, so I ran and took it away from the house. Brannen will protect Mum. Actually, if it comes to that, he's pretty good at keeping her safe: it's about the only thing I like about him."

"Good," said Annabel, feeling a twist in her stomach straighten out. "Blackfoot, what do you mean, used up? Grenna's magic is used up?"

She's used up, too, Blackfoot said quietly.

"She's dead?"

Yes.

Peter dusted himself off impatiently. "Stop talking to the cat and talk to me! What do you mean, Grenna's dead?"

"That grey cat, the Mordion one," Annabel said. "Grenna made a spell for him to use me and Blackfoot but we got him out and so Mordion took Grenna's magic instead."

"Phew!" Peter whistled. "No wonder the spell was so different. Where's this Mordion got to, then?"

That's what I'm trying to tell you, said Blackfoot impatiently. *We need to move further in, Nan. It won't be long before he works out what has happened, and I can't guarantee that the sealing will last against him for more than a day or two if he gains access to more magic.*

"Blackfoot says we should move further in," Annabel reported, climbing awkwardly to her feet. She still felt as though everything inside her wobbly, soft outside had been shaken with great force.

"Further in, *where*?" said Peter. "It's not like there's much of the ruins left, is it? We can go further into the centre, but what good will that do?"

"Don't know," Annabel said. She pointed toward the edge of the ruins. "But that spire wasn't there yesterday, was it?"

"What–? That– that's impossible. That wasn't there yesterday."

Annabel gazed up at the spire. "That's what I just said."

It wasn't exactly a spire: it was the outer edge of a tower, tall and precarious and out of place, and it certainly hadn't been that tall or that *new-looking* yesterday, either.

The Castle, said Blackfoot, his tail lashing, *is–*

Peter yelped, and Annabel found herself being dragged sideways and behind one of the outcroppings. "Ow! What–?" she began, but Peter clapped his hand over her mouth.

"Shhh!" he hissed. "There's a man over there!"

Annabel looked up with a sinking feeling in her stomach. Sure enough, it was Mordion, standing on a piece of rubble just outside the ruins, his head turning carefully this way and that as his narrowed gaze passed over the crumbled masonry.

It's all right, said Blackfoot. *He can't see us. Not yet.*

"Blackfoot says he can't see us," said Annabel. She still felt uncomfortably exposed crawling back out from behind the bricked outcrop, and Peter must have felt the same way, because it took him even longer before he joined Annabel and Blackfoot in the open courtyard.

"Is that–"

"Yes."

"What's he doing?"

"Looking for us, I think," said Annabel. She felt like shivering again. "Blackfoot, why is he still looking for us?"

Because he still needs you.

"He needs *me*? Why? I thought it was you he needed."

We should go further in first, said Blackfoot. His tail was lashing again– in a combination of impatience and anxiety, Annabel rather thought.

"Blackfoot still wants to go further in," she told Peter.

"Oh, well, if the *cat* wants to go further in!" said Peter.

Annabel rolled her eyes at him. "You can't ask me what the ca– what Blackfoot is saying all the time and then go back to not believing he talks!"

"I can do whatever I want," Peter said. "You're the one to talks to yourself. You can't turn up your nose at me."

"Fine," said Annabel, following Blackfoot, who had padded away as soon as they began to argue. "You stand here and watch *him*. I'm going to go further in with Blackfoot."

Peter hurried after her. "I didn't say I wasn't going to come!"

They left the outer wall and Mordion behind, following Blackfoot further into the untidy ruins. Annabel, who was still sniffling occasionally, wiped her nose on the front of her flannels and came to the gloomy realisation that her flannel nightgown was now her single piece of clothing. She looked enviously at Peter, who must have been dressed when her message came through the tickerbox. Not only was he fully clothed, but shod, his hands comfortably in his pockets.

"Are we stuck in here now?" she asked Blackfoot.

"Probably," said Peter, scuffing his shoes along the flagstones.

For now, said Blackfoot. *But if things go right, if I'm right–*

"If you're right about *what*?" demanded Annabel. "Where are we going to sleep?" And then, appalled: "What are we going to *eat*?"

Peter gave a rude crack of laughter. "It never fails!"

If I'm right, said Blackfoot, *something should start to happen. I don't know exactly what, but I think the castle might come back.*

"Blackfoot thinks the castle might start to come back," Annabel said to Peter, more because she thought it might annoy him than because she though he'd believe her.

"Rubbish!" said Peter. "What utter rot! How can it come back? Come back from *where*, exactly? It'd have to come back from the past, if it was coming back from anywhere, and time travel is impossible!"

Not impossible, said Blackfoot, his voice more particularly caustic than usual. *Just very, **very** difficult.*

"Don't tell me," Peter said, shoving his hands even further into his pockets and curling his lip. "The cat has just said that it's not impossible."

"Yes."

"I told you not to tell me," complained Peter. "I don't want to hear it. It *is* impossible, and nothing your imaginary voice tells you is going to make that any different."

He's quite an irritating little thing, isn't he? said Blackfoot.

"Well, yes, but Grenna said it's impossible, too," Annabel said, grudgingly fair to Peter.

Grenna isn't the repository of all magical knowledge, Blackfoot said, just as Peter said: "That's no proof, Ann: what Grenna didn't know about magic could fill a whole bookcase of books."

"Oh shut up, both of you," grumbled Annabel. "I don't know why you can't get along: you both say the same thing most of the time."

Don't compare me with that cocksure young dribble, protested Blackfoot.

Peter said: "Thanks a lot, Ann! I'll have you know that my intelligence–"

"Oh, shut up," Annabel said to Peter. To Blackfoot, she said: "You were probably just like him when you were a kitten." Then she left both Blackfoot and Peter spluttering their outrage behind her and stomped further into the ruins.

Blackfoot soon took the lead again, with the rather snide question of: *Do you know where you're going, Nan? No? I didn't think so. **This** way.* Annabel didn't really mind. She was still feeling shaken and not quite sure of anything, and it was comforting to follow the familiarity of Blackfoot's lead. Peter continued to grumble as he trailed behind them, but he didn't try to do anything but follow Blackfoot either. Annabel wondered if he was as frightened as she was, and came to the surprising conclusion that yes, he probably was.

By late morning, they had found their way into the old throne room. Annabel and Peter had found it once before, but it was so deep in a vicious snarl of blackberries and raspberries that they hadn't tried to visit it again: Annabel, because it took far too much effort and sweat, and Peter, because he cared more about his tickerboxes anyway, and the light wasn't as good in the throne room.

Annabel, sweaty, scratched, and tired of pushing through

brambles, sank down on the dais and wished it wasn't so stuffy in the throne room. It was the only place in the ruins where you couldn't see the sky, and she resented not being able to see it.

Peter looked around critically. "Is this where we're staying, then? Good. There are some things I want to know about."

I wondered how long it would take, said Blackfoot, his voice somewhere between resigned and amused. *Nan, why do you always wait for Peter to ask the questions? Have you spent so long pretending to be stupid that you actually believe it now?*

"Because I can't think of any to ask," Annabel groaned, flopping on her back to feel the coolness of the marble slabs beneath her. "I told you. I'm not the clever one: Peter is."

"Shut up for a bit, Ann," Peter said impatiently. "I want to know how the cat knew the ruins were going to seal up. I also want to know why that Mordion came after me, and what on earth he wants with you."

Annabel sat up again, crossing her legs, then leant her elbows on her legs and her chin on her fists. From there it was easy to give Peter her best stupid, expressionless look.

"What now?" demanded Peter in annoyance.

"I thought you wanted me to shut up. And I *also* thought you were back to thinking Blackfoot can't talk."

Peter scowled. "I don't know. But I know *you* wouldn't know about the ruins sealing, so something's up."

It was more of a guess than anything, said Blackfoot, licking a paw.

"What if you'd guessed wrong?" Annabel demanded.

Blackfoot, very calmly, said: *Then we would all have been dead.*

"But– but–"

What were your other choices? It was die there or die here, and there was slightly less chance of dying here than there was of dying there.

"Well?" said Peter impatiently. "What has the cat got to say for itself? And don't say that I don't believe it talks so what's it to me, just answer me."

Annabel made a face at him. "All right, clever clogs! He says it was a guess, and that's all there was to it. We're just lucky he was right."

"What guess? What made him guess that? Why? Wait! Ann, stop your cat from walking away while I'm talking to it!"

Annabel dispassionately watched as Blackfoot sprang up onto the partial wall-section behind the dais, climbing light-foot through the precarious bricks, and said: "You should be more polite if you want him to listen to you."

"It's. A. *Cat.*"

"That's no reason to be rude," said Annabel, just slightly more smug than she had been before. "Even if he is just a cat, he's still a cat you want something from. You should use your manners."

Peter, instead, hurled his shoe at Blackfoot. He was usually a very fair shot, so Annabel could only assume that he had meant it to fall short of Blackfoot and drop back onto the dais for him to put on with a sour expression.

"I'll find out about the sealing myself, then," he said, and vanished back into the brambles.

Blackfoot, by contrast, dropped a blackberry beside Annabel and said: *You wanted something to eat, Nan?*

"I meant porridge or scones or bacon," said Annabel grumpily, but she ate the berry anyway. That reminded her stomach that she hadn't eaten since last night, and she spent the next half hour picking and eating berries right off the canes before she was sated enough to gather some for Peter as well.

Peter didn't come back for his berries until the late afternoon heat from the triad had begun to make the stuffy throne room even stuffier. While he was gone, Annabel, her face too hot and distinctly sticky, drew with her tiny pencil nub in the small book of paper that Peter had given her yesterday, shading carefully so as not to ruin the drawing. There were only so many palm-sized pieces of paper to a book, and she didn't want to waste any of them.

She drew the throne room free of brambles, the way she would have liked it to be, and sketched in a door that had long since been bricked up by rubble at the far end of the room. By the time she was working on the walls of the throne room, Peter tumbled back through the brambles, panting.

"I haven't ever seen anything like it!" he said, eyes glowing. "Ann, you should see it!"

"Well, I can't," said Annabel. "There's no need to rub my face in it, either."

"What's wrong with you? Too hot, are you? Look: I brought you some water."

Annabel brightened. "Really? Where did you get it?"

"There's a magic-crank pump in the bit that used to be the laundry or something."

"Wasn't that broken?" asked Annabel, remembering a similarly stuffy day when she had been unable to slake her thirst until they left the ruins for the creek.

"It was," said Peter offhandedly, tossing her a flask. "I fixed it. I thought it'd come in handy if we're in here for a while."

"Yes, but will we be in here for a while? Won't Mordion get sick of trying to get to us? Blackfoot?"

"It doesn't matter if he gets sick of us or not," said Peter, while Blackfoot batted a stray leaf across the dais without giving any sign that he'd heard her question. "That seal around the castle: it's not going anywhere. And we can't get out, either. I tried."

"You *tried–*"

"Oh, well, someone had to try," said Peter. "I didn't see you or the cat wanting to try, what with Mordion being out there and everything. It's really strong magic, Ann: I haven't seen anything that strong before. Even *my* magic–"

Blackfoot laughed in Annabel's mind. *Good heavens. He's comparing his magic with the magic Rorkin worked on the castle.*

"Even my magic–" Peter said again, uncertainly; and then, "Ann, is the cat laughing at me?"

Annabel blinked into her best expressionless face. "No."

"It always looks so satirical," said Peter, unconvinced. "Anyway, what I really meant to say is that we can't get out of here today or tomorrow or maybe ever, so we're going to need to fix a few things around the place."

Annabel, who was about to remark that the last time she'd needed water and had asked him to operate the pump, he had only looked at it and said: "It's broken", decided that on the whole she'd rather drink the water than begin quarrelling again. Accordingly, she drank the water.

"What about Mordion?" she asked, between sips. "Has he gone away yet?"

"I didn't see him," said Peter.

Blackfoot said: *No. He's still there. I can feel him pressing up against the sealing, trying to find a way in.*

"Blackfoot says he's still there," Annabel said, passing Peter the stained handkerchief full of berries that she'd picked for him.

"I know that," Peter said loftily. "I said I didn't *see* him. Anyone could sense him doing magic against the seal."

Anyone with stronger-than-usual magic, said Blackfoot. His voice still sounded sarcastic. *Nan, I'll never understand why you associate with this horrible little boy. You've got enough bad habits of your own without learning his as well.*

"Hey," said Annabel, only mildly resentful. She *did* have a lot of bad habits, after all. "You're not exactly perfect yourself."

Peter said: "What?" in surprise, and then: "I wish you wouldn't talk to the cat at the same time as talking to me, Ann. It makes you look really mad, you know."

Annabel shrugged. She was used to people thinking she was mad, or not quite all there, or stupid. Most of the people she had met at Grenna's cottage had looked at her round, expressionless face and rolls of fat, and had assumed she was stupid. It had been a very useful screen for Annabel.

"What are we going to do, then?" she asked. "Are we going to stay here forever?"

No, said Blackfoot. *Don't worry, Nan: things will work out. The castle is the safest place we can be, right now.*

"I'll do some tests tomorrow," said Peter. "That Mordion, though– his magic is barely anything. I don't see him getting through that seal in a hurry."

That's the problem with Mordion, said Blackfoot, and Annabel thought that his voice was a little bit bitter. *He never seems exactly strong, but somehow he always manages to wriggle back to the top every time someone throws him to the bottom of the pile. He's already taken Grenna's magic and used it up. He'll come back when he's replenished himself again.*

"He's going to kill someone else? Peter, Blackfoot says Mordion will just go and get magic from someone else."

"Oh," said Peter. "In that case, I don't much like the idea of being stuck in here while he goes off to get more magic. We should be trying to get away while we can."

*I'm sure that would be a very useful attitude if we **could** get *away*, said Blackfoot. *But since we can't, perhaps Peter could turn his mind back to fixing things again.*

"The cat's giving me that look again," said Peter.

"He says we can't get out," Annabel reported, weary of translating. "So it's no use trying."

"That's stupid," Peter said. "It's like saying that it's impossible to fly without magic, so we should stop trying to invent machines. It *is* possible, it'll just take some work."

Blackfoot flicked his tail and sat down neatly next to Annabel. *Or like saying that time travel is impossible without ever trying to make it happen?*

Annabel snickered, and made another face at Peter when he said an annoyed: "What?" That, of course, annoyed Peter enough to send him out to study the seal again, leaving Annabel free to sketch, and Blackfoot free to make the occasional sarcastic remark at either Annabel or Peter's expense.

Annabel ignored them as she almost always did. Sometimes she thought that Blackfoot made sarcastic remarks at her for the pleasure of having them ignored, soaking into her thick skin without making a mark. She gave up on her drawing of the throne room for the time being: she had been trying to draw it without the blackberry and raspberry brambles, the way it must have been so long ago, but she couldn't see enough in the shadows to draw it right, and she didn't like to draw things if she couldn't draw them correctly. Instead, she was working on a portrait. It wasn't a quick sketch of Peter as most of her portraits were; this one was a sketch of a man that Annabel was quite sure she hadn't met, but whose face she was equally sure she knew. In its way, it was just as hard as trying to draw the throne room in all the shadows. She drew in a sharply angled eyebrow and then erased it, only to draw it back in with very little adjustment; shaded beside the vague suggestion of a nose only to realise that it should certainly be thinner and more aristocratic.

In the end, she left the portrait unfinished as well. Nothing was sitting quite right with it, and she couldn't for the life of her decide how the mouth should be drawn in. That was annoying, because Annabel was quite sure that she knew exactly how it looked: it was just that she didn't seem to be able to *draw* it.

Giving up? Blackfoot said, his head popping up to nose into the paper block. *How unusual of you.*

Annabel rubbed his stomach with her free hand for the pleasure of seeing him fail to resist purring. He could be as prickly and sarcastic as he liked, but when she scratched his stomach everything gave way to purring. His irritated and slightly offended pleasure always amused Annabel.

Don't think you can get around me by scratching my stomach, warned Blackfoot, but he flopped down with his head on her knee anyway. *Your habit of giving up on things when they get too difficult is likely to come back and bite you, you know.*

"So are you, but I still keep you around," said Annabel, and went on to a more amusing drawing where the castle grew in spires and random stair-ways to the clear sky.

Annabel was stiff and sore when she woke the next day. To her relief, the throne room wasn't as stuffy as it had been when she went to sleep, a fresh, cool breeze rolling across the marble floor to tease her hair. It wasn't until she sat up, careful not to disturb the still-sleeping Blackfoot, that she saw the reason for the freshness: the door at the other end of the room was now mostly free of rubble, and quite a few of the berry-canes were also gone.

"Good for Peter," yawned Annabel, climbing rather grimily to her feet. Peter must have worked quite hard to clear all that away. He wasn't anywhere in sight, which probably meant that he had gone back to his study of the seal– or, thought Annabel hopefully, to look for somewhere that they could bathe. Her flannels were very much worse for the wearing, now, stained from climbing about the ruins and stiff and smelly from running until she sweated last night. She could see a frizz of brown hair in her peripheral, which meant that her hair was in much the same state, and when she tried to run her fingers through it there were so many bramble strands that she gave up and simply pushed the frizz back from her face.

She wandered over to the cleared doorway, wondering if Peter had gone through it instead of back to the edges of the sealed up ruins, but when she called out his name into the darkness of the newly uncovered corridor, there was a scrabbling from behind her.

"What?" said Peter's voice, grumpily.

Annabel turned her head and blinked stupidly at him. She hadn't seen him asleep by the side of the raised dais: his brown trousers and green shirt had blended right in with the leaf-litter there.

"Oh," she said. "I thought– wait, didn't–"

Peter sat up, yawning, and saw her by the cleared doorway. He whistled. "Ann! You cleared that?"

"*I* didn't do it," said Annabel, staring. "I thought *you* did it!"

"Really?" Peter scrambled eagerly to his feet and hurried over to her. "I wonder if the ruins shifted in the night?"

Annabel, chewing anxiously on the collar of her flannels, said: "We would have heard it. Wouldn't we?"

"I suppose so." Peter stuck his head through the door

frame, turned it left and right, and pulled it back in again. "It's a bit dark, isn't it? I would have thought there'd be more light."

"There wouldn't, you know," said Annabel, mentally piecing together a map of the bits of the ruins that they knew. "It goes into the bit that's all lumpy and fallen, doesn't it? It's probably buried under too much rubble to get the sunlight."

"Should we– we should have a look, shouldn't we?"

"Yee-eees," agreed Annabel doubtfully. "But shouldn't we bathe first?"

"Good idea," said Peter, and it occurred to Annabel that he was just as nervous of going down that dark hall as she was. "There's the pump I fixed last night. It'll be a bit cold if the triad's not up, but at least we'll be clean."

By the time they had grubbed their way out of the brambles again, Annabel was so hot and scratched that it could have been a fine winter's morning and she would still have put her head under the pump for washing. It was very far from being a fine winter's morning, however: the first sun of the triad was certainly up and hot, but there was a humidity to the air that suggested a storm. Annabel, who had been feeling more than slightly suffocated in the throne room, found to her dismay that it was hardly less stifling in sight of the sky.

By the time she and Peter had finished washing, Blackfoot was sitting in the partial doorway to watch them splash each other. Peter had scrubbed the blood from Annabel's face, and Annabel had returned the favour by scrubbing the back of his neck for him, so they were both rather cleaner than usual, though Annabel was still flapping about in her now wet flannels.

"Never mind, Ann," said Peter, grinning. "If we find the secret treasury, maybe we can get you some clothes that aren't completely moth-eaten!"

"I don't care if they *are* moth-eaten," said Annabel, who was beginning to feel hot and heavy again. "So long as they're not flannel!"

There is no secret treasury, Blackfoot said. *It's just a story told to gullible children.*

"How would you know?" demanded Annabel, rescuing her note-pad and pencil from the swiftly approaching puddle of water that was encroaching on them. "You're a cat."

"Cat being rude again? I don't know why you keep it, Ann."

I don't know why she keeps you, if it comes to that, said Blackfoot, sending a particularly glassy look up in Peter's direction. That made Annabel giggle, but since it was too hot to be arguing with Peter, she avoided his suspicious inquiries and led the way back to the throne room, this time more slowly.

It was still too hot in the throne room, but Annabel's wet cuffs were pleasant to wipe her face with, and there was an ominously cool breeze coming from the newly cleared doorway.

"Makes you wonder, doesn't it?" said Peter. "What's down there, I mean. If there's a breeze, there has to be another opening in there somewhere, but I've never found another entrance to this part of the castle."

This part of the castle wasn't here yesterday, Blackfoot said. *As for it being another entrance...well, I suppose we can **hope** that's what it is.*

"What do you mean?" asked Annabel, alarmed, but Blackfoot had already vanished into the darkness of the corridor without waiting to answer her.

"What?" said Peter, who was watching her.

"Blackfoot's being mysterious," Annabel said. "I *hate* it

when he does that. Most of the time I think he's just pretending to know things."

Blackfoot sniffed somewhere at the back of her mind, but Peter looked as uneasy as she felt. "Oh, well, there's no use standing around here, anyway. We'd better follow the cat."

They entered the corridor together, and the coolness of it immediately sank through Annabel's wet flannels with blissful effect.

"Ugh," said Peter at the same time. "Cold!"

Annabel, on the other hand, found herself walking more swiftly. "It's nice," she said. "Sort of refreshing. I can't see Blackfoot, can you?"

I'm here, said Blackfoot, twining around her ankles a second later. Annabel, who would have shrieked if it hadn't been for the split-second of warning, still jumped. *Stop quivering, and follow me.*

"Never mind," she said. "He's right at our feet. Where are we going, anyway?"

"That's what I want to know," complained Peter. "It's all very well to be exploring dark tunnels and unseen parts of the castle, but why? Shouldn't we be working on getting safely out of the castle? Or at least trying to get rid of Mordion?"

What a good idea, said Blackfoot. *What a shame I didn't think of it.*

There was a brief silence, into which fell footsteps. Then Peter said: "What? What did the cat say?"

"He says he already thought of it and it's no good," Annabel said diplomatically. She listened to Blackfoot's explanations for an uncomprehending few moments and added: "He's saying something about the only way out being to go further in. It doesn't make sense."

Don't paraphrase me, Nan, said Blackfoot. *You invariably get it wrong.*

"I do that on purpose," Annabel said. "If you want Peter to know what you're saying, talk to him yourself."

I couldn't broach that level of self-contained disbelief if I tried, remarked Blackfoot. *And I prefer not to try while that disbelief continues to be upheld by such disgustingly powerful magic.*

"What's it saying?"

"He's complimenting your magic," Annabel said, with the vocal equivalent of her solid, stupid look. "He's impressed by how powerful it is."

From Peter there was suspicious silence, from Blackfoot silence that could have been either amused or annoyed. At last, Peter, ignoring the issue completely, said: "Well, it *could* make sense, Ann. It depends on what sort of magic someone used on this place."

"I thought you said there was no magic in the ruins."

"Well," said Peter, "it's not so much that there wasn't magic: it's that it was far too strong for me to be able to notice it."

"You mean you were wrong."

"It was incredibly well hidden!" protested Peter. "How can I be expected to see something that strong?"

Annabel made a face in the darkness. "That doesn't make sense, either."

"It *does*," said Peter. "Magic is easy to see–"

"For *some* people–"

For most people, said Blackfoot. *You're just special.*

"Hey!"

"What now?"

"Blackfoot's being sarcastic," said Annabel. "Never mind."

"As I was *saying*, magic is easy to see, even the small stuff. And if you're really good at it, and know how to hide it, that's when it gets hard to see."

"So you were wrong–"

"*Ann–*"

"–and there's actually a *lot* of magic in the castle?"

"Well, if you're going to put it that way," said Peter crossly, "yes! I was wrong, all right? With this amount of magic, and how strong it is, the castle could have something as complicated and clever as an inverted exit spell."

He's not wrong, said Blackfoot. *He's not right, either, but at least he's trying.*

"It's no good my trying," said Annabel. "I can't see magic and I don't know how it works. Peter might as well work at it: at least he likes magic."

"Actually–" began Peter.

Now *you've started it!* muttered Blackfoot.

"*Actually*, I *don't* like magic," said Peter, with the air of one about to give a speech.

Annabel, hurriedly, said: "Yes, yes, I know. You don't like magic, you just use it when you need to and the future is in cogs and wheels and tickerboxes and metal blobby things."

"They're *solder nodules*," Peter said. "Honestly, Ann: you don't even listen!"

"Anyway," Annabel said, even more hurriedly, "what do you mean by an inverted exit spell?"

"Well, what the cat said made me think: if someone put an inverted exit spell on the castle, we *would* have to go deeper to get out."

"Oh," said Annabel. "So we *can* get out."

"Yes," Peter said. "Theoretically."

Blackfoot said: *No. Not like that, anyway.*

"Why do you know so much about it, anyway?" complained Annabel. Peter opened his mouth to answer, then realised she was talking to Blackfoot, and closed it again.

Be careful, said Blackfoot. *There's a hole here.*

His warning came too late: Annabel had already put her foot in the hole. There was the sensation of horrible, unexpected absence, then she pitched forward onto the corridor floor.

FOUR

"Ow!" said Annabel, rolling in the dust. Something was bouncing slightly, and it could have been her, but she didn't think so. "Oh! Blackfoot! Should the floor be movin–"

This time, the entire section of flooring betrayed her, vanishing beneath her as utterly as it had vanished beneath her foot. Annabel gasped in a dusty breath as time seemed to stop, then something hit her hard *everywhere*. For a moment she lay where she was, and the everything that had been hit hurt too much to do anything but stay still and groan, or sob, or perhaps she was just breathing.

Annabel became aware of the blood and Peter's voice at about the same time. When the first frozen, dream-state of pain had abated a little, they were both waiting for her, bothersome and insistent. She dealt with the blood first, letting it pool at the corners of her mouth where it could drain away into the dust beneath her without having to spit, then mumbled: "Shudda Eter."

"That's right," said Peter encouragingly. "Tell me to shut

up. I did try to catch you, Ann, I just wasn't quick enough. I'm coming down."

"Don'," Annabel said thickly. "Too 'ar 'own."

"I'll be all right," Peter said. He was still sounding encouraging, which worried Annabel. It meant that she was probably hurt worse than she'd thought– or at least, that Peter thought so. "Don't move, Ann. The cat's already down there somewhere."

So that's what the furry warmth against her cheek was. Annabel, who only seemed to be able to feel the cold at the moment, had vaguely noticed it somewhere in the back of her mind where she kept Blackfoot's voice.

As if that had woken her ability to hear him again, she faintly heard him say: *Nan? Have you lost any teeth? Broken any bones?*

Annabel considered that, but the question was too involved to answer with her crushed and bloody mouth, so she merely pushed herself up on her forearms and dribbled another warm string of blood into the dust. Her arms, pleasingly, held her up better than she'd expected, and when it was possible to breathe without everything hurting quite so much, Annabel clumsily turned herself over. Her pencil was digging into her palm, and the other sharpness there was the corner of her notebook, she rather thought. Annabel scrabbled them together with a decent assortment of dust and debris, and shoved them into her dirty pocket, regardless of the fact that it was still slightly damp. Then she gazed up at the gaping hole in what had been the floor, surprised to find that she could distinctly see it. She'd thought it was dark in the corridor, but down here beneath the corridor it was darker still, and the hole was a patch of greyish dark instead of the pitch black around her.

"All right, Ann?"

"No," grumbled Annabel, through rubbery lips. She painfully turned her head into her shoulder and wiped her mouth against her flannels. That hurt, but it was better than feeling slimy *and* painful. She touched her fingers to her lips carefully, then said: "Nothing's broken. I think. My stomach broke the fall. And my mouth."

She heard Peter drop clumsily to the floor at last. "Finally!" he said, and there was the click of his fingers snapping. At once light, soft and pulsing, pushed back the darkness.

Annabel squinted at him, and as she did so, she felt the pull of something painful across her cheek. "Ugh. Why didn't you make your light *before* you climbed down? You could have fallen."

"You know how I am with heights, Ann! If I'd been able to see it, I *would* have fallen. It's awfully high."

"I know," said Annabel. She was sitting now, which was nice. Nicer still, it wasn't hurting quite so much to keep breathing, and the distant, cold feeling had faded away. Her body once again felt like one piece and not several broken parts. "You can stop biting my sleeve, Blackfoot: I'm fine."

"You don't look fine," Peter said brutally. "Your mouth is all bloody and you've got a big cut across your cheek. You've probably broken some ribs, too."

"I haven't, you know," said Annabel, padding about with her hands for somewhere that wasn't rocky to push herself up from the ground. "I think I was just winded. It's a good thing I'm so well-padded."

Don't stand up! said Blackfoot's exasperated voice. *You're still dripping blood on your flannels.*

"All right," Annabel said, still too shaken to feel like fighting about things when it was simpler just to do as she was told.

Peter was gazing around them, his lively glow of light as curious as he. "Might as well explore while we're down here," he said. "Maybe we really *have* found the treasury, Ann! Well, the hidden tunnel that leads to it, anyway."

Annabel wiped her mouth on her flannels again, gloomily. "If *we've* found it by accident, someone else is sure to have found it by now. It'll be empty."

Blackfoot's voice had a distinct sigh to it. *I suppose it's impossible to convince you both that it's **not** the treasury?*

"Not impossible," said Annabel. "We just don't want to believe you. Well, would you rather find gold or spiders?"

Blackfoot gave an unexpected laugh at that, but Peter said in a superior sort of way: "Not *gold*, Ann: magic! Why would they put boring old gold and jewels in a treasury?"

Annabel laughed rudely. "Maybe they should have. Maybe they would have been able to last through the war instead of being over-run. At least you can hire soldiers with gold and jewels."

Blackfoot laughed again at the back of her mind, and said: *There were gold treasures and magical treasures. But this tunnel doesn't lead to the treasury.*

"Blackfoot says–"

"I don't care what the cat says. What does it know about treasuries?"

Oh, nothing in the world, said Blackfoot. *It's not as though I spent my youth–*

Annabel stared down at him in surprise, ignoring Peter, who had already wandered away. "What? What did you do when you were young?"

I did as I was told and didn't ignore my elders, Blackfoot said.

"Were you this sarcastic when you were a kitten?" demanded Annabel. "What turned you so bitter?"

I never was a kitten, said Blackfoot.

There was another brief, conscious silence, where he seemed to realise that he'd again said something that he shouldn't have said. Annabel broke it to ask: "How can you *not* have been a kitten?"

And I was always this bitter, thank you very much.

"I don't believe you," said Annabel, scruffing behind his ears to make him purr. Sometimes, Blackfoot could even be lovely. "Where has Peter gone, do you think?"

Don't worry, said Blackfoot, and Annabel heard a distinct purr of laughter to his voice. *He'll be back very quickly, I should think.*

Annabel was about to ask suspiciously *why* Peter would be back so very quickly, when she heard running footsteps and something hissing loudly above that. Peter's light came back into sight again, bobbing a little, but when Peter himself came into sight he was only walking a little more quickly than usual, his hands stuffed into his pockets. Annabel heard Blackfoot chuckle in the back of her mind, and was quite well aware herself that Peter had only slowed down at the last moment to put on a good front.

He said, just a little more breathlessly than usual: "Bit of a tricky door through there, actually."

"What sort of a tricky door?" asked Annabel, giving Blackfoot's ears one last tickle.

"Magic locks: huge ones. They're snakes, and they're pretty angry."

Annabel tilted her head to one side. "Why are they angry?"

"That might have been my fault."

I wouldn't believe it for a minute.

"What did you do to it?" Annabel asked, gloomily unsurprised.

"I let the tickerbox have a go at it," said Peter. His voice became indignant. "They nearly crushed it, too! It only just managed to get through: I can hear it ticking away behind the door now. It wants to come back but I don't think it dares."

"You've probably lost it, then," said Annabel. "If your tickerbox can't pick the lock, what can we do?"

"Don't be like that, Ann," Peter said coaxingly. "We *have* to get it back. We might need it later."

Annabel sighed, and licked her damaged lips. "Might as well try, I suppose."

"Oh, here," said Peter, poking her forehead with one finger to tilt her face. She couldn't see what he was doing, but her mouth felt better at once, and even the cut across her cheek began to feel itchy. "I've sped up the natural healing. It'll still be a bit sore and itchy, but it shouldn't hurt as much."

Oh, well done, said Blackfoot, his voice particularly caustic. *It only took you half an hour to realise that you should do something that took all of five seconds.*

"He can't help it," Annabel said excusingly. "He gets carried away when there's something new to explore."

Blackfoot's sarcastic comments didn't stop, but they did sink into a vague, grumbling murmur at the back of her mind instead. They continued as Annabel followed Peter and his bobbing light, and only stopped when the light threw forward and glanced off brasswork at the end of the hall.

Then he said: *Oh. That's a bit different to what I pictured.*

"Oh!" said Annabel, as close to cooing as she ever came. "Oh, aren't they *nice!*"

There was a hissing kind of silence as the brazen snakes unfurled themselves, all golden and soft and glowing in Peter's magic light, then Peter and Blackfoot said at the same time: "*What?*"

"I'm drawing them!" Annabel said, her fingers already groping for her pencil and her notebook. "They're so smooth and glowy! Don't do anything to them until I've finished, Peter!"

"Do anything to them! *Do* anything to *them?*"

Well done, Nan, said Blackfoot, sinking down on one of the flagstones and curling his tail around himself. *I don't think I've ever seen him so lost for words. Incidentally, since when have you had an affinity with snakes?*

"I've always loved snakes," Annabel protested. "They're so soft and pretty, and I had one when I was a baby."

"No, you didn't," Peter argued. "You couldn't have! Grenna hates 'em, and even if your parents had loved 'em, who's going to give a snake to their child?"

"Well, I did," said Annabel positively. "He was a little garter snake and he was green. He only bit me once, and that was because I accidentally stepped on his tail. I fed him crickets and grasshoppers."

"You're not even drawing them right," muttered Peter, who was obviously in an argumentative mood. "You're drawing them with their eyes closed."

"That's how they were when I first saw them," Annabel said, ignoring his rancour. She'd drawn one of the snakes with its eyes closed, its head curved beneath a coil of the other snake. The second, she'd drawn with its glowing eyes open just a slit, sleepy curiosity wakening like the embers of a fire. "They look nicer like that, anyway."

"Come *on*, Ann! We've got to rescue my tickerbox!"

"You're the one who did something stupid," countered Annabel. "I don't have to do anything. And I'm *drawing*."

"You're always drawing. It's boring– look, even the snakes are falling asleep! Even the magical lock is falling asleep waiting for you to do something!"

"Well, that's all right, isn't it?" Annabel said reasonably. "If they're asleep, maybe we can unlock them before they wake up again."

"I'm not putting my hand near them again!"

"I'll do it," Annabel said. "But I'm finishing my drawing first, so there. I want to remember how lovely they were."

"Ann–"

"No," said Annabel, her chin mulish.

"What do you mean, no? I didn't get to ask you anything."

"I'm not going to try anything until I've finished my drawing."

"You don't know that's what I was going to ask!"

"All right," said Annabel, without ceasing to shade the smooth scales of the second snake. "What were you going to ask me?"

"Well," said Peter, and stopped. There was a silence where Annabel's scratching pencil was very loud, then Peter said: "Well, but do you *have* to draw all the time, Ann?"

"Yes," Annabel said. "I haven't got perfect recall like *some* people. This is how I remember things."

"This is how you waste time when you don't want to do something," muttered Peter.

Annabel only shrugged. It was true, after all: she didn't see why she should risk her limbs for Peter's errant tickerbox. She was very fond of snakes, but she was also sensible enough not to get too close if she didn't know whether or not one was poisonous.

There was another scratching silence before Peter said sulkily: "But you *like* snakes, Ann!"

As do I, remarked Blackfoot. *They're quite reasonably tasty if you can get past their infernal teeth. I tend to avoid ones that are big enough to swallow me whole, however. Nan, there is no earthly reason you should put yourself into danger to help an insensate piece of machinery.*

"I'm not sure it *is* insensate," Annabel murmured. "It's one of Peter's after all."

"Of course it's insensate," said Peter moodily, catching on to the conversation. "It's a machine, just cogs and gears and–"

–a vast amount of undirected and uncannily powerful magic, said Blackfoot, in a loud aside. *If it comes to that–*

"Oh, wait!" said Peter suddenly. "They're– Nan, they really are going to sleep!"

"Shhh, then!"

Peter hissed: "No, but Nan! Their tails are dropping back into the slots as they fall asleep: they were like that when I first saw them. When their tails are in those slots, the door is unlocked."

"Huh," said Annabel. "Keep quiet, then. If they're asleep by the time I finish my drawing, I'll try to reach the doorknob."

She'd already seen their tails sinking into the slots, but it hadn't occurred to her that it was all part of the lock. Annabel smudged a little with one finger, and began to draw the tails of her sketched snakes in their slots as well. The snake locks were already coiling wider as their tails settled, and through the coils, she could see the two doorknobs. They hadn't been visible before.

Beside her, Peter bounced up and down in his impatience, but Annabel ignored him until she had finished shading around the tiny gleam in the eye of the second, almost sleeping, snake. It was a friendly gleam, she thought as she looked from her drawing to the door: the real snake had the same one. She tucked away pencil and sketch book, and said: "All right. Let's go."

"Be careful, Ann," Peter said anxiously. She heard the shuffle of his foot back and forth, then felt his warmth at her back. "They're awfully fast!"

Nan, I really think it's better for you not to do this.

"It's all right," she said, catching the final, friendly gleam in the second snake's eyes just before they winked shut. She reached through the coils, careful not to touch the silken scales that curled around the doorknobs, and turned both at once.

Carefully does it, Nan. Don't touch them.

"I won't," sighed Annabel, though she would very much have liked to touch them.

"Won't what?" Peter asked, sidling through the doors after her. He skirted around her back to keep her between himself and the snake locks. Annabel didn't blame him: she was quite sure that one of the second snake's eyes had cracked open again, and that a glow of consideration was rimming the crack.

"Touch them."

"I should hope not!"

"Just because they didn't like you–"

"They're *snakes*. They don't like anybody."

"Maybe they just didn't like you," retorted Annabel. "They didn't try to bite me– or Blackfoot."

"Oh, never mind!" muttered Peter, hurrying further into the room. There was a swishing—of paper, perhaps—and the *tick tick*ing of the tickerbox further in.

Not so bad, said Blackfoot cautiously. *But I wouldn't close the doors just yet if– Nan! Why did you close the doors?*

"Hey!" Peter protested, as the faint light from the tunnel vanished. "Why did you close the doors, Nan?"

"Didn't," said Annabel guiltily. Strictly speaking, she

hadn't. She'd given them a bit of a push out of the way, and hadn't expected a sharp draught to send them shuddering together again. She heard the sound of hissing from the other side, and the distinct sound of a lock clicking into place. "The breeze–"

Peter sighed, and conjured another light. The darkness sank back as the light rose, and after a moment, Peter sent another two lights high into the air, lighting the room right to its edges.

"Oh," he said, his voice flat with disappointment. "It's not the treasury."

"No," agreed Annabel. The room was far too small to be treasury, for a start. Worse, it was filled with shelf upon shelf of books, and several dilapidated desks around the room were piled high with papers made thick and clumsy with dust, and ancient quills that were now only spine instead of feather.

"And tell your cat to stop looking at me with that expression! He might as well say *I told you so!*"

"He can't help it," Annabel said. In fact, Blackfoot *had* just distinctly said: *Didn't I say so?* "He has a naturally smug face."

Naturally– Nan, I'll have you know that my face is naturally sarcastic. The smugness is a perfectly normal response to that boy's superior attitude.

Annabel only made a face at him. "Where's your tickerbox, Peter?"

Peter looked around with new interest. "Good point. Where did the little nuisance get to now?"

It seems to be tunnelling into the books, said Blackfoot, with interest. *I wonder why it's doing that?*

"Blackfoot's found it," Annabel said, wandering over to one of the desks. She brushed the oily dust off a few of the papers and wiped her hands on her flannels. With her predilection for drawing and the scarcity of paper in her life, paper never failed to draw her attention. "What a waste: they've only used one side. Oh! These are *old*, Peter! Look, this one is in the old form writing– you know, the one that's all joined and flowing. Wait, though. This– wait, this can't be right! It says, *Sorry about this, your highness. Try not to get hurt, won't you? And don't forget to duck.*

Peter emerged from one of the bookshelves, his hair ruffled and festooned with cobwebs. "You must be reading it wrong," he said. "Someone using that form wouldn't be using modern words. Sometimes the old form cursive is hard to read: our minds recognise patterns and translate them as familiar–"

"I can *read* old form cursive!" said Annabel crossly, snatching up a handful of the half-used paper to save for later. "I used to read Grenna's spell books to her all the time!"

"You must be out of practise, then."

Annabel made a face at him and dusted off more of the documents. Blackfoot leapt onto the desk and padded over the shifting mass of papers, and something slithered in the depths of the piles of paper, prompting Annabel to hope that it was only the rolls of heavy dust that she'd removed slipping down between the leaves. "Don't be so superior," she said. "It makes you look smug. Oh! Look at this one: it's talking about something called Black Velvet and the re-establishment of the–"

There was an explosion of paper and dust that sent leaves and dust-bunnies flying through the musty air, while Blackfoot's claws shredded the air with frantic haste. Annabel shrieked and flailed in the whirl of paper, and caught Blackfoot, who had launched himself at her. She sat down rather more suddenly than she'd intended, and Blackfoot, his claws still rigidly gripping her flannel collar, flopped against her face. "Blackfoot! What *are* you doing?"

There was an embarrassed kind of silence before Blackfoot's claws retracted. *Ah. Yes*, he said, climbing away carefully to avoid scratching her. *There were spiders. Big ones.*

"What?"

Spiders.

"You– you're afraid of *spiders*?"

They were big ones. Stop stirring up the papers: they're hiding underneath them.

"Ugh," said Annabel, scrambling to her feet. She'd *thought* there was something moving amongst the papers. "Ugh, let's get out of here, then."

She followed Blackfoot, who was now nudging at Peter's tickerbox with his nose, and crouched curiously beside Peter, trying to shake off the phantom feeling of spider legs against her neck.

"Is it trying to get out?"

"Don't know," said Peter. "This one's completely off-program. I didn't tell it to do this sort of thing."

"Maybe it knows something we don't know."

Peter shrugged. "Maybe. There's an awfully strong draught around here for a room that's below ground and doesn't have a second door."

"There are draughts everywhere," Annabel said. "There's only part of the castle left."

Peter, doubtfully, said: "We're pretty far beneath the court-yard level, Ann."

I don't think the box has scented fresh air, Blackfoot remarked coolly, nosing the tickerbox aside. *I think it's scented magic.*

"I thought the whole ruins was stuffed with magic," said Annabel doubtfully. "Why has it gone for this particular bit?"

"The whole ruins *is* stuffed with magic," Peter said, scrambling onto his stomach. "Wait, there's something here, all right! Help me clear away the books, Ann!"

Annabel lazily pawed books away from the lowest shelf while Peter did the same with terrier-like speed on his side. When the last of the books were cleared away he laughed in delight.

"What?" she said gloomily. She was occasionally disheartened by the way Peter and Blackfoot saw things that she couldn't: and, just as occasionally, that made her wonder if Peter was merely annoyed that he couldn't hear Blackfoot, and not actually sceptical. He did so hate not to be the best, the quickest– the most perceptive.

"It's a door! Well, a sort-of door: it's only one way. We can get out, after all."

Clever little thing, observed Blackfoot. *Nan, wriggle over, will you? I want to have another look at this thing.*

Annabel wriggled over and Blackfoot brushed past, tickling her ear with his whiskers. "What's clever about it?"

"Clever? Well–"

Annabel kicked him. "Not you."

It's...well, let's just call it ahead of its time. Or perhaps it's me that's ahead of my time.

"I don't know what that means," Annabel said, even more gloomily.

It means that someone established value long before we got here, and that they knew how to do...something I thought no one else knew how to do.

"It's actually a fascinating spell," said Peter.

"Yes, yes," Annabel said hastily, because the lecturing tone was back in his voice. "That's what Blackfoot says. He says it's from someone es– doing what? Oh, establishing value."

"It's a door that's not a door, only it's more like a tunnel. It's activated by touch, I think."

"How?" asked Annabel, nudging Blackfoot aside to peer at the back of the shelf. In the dim light she could just see Peter's fingers pinching around a tiny knob: pushing, pulling, and finally attempting to turn.

"Bother!" he muttered. "It's really tight!"

"Let me try," Annabel said impatiently, elbowing him. "This knob has to turn?"

"You won't be able to get it. It's too stiff."

Annabel felt the tiny knob at the back of the book shelf, smooth porcelain. She gave it a small, testing twitch with her forefinger and thumb, and it turned at once. "There," she said, with a slight trace of smugness. She sat up in a slither of dust and cobwebs, and watched as the bookshelf spiralled in on itself. "Done."

Peter sat up hastily to avoid being sucked into the vortex, his mouth open incredulously. "What? How did you do that, Ann? It was– I couldn't even get it to *budge*!"

"It just turned," said Annabel, gazing into the inky blackness of the tunnel that had formed. "Maybe your fingers are too big."

"My fingers aren't too big!"

I'm beginning to get a headache.

"What do you suppose it was used for?" Annabel asked. She climbed to her feet rather stiffly, and beside her, Peter did the same with a great deal more ease. "There's the front door, after all, even if there are snakes."

Peter, who was frowning to himself, said in sudden excitement: "Burn room! It's a burn room, Ann!"

Annabel touched a cautious finger to the rough edges of the tunnel where it had carved out a space for itself from the bookcase and surrounding wall. It felt like wood, then brick, then cold and dust. "What's a burn room?"

"It depends. It can be for secrets, or for people, or for- well, for anything, really. One way in, and one way out, and you make sure you can turn it inside out from the outside if you need to collapse it on anything. I bet there are little magical charges all around the room that can be set off remotely."

"Someone could collapse this on us?"

If there were anyone around to do so, yes, said Blackfoot. *It's a rather savage form of secret keeping.*

"Then I'm getting out of here," Annabel said firmly.

Wait! Blackfoot said sharply. *The tunnel could also collapse on you if it's not done correctly.*

"We should explore down here a bit more, first," protested Peter. "We might not be able to get back down here once we're out. I want to see if there *are* magic charges, and I want to know what secrets they were hiding down here."

I'll go first, sighed Blackfoot.

"But- but what if it collapses on *you*?"

Oh, I shouldn't think it will, said Blackfoot coolly. *Wait for a moment before you follow me, Nan.*

"Where's the cat going- where are *you* going, Ann?"

"Up and out," said Annabel, watching anxiously as Black- foot's inky form disappeared into the darkness of the tunnel. The tunnel didn't seem to be in any danger of imminent collapse, so she stepped after him tentatively. Over her shoul- der, she said to Peter: "You can stay if you want."

"But Ann-"

"You can stay if you want," Annabel said again. Blackfoot was already outpacing her, and she thought she could hear his voice murmuring: *Yes, yes, just as expected. Powerful: but then, power isn't what matters with this one. One could pride oneself-*

She caught up with him as the thoughts slowed and stopped. "What are you priding yourself on?"

Oh, you could hear that, could you? I was just remarking–

"Yes, but who were you remarking *to*, if you didn't know I could hear?"

I would like you to know, Nan, that– Good heavens, what a bad influence the both of you are on me. I refuse to squabble with you. Is the boy following?

"I think so," said Annabel, with a cursory look back. A light was bobbing along behind them, and Peter was no doubt behind that.

Very good, Blackfoot. I didn't like to mention it, but if we go out before he catches up with us, the tunnel could collapse on him, too. It's not a very good one.

Annabel looked apprehensively behind them again. "I thought you said it was very strong!"

It is. But strong magic isn't necessarily better than crafty magic, and in this case, crafty would have been a great deal better than strong.

"Oh," Annabel said. It was mildly pleasing to find that she understood that. "You mean someone like Peter was using a spell they didn't really know much about."

Exactly that, said Blackfoot. He also sounded mildly pleased with himself, though Annabel didn't know why.

"What do you mean, someone like me?" Peter's voice said indignantly. "Are you discussing me with the cat again, Ann?"

"Not really," Annabel said. "We were just talking about the person who made this tunnel spell: Blackfoot thinks it was made by someone quite strong who wasn't familiar with the spell."

"I wouldn't know," said Peter, stiffly. "*Someone* ducked down the tunnel before I could study the other room. *Someone* was already out of sight before I could study the spell from the other side, too. And *someone–*"

Something loomed, and Annabel ducked instinctively. Peter, who was still talking, walked into the wooden board that was fastened just a little too low to miss. "Ow! What–?"

"Oh, look!" said Annabel, surging ahead until she was out in the open. She blinked back at the others, her eyes watering with unexpected light. "We're at the end. We've come out at the stables."

Peter staggered out after her, Blackfoot weaving between his feet. "What a stupid idea!"

On the contrary, a very clever one, said Blackfoot. *Especially if one happens to be evading pursuit.*

"Blackfoot says it's for knocking out people who are chasing you," Annabel said cheerfully. "Oh! That must have been what the note was about. They must have had to sneak the king or queen out through there."

"Maybe I can keep it open so we can go back through," said Peter, squinting at the rough edges of the tunnel that made a hole in the stable wall. In older days there would have been tack hanging from the pegs that spanned the top of the tunnel: those were probably used to slow down any pursuers, too, Annabel thought.

There was a ghostly laugh. *I doubt it, but by all means go ahead and try*, said Blackfoot. When talking to Peter, his voice was usually amused and somewhat curious. This time it was casual and quite certain, and Annabel wasn't surprised when, for all Peter's hasty efforts, the tunnel swirled once again and closed itself.

She patted a cautious hand against the brickwork and tugged at the pegs that lined the panel she had only just avoided. "Oh well," she said. "We'll just have to climb back down the hole I made if we want to get back down there."

Peter made an unsatisfied noise, and put his tickerbox in his pocket. "I suppose."

Nan, said Blackfoot's voice suddenly. *Ask the boy if he senses anything about the castle.*

"I want to eat," Annabel said instead. "Can't I ask him later? Peter, I'm *hungry*. Let's go back to the throne room."

"Wait," said Peter, looking around with a frown. "There's something wrong. Something's changed."

Annabel looked around too. "What? What's different?"

"Don't know," Peter said uncomfortably. "There's something...I don't know, *smaller* about the castle."

Check the sealing around the Castle, said Blackfoot sharply. *Quickly!*

"Blackfoot says to check the sealing around the castle," Annabel said hastily. "I think you'd better, Peter."

Peter said preoccupiedly: "Already doing it. That's– oh, that's funny. I don't think that should be happening."

Blackfoot's voice sounded pained. *Don't tell me– the workings have moved further into the Castle courtyard, haven't they? And our safety net is now just a little bit smaller?*

"The safe bit is smaller," said Peter, at the same time. "That Mordion: he's– I think he's sort of *pushed* it inward."

"Can he do that?" squeaked Annabel. "I thought he couldn't get in!"

I told you it would only be a matter of time before he managed to get himself more magic, said Blackfoot. *If there's one thing Mordion is good at, it's siphoning off magic from unsuspecting civilians. I did think we'd have a little more time, however. Can either of you see him? He must be around here somewhere.*

"The whole protective wall is about a foot smaller," observed Peter. "If it keeps going at that rate, he'll have us in a few weeks– if the hunger doesn't get us first."

"Yes," Annabel said gloomily. "I'm tired of berries. Can you see Mordion, Peter? Blackfoot wants to know where he is."

"Forget the cat! *I* want to know where he is!" He stomped away across the courtyard, ignoring Annabel's calling, and vanished from sight around the piles of rubble.

"Don't expect me to be able to see him," said Annabel to Blackfoot, and sat down on a flagstone that rocked amusingly back and forth.

I wouldn't dream of it, said Blackfoot. *Imagine having to put yourself to any effort! The thought curdles the mind.*

"Well, what can *I* do?" demanded Annabel, stung.

That's what I constantly find myself wondering, said Blackfoot. *I find myself wondering what you could do if you'd only put yourself to the effort of trying something. You always sit just where you are and refuse to move, or try, or do anything. But every time I think you're a hopeless cause, I remember that you're the girl who convinced Grenna for years that she was one step removed from being the village mumbler, not to mention saving that young idiot from certain pain and death. When I remember that, I can't help thinking that maybe you won't turn out so badly after all. Perhaps I'll even live to see the day when you won't need to be **nudged** to do things.*

"But I don't have magic!"

*Since you've arms and legs and scarcely seem to use **those**, I can only imagine that you'd do the same if you had magic.*

"That's–" Annabel stopped, biting her lip, and said: "That's *mean*."

Yes, said Blackfoot. *But it's true. What are you going to do about it?*

Annabel mumbled: "I'm going to climb up on the wall there and see if I can see anything."

That's not exactly what I meant, said Blackfoot, but he briefly buffed his head against her shin. *Good girl. Don't fall, will you?*

"I won't," said Annabel. She tried to say it in a cold, mature way, but it came out sounding sulky instead.

Politely, Blackfoot said, *I do beg your pardon,* and sat down to watch her climb. The nearby wall was much higher than it used to be, but despite her chubbiness, Annabel was a goatishly nimble climber, and could scale the uneven slabs almost as swiftly as Blackfoot himself.

She hefted herself to the first flat place, tearing her flannels as she went, then scrambled up the steep slope more easily, her palms and the soles of her feet rapidly growing chalky with dust and mortar. She saw Peter as she climbed, still marching around the outer edge of the ruins, and it occurred to her at the same time that the ruins were larger—much larger!—than she remembered them being. Peter must have realised the same thing at much the same time, because his far-away figure stopped walking with an attitude of annoyance that clearly telegraphed across the distance.

Annabel snorted to herself and kept climbing. Peter had obviously decided that the ruins were now too large to walk around, even if he was in a snit. Now that she had started climbing, she would like to be able to tell him when he returned that she knew *exactly* where Mordion was.

Unfortunately for that particular aim, Mordion was nowhere in sight when Annabel reached the highest point of the growing wall. She couldn't see the entire circumference, of course: far too much of the castle had grown back since yesterday. From this height, there was more than she'd thought at first. Here and there, there was even the wink of glass catching sunlight. Annabel knew that there were no unbroken windows around the ruins: she'd broken the very last one herself. It had been an accident, but she'd felt badly about it anyway.

Now, looking out at the brand new windows, and the very definitely bigger ruins, Annabel felt a distinct chill of fear. It was one thing to hear from Blackfoot that the ruins could grow back: it was quite another to be able to see it actually happening. Annabel's eyes went back to where the distant figure of Peter turned in a circle with an air of helplessness. As she watched, he turned on his heel and began to come back. Annabel scrambled back down as well, and by the time Peter made it back to the outside of the stables, she was just dropping down to meet him.

"Well, the good news is that the ruins have got bigger," said Peter. He sounded almost as breathless as Annabel felt.

"I know," Annabel said. "I saw. Why is that good news?"

"Because the bad news is that the safe zone has definitely shrunk."

FIVE

Peter, having delivered the statement with the most portentous of accents, added: "Well, actually, it's only sort of shrunk."

"What do you mean, *sort of*?"

"It's shrunk in relation to the ruins, but not in relation to itself, because the ruins have got bigger."

Well, well, said Blackfoot. *A little breathing room. Perhaps we should see what else has grown back in the ruins, now that we're above ground again. What did you see when you were on the wall, Nan? Which sections have grown back the most?*

"It's mostly staircases and lower levels," said Annabel, without enthusiasm. She'd already scaled a wall, and she felt that she'd made enough effort for one day. Despite the nagging feeling that Peter's worry gave her, it was difficult to feel as frightened as she'd felt when she could physically *see* Mordion, and it made her less motivated to work on finding a way out of their predicament. "What if the castle ruins keep getting bigger? Won't we stay safe?"

Peter, impatiently, said: "That's just like you, Ann! I don't want to stay in here indefinitely! Mother's bound to be worried already; and anyway, even if the safe bit is bigger than it was yesterday, the castle's bound to stop growing before long. Then the shrinkage will catch up with us."

The castle will only keep growing until it reaches its original size, said Blackfoot, and added: *Well, at least, so I suppose. What will happen after that is hard to guess.*

"Well, then, *you* find a way out," grumbled Annabel.

Was that directed at me, or the boy?

"Both of you!"

Don't be cross just because I shamed you into bestirring yourself, Blackfoot said mildly. *Of course we're working on getting out of the castle–*

"I don't think you are working at it," Annabel said. "You're just following us around and making sarcastic remarks. Maybe you should work on that instead. People don't like sarcastic pe– cats."

*I wouldn't like to arrive at perfection so quickly. A cat must have **some** failings, after all.*

"Ann, do you think you could *not* quarrel with your cat?" complained Peter. "It's off-putting. And if you were talking about me, I *am* working on getting us out of the castle: it's not easy, you know!"

You can rest assured, Nan, that I won't allow you to be killed. It may simply take some time to find our way out of this mess.

"You're the one who got us into this mess in the first place!"

I'm so sorry to have saved your life. It must be very difficult for you to bear.

"Ann!"

Annabel, glaring at Blackfoot, said: "Blackfoot is being sarcastic again."

"Oh well, at least he's not being sarcastic about me this time. Wait, is he being sarcastic about me?"

"Why do you care?" Annabel said sourly. "You can't hear him."

"No, but– *Ann!* Now you've pulled me into your figment again! Stop it! I'm trying to find a way out of here, you know."

Mildly diverted, Annabel asked: "How?"

"The sealing is pushing against Mordion's magic," said Peter, his face lighting up. He had probably, thought Annabel rather crossly, been waiting for just this chance to let her know how clever he'd been. "There's a lot of power going to waste around there, just crashing up against the other side, so to speak. If we can harness some of that–"

–then we can hope to create the single biggest magical fallout that the Two Monarchies have ever seen, sighed Blackfoot.

"Blackfoot doesn't advise it," said Annabel.

Advise it? I forbid it!

"He feels very strongly about it."

Did I not already tell you both that the only way out of this castle is to go further in?

"Didn't you decide that the best way to get out was to go further in?" Annabel asked. "You said it made sense."

"That was just one idea," said Peter. "I have *heaps*: I just don't have enough information yet. For instance, I still haven't determined if the sealing goes all the way up–"

It does.

"–and all the way down–"

It does.

"–so I have to find out about that first. Why don't you sit here with your cat and draw things? I'm going back to the edge of the seal and Mordion's magic."

"Blackfoot says the sealing is all the way over and under the castle."

"Of *course* he does. Sometimes I think he just says what you want to hear, Ann, so you don't have to put yourself to the trouble of doing anything. Ow! *Ann!* Tell your cat not to bite me!"

Annabel, who was still feeling slightly raw from hearing Blackfoot say much the same thing earlier, patted his head and said: "Bad cat."

Peter huffed and went away again, presumably to study the sealing once more. Blackfoot watched him go and only flicked an ear in Annabel's direction when she sat beside him and said: "You said the same thing yourself. Why are you biting Peter?"

I'm your cat. You're my human. It's my job to tell you the unpleasant things. It's none of his business.

"That's probably because we're going to be married when we grow up."

As delightful a prospect as that must be, Nan, why would you ever consider marrying that top-lofty young jackanapes?

"Well, who else is going to marry me?" Annabel said reasonably. "Plump girls aren't fashionable, and I like food too much to be a slender girl. Peter doesn't care about that."

Who knows? Plump girls could come back into fashion, Blackfoot said. *Stranger things have happened, after all. It only takes one well-known woman to be comfortably plump, and fashion changes again.*

Annabel, ignoring this as the nonsense it was, said: "Anyway, we know each other, and it would be such a bother to get to know someone else that well. Peter's all right."

I suppose I've heard stupider reasons for marrying someone, said Blackfoot, giving the feline equivalent of a shrug. *What will you do now, Nan? Your betrothed is bound to be quite some time, if I'm any judge.*

Annabel hesitated. She had been planning, insofar as succumbing to long years of habit could be called planning, to sit exactly where she was and draw in her book for as long as it took Peter to collect whatever data he was trying to collect. Now that Blackfoot had asked the question, however, it seemed impossible to do just that.

Annabel said cautiously: "What do you think?"

It was Blackfoot's turn to hesitate. At last, as if not quite sure he was allowed to answer, he said, as cautiously as Annabel: *I suppose asking for advice is a forward step, after all.*

"Pardon?" Annabel said, startled.

I said that we could try looking inside some of the new rooms that have spawned through the castle. I really applaud your proactive attitude.

"Oh, shut up," said Annabel, grinning. "How do we get in?"

The servants' entrance, said Blackfoot. *Or at least, so I suppose. Your faith in me is touching, but I'm not sure why I should be expected to know more about castle entrances than you do.*

In the end, it wasn't so much a matter of find the servants' entrance as it was finding *any* door. There was still a great deal of rubble around the base of the castle itself, though there was more around the stables and the courtyard in general, and if there had originally been more doors, they were now inaccessible. Annabel and Blackfoot, skirting around the worst of the rubble, eventually came back to the laundry where Peter had fixed the pump, and found a small, narrow stairway up and into the castle itself.

"At least we don't have to wriggle through," Annabel said

in relief. The day wasn't as hot as it had been yesterday, but the triad was still distinctly summery, and she didn't feel like struggling her way into the bowels of the castle as they had had to do to get to the throne room.

She was shortly to know her mistake: she and Blackfoot may not have had to struggle through briars and tangled rubble to forge further into the castle, but they did have to climb a great many stairs. And most of those stairs, to Annabel's rue, climbed *up* into the castle. There was the occasional landing, and even a hall or two, but most of the halls ended abruptly, dangling their half-finished selves out into cold, empty space while Annabel gazed into the empty centre of the castle.

"It's like it's building itself a skeleton," she said to Blackfoot. If she was careful about how she craned her neck, her feet a safe distance from that treacherously ragged edge of stonework, she could even see up into the sky, where the triad's last two suns were searingly visible. "And– and– wait. Blackfoot, if I can see the suns up there, why can't I see what's down *here*?"

She hadn't realised it until that moment, but Annabel couldn't even see the rough ends of any of the other corridors they'd come across, and if there were unfinished halls on this side of the ruins, there should certainly be other, unfinished halls across from them. Instead, there was only dense, impenetrable darkness, soft and inclined to swallow sound.

Don't get too close to the edge, Nan, was all Blackfoot said.

Annabel gazed into that darkness for a little while longer, then, with a brief shiver, went back to climbing stairs again. A little further up into the skeleton of the castle, they came across a landing that was almost complete, with just a small patch of darkness at the far end. Annabel, who was already panting and wishing that she'd never begun to climb the stairs, puffed out a sigh of relief and leaned into the wall.

Now that's interesting, Blackfoot said. *Doors. I didn't think we'd see doors until there was a bit more wall and floor.*

"Oh!" said Annabel, who hadn't noticed. "So there are! What do you think is inside?"

I understand that the easiest way to discover what's in a room is to open the door, said Blackfoot.

Annabel ignored that, because a bright hope had blossomed within her. "I wonder if one of them has clothes?" She scrambled to her feet with a new kindling of purpose, and approached the door closest to them, Blackfoot padding along curiously behind her.

Be careful, he warned. *The Castle is fragile. It might not mean to kill you, but there is so little of it here that mistakes could happen.*

"*Mistakes,*" muttered Annabel, but she was careful about how she opened the door. It swung inward, and despite all her care, if she hadn't had a very good grasp on the door handle, she would have pitched forward into empty space for the second time that day. She squeaked and pulled the door closed as she jerked herself backward.

That was particularly graceful, said Blackfoot, when Annabel was in a clumsy heap on the hallway floor. She puffed a dismissive breath at him and propped herself up against the opposite wall until her heart stopped beating quite so quickly.

When she wasn't so breathless, she said indignantly: "How silly! What use are rooms without floors?"

Blackfoot gave his cat-shrug and licked one paw.

"But the rooms that were still there from before had floors!"

Just barely, if you recall.

"Yes, but there was a floor *to* fall through," argued Annabel, climbing carefully to her feet. She looked cursorily into each of the other doors, but there were no floors or walls there, either: just the same, bouncy, impenetrable blackness. "There isn't even a floorboard to be seen in that lot."

Perhaps the floors will follow tomorrow.

"And perhaps I'll fall through those as well," said Annabel, disgruntled. She had, she thought, made a great deal of effort today, and for no reason whatsoever. "I'm going back down."

I suppose you want a pat on the head, said Blackfoot; but he followed her back down the myriad winding stairs without making any other sarcastic remarks. Perhaps he also felt that she'd made a great deal of effort today.

There was no sign of Peter when they made it back to the overgrown court. Annabel, reverting to old habits, promptly sat down and fished out her pencil nub, and spent a happy hour drawing. From inside, the skeletal stairways and abruptly ending corridors were confusing and perilous: from outside, they were beautiful and mysterious. They also gave the impression that they were growing every time she looked away from them.

She was cross-hatching the rubble at the base of the main castle when a shadow fell over here, and Peter's voice said irritably: "You've drawn it wrong, Ann!"

"What do you know about drawing, anyway?" Annabel said placidly. She knew she hadn't drawn it exactly as it was: there were bits of rubble at the base of the castle that had once obviously parts of the towers above, and she'd drawn them back where they should have been. "It's better than the blank spaces, anyway. They're frightening."

"What blank spaces?"

"The ones inside the castle. What about the warding? What did you do?"

"There's nothing *to* be done," said Peter, in a rather disgruntled way.

As if the Castle is doing it to spite him, murmured Blackfoot, making Annabel giggle.

Peter ignored her loftily. "It's too strong to touch, that's all. I *could* do it, but I couldn't predict the outcome."

"Isn't that what Blackfoot said before?"

"I suppose you've been drawing all afternoon," added Peter, more loftily still.

"Then you suppose wrong," Annabel said smartly. "Blackfoot and I have been exploring the new rooms."

Peter's lofty tones immediately descended to eager interest. "Anything interesting?"

"I told you," said Annabel. "There are blank spots everywhere in there. None of the rooms have floors, or proper walls, or ceilings. And also the corridors are only partly there."

"How can they be *partly* there, Ann? And how–"

"Don't argue with me about it!" snapped Annabel. "Go and look for yourself. I'm going back to the throne room."

Peter caught at her arm. "Don't be like that, Ann. We still have to try a few more things today."

He means that he wants an audience while he shows off how clever he is, Blackfoot muttered. *Nan, your face is very colourful. You should probably splash it with some cold water.*

Annabel cautiously wrinkled her nose and found that her whole face was stiff and disinclined to move. She prodded it just as cautiously, but it was only slightly painful.

"It's all right," Peter said. "I put a lot of magic into it. It's accelerated right past the sore bit."

He said it expectantly, and Annabel, feeling that something was expected of her, said: "Thanks."

"Oh, well, it wasn't anything much."

Not as much as all that, agreed Blackfoot. *He's waiting to be thanked again, Nan. He'll accept it bashfully.*

Annabel giggled, earning a slightly indignant look from Peter, and said meekly: "Blackfoot was being sarcastic. Never mind: what are we supposed to be trying?"

"The thing is," said Peter, in his lecturing tone, "the thing is, that we really need to know what Mordion's up to. That thing that's pushing the safe space in– it's got him all over it. I recognise it, even if it's with different magic this time."

With the air of one making a concession, Blackfoot said: *Well, he's had stupider ideas.*

"I can probably piggyback off the castle's workings," added Peter. He was straightening his collar with one berry-stained hand, which was his particular quirk when he was doing something that was very clever, and something that Annabel should *recognise* as very clever.

Annabel tried to make her face more suitably congratulatory, but it was stiffer than it had been before, and she couldn't quite manage it. At the back of her mind, Blackfoot's voice sighed: *Oh, and we were doing so well just a minute ago! Tell the child not to piggyback off the castle's magical workings, Nan.*

"Blackfoot doesn't think it's a very good idea," Annabel said instead. Peter would hardly react well to being called a child. Sometimes she thought it was quite a good thing that he couldn't understand Blackfoot.

That's not what I said.

"What would the cat know?" demanded Peter. "I've never seen *it* do magic!"

By all means, go ahead, said Blackfoot. *I'm sure the castle will just **love** having an ignorant and undeservedly powerful young wizard interfering with its workings.*

"Neither have I," said Annabel. "That only means I can't

see it, though. Weren't you saying just before that sometimes magic is so good it's unseeable?"

Peter opened his mouth and closed it again. "Stop trying to pull me into your delusions, Ann! The castle workings already recognise Mordion. It's just a matter of trying to use that recognition to run a Tracer, and then hitching *that* to a standard Look-See."

*Oh, this is **hard**, said Blackfoot. There are so many biting comments to be made here, but the child really is ridiculously clever about his workings. He might as well try it: he's just strong enough to perhaps get away with it– and if he doesn't, it'll be a well-deserved lesson.*

"Blackfoot still doesn't recommend it," Annabel told Peter, who was already preparing for his spell. Unlike Grenna, who had to do item-based spells and scratch conduits and wards on the ground, Peter did very little in the way of preparation. He simply looked around for a few moments—whether that was in order to find a magically ideal spot, or to find the most comfortable spot, Annabel wasn't sure—and then sat down with his back against a wall that faced one of the new, sparkling windows, so that he wouldn't fall over if he sank too deeply into his working to keep control of his body.

She wandered closer, looking around in some interest at the spot Peter had chosen. "And he says it'll serve you right if you get it wrong and the castle does something nasty to you."

Nan, began Blackfoot, and then added more mildly: *Well, I suppose that's close enough. What a forward-thinking child he is: he's going to use the window as a view-screen.*

"Blackfoot's impressed by you using the window as a view screen," said Annabel. She didn't like to compliment Peter too much, since it made him more than usually difficult to deal with, but complimenting him in Blackfoot's name was oddly satisfying. He couldn't take it at face value, since he still didn't believe Blackfoot was anything more than an ordinary cat.

Peter looked wary, but wasn't able to resist continuing on in his lecturing voice: "The window is an important part of the spell, actually–"

Good heavens, I'm sorry I mentioned it.

"–since it gives the picture from the Look-See more depth. It gives it a three dimensional effect that makes it seem more real."

*That could be because it **is** real.*

"It *is* real," said Annabel, at the same time. She had, quite against her will, learned more about magic from watching and listening to Peter these last few years than she had in her entire time with Grenna. "Just because you're seeing it through a spell doesn't mean it isn't real."

"I *know* that," Peter said in annoyance. "What I *meant* is that the picture is better than you'd get from say, water, or ink. The window has more depth, you see—an inside of its own—and it gives the spell a corresponding depth."

Annabel tried to make a face at him, but her face was too stiff for that, too. Peter, caught up in the spell and in his own cleverness, didn't notice, and before long the glass in the window frame became opaque.

"Anyway," said Annabel, "wasn't this window broken yesterday?"

"You're imagining things," Peter murmured, peering at the cloudy glass.

"Blackfoot?"

I told you about this before, sighed Blackfoot. *You should really start to listen to me, Nan. I told you that the castle would start coming back.*

"Blackfoot says it *was* broken yesterday–"

I didn't say that.

"–and that it's just the castle coming back like he said it would."

"It doesn't matter," Peter said impatiently. "What do a few windows matter? Bother! Why won't it establish a connection with the castle's sealing?"

"Why are you looking at me?" demanded Annabel. "*I* don't know anything about it."

"It was a *rhetorical* question, Ann! I didn't really think you'd know the answer."

"Oh," Annabel said, and listened to Blackfoot's murmur at the back of her mind. "Well, Blackfoot says you haven't established value, whatever that means."

Peter stared at her. "Haven't est– what– wait. Where did you learn about that, Ann?"

"Is that a real question?"

"*Ann.*"

"I didn't learn about it. It's what Blackfoot said. Why? Isn't it right?"

Faithless child.

"No, it *is* right," said Peter, still looking at her narrowly. "That's why I'm surprised. The castle workings have no reason to accept a piggy-backed spell unless it directly benefits the workings. My spell needs to provide a building block for the workings, or give it a direct benefit it doesn't normally have."

"Oh," Annabel said again. She still didn't understand. "Then establish value, I suppose."

"I'm thinking," said Peter, with dignity.

In the back of her mind, Annabel heard Blackfoot laugh. *A remarkably strong-headed boy, isn't he?*

"Is that what you'd call it?" muttered Annabel. "I would have called it pig-headed."

"Don't insult me to the cat, Ann."

"Why? You don't think he talks, anyway."

Heatedly, Peter said: "That's exactly why! You're insulting me to your imaginary friend."

Blackfoot bit Peter's ankle. *Imaginary, am I?*

"Ow! *Ann!*"

"What? If he's imaginary, it shouldn't have hurt you."

"I need to *concentrate*. Stop talking at me!"

Annabel stuck her tongue out at him and went back to drawing. Peter wouldn't admit he didn't know what to do, and he was clever enough to figure out what to do if she left him alone, anyway. She drew more windows into the sketch of the castle, making them bright and reflective, and pencilled in blocks up the front of the castle so that the blank inside was hidden. Of course, it was still in there behind the bricks, but Annabel was a firm believer in the idea that if she could cover up something enough, it would eventually be forgotten and cease to trouble her. And that slightly springy, dense darkness *did* trouble her.

*What **are** you doing, Nan?*

"Bricking it up," said Annabel. "It's ugly and makes me feel wobbly inside. I like my drawings to be happy."

That, said Blackfoot rather dryly, *is not a happy drawing.*

Annabel looked at it again and hunched her shoulders. It *wasn't* a particularly happy drawing: the blocked up bit was blank and deliberately bland—a bit like her own blank look, thought Annabel, startled—taking away from the pretty, spindly look of the skeletal castle without doing away with the menace it currently exuded. And, like Annabel's blank look, it gave the impression that there was something else going on underneath.

On the other hand, Blackfoot remarked, *it's a particularly typical example of–*

"Oh, shut up!" said Annabel. Now that she looked at her drawing again, the block façade made her feel as uncomfortable as the empty, black space had done. She carefully erased through the block segment, leaving a deep gash in the space she'd just filled, but left some blocks edging that section. That left it looking like the rest of the castle: incomplete, sprawling, and lively.

Then, to make herself feel better, Annabel turned the page against the deep blackness that the segment revealed, and began to draw room interiors instead. Blackfoot made a rather derisive sound when he saw the interiors, all clothes and food and pretty furniture, but he didn't find it necessary to make any remarks. In fact, thought Annabel, with one eye on Blackfoot and another on her drawings, he must have been in a good mood: when the window opposite them began to show something other than a bright reflection of them in the courtyard, and shadowy depth behind, he sat up in distinct interest. Moreover, he didn't make any sarcastic remarks about Peter, either, *or* repeat his gloomy warnings with the rather macabre glee of someone who knows he will not be attended to.

"Got it!" said Peter, his voice thick with satisfaction. A shadowy scene had replaced their reflections in the window, rapidly becoming clearer as Peter's spell refined itself and pulled closer.

Oh, very nice! Blackfoot said, sitting with all the prickly interest of a cat who has seen its prey. *I've not seen such precision of spell refining since– well, since working with another particularly irritating wizard, actually. No, don't tell him that, Nan.*

"I won't," Annabel grinned.

"You won't what?" demanded Peter.

"Nothing," said Annabel provocatively. She was quite well aware that Peter was needled because she wasn't paying enough attention to his cleverness. More provocatively still, she added: "We were talking about your spell."

"What about my spell? Is the cat saying rude things about my magic again? Ann, stop trading rude remarks about my magic with the cat! What does it know about magic, anyway?"

Nan, you beautiful child. I think you've broken him.

"It wasn't anything much," Annabel said, relenting. "Oh, look! That's Grenna's cottage, isn't it?"

Disgruntled, Peter said: "I suppose so," and looked his spell over with a professional eye. "We should be able to see Mordion properly soon."

"Wait," said Annabel uncertainly, as the picture refined itself into clear lines. It was certainly a man there in Grenna's cottage, but where she had been expecting an older man, this one was young and insolently energetic. "That's not– that's not him, is it?"

"It has to be him," Peter said. "I set the parameters from his signature."

Annabel gazed dubiously at the living reflection in the window. "It doesn't look like him, though."

It does look like him, said Blackfoot, in a particularly grim voice.

"But he was *older* than that!" protested Annabel, who distinctly remembered the thin, grey face of the man-cat who had crawled out of the spell in pursuit of her and Blackfoot. "His hair was grey and his eyes were–"

Her voice trailed away, because the man had looked up, his eyes dark blue and terrifyingly reflective. Annabel knew those eyes very well: she'd seen them looking steadily at her as she waited for Peter at the cusp of the castle courtyard. She'd seen them since in her dreams, unhurried, unworried, and certain of their eventual success. Now they were clearer and crueller, in a smooth, unlined face that spoke certainty and arrogance in every beautiful line of it.

This is how Mordion looks at his best, Blackfoot said quietly. *He must have found a particularly strong source of magic.*

"Does that mean– does that mean there's another body out there, like Grenna?"

Nan–

"Of course not," scoffed Peter. "Grenna only had a spark of magic to take. If he got all of *that* magic from one person, there wouldn't have been enough of them left to leave a corpse."

Oh, for hands to box his ears!

"Peter, he's looking at us."

Peter briefly assessed his spell. "He can't be. He can't see us– or hear us, for that matter."

"That," said Mordion, with a particularly beautiful smile, his eyes pinioning Peter, "is not entirely correct."

Six

Mordion gazed at Peter for a long time, those dark blue eyes velvet and shadowed and bottomless. At last he said, still with that beautiful smile: "Now, this is *very* interesting. You didn't have to go to these lengths to meet with me, Peter Carlisle. Step outside the castle and I'll be glad to speak with you. Better still, send out my plump little friend: she and I have much to discuss."

Annabel looked at him in dislike. Somehow, it was worse hearing Mordion caressingly call her his 'plump little friend' than it was to hear Peter refer to her bluntly as being fat. "We don't have anything to talk about," she said. "And we're not friends."

"That's not very polite, darling," said Mordion. "I've been searching for you for quite some time now. I've put a lot of effort into finding you, as a matter of fact."

Annabel, in her discomfort, retreated into her blank, slack-jawed face and simply stared at him.

Tell Peter to cut the connection, Nan, said Blackfoot sharply. *It's one thing to be sneaking a look at Mordion when he doesn't know about it: it's quite another to give him any more information about ourselves than needful.*

"You really shouldn't do that, darling," said Mordion. "It's unattractive, and I'm hardly likely to underestimate you twice, no matter how cow-like you appear to be."

"Blackfoot says to cut the connection," Annabel told Peter, ignoring Mordion.

Mordion smiled again, and this time there was more than insincere friendliness to it. "So you *do* communicate with each other. I wondered."

Nan! This time, Blackfoot sounded distinctly exasperated. *How much more information are you prepared to give him? Sever the link!*

"Stop the spell, Peter!" Annabel said crossly. "It's gone wrong anyway!"

Hotly, Peter said: "It hasn't gone wrong! There's just *more* of it than usual: in fact, it's a lot stronger than it would normally be."

"What's the use of that?" snapped Annabel. "What's the use of being stronger if it's doing things we don't want it to do?"

Mordion shrugged elegantly. "You may not have considered the effect of the castle magics. Still, it's an impressive working, Peter Carlisle: you might even be as strong as I am."

"As strong?" said Peter, in his most lordly tone, "I'm stronger!"

Now we're in for it: they're going to have an argument about which one of them is the stronger.

"Shut *up*, Peter!" hissed Annabel. "Stop the spell!"

Peter sighed gustily. "All right, all *right*, Ann!"

"You take your marching orders very well, Peter Carlisle," said Mordion, his smile thin-edged. "It is painfully obvious that you're the younger friend: do you always do as you're told?"

"You can shut up, too," Peter said briefly. "It's no use trying to make me annoyed with her."

"Now, that's very touching," said Mordion. "You're such firm friends?"

"No," said Peter, and cut the connection. To the empty, reflecting window, he said: "She annoys me all the time, anyway. I'm used to it."

The next morning, the coloured glass that had once lined the throne room was again whole, and coloured light was beginning to edge through the vines and rubbles.

More importantly, there was a man *in* that glass when Annabel returned from washing under the pump. She squeaked in her shock, but unlike Mordion, he didn't seem to be able to see her in return. That being the case, Annabel scrambled up and approached the coloured windows, her eyes running over the whole series of glass in fascination, throughout which the scene showed. The man was busily scribbling a few sentences on a piece of paper, his long sleeves dangling in the ink and nudging papers off the already heavily laden desk. He was a lanky, dark-skinned man with very long, very knobbly arms and legs, and an even longer, hooked nose. Annabel wasn't very sure about the countries further afar than Glause, but she concluded cautiously that he was probably Caliphan.

More importantly than that, Annabel was sure that he was in the throne room, too. His version of the throne room was less inclined to cobwebs and the berry canes, but it was just as untidy as her version. The desk was distinctly out of place in front of the dais, with all its papers and sludgy ink, but after the man had stopped writing and read his note over in a pleased sort of a way, the whole desk, note and all, vanished in a wave of his hand.

"Hey, wait!" said Annabel. "That's the desk– that's the note! Hey!" She thumped at the glass with her flat palm, bouncing impatiently, and the other version of the room vanished completely.

"What?" Peter mumbled. "What's'matter?"

"Bother!" said Annabel, feeling instinctively for her pencil and sketchbook. She found it and dashed down the base lines for the Caliphan's face, nudging Peter with her toe. "Peter! There was a man in the glass!"

Peter groaned and opened his eyes. "Oh, *Ann*, not another imaginary friend!"

"This one's not imaginary, either," said Annabel, busily drawing. "Besides, he's not a friend. He's just a man I saw in the glass along the wall there."

"There isn't any gl–" Peter sat up, catching sight of the colourful progression of glass and said, "Oh. That wasn't there yesterday, was it?"

"It must have come back last night," agreed Annabel.

Peter scratched his head. "Must be less rubbish outside now, too. The sunshine's coming in a bit."

"Much less," said Annabel, who hadn't actually checked any such thing on her way to wash. She sketched in the man's awkward adam's apple and tried to shade his eyes just right, but she couldn't seem to catch the hawk-like gleam they'd had. She huffed her annoyance in the dusty air, and said: "What a pity he was so tall and odd: I can't get his eyes to work, now."

"At least your figments are becoming human now,"

observed Peter, in a congratulatory kind of way. "That's probably an improvement."

Blackfoot sat up, lashing his tail. *It's entirely too early for that amount of concentrated superiority. Show me the drawing, Nan.*

Annabel kept drawing, but tilted it for his inspection.

Hm. Not bad. Are you sure you weren't still dreaming?

"Of course I am!" Annabel said indignantly. "He *was* there, and I *wasn't* imagining him, and I *wasn't* dreaming."

"Oh, that's a bad sign," said Peter, tying his shoelaces. "Even your imaginary friends think you're potty."

Annabel made a face at him. "Where are you going, anyway?"

"To check on the sealing. What about you?"

"I'm going to see what other parts of the castle have come in since yesterday," said Annabel. Blackfoot couldn't accuse her of not doing anything if she was exploring. Besides, she was hoping that the new rooms had filled themselves in by now: perhaps she would be able to find something else to wear other than her flannels. And perhaps the larder would have filled itself, too.

Peter raised his eyebrows at her, but she ignored him. "All right," he said. "I'll come with you, then. I can look at the sealing after we've explored a bit more. Maybe this old pile has some useful spells and books lying about somewhere."

Annabel, remembering her drawings from the night before with some wistfulness, said: "Maybe." She would rather find clothes than books, at this stage. "I've already washed. You can use the pump if you want it."

"Might as well stink this morning," said Peter carelessly. "We're going to be exploring, anyway. There's probably more cobwebs and dust around the place. Starting at the lower levels?"

"Mid levels," Annabel corrected. "The lower ones we went through yesterday are all kitchens and middens and cooling systems. Blackfoot says the mid levels should be more interesting if they're filled in by now: guest quarters and galleries, and maybe a library or two."

Peter considered this, and said handsomely: "Well, we'll do it your way today, then. Mid levels it is. I wonder how high the castle has got today?"

The castle had become dauntingly high overnight, as it happened. Now that it was warmer, Annabel felt the cool shadow of it as soon as she pushed through the last remaining vines, and Peter whistled as he exited behind her. There were at least two more levels than there had been yesterday, though the skeleton of the castle was still climbing to the sky in crooked fingers of unattached stairways and teetering spires of stone.

Annabel, who should have seen it earlier when she washed, but had been too much asleep and too little curious, said airily: "Pretty big, isn't it? I think all the really big blocks that were around the throne room are up in that bit, now."

Peter whistled again. "It is pretty big. I like that big diamond thing it's done along the front: what is it, a view-station?"

Something like that, said Blackfoot. *That's the court wizard's quarters.*

"Court wizard's quarters," Annabel said knowledgeably, and heard Blackfoot snort.

"All right," Peter said, for once ceding to someone else's knowledge. "Where do we start, Ann?"

"The same place as yesterday, I suppose," said Annabel, thrown off-guard. She wasn't used to Peter asking her what to do. Despite the fact that he was a year younger than she was, Peter had always taken the lead. Annabel wasn't sure if he had done so because, Peter-like, he considered it his due, or if it was simply that she had never tried to assert leadership before. "We got in by the laundry. Can you do something to make sure I don't fall through any of the floors again, though?"

It was Peter's turn to look surprised. "That's a good idea. Only, maybe it wouldn't be a bad idea to fall through a few more: I'd like to get back to that snake-room, actually."

I doubt you'll have a chance to fall through any more floors, unless you're very careless, Blackfoot remarked. *The castle is looking rather more solid today than it did yesterday.*

"Yes," agreed Annabel, who didn't much care, so long as there were floors in the rooms today. "Hey! What's that?"

"A nice, handy little spell," said Peter, grabbing the wrist she tried to pull away.

"Yes, but why are you tying string around my wrist?" protested Annabel. "That's just silly."

"Stop wriggling, Ann! I've put the spell in a bit of string I had."

Annabel stopped pulling away, but said: "Why, though?"

"Because you don't have any magic, and things get really sticky when I put them on you without putting them in something else first. Lack of magic creates a vacuum– Ann, I've *told* you this before!"

"Not that," Annabel said impatiently. "I meant why do you have a bit of string?"

Peter, momentarily taken aback, said: "I don't know. It was around somewhere. I thought it would come in useful. Well, if it comes to that, why do you always have that scrubby little pencil on you?"

Blackfoot, interrupting Annabel's protests that a pencil

was *much* more use than a random piece of string and Peter's meaningful look at the string bracelet around her wrist, said: *This discussion is, of course, very interesting, but who knows? perhaps exploring the castle will prove to be exciting as well.*

Annabel made a face at him and was pleased to find that her face was no longer too stiff to do so. "Blackfoot wants to get on with exploring the castle," she said.

"I don't know why the cat is so eager to explore," muttered Peter. "If Mordion gets in, do you think he's going to bother to chase a cat? *We're* the ones he'll come after. If anyone wants to be exploring the castle, it should be us."

So I would have thought, said Blackfoot. *And yet, here we are, still in the courtyard.*

"Oh, shut up," Annabel said amiably. "I can't be bothered telling Peter everything you say, so you might as well stop being clever at his expense."

"Hey!" said Peter indignantly. "What did the cat say?"

Annabel, ignoring him, started across the courtyard again, her eyes running along the base of the castle. It looked differently than it had looked with all the rubble around it, and she wasn't quite sure of her ability to find the same door they'd used yesterday. At Peter, who hadn't moved, she called over her shoulder: "Didn't you want to see if you can find a way out by going further in?"

"Don't know why you're so active this morning," Peter muttered, but he caught up with her anyway. "It's not like you know what I mean when I say we should be trying to get out by going further in."

"You didn't say it," sniffed Annabel. "Blackfoot did. You just agreed. Oh! There it is!"

"Don't change the subject."

"I'm not," Annabel argued. "The castle *was* the subject, and– oh! Why won't it open?"

"Let me try." Peter pushed her aside, but to his obvious chagrin, couldn't push open the door any more than Annabel had been able to do so. "Ann, I think it's locked."

"It wasn't locked yesterday," protested Annabel. "Why is it locked today?"

Well now, said Blackfoot, sounding pleased. *That's progress. We can be reasonably certain that most of the inside will be complete today, in that case.*

"It could be a good sign," said Peter, at the same time.

"That's what Blackfoot says. Can your tickerbox unlock it?"

Peter fished about in his pocket and brought out the small box, but when he held it up to the lock, it scrambled back across his palm on its spindly legs and tried to crawl down his collar.

"I think it's scared!" Annabel said, much amused. "It probably remembers the last lock you tried to get it to pick."

"It can't be scared: it's a clockwork box. As for remembering– well, I suppose it could be. I've been working on a special program to make it able to remember and learn. It's not exactly remembering, but it's close and–"

Nan, you've set him off again, said Blackfoot, reproachfully. *At this rate, we'll never get into the castle.*

"*Peter.*"

"Oh, right. Sorry." Peter reclaimed the tickerbox from his collar and shoved it at the lock again. This time, the tickerbox only pranced back and forth worriedly once or twice before it settled itself over the lock. Beneath its regular ticking, Annabel could hear fainter clicks. Peter said: "Got it!" a moment later, and when Annabel tried to push the door open, it moved.

"Up we go, then!" said Peter.

Annabel, who could smell a gloriously familiar smell, said: "Wait!" She pushed through a door that had yesterday only been an empty doorway, and through two more successive doors that hadn't been there yesterday.

Peter, following behind, said incredulously: "Is that bread I can smell?"

Annabel charged down a few curved steps that led to the kitchen, and made directly for the huge ovens at the opposite end of the room. They were, unaccountably, lit, and from all four of them came the distinct aroma of freshly baked bread. "Yes!" she said. "So much bread!"

"But that's impossible!" protested Peter.

Annoying, isn't it?

"Don't just stand there!" Annabel said. "Help me get the bread out! It's going to burn if it stays in much longer."

Peter helped, but she could hear him muttering: "It's not possible! Where did it come from? There's no reason for bread to reappear with the castle!"

Annabel shrugged. She didn't care: there was deliciously fresh bread to eat. "It might have been cooking when the castle disappeared."

"That's– actually, that's something to think about," Peter remarked. "I still don't hold with the idea of time travel, but it really does seem like the castle is coming *back* from somewhere."

A difference so fine as to be almost invisible, sniffed Blackfoot. *Good heavens, Nan! Are you inhaling or eating?*

Annabel, who had her mouth full, only mumbled at him.

"Don't eat it *all*, Ann. Pack up some for later: we can't expect the castle to keep coming back with food inbuilt."

Annabel mumbled again.

"What?"

Annabel gave up on mumbling and trotted across to the series of cold-boxes that lined the inner wall, clutching the remains of a bread loaf to her chest. She couldn't see the spells on the cold boxes, but when she was near enough she could feel the cool seeping from them. Triumphantly, she threw open the door of the first, displaying a dizzying amount of cold meats, pies, open preserves, and cream.

Peter's mouth dropped open. "What? *And* the cold-boxes! This is– this is– I'm having a pie, then."

"Think the cupboards are full as well," Annabel said, still a little thickly. "'T'least we won't have to worry about food for a while. Oh! If you're getting one of the pies, get me one, too. We can take them with us."

"You could get your own if you weren't so busy stuffing your face with bread," Peter pointed out, but he picked up two of the apricot pies anyway. "All right, we'd better keep going. There isn't anything else in the ovens, is there?"

"No," said Annabel regretfully. Even more regretfully, she followed Peter back up the stairs.

Further in, further up, the corridors were almost whole. Still munching on her pie, Annabel was pleased to find that there was far less of the unsettling darkness lurking, and that her stomach wasn't doing the odd, squishy thing it had done yesterday.

The rooms that had doors to them were whole, too. There was still the odd doorway with no door, opening into that awful stretchy blackness, but by and large, the lower level of the castle nearest the kitchen was complete. Annabel and Peter opened doors to galleries, libraries, and a small receiving room in which Annabel would have liked to stay a little longer.

"Not interesting," said Peter, and foraged onward.

On the second level, things became more interesting. The corridor was less complete there, and Annabel could feel a subtle chill to the air that suggested there were still quite a few holes in the higher sections of the castle. That sensation of incompleteness was overshadowed, however, by the fact that the first door they opened on the second level led to a particularly useful room.

"Ugh," said Peter, leaning into the door. "Boring."

It was a whole room full of clothes. In fact, it was a whole room especially dedicated to displaying clothes.

Peter gave it one more look of disgust. "Nothing here, then." He wheeled and went on to the next door, but Annabel, her fingers closing tightly around the doorknob, said: "Wait!"

"What? There's nothing here."

"Yes, there is!" said Annabel. "I've been wearing these flannels for *days*. I can finally change!"

Peter made a face. "Fine. But I'm going on to the other rooms."

Annabel made a face in retaliation, but he already had his back to her. Shrugging, she pushed back through the door and looked around the whole room with gleeful anticipation.

Good heavens, said Blackfoot, padding a swift circle around the room. *I could have sworn that you only look at food like that.*

"I've never had any pretty clothes to look at," Annabel said, hugging herself with delight. "Look at all the colours! I'm going to wear this one!"

*Nan, **no**. Not that one. It's by far too long for you– and red, for heaven's sake!*

"But it's so pretty!"

We'll agree to disagree, shall we? By all means, wear it– if you have no objections to looking like a particularly over-ripe tomato.

"I'm going to try it," said Annabel, unheedingly. She began to wriggle out of her flannels, and Blackfoot disappeared like a whisp of smoke. He always did when she changed, though Annabel, who had spent many summer days swimming in her small-clothes with Peter, and had no modesty to speak of, didn't know why he should be more circumspect than she. He was a cat, after all.

The red dress was delightfully light and cool after her flannels, and although it was, as Blackfoot had warned, a little too long, the petticoat that Annabel found to go along with it pushed it out sufficiently so that she only had to lift the skirt a little when she walked. She tied the sash around her waist—more tightly than it was possibly used to being tied, since it subsequently folded in on itself—and twirled in front of the mirror. Then, very much pleased with herself, she emerged from the room to find Blackfoot, and, in turn, Peter.

She found Blackfoot at the end of the hall. He stared at her in silence for quite some time before she heard him say in a pained sort of a way: *And the worst of it is, the child is actually **proud** of looking like a tomato.*

"Hey! I can hear you, you know!"

Is that so? I would beg to differ, since you've completely ignored my advice.

Annabel glared. "What advice? It was an insult."

A statement of fact.

"Well, I like it!" said Annabel sulkily. "I think it's pretty."

There was a sigh. *I'm regretfully aware of that.*

"What does it matter what you think, anyway?" Annabel demanded. "You're a cat! I've never had a dress as pretty as this before."

There was another moment of silence before Blackfoot

said, more mildly: *That's a good point. Oh well, so long as you're happy, Nan. Don't trip over your hem, will you?*

Annabel beamed at him, and twirled her way around the next corner. "I won't! Did you see the rosettes around the hem, Blackfoot?"

I could hardly help seeing them, said Blackfoot, following her languidly. *They're rather large and quite red. Where has this dreadful child hidden himself, I wonder? Could we be fortunate enough to have had the castle spirit him away somewhere?*

When they came upon Peter again, he was in one of the other rooms, half-way in and half-way out of a shirt that was much finer than his now stain-ridden original. She stayed in the doorway, smirking, until he turned about in his attempts to wriggle into the shirt, and saw her.

"All right, all right, don't just stand there grinning," he complained. "Help me pull this thing down! It's tighter around the shoulders than I expected."

"You should have unlaced it a bit more," said Annabel, coming far enough into the room to yank on the hem of his shirt. Peter emerged, flushing and untidy, and straightened his new shirt.

"Good grief, Ann! What *are* you wearing?"

"Don't you start, too! It's pretty!"

Peter looked her up and down. "You look like a tomato that someone's sewn around the middle."

"Well, you look like a grubby little boy dressing up in his older brother's good clothes," snapped Annabel.

Oh, well played, Nan!

Peter went slightly pink. "I thought I should get something to wear if you were getting something, too."

"Rubbish," said Annabel. "You were just pretending to be

above clothes because you thought there weren't any for you. You went out and looked for boys' clothes, didn't you?"

"I don't care *what* I wear," Peter said. "They only get oily and messed up when I take things apart, anyway, so–"

Annabel folded her arms. "So put your own shirt back on."

"Ann, I *just* changed," argued Peter, marching from the room. "I'm not going to change again."

"Isn't that convenient," Annabel muttered, and followed him. "Where are you going now?"

Peter, very haughtily, said: "We weren't here to look for clothes, Ann. I'm going back to looking for the source of the castle's magic."

A delightful idea. Do you suppose he makes an effort to be so very **emphatic** *about it?*

"Blackfoot says you need to be more careful about how you go looking for it."

"Stop telling me what the cat says! I don't care."

Of course not. That would be the height of stupidity. It's always turned out so well for you when you ignore me, after all.

Annabel rolled her eyes at Blackfoot. "You will if you do something wrong."

"Well, I *won't* do something wrong!"

Was that me snorting with laughter? Dear heavens, how rude of me.

"That's what you always say and it's not always true," said Annabel, but she said it to deaf ears. Peter was already outpacing her along the hall. She groaned and tried to walk more quickly, but her breakfast of bread and pie was beginning to weigh her down. "I think I ate too much."

Now, what can have given you that idea? wondered Blackfoot. *I wonder if our young idiot is trying to get further in, or find the source of the castle's magic. He seems to vacillate between the two.*

"Blackfoot," said Annabel, panting a little as she trotted after Peter, "what *do* you and Peter mean when you say that the only way to get out is to go further in?"

Will wonders never cease, the child is asking questions!

"Just say so if you don't want to tell me," Annabel said sulkily. "*I* don't care!"

It means, Nan, that the whole spell with the returning castle is a cycle spell. It's set to bring the castle back, so if we can speed it up and complete the parameters of the spell, we should be able to get out more quickly. The only way to get out of a cycle spell is to complete the cycle.

"Oh," said Annabel, mollified. "Well, I suppose that makes sense. Anyway, whether Peter's trying to find the source of the castle's magic or trying to go further in, he's sure to find something. That's what Peter *does.*"

That's all very well, Nan, but if he keeps going about things this way, he's going to get you both killed, or maimed, or worse.

"What's worse than being maimed or killed?"

Blackfoot's voice was uncharacteristically serious as he said: *I hope you never find out, Nan. Pick up your skirts: we should try to keep up with the young hot-head. Do you know, it continually surprises me that you're both such good friends.*

Annabel, who was still sometimes surprised at it herself, said: "Yes, I suppose so." She picked up her skirts and hurried around the next corner with Blackfoot, more resigned than annoyed at Peter's behaviour. Once around the corner she stopped, dropping her skirts again, and said uncertainly: "He *did* come around this way, didn't he?"

Blackfoot, padding around her skirts, said: *Of course he—ah. How unfortunate.*

"What happened?" demanded Annabel, turning in a circle to take in the empty hall they had just come from, and the suit of armour that was guarding an alcove behind them. Inevitably, she came back to the sight she had just taken in such disbelief. The corridor ahead of them was gone. It existed as far as a few steps beyond the corner, but after that it ceased, in a ragged, uneven sort of way, into thin air. The breeze, warm and summery, swept freely through the gaping hole in the castle, and Annabel, who was beginning to be used to the castle being more complete again, could only say again: "What happened?"

Because it wasn't just the rest of the hall that had vanished. Peter, too, was gone.

SEVEN

"What happened? Where's Peter?"

Blackfoot, sounding very much as if he were trying *not* to mention that he had warned Peter, said: *I think the castle has taken punitive measures. At a guess, I'd say that Peter is wherever the rest of the hall is.*

"Yes, but where is the rest of the hall?" wailed Annabel. There was a sickening pit of fear in her stomach. "What if Peter's *dead*?"

Peter isn't dead, said Blackfoot, but Annabel heard the uncertain note to his voice. *He's more likely to be back where the rest of the castle is– in the past. I'm sure he'll turn up again, just as annoying as ever.*

Annabel, who had been leaning against the wall in a fatalistic kind of way, prepared for it to vanish too, slid to the floor in a puff of airy red satin. She was quite certain that the hall had been there moments before: she would have felt the strong summer breeze that was currently sweeping through and tugging at her hair.

"What–" her voice cracked, and she tried again. "What are

we supposed to do now? Peter's the one with magic. I don't know how to find him! Even if I did, how could I get him back?"

That, said Blackfoot, *is the question, isn't it? Nan, what are you doing?*

"I'm going to find Peter," said Annabel, her voice snubby with tears and worry. "He's got to be around here *somewhere.* He's Peter. He'll come back, somehow."

The castle is unsafe, said Blackfoot, considerately ignoring Annabel's self-contradictory assertions. *If there's anything we can take away from today, it's that none of us should be wandering this section until it's fully complete.*

"You can go back down, then," said Annabel. She edged closer to the brink of empty space, feeling the warmth of summer on her face, and said: "This one's different."

I find myself wondering why it is that you only bestir yourself into action when you're about to do something I particularly don't want you to do, said Blackfoot, in some exasperation. *No, never mind, Nan. I'm quite well aware that you'll only ignore me. You said this is different? How is it different?*

"The other bits that are gone, they're different," Annabel said slowly, to give herself time to think about why that was. "Well, there's no black stuff. The other bits have been coming back as if they've been *pulled* out of something– out of non-existence, or the past, or whatever that awful stuff is. But this bit has just gone, and there's real space left behind where it should be: look, I can see right down into the floor below, and the sky through where the wall should be."

That's all well and good, Nan, said Blackfoot, prowling along the edge beside her. *But what does it mean?*

"Don't know," Annabel said. Her voice was less snubby now, and it didn't shake, either. As little sure as she was about why the corridor had suddenly disappeared, was she sure of why that should be, but she thought it might have something to do with the distinct feeling that she was, in some indefinable way, a step closer to finding Peter.

The throne room was unnaturally quiet that night. Annabel, who was used to hearing Peter's heavy breathing when they slept in the same room, found it distinctly ominous. She had spent the rest of the day searching the parts of the castle that had come back—and were, more importantly, still *there*—too intent upon finding Peter to be able to concentrate on anything else. He was nowhere to be found, and having wearily traversed dozens of flights of stairs, Annabel eventually had to admit defeat. She collapsed on the dais with a face as red as her new dress, and sought comfort in her stubby little pencil and sketchbook. Unusually enough, it wasn't the soothing past-time Annabel was used to it being, and instead of starting on a new drawing, she found herself paging through the drawings she had already completed. She added a few lines to the face of the man she'd seen in the glass that morning, and looked up instinctively to see if he was there again; but he wasn't, and she still couldn't seem to get his eyes quite right. Despite her recent exercises of effort, Annabel still wasn't in the habit of pushing herself to do what she found to be too much hard work: she left the drawing. She dabbled at the other unfinished sketch instead, shading the eyelids she'd drawn earlier, and this time she was satisfied with the result. Whoever this other man was, he looked out on the world through slightly mocking eyes that were only partly open. He could have been sneering, but Annabel still wasn't sure about how to draw his mouth, and after minimal work around his eyes, she left that sketch, too.

After that, she flipped through the book in a lacklustre kind of way, looking cursorily at the rough sketches she'd made of the castle as it came back. It afforded her a small, colourless pleasure that she had managed to draw a very good guess of what would come back next in several of them, and that she'd correctly replicated most of the rubble that was now back in its place around the castle. If Peter had been there to share in her success, she would have been very pleased with herself. Now that he wasn't, the triumph was significantly diminished.

It's no use fidgeting, Blackfoot said, batting at her foot through the red satin. He had banished the spark of magical light he'd given her quite some time ago, but there was just enough moon shining through the newly vine-free skylights to keep going, despite his obvious disapproval. *Stop wriggling and twitching, and go to sleep. We'll find Peter tomorrow.*

"I *am*," Annabel told him crossly, but although she leaned back against the dais and stared at the moon through the skylights, it was a long time before she fell asleep.

She went to sleep with her book and pencil stub in her lap, and woke with them there. That was a fortuitous circumstance, since the first thing Annabel saw when she opened her eyes was the Caliphan stranger in the coloured glass opposite.

Annabel squeaked and flailed. "Blackfoot! Blackfoot! He's back! Look, there in the glass!"

He's been there for quite some time, Blackfoot said, his voice particularly bored.

"Well," said Annabel, taken aback. "Well, you should apologise, then."

I'm quite sure he's not there because of any effort of mine. That child's proof of value has obviously been adopted by the castle.

"That's not what I meant!" Annabel complained. "You and Peter both thought I was going mad. He– oh…"

Nan, said Blackfoot. *Please don't cry. Look, you've dropped your pencil. Pick it up, there's a good girl. Draw the Caliphan so you don't forget him and then we'll visit the kitchen for breakfast. We'll look for Peter when you've eaten.*

"I don't want breakfast," said Annabel, but she said it very quietly, and it was likely that Blackfoot believed it as little as she herself believed it. She was rather surprised, therefore, upon entering the kitchen, to find herself opening and closing cold-box doors with as little enthusiasm as she had tried to draw the previous night.

Blackfoot, who was prowling behind her, said curiously: *Are you ill, Nan?*

"No," Annabel said, and surprised herself yet again by adding: "I'm not hungry, I think. Let's go look for Peter again."

I never thought I'd hear myself say this to you, Nan, but you should eat.

"Don't want to," said Annabel. It wasn't so much that she wasn't hungry: the thought of food was simply and completely unappetizing. Even the apricot pies that she and Peter had eaten with such relish yesterday weren't appealing. "Let's just go back to where Peter vanished yesterday and see if the corridor has come back yet. Maybe it's come back and brought Peter back with it."

I wouldn't expect too much if I were you, Blackfoot warned, but he padded along behind her again as she climbed the stairs, anyway.

Annabel was steadfast in her determination to expect exactly what she wanted to expect, but she wasn't given the chance to find out if her determination was warranted: shortly after they began climbing stairs in their quest for the missing hallway, they found themselves back in the kitchen.

"Hey!" said Annabel in surprise. "What happened? We've been climbing *up* the whole time!"

Oh, this is interesting, Blackfoot said. *Or is it terrifying? I can't decide.*

"Maybe it's another kitchen?" Annabel suggested, though she sounded unconvinced even to her own ears. The kitchen they were now in was very obviously the same one they had just left: she could even see her own and Blackfoot's dusty footprints going through the opposite door.

A kitchen above stairs? I think not. I have the horrible feeling, Nan, that Mordion has given the castle a proof of value.

Annabel peeked into one of the cold-boxes and was gloomily unsurprised to find it stacked familiarly with pies and sauces. "Does that mean he's in the castle right now?"

For the first time since she and Peter tumbled into the castle ruins, Annabel heard the sound of fear in Blackfoot's voice. *It shouldn't be possible. He shouldn't be able to get in here. Even if the castle accepted his proof of value, it shouldn't have given him access to the castle itself. No: it's far more likely that he's playing games with the corridors and stairways to make it harder for us. Even that would be a stretch– nothing should be able to affect the castle's growth at this stage.*

"Oh!" said Annabel, as a far-too-belated thought struck her. "Then *Mordion* took Peter!"

I find it extremely unlikely, Blackfoot said. *The castle won't let Mordion in, even if he's given proof of value. All that proof of value will give him is the ability to piggy-back a spell on the castle's magics.*

"Well, but all he'd need to do is take away some of the corridors," argued Annabel. "He could do that, couldn't he?"

*That– Nan, it's unlikely in the extreme! Do you never listen to me? I **told** you about proof of value!*

"I still think it's Mordion," muttered Annabel, and stomped back out of the kitchen. "You *said* that he could establish proof of value, too."

Where are you going, Nan?

"I'm going to find Peter!"

We've already come this way.

"We're going to *keep* coming this way until it goes upstairs instead of back to the kitchen," Annabel said obstinately.

***Nan**– oh, very well, if you **must** trudge up and down myriad stairways, at least wait for me! Who would have thought the child was capable of such a turn of speed?*

"I can *hear* you," Annabel said coldly. She bunched the red satin of her skirts to her chest and climbed determinedly back up the stairs with Blackfoot padding behind her on silent feet. Unfortunately, his voice wasn't as silent as his feet, and he continued to mutter in the recesses of Annabel's mind as she tried to retrace her steps through the castle.

This time, the route was longer and more circuitous, but it ended in the same place that it had begun: the kitchen. Annabel stared at it for a pent moment and then wheeled and stomped up the stairs again.

How exciting, said Blackfoot. *Whatever will we see this time, I wonder? More staircases? New window frames? Perhaps we'll be lucky enough to spot a new corridor! How will I manage the exhilaration?*

"I'm not listening to you," Annabel said. Instead of trying to retrace her steps, or even trying to find her way back to the partial hallway where Peter had disappeared, she didn't choose her way. She simply climbed stairs and wandered hallways, and wherever her steps took her, she went. There was certainly something different about the castle this morning: it was more whole and less inclined to sudden, gaping spaces where walls should be. The effect, unfortunately, wasn't to put Annabel more at her ease, since she found herself even less sure of her surroundings than she had been before. She was quite certain, however, that in her scurryings around the castle, she saw the north and south views in the blinking between one window and the next. There were *more* windows, too, their views never quite consistent, and when she grew dizzy with trying to keep her position straight in her mind, Annabel stopped looking out of them entirely. Instead, she watched the reflections, and in those reflections saw not only a clear echo of herself, marching determinedly through the traitorous halls, but the same Caliphan she'd seen earlier. Like herself, he was hurrying through the castle, but where Annabel was confused and angry, the Caliphan seemed surprised and inclined to nervousness. She wasn't quite sure why, but Annabel got the feeling he was being pursued by someone or something.

"He's still there," she said to Blackfoot. "He looks worried. Maybe Mordion is playing with his version of the castle, too."

There was a silence before Blackfoot said: *Even if it's possible for Mordion to be interfering with the castle, how could it affect the castle in the reflections? One problem at a time. And speaking of problems, do you think we've wandered enough? Shall we return to the kitchen and try to think of another way to proceed?*

Annabel scowled. "No. We're going to start opening doors."

Blackfoot seemed to sigh. *Of course we are. I hate to seem to complain, but what exactly is your plan? Are we to continue wandering the castle at random, and opening convenient doors, or is there more to your thoughts?*

"If someone is making the corridors go where they don't usually go–"

I believe I've explained about the castle. Nobody should be capable of affecting its growth or removing sections: not even Mordion.

"If the castle is making the corridors go where they don't usually go," continued Annabel, not put off, "then it's doing it for a reason. I've seen this hallway three times already, actually. So now I want to know why the castle keeps bringing us here."

All right, Blackfoot conceded. *We'll suppose you're right.*

"Thanks."

Don't be sarcastic, Nan: it's my particular pleasure to provide any and all commentary of a sarcastic nature that is required in your life. We'll suppose you're right–

"Yes, we'll suppose I'm right," said Annabel, grinning in spite of herself. "Someone or something keeps bringing us back here, and I don't think that door is locked."

Blackfoot's velvet nose turned cautiously this way and that, between two doors. *Which one?*

"This one," said Annabel, and flung open the door. She recognised the figure it revealed as a person instinctively before she was aware of it rationally, and flinched back into the hall as the door hit the inside wall.

The sound of metal connecting with quarried stone sounded loudly in the uneasy silence of the hall as Annabel's pale blue eyes met Mordion's vibrantly sapphire ones. She heard her heart thundering loudly in her ears, but even with the shock of it all, Annabel was quite sure that Mordion was just as startled as she was. He was still a pace or two away from the door-frame, as though he'd been approaching it from his side.

To Blackfoot, Annabel said: "You said– you said he couldn't get in!"

"I really wouldn't listen too carefully to what your cat says," Mordion said. "He's a quite a slippery sort of cat: you're never entirely sure you've got him pinned down."

I could say the same thing of him, said Blackfoot. *Nan, back away, please.*

"He's returning the compliment," Annabel told Mordion, and shifted her weight as imperceptibly as she could. Mordion's eyelashes flickered, and she saw him smile faintly.

"I really hope you're not planning on running, darling."

"Of course I'm planning on running," she said. "What else would I do?"

Just two steps back now, Nan, said Blackfoot's voice; and it was so calm that even though Mordion took one step forward for each of those two steps she retreated, Annabel found herself less afraid than she'd expected.

As leisurely as ever, Mordion rested his hands against the frame of the doorway. "Now I'm curious. Where exactly is it that you're planning on running?"

"There are a lot of hallways and stairs and rooms," Annabel said. Perhaps she wasn't as unafraid as she'd thought: her heart was beating steadily and she felt very wide awake, but it was strangely difficult to speak without gasping.

"There are," agreed Mordion. "Now don't take this the wrong way, darling, but I've seen you run. You're not particularly fast, and what in the Three Monarchies makes you think that I'd be so disingenuous as to underestimate you a second time?"

And one more step, Blackfoot's voice murmured. *Mind the gap.*

"It's the *Two* Monarchies, actually," Annabel said coldly,

and took one more step backwards. Belatedly, she squeaked: "What gap?" but by then her foot had stepped onto nothing, and she was falling: coldly, slowly, inevitably.

In the coldness of the fall, Annabel heard Mordion swearing, and the corridor that she was somehow falling *through* seemed to shudder around her. Then her back hit something cool that gave a little under her but held, and there was a sensation of furry warmth beneath her neck while something squeaked in a distinctly undignified manner.

"What?" panted Annabel, staring up at the curved darkness above her. "Where's Mordion? Where are we?"

Nan–

"What happened? Have we disappeared too? Where's Peter?"

Nan–

Annabel wailed: "Why did you tell me to step backwards? Now look where we are!"

Nan, do you think you could lift your head a little? I'm finding it a trifle difficult to breathe.

"Oh," said Annabel, and sat up. The furry warmth that had been beneath her shoulder and neck scrabbled in the darkness, a shadow against shadow, and sat down next to her with a series of mental groans and mutters. "Was that *you* squeaking?"

Blackfoot, in a decidedly stiff manner, said: *It seems that when a significant weight falls on a per– cat unexpectedly, they tend to be startled. They also, Nan, tend to gasp.*

"That wasn't a gasp," said Annabel. "It was a squeak."

Nan– oh, never mind. Can you stand?

"Oh yes," Annabel said. "I didn't hurt myself: it's pretty springy here, actually. Blackfoot, where *is* here?"

Why ask me? Blackfoot demanded, still stiff.

"You're the one who told me to step backwards!" Annabel said indignantly. "I didn't do this!"

The wall disappeared: I thought it was a good opportunity to get away while we could.

Annabel looked around at the velvety darkness dubiously. "So it was the castle that did it? Then we *have* disappeared, too! Maybe Peter's in here?"

I very much doubt it, said Blackfoot. *Nan, **must** you scrabble about like that? That was my tail!*

"Oh, sorry." Annabel climbed to her feet rather more carefully, and felt Blackfoot twining around her ankles. "If you're going to do that, don't blame me if I step on you."

There was a sigh at the back of her mind. *You'll have to pick me up, then.*

"Why?" demanded Annabel, but she picked him up anyway. "You've got legs!"

It's too dark. I don't want you to step on me again. Nan, do you suppose we can at last return to the kitchen? I may not have to eat quite as often as you, but I'm really quite hungry.

"How should I know?" Annabel peered around her in the darkness again, and found it just as murky. She took a few steps forward with Blackfoot in her arms, feeling her way carefully. She'd fallen down often enough in the castle. "For all I know, this tunnel goes to– oh! That's– that's the kitchen! How did we get back here?"

Goodness knows, said Blackfoot, springing from Annabel's arms as she stepped out from darkness into the kitchen. Annabel thought that he sounded smug, having got his own way without having to make any effort toward it, and made a face at him. *How fortunate. Mind your skirt, Nan: the tunnel is closing up again.*

Annabel hastily twitched her skirts out of the way and

watched the hole in the wall as it vanished. One moment there was a soft blackness to the wall, the next there was only regularly spaced, smoothly quarried stone. "Wait," she said. "Wasn't it the same as the spell in that room? The one that took us to the stables?"

Good grief, no! said Blackfoot. *Completely different. Not that I expect you to realise the difference, Nan, but the tunnelling spell that led us to the stables was a clumsy sort of copy of this one. It was nothing like as stable, nor was it as elegantly winding.*

"All right, all right, there's no need to rub it in!" grumbled Annabel. "I can't help not being able to see magic. What do you mean, anyway, *elegantly winding*? Winding around what?"

The black squishy centre, of course. There were huge branches of it all around us as we walked through the tunnelling spell: it wound around them all.

Annabel shivered. "Ugh! I'm glad I didn't know! And that reminds me: you told me that no one could get in to the castle! Why didn't you know Mordion was here?"

I did, agreed Blackfoot. *And I've certainly no idea how Mordion got in. How utterly revolting. I'm afraid that things are becoming more complicated, Nan.*

"That settles it," Annabel said firmly. "It was Mordion that took Peter."

Let's not rush to conclusions.

"It's not rushing. Mordion is in the castle and you said he couldn't get in, and you *said—*"

Thank you, Nan, I remember what I said.

"Well, you were wrong."

Yes, Nan. Believe it or not, you were quite clear the first time. Blackfoot sat where he was for silent moments, his tail twitching, and said at last: *Nothing is going as I anticipated: I have no idea what to expect any more.*

Uncertainly, Annabel said: "Oh." She wasn't used to Blackfoot being so unsure of himself. "Well, it's not your fault, after all."

Blackfoot sighed. *Perhaps not directly, but I'm beginning to regret that I brought us into the castle. I thought—I was certain—that you would be safe here.*

Annabel shrugged. "I'm safe enough at the moment: it's Peter who isn't safe."

Peter will take care of himself. Blackfoot licked a paw and wiped it over his whiskers reflectively. *If it comes to that, right now it's the thing I'm most certain of: that Peter is perfectly safe.*

"Yes, but you've been wrong about a lot of things," said Annabel. Blackfoot hissed at her, but she ignored it. Now that the shock of Mordion's sudden presence had come and gone, she discovered she was once again quite hungry. The cold-boxes were conveniently close, so Annabel found herself a fat little bottle of preserves that was already open, and rummaged around until she found the remains of yesterday's fresh bread.

Blackfoot seemed to stare at her in horror. **Don't** *eat that, Nan! You don't know how long it's been in there!*

"Prob'ly a couple hundred years," Annabel said. "If it's from the past like you said. But you've been–"

Yes, yes, I've been wrong about a lot lately. Nan, it's a dreadful habit in a little girl to be pointing out every time people make mistakes.

"You want sausages?" Annabel asked through a mouthful of bread and preserves, a little more thickly than before. "Pork or chicken?"

There was a dignified silence before Blackfoot said: *Chicken, thank you.*

They ate in peace until the bread and sausages were gone. Then, sitting on one of the preparation tables with an apricot pie in one hand, Annabel said thoughtfully: "Do you know, I don't think Mordion could get out of that room."

An interesting theory, said Blackfoot, licking his chops. *What makes you suppose it?*

Annabel had to think about that for a longer time. At last, she said reluctantly: "Don't know. But he did that same thing."

Nan, it may interest you to know that I can't, in fact, read your mind.

"That thing he did the first time," Annabel said slowly. "Where he tried to frighten me into staying in Grenna's garden because he wasn't strong enough to keep me there himself."

Well now, said Blackfoot, and he sounded startled. *That's something to think about. I wonder– I really wonder, Nan, what exactly it was that Mordion used to establish value with the castle.*

Annabel scowled at her pie. "And I want to know how he took Peter. You said–"

I warn you, Nan: if you're about to tell me how I was wrong again, I'll bite you.

"It's not that. You said that Mordion gets magic by taking it from other people– does that mean he doesn't have any of his own? When it runs out, I mean, how does he get more? Because even if he took a lot of magic from someone else, won't it run out soon if he's going around doing big magic like stealing people?"

Mordion has magic of his own, Blackfoot said. *If he didn't, he'd attract all the magic he could desire. Because, Nan–?*

"What?" Annabel blinked at him, then said glibly: "Oh! Because a complete lack of magic creates a vacuum."

Exactly so. Of course, it wouldn't do him any good, since he wouldn't have the ability to use what he gathered, and Mordion *is **very** good at putting to use the magic that he gathers. So to answer your questions, Nan–*

"Oh good."

*To answer your question, Nan, repeated Blackfoot repressively, Mordion **does** have magic, albeit very little, and what he gathers does run out, in time. If he had kidnapped Peter—**if**, Nan—his resources would diminish much more quickly.*

"So he should be weaker now," Annabel said darkly. "Now that he's taken Peter, I mean. We should hit back while he's weaker."

Blackfoot sighed.

"What?"

Nan– oh, where to start?

"If you're going to be superior, I won't give you any more sausages," warned Annabel.

I suspect you're overestimating my love for sausages, said Blackfoot. Not to mention underestimating my love of being superior.

"Pft," said Annabel. "I saw you eating the old sausages Grenna threw away that time."

I was particularly hungry.

"*And* I saw you catching the pieces of sausage Peter threw at you last week."

*The point **is**, interrupted Blackfoot, that we have no reason to suppose Mordion took Peter. And if he didn't, then your confidence that Mordion is in a weakened state could prove to be a costly mistake.*

Annabel, for once quite sure of her own reasoning, shook her head. "Yes, but you don't understand. You said Mordion must have established value. All right, suppose he established value with something that can move corridors and walls? It was after Peter established value with his seeing spell that I started seeing that Caliphan in the windows. What if the castle reacts to the value spells? Like little hiccoughs of magic."

There was a ghostly laugh at the back of Annabel's mind. *Nan!* said Blackfoot. *Well, I never!*

"All right, all right," grumbled Annabel. "There's no need to laugh at me. It was a stupid thing to say."

On the contrary: I've never heard you reason so deductively before! I was merely taken by surprise.

Taken aback, Annabel said: "Well! Then we'll go looking for Mordion tomorrow."

That's not even remotely what I was suggesting.

"Yes, but–"

In light of the fact that Mordion seems to be able to wander the castle at will–

"We're not sure of that–"

*–**seems**, I said, Nan: **seems** to be able to wander the castle at will, and that we have no way of knowing how strong he is, what in the Two Monarchies makes you think it's a good idea to deliberately look for him?*

"Well, what else are we going to do?" Annabel said reasonably. "Wait until he finds us? He'll probably have found someone else to drain of magic by then."

***Now** you take my advice to start thinking for yourself and ask questions,* muttered Blackfoot. *Oh well: better late than never, I suppose. Tomorrow, then. But if he kills us both, don't come crying to me about it.*

EIGHT

"Hey!" said Annabel indignantly. "Two of the apricot pies have gone!"

She'd been looking forward to those pies ever since she woke to the now-familiar sight of the Caliphan stranger rushing about in the coloured glass of the throne room. Annabel had watched him, thinking of pie, then guiltily of Peter, then of pie again. The yearning had only grown stronger as Annabel performed her rudimentary morning ablutions under the pump, and by the time she reached the kitchen, she could almost taste them. Great was her indignation, therefore, to find that there were two less of the treasured treats than there had been the day before.

Annabel looked wrathfully into the pillaged cold-box. "Who's creeping around the castle *now*?"

Nan, this is no time to be taking stock of pies. There are more important things that demand our consideration, not the least of which is your rash determination to seek out Mordion.

"Pies *are* important!" Annabel insisted. "And I know there are two missing because there were five stacks of four in the top shelf of this cool-box yesterday, and now there are only two in this pile. Who's been getting into our kitchen?"

*Leaving aside the obviously insurmountable importance of the missing pies, perhaps we could consider that the more important question is who **else** has gotten into the Castle through the wardings,* remarked Blackfoot. *If you're right—*

"I am."

*If you're right—Nan, don't throw that at me—then there's the distinct possibility—I said **don't** throw that at me—that yet another person has made it through the castle wardings. If that fails to move you, only think of how many pies you stand to lose now that there's another dangerously strong player in this game.*

"What game?" demanded Annabel. "Peter has *gone*, and Mordion is popping up in corridors where he shouldn't be, and you're calling it a game?"

Why are you trying to pick a quarrel with me, Nan?

Annabel sank into herself sulkily, staring at him with her best cow face. "I'm not trying to pick a quarrel. You're sarcastic and horrible and flippant."

I'm always sarcastic and horrible and flippant. What's the particular objection today? And it's no use doing that face at me, Nan: if I'd not learned your tricks by now I wouldn't be able to hold my head up again.

"Don't know," Annabel said, hunching her shoulders. "Anyway, I don't think it's Mordion doing it."

Why? Because of your theory that he can't move through doors?

"No," said Annabel. "I don't think he'd want to dirty his clothes or his hands. I think he'd have picked something less messy to eat."

There was a breath of laughter from Blackfoot. *That's a good point. Then who else is there? Your Caliphan?*

Annabel considered this suspiciously. Between Mordion and the Caliphan, she could far more readily see the Caliphan sneaking pies out of the cold-box and guiltily scoffing them while Annabel and Blackfoot slept.

"Where is he, anyway?" she asked. "The Caliphan, I mean? Or maybe I mean *when*. When Peter did the spell before, it showed Mordion, *now*. Does that mean that the Caliphan is in the *now*, too? Or is the castle showing bits from the past? I thought it was showing bits of the past—you know, before the castle vanished, or went wrong, or whatever happened—but now I'm not so sure."

She was remembering the flash she'd seen of the Caliphan that morning: she'd been drawing near by the windows to get some light that wasn't coloured by the coloured glass behind the throne itself, waiting for Blackfoot to wake up. It took a while for the feeling of being watched to sink in, but when Annabel became aware of it she only assumed that Blackfoot had woken, and kept working on the drawing she had started. She was trying to draw the Caliphan again, and although she'd managed to get his gangly limbs down on the paper, his eyes still wouldn't come out right. Annabel left them for last and smudged shadows to make the adam's apple on the Caliphan's knobbly throat instead. She slid a look across at Blackfoot as she wiped her pencil-smudged hand carelessly on her skirts, expecting to see him watching her, but he was still curled in circle by the dais where she'd woken earlier.

Annabel didn't think about it: instinctively, she looked up at the window beside her. The Caliphan was there, closer than she'd ever seen him before, his head bent as if he was looking at her drawing. Perhaps he sensed the movement of her head: he looked up, too, and for the barest moment, their eyes met. He looked away at once, and wandered away from the window, but his gaze was just a little too studiously unaware of her presence. Annabel had spent the rest of the morning certain that just as she'd seen him, he had seen her.

How could he be here and now? Blackfoot's voice was sceptical. *We would have seen him in the flesh before now.*

"Oh," said Annabel reluctantly. "I suppose we would have. But what if– well, what if he's in the *now*, but in a bit of the castle that hasn't come back yet?"

The bits of the castle that haven't come back yet are still in the past, Blackfoot said dampeningly. *That's why they're not here, **now**.*

Annabel looked at him accusingly. "Then what about the black squishy stuff? You can't tell me that's stuff from the past. It's right here, now."

There was a slight fuzziness in the part of Annabel's mind that spoke Blackfoot's words, as if he were deliberating upon which words to say– or simply choosing which particularly sarcastic barb was best to use. At last, she heard him say: *That... well, that's not really here **or** there. It's more of a– well, actually, I have no idea what it is.* He sounded distinctly annoyed. *I've been working on the assumption that the castle was coming back from the past.*

"Ugh!" said Annabel, disgusted. "You and Peter are just the same! So certain of yourselves!"

With good reason, I must say, Nan, objected Blackfoot. *I've not been badly wrong in quite some time. I'm still not convinced that I **am** wrong. The castle disappeared shortly before the Civet invasion, and slightly after the staff and royal household escaped, in anticipation of the invasion. There was a lot of magic flying around everywhere: here, the Frozen Battlefield– the whole country was thick it. Somewhere in the middle of the melee the Battlefield shifted, people were encased in magical amber, and* *they lost the castle. It came back, but by then the King and Queen were dead and all the heirs were either dead or gone, anyway. The Council never tried to make use of it—I assume they knew better than to interfere with it—and over the last three hundred years it simply crumbled apart.*

"Where did it go when it vanished?"

No one knows.

"Peter says there was a story about the heirs coming back when the castle comes back."

Heir, corrected Blackfoot. Old Parras only allowed for one heir to be named.

"Well, *the* heir, then."

That- well, I suppose there is. It's not a very interesting story, however, Nan. The interesting story is the one about Rorkin and his staff-

"Yes, but what if the heir has shown up, and that's why the castle is coming back?"

*Well, what if that **is** why?*

"Then the castle might not be coming back from the past. Maybe it's coming back from wherever it went when it disappeared that time. People would have noticed all that black stuff. And if the black stuff isn't from back then, maybe the Caliphan isn't, either."

And if he isn't?

Annabel glared at him. "*I* don't know! I was just supposing! If you're just going to sit there and mew questions at me, we might as well start looking for Mordion."

Nan, I really don't think it's a good idea to go looking for Mordion.

"Neither do I," said Annabel, jumping down from the kitchen table where she had been eating breakfast. "But if he's got Peter, we've got to find him."

That's not a certainty, either! hissed Blackfoot, but he followed Annabel up the stairs when she left the kitchen anyway. *I'm curious, Nan: do you have a better method of finding your way around the castle this morning than you had yesterday?*

"What? It worked yesterday!"

Only in the very slightest approximation! May I point out that putting on a blindfold and attempting to find the edge of a cliff will also generally be quite successful?

"I don't know why you ask things like that," said Annabel coldly, "when you're only going to say what you want whether or not I agree."

Let it be a life lesson to you, Nan.

"*What* life lesson?" demanded Annabel, who was still more than reasonably sore about Blackfoot's comments upon her laziness. They could be—*were*—quite true, but she was still having the odd moment where she would remember them, and feel as though she had to act upon them. It wouldn't have been so bad if she could simply have forgotten them– or at least, decided not to let them affect her. After all, why should she be indebted to a cat for her moral betterment?

A reminder that people will say whatever they want to say, no matter how much you don't want them to do so, said Blackfoot.

"You're not even a person!"

That's unkind, Nan.

"It isn't a life lesson! It's just a reminder that cats are awful and that I've never liked them."

Oh, very roundly dismissed! Well done!

"*Anyway,*" Annabel said coldly, "I don't see why we should do anything differently today. I think the castle is a bit sneaky: it takes us where *it* wants us to be, so it's no use trying to get anywhere else, really. It was the castle that made us run into Mordion yesterday."

There was a mutter of *Oh, for pity's sake!* in Annabel's mind.

"And it's no good telling me not to– to anthrop– anthrop– not to pretend the castle has feelings. Not after we couldn't get back to the hallway where Peter disappeared and Mordion popped up like that."

Nan, has it ever occurred to you that Mordion was the one who pulled you toward himself?

"Yes, but I don't think it's right. He was just as surprised to see us as we were to see him."

*You think **the castle** let Mordion in?*

"No," said Annabel, and stopped. "No. Well, that is– Blackfoot, you're confusing me! I told you yesterday: I think Mordion used a spell as proof of value to let him piggyback off the castle's magic, and that the castle has been using it ever since."

*Yesterday you were **convinced** that Mordion was the author of all evils.*

"Yes, but– well, maybe not all of them. He *must* have kidnapped Peter, and he's still trying to get to us. I think the castle is trying to help us."

Better and better, muttered Blackfoot. *Then, Nan, if you're quite finished inspecting the stores, perhaps we'd better get started. I can only hope you're right about the castle: perhaps it will prevent you from getting to Mordion.*

Annabel, who was privately quite sure that the castle would help them in finding Peter again, only sniffed at him and wrapped two of the pies in her handkerchief for later.

· · ·

If the castle had been confusing yesterday, it was positively dizzying today. Annabel sturdily climbed stairs, only to find herself passing through dressing-chambers at the half-way landings; wandered through maids' quarters, only to discover that she'd opened a door into a gallery that overlooked the ballroom. Once, returning through the same door by which she'd entered, she found herself in an entirely different room than the one she'd just passed through, and when she stumbled into what was obviously the king's suite, it was only to discover that the midden was behind his dressing-room door.

"Ugh," said Annabel. It hadn't occurred to her that if food had come back with the castle, waste was also likely to have returned. She looked around her with a wrinkled nose, holding her skirts high, and added hopefully: "Maybe Mordion will fall in."

*We can only hope. **Must** we stand in this disgusting cess-pool, Nan? I'll never get the smell out of my fur.*

Annabel scooped him up. "Oh, sorry. We'd better go back this way: it'll probably be a different room now, anyway."

But this time when she went back through the same door, she entered the king's suite again. Blackfoot, springing out of her arms, deliberately padded all over the king's bed with his squishy feet, and spent what Annabel considered to be a disproportionate amount of time kneading the bedspread. He refused to be rushed or shamed, and in the end she simply sat down on the bed as well, shuffling her own feet on the rug and picking apart the knots in her handkerchief to get to her pies.

A little before lunch time, they found themselves in the kitchen again. Annabel, with her pies already eaten and uncertain about how soon—or even *if*—they would make it back to the kitchen, raided the cool-boxes again and made off with half a loaf of bread to round things out. Blackfoot made a *pft* noise at her, but he didn't complain when she brought along sausages for him to eat, so Annabel concluded that it had been a habitual sort of sneer rather than a felt one. She found a flask in the kitchen as well, and filled it from the pump. The castle was inclined to make her climb quite a lot of stairs, and she had felt the lack of something to drink more than once that morning.

It was much to her relief, therefore, that their afternoon proved to be a more sedate, flat affair. Shortly after she left the kitchen for the second time, Annabel found herself on the third level, and although the windows still tended to show distractingly different views from one to the next, there didn't seem to be any stairs in sight.

Suites, said Blackfoot dismissively. *Nothing very useful here.*

"There might be something," protested Annabel, who was merely thankful for the lack of stairs. "Oh! Look! Isn't that the wizard's quarters?"

It may have escaped your notice, Nan, Blackfoot said coldly, *but I can't actually **see** out of the windows.*

Annabel muttered to herself, but picked him up with her free hand. "Look: that bit over there, the diamondy-shaped one. I put that in one of my drawings and you said it was the castle wizard's quarters."

Well, I never! said Blackfoot. *Nan! You listened to me!*

"I listen to you all the time," mumbled Annabel. "Can't do anything else, actually: you never shut up."

Blackfoot, ignoring that, mused: *I wonder if we can get there.* His ears had gone up and forward, and even his slightly smelly paws, which were usually placed precisely together in a dignified stance, were padding at the arm that supported him, as if he were preparing to spring from the window.

"Why should we get there? I couldn't use any of the spells, even if there were some spells still lying about."

There's food still lying about, so why not spells? demanded Blackfoot. *And if it comes to that, you may not be able to use them, but I certainly can!*

Annabel pondered this for a brief moment. "That's a good point," she said at last. "All right, we'll try to find it first, then. We might as well be prepared for Mordion if we can."

A day of wonders indeed, murmured Blackfoot. *But I do wonder if it will be any easier to find the wizard quarters than it is to find Mordion. As far as I can tell, we've been aimlessly wandering through every possible part of the castle for the last few hours.*

"At least we're on the right floor to find them," said Annabel, peering at the outside of the castle. "Goodness knows where Mordion is. Maybe the castle doesn't want us to find him today."

Nan– oh, never mind. Very well then: the castle doesn't want us to find Mordion today. I'm grateful to it. Shall we see if we can't find our way to the wizard quarters?

"I suppose so," Annabel said reluctantly. She would very much have preferred to meet Mordion and get the whole thing over with. She had been rehearsing bits and pieces of what she was going to say in her mind, and she was very much afraid that if she didn't get the chance to speak them soon, she wouldn't remember them. "Let's go through this door."

*That door is in **exactly** the wrong direction. You couldn't get any further from the right direction, in fact.*

Annabel, in great satisfaction, said: "That's right. And I bet it takes us in the right direction anyway."

What could possibly make you think such a thing? demanded Blackfoot, in despair.

"Well, *that* window is looking out over the wizard quarters. *That* one is looking out over the hills at the south."

What of it?

"They're right next to each other," Annabel said reasonably. "And every time we've tried to go in the right direction to get where we wanted to go lately, we've ended up in the opposite direction. If the castle is trying to help us– sorry?"

I said nothing. I merely choked on my spleen.

"–if the castle is trying to help us, then we'll end up there no matter which way we go. I'm testing my theory. Isn't that what you're meant to do with theories?"

Yes, Nan. In a controlled environment with controlled conditions.

"We haven't got a controlled environment," said Annabel. "Well, it's not us controlling it, anyway."

I am painfully aware of that.

"So we should go through this door," said Annabel, and opened the door. It opened into a vast, wooden-boarded space that echoed beneath their feet and through the beams of the oddly-slanted ceiling.

It was broad, spacious, and seemed to converge upon the single window that let in an impossible amount of light through its crystal-bright surface. It was also completely empty.

"Oh!" said Annabel in wild triumph, recognising the way the faceted ceiling met with the window. "Blackfoot! I think we're there! The wizard quarters, I mean. Why is it so empty, though?"

I wouldn't like to hazard a guess, Blackfoot said. He sounded both resigned and puzzled. *My surmises haven't been the most accurate, lately. And yet, the rest of the rooms we saw on this floor are whole: why not this one?*

"The castle is–"

Blackfoot prowled into the centre of the room and sat down very precisely. *Yes, yes, the castle is doing it, so you said. There's something odd about this room.*

Annabel wasn't surprised when he got up again and stalked around the entire room, stopping only at the window, which he sniffed suspiciously. Since it seemed likely that he was intent upon his investigation and wouldn't speak to her for some time, she sat down near the window and made herself busy eating the food she'd brought with her. Blackfoot passed by to eat a sausage every now and then, but when he stopped to say: *We can go back down now if you want, Nan. I have all I need*, it was Annabel who said pathetically: "I just want to sit down for a bit, Blackfoot. My legs are sore."

Blackfoot sniffed, but since he didn't do anything else except go back to padding around the room, Annabel gathered that he was by no means as finished with the room as he had said. Since he seemed content to wander the room, doing magic that she could neither see nor feel, Annabel wriggled a little closer to the window and pulled out her sketch-book and pencil nub.

After traversing half of the castle in a day, it was pleasant to sit without doing anything but drawing. Annabel would have felt more pleasure in it if it wasn't for the small, persistent reminder of Peter's absence that the sudden silence created. Even if Peter didn't always talk, there was always a ticking, shuffling kind of energy to his presence: his tickerboxes and his habit of always being busy with some small project or another meant that there was rarely a silent moment in his company.

Annabel bit her lip to stop it wobbling, and looked back down at her little notebook. While Blackfoot nosed his way into the corners of the room, she'd somehow drawn Peter: he was sitting at a table somewhere in the castle, his head bent over a mess of wires, cogs, and other disassembled clockwork. Annabel left the drawing unfinished, hugging her arms around her knees, and looked up at the window in the hope of a distraction.

She was to have one: the Caliphan was there again, peering out from a black background that was more than slightly springy, his dark, shrewd eyes scanning her drawing.

Annabel yelped, startling Blackfoot into a lithe leap sideways. "Blackfoot! He's watching me again!"

Blackfoot stalked back to her side. *Do you think you could refrain from sudden noises?*

"But he's watching me!"

I'm sure he's not, Nan. How could he see us if he's not even here?

"I don't know, but he won't stop looking at my drawings!"

I'm sure a phantom Caliphan has better things to do than look at your sketches, Blackfoot said dampeningly.

"Then why isn't he doing them!" wailed Annabel. "Why is he looking over my shoulder?"

Whatever he was doing, he's gone now. Do you want to leave?

Annabel, who had discovered that she was rather too full to move comfortably, said a snubby sort of "No," and hunched her shoulder over her notebook.

You look like a hunchback, Blackfoot told her, and went back to his silent stalking of the room.

Annabel had given up on finding Mordion by the time the first sun in the triad was beginning to dip beneath the horizon. By then, she and Blackfoot were rather tentatively on the way back to the kitchen, with the nebulous idea of being able to escape the unsettled castle that way, and the hallways were darker than

Annabel quite appreciated. There were pools of shadow here and there that reminded her uncomfortably of the squishy blackness around the castle, and as they turned down stairwells and walked through archways, it seemed to her that at least a few of the shadows may not have simply been shadows.

Even Blackfoot, who had been trotting well ahead of Annabel, fell back at the sight of some of the darker patches, and once he steered her away from a doorway that wasn't, he said, *quite right.*

"It's that black stuff again, isn't it?" Annabel asked, bunching her satin skirts in damp hands. "Is there more of it now? I don't remember there being this much of it."

I'm sure there's not more of it, Nan, said Blackfoot, and although he didn't sound exactly certain of himself, Annabel chose to believe him.

After that one doorway, the castle seemed to grow lighter again. Before long, they even found a mid-way landing where the triad shone through a window and left a molten gold patch on the stones, warming the air and stones alike.

Annabel, unwilling to travel out of that piece of warmth, sat down on the top step and groaned: "I need to sit down."

I really wouldn't, Nan, warned Blackfoot. *The castle is— well, I suppose you could say it seems to be in an odd mood tonight. I don't want to have to travel through any more tunnels.*

"That's another thing," said Annabel, willing to waste a little time in her endeavour to stay in the sun-light. "I want to know who gave the castle that bit that makes tunnels. If Peter gave it a way to see people who aren't *here*, exactly, and Mordion gave it the ability to change bits of itself around to make people go where it wants them to go, who gave it the tunnels?"

The tunnel in the burn room was already here when the

castle started to come back, sighed Blackfoot. *And we've not yet established that Mordion did any such thing. Nan, do you think it's possible for you to try very hard at just one thing at a time, instead of making a slapdash effort at three or four different things and giving up on each of them when they get too hard?*

"I tried very hard at lunch," said Annabel. "You should try to eat with a girdle that won't untie! Anyway, I'm just sitting down for a little bit, to catch my breath."

That's what you said when you sat down for lunch, said Blackfoot. *If I recall, we were in the castle wizard's quarters for at least two hours.*

"That's because I ate too much."

Whose fault is–

"And I had to let it settle," Annabel said, more loudly. "And then Rorkin was there watching me draw, so you argued with me about whether or not he could see me."

I was there, thank you, Nan.

"And anyway, you were just as busy sniffing around the castle wizard's room."

My point exactly, remarked Blackfoot. *I was **busy**.*

"So was I," Annabel said firmly. "I was busy eating."

I don't think you'll enjoy it if the light fails while we're still in this part of the castle.

Annabel climbed sulkily to her feet. "Oh all *right*."

Good girl, said Blackfoot. *Look, there's a door at the bottom of the stairs: if I'm right, that should be the kitchen.*

Annabel said "Pft!" loudly, but she reluctantly descended the stairs and opened the door anyway. She would have liked to tell Blackfoot he was wrong, but it *was* the kitchen, and Black-foot's trot as he passed her and darted into the kitchen again told her how pleased he was with himself.

"There's no need to be smug," she said, and pulled open the door to the outside courtyard.

There was no courtyard there. Instead, there was a very richly furnished room and a very surprised Mordion. Annabel stared at Mordion, and Mordion stared at Annabel, one of his brows rising.

Bother! said Blackfoot, in vexation. *And to think how close we were to being out safely!*

"*There* you are!" said Annabel. "I've been looking for you!"

Mordion's other eyebrow went up. "Of all the things I expected you to say, that was not one of them," he said. "If I'd known you were looking for me, darling, I would have made myself more readily available. It's very bold of you, by the way, to stand so easily in reach! Or do you think that another spell will save you?"

"Hah!" said Annabel. "As if I didn't know you can't get past the doorway!"

Mordion's face didn't change, which would have worried Annabel if she hadn't noticed how *very* much it hadn't changed. As if it had frozen in that look of mocking superiority. And if there was anything Annabel knew, it was how to hide her feelings behind a blank mask.

"Now what makes you say that, darling?" he said.

Annabel threw her lot recklessly. "You can't get past any of them, can you? You keep trying to get me to go through them instead. Well, I won't, so don't waste your time."

Mordion's face unfroze enough from its mocking superiority to fade into a rather humourless amusement. "You're surprisingly clever sometimes, little cow," he said.

Blackfoot hissed, but Annabel, who was quite used to being called worse by Peter—and calling him worse herself—

and who much preferred an insult to one of Mordion's sickeningly smooth *darling*s, smirked faintly.

"That's the thing about cows," she said. "You think they're big and stupid, so you get too close to them. You forget they can kill people if people get between them and their calves."

"Who is the calf in this scenario, I wonder?" Mordion's eyes were very bright. "Your little friend Peter? The cat, perhaps? Shall I tell you a few things about him?"

"Don't bother," said Annabel, ignoring the mutter that was Blackfoot. "I wouldn't trust you to tell the truth, anyway. You might as well spare your breath."

"Now darling–"

Annabel looked at him in dislike. "Don't call me *darling*."

"That's not very polite of you."

"It wasn't very polite of you to try to use me in a spell, either," retorted Annabel. "What have you done with Peter?"

Unexpectedly, Mordion laughed. "Peter Carlisle? I? Nothing. You might as well ask him what he did to me."

"I *can't*," said Annabel, more furious than she'd ever been in her life. Mordion had taken Peter, and now he was joking and playing games with that fact, too. "I can't because you took him away! What have you done with him? Where did you put him?"

Mordion smiled at her quite pleasantly and said: "Wouldn't you like to know? It seems to me that it's the sort of information that's very valuable. What can you give me in return?"

"Nothing," said Annabel bluntly. "I haven't *got* anything."

"I beg leave to differ, darling. You have one thing I want very much."

Nan! Blackfoot's voice was distinctly annoyed, and Annabel wondered why until it occurred to her that she'd been ignoring him since the shock of seeing Mordion so suddenly. *Nan, pay attention to me! You should walk away now. When he smiles like that, only bad things follow.*

"I know," Annabel said. "But I can't do anything about that."

Mordio threw a quizzical look at her. "On the contrary, darling: you can do a great deal about it."

"What?" Annabel blinked at him, then frowned. "What are you talking about? Look, can you be quiet for a minute? Blackfoot is saying something."

There was a quiet kind of *hui hui hui* floating around in her mind. It took Annabel a moment or two to realise that Blackfoot was snickering.

"What?"

His face! giggle Blackfoot. *I never thought I'd see an expression like that on his face! Nan, we really have to work on your communication skills: in particular, your habit of blanking me out as entirely as you've just blanked out Mordion, whenever you walk into a situation that startles you.*

"Yes, but not now," Annabel objected. "We're too busy for that."

"We are," agreed Mordion, leaning against his doorframe in an invasive kind of way that made Annabel want to back away. She didn't, because she didn't want him to know how much afraid of him she really was. Instead, she glared up at him as he smiled rather blindingly at her and said: "Darling, do please keep your cat out of our conversation: I can't imagine he has anything important to add to our discussion and I'd really rather discuss it with you."

"Blackfoot quite often doesn't have anything important to add to the conversation," Annabel said, as bluntly as before.

"He just likes to make remarks. What have you done with Peter?"

"Ah," sighed Mordion. "So we're back here again! There's something you'll have to give me if you want to see your young friend again."

"What? What is it you want?"

Mordion's dark blue eyes laughed at her through his lashes. "You, of course! What else would I still be wanting from this castle?"

"You want me to swap myself for Peter? How will that make me able to see him again?"

"That was a slight shading of the truth," admitted Mordion. "You will see him again, just not for a great deal of time. You'll have to resign yourself to knowing you made a great sacrifice, and that he's safe."

Peter won't be safe, warned Blackfoot. *No matter what he says, Mordion will not leave any of us in the castle alive after he has you.*

"I see," said Annabel slowly, as much to Blackfoot as to Mordion.

Mordion smiled lazily at her, a provocative, teasing thing. "Who knows, darling? We could get along very well together."

"That won't work," Annabel said. "I've seen you when you were all smudgy and catty and human at once. It wasn't very pretty. Also, why are you flirting with me? I'm fourteen. That's disgusting."

Mordion shrugged without signs of any emotion other than faint amusement. "It's usually quite successful, as a matter of fact. Very well, then truth: you and I will not get along well. I will almost certainly use you up in my spells, sooner or later. You won't die well, and your death is unlikely to do more than bring me much closer to my end goal."

"All right," said Annabel. "You'll have to let me think about it."

"A surprisingly prosaic attitude. Don't you care about the well-being of your friend?"

Annabel shivered a little. "Yes," she said. "But I also care about what happens to them after I'm dead. So you'll have to wait a bit longer before I give you an answer."

"Don't wait too long, darling," said Mordion, smiling a sparkling smile at her. "Don't forget that if you wander into any parts of the castle that are mine, I won't need to bargain with you. Just step through one wrong door way: you'll be mine, and Peter will be mine."

"I'll remember," Annabel said, and there was a certain grimness to the sick feeling in her stomach. "You won't see me again until tomorrow."

NINE

Annabel slept badly. Her dreams revolved and twisted until they were nightmares, where a vast blackness chased the Caliphan up and down shifting castle halls until it subsumed him, then turned and chased Annabel and Peter. She woke far too early, sweating and shivering, with her pencil and sketchbook clutched tightly in damp hands, and spent the early morning sketching the Caliphan out of the blackness by way of comforting herself. That made the shivering go away, but the cold feeling still ran up and down her back in a crawling kind of a way, so Annabel occupied herself with drawing elegant castle walls around it in her sketchbook, making a core of blackness to her castle sketches.

By the time Blackfoot also woke, stretching and yawning, Annabel was feeling better.

Well, Nan? he said. *I trust you've spent the night thinking better of your rash actions yesterday.*

Annabel, who hadn't, in fact, thought about Mordion at all, came to the startling realisation that her decision was already, irrevocably, made. Perhaps it had been made some time during her consolatory drawing time: perhaps she had already decided before that. "We'd better get some breakfast," she said. "Then we'll find Mordion. Perhaps you should stay here, Blackfoot."

No need, Blackfoot said, and Annabel couldn't decide if his voice were resigned, exasperated, or frustrated. *Once Mordion gets his hands on you, there's nowhere in the castle that will be safe for me. If it comes to that, there's nowhere in the Two Monarchies that will be safe for me– or anyone else. You won't save either Peter or me by giving up yourself to Mordion.*

"I know," said Annabel. "But it'll give you a good running start from here. If you stick with Peter, you'll be all right. What will Mordion do with me?"

*Oh, so **now** you're asking that?* This time, it was certainly exasperation in Blackfoot's voice. *I thought you were prepared to go to your fate in wilful ignorance.*

"Yes, but I don't understand," complained Annabel. "Grenna was always using me in spells, too, and they both used me in the one that brought Mordion back. Is Mordion going to use me in his spells? Why? Can't they use just anyone?"

The thought left a horrible chill just under her skin. It had been bad enough being used by Grenna in spells that killed animals: Annabel didn't think she could bear to be used in spells that stripped people of their magic and killed them. It was bad enough that Grenna had died that way, and Grenna, it could be said, had deserved to die in that way.

Mordion will certainly use you in his spells, said Blackfoot, and his voice was particularly flat. *You're a useful commodity, after all.*

"It's because I don't have magic, isn't it?" Annabel said.

"Peter says I have a little bit, but I don't think so. Grenna always had trouble keeping track of me at first: I think she put something on me in one of the spells."

You have a particularly dense lack of magic, Blackfoot agreed. *That young whelp might think he does what he does by clockwork and talent, but he's been working with the best enhancement field in the Two Monarchies, and that combined with his natural overflowing of magic– well, it's exasperating, really.*

"Yes, but absence of magic creates a vacuum. What about that?"

It constantly astounds me that **that** *is the sum of your magical knowledge, Blackfoot said, in exasperation. If you'd known a little more– no, if you'd known that well enough, instead of repeating it parrot-fashion every time someone mentions it–! Well, Nan, we might not be in this situation!*

Annabel felt her chin trying to crinkle, and pushed the feeling away. There was no time for tears today. Instead, she said in a voice that was as cool as Blackfoot's was hot: "Why are you trying to pick a quarrel with me? What did I do?"

You– oh, never mind, Nan. I'm sorry. We won't quarrel today. Just don't expect me to go along with your plan without doing a little planning of my own.

"All right," agreed Annabel, because what could a cat do, after all? She'd never seen Blackfoot do anything but the smallest of magics that Peter had been able to dismiss with a snap of his fingers. "But tell me about Mordion first."

Very well. Then I'll tell you a very curtailed version of a tale involving a princess, a spindle, and far too many cats.

· · ·

The castle was even more inclined to playing tricks that morning. Stairways led to dead ends, suite doorways opened into wardrobes, and although there seemed to be a truly astounding amount of tunnels dimpling the walls around them, the only place those seemed to lead was back on themselves.

Blackfoot, who had stalked away into the first without waiting to see if Annabel was following, at first expressed his disapproval by stalking straight into the next tunnel entrance without stopping. Later, when they walked for fifteen minutes and emerged only two steps away from where they'd originally started, this disapproval became more clearly marked by a series of increasingly sour remarks at the back of Annabel's mind.

"Why are there tunnels if they're only going to take us in circles?" demanded Annabel pettishly. "The last one was there to save us from Mordion, but since we didn't really need saving from him, that was pointless, too! Why are there so many! Wait! Why are you going into another one?"

The first one wasn't **completely** *useless*, Blackfoot said, disappearing into the next tunnel. *If Mordion had been able to get through the doorway, it would have been very useful.*

Annabel, annoyed to find herself in yet another winding tunnel, and unwilling to concede even that much, said: "Yes, but he *wasn't*."

Well, Nan, if your theory that it's the castle doing all this is correct, perhaps you should be paying attention. The castle obviously doesn't want you meeting with Mordion, or tunnels wouldn't be turning in on themselves.

"Rubbish. It's probably just in a bad mood this morning because we woke it up early by stomping about on its stairs. Blackfoot, I think this tunnel has lost its way."

Blackfoot, after a brief silence, said: *Perhaps it's confused.*

We seem to be surrounded by rather a lot of stonework that wasn't here yesterday. It's been growing ever since we stepped into this tunnel, and now the tunnel doesn't know how to get out again.

"But the tunnels *appear* in the walls! How can they not get back through?"

That's what I'm trying to figure out, muttered Blackfoot. *It may simply be the perennial case of an unstoppable force meeting an immovable object, but there does seem to be rather a larger amount of concentrated darkness in this area than there was yesterday. Perhaps the castle is confining the blackness to its centre.*

"This tunnel goes through the squishy stuff? Why didn't you tell me!"

I assumed that you would rather not know. Ridiculous, I know, but it occurred to me that you would panic.

"I'm not panicking!"

Of course not. You're calmness itself. Nan, **must** *you step on my tail?*

"I didn't do it on purpose!"

I'd rather be carried if you're going to make a habit of stepping on me, added Blackfoot, and although Annabel was perfectly well aware that he was only saying it because he knew she would be comforted by holding him, she still picked him up. *Let's see now,* said Blackfoot, when he was making a warm, furry weight against her stomach, *straight ahead now, I think.*

"It's all black there, too," Annabel said, but she took a few tentative steps forward anyway. The darkness didn't grow any less, but the tunnel did seem to twist and turn less than it had previously, so she kept walking with Blackfoot held tight in her arms.

It was a relief to find herself stepping out of the tunnel just a few minutes later. It was so much of a relief, in fact, that Annabel was able to ignore both the circumstance that it was strangely difficult to take that one step from darkness into light, and the circumstance that they were again back exactly where they had started. Opposite them was the very tunnel mouth by which they had entered.

"This is ridiculous," said Annabel. "Don't go down any more tunnels!"

Blackfoot tut-tutted soothingly at her. *You can put me down now. You'll feel better after you've eaten: I trust you brought sausages?*

Annabel, with a wary look at both tunnel ends, scuttled further away and sat down with her back to one of the walls. From there, she could just see the insides of the walls before they vanished into darkness.

"There *are*," she said, unwrapping a handkerchief full of bread, cheese, and sausages. "There are more walls in there than there were yesterday. Yesterday the castle was moving about, but all the rooms were normal-shaped rooms. Now they're just a little bit smaller toward the centre of the castle."

It looked familiar, in fact. Annabel gazed at it for some time, wondering what it was about those walls that was so recognisable, but they were only walls, after all: plain block work with nothing unusual about them except their placement.

Sausages, Nan, reminded Blackfoot, and Annabel put one down for him.

"You said yesterday that Mordion is hundreds of years old," she said, through a mouthful of bread. "How did they manage to turn him into a cat, then?"

It's not really something you can foresee, Blackfoot said

reflectively, *being turned into a cat. I don't think he was expecting it.*

"Well, how did you come across him, then?"

That? Well, that was something of a rash decision on my part. Even as a cat he looked like trouble, and I was already pretty familiar with the kind of things that he got up to. It was more of a glancing carom, actually: I bounced off him and found you, and by then it was obvious that he was looking for you. I thought it would be a good idea if he didn't find you.

"Because of my–" Annabel stopped, and then started again defiantly; "because of my lack of magic? You were afraid he'd use me to amplify the little bit of magic that he *did* have, and change back to being a person again."

He never really stopped being a **person**, Blackfoot said, even more reflectively. *Well, as much of a person as he ever was. Being an animal over the course of several years doesn't change the person bit of you. It was more that he wanted to change his form back.*

"It's a pity we couldn't stop that," said Annabel sadly. "Things would have been so much easier."

Blackfoot finished a sausage and licked his paw. *Yes. I was rather expecting to be able to stop that, as a matter of fact. I'm still not sure how things went so badly.*

"Don't worry," Annabel said, patting his head. "You couldn't have stopped it. I don't blame you."

Thank you so much, said Blackfoot. He sounded amused and perhaps a bit rueful.

"You're afraid he's going to use me to keep stealing magic from people, aren't you? Like he used the Sleeping Princess to keep himself in magic for hundreds of years."

I'm certain of it. And with his natural powers amplified by you, there's no reason he shouldn't try for the throne again.

Annabel shivered. "I'm sorry, Blackfoot."

Then don't do it.

"It's Peter."

I know. I will point out once again that Peter is quite capable of taking care of himself, and that you will not necessarily save Peter by giving yourself up.

"Yes, but it's *Peter*."

Very well, said Blackfoot. *Then where shall we start, Nan? The tunnels that turn back on themselves, or the doors that open into closets? You could get yourself a new dress.*

"Doors," Annabel said, rather more flintily that was her norm. "We'll just keep opening them. This one–" she scrambled to her feet and tugged at the closest door, disclosing a small cleaning cupboard that was smaller than the door itself, "and *this* one–"

Every door in reach, in fact, sighed Blackfoot. *Hoping to achieve something by sheer obstinacy. It's a plan, I suppose. You missed one, Nan.*

Annabel made a rude noise at him, but opened the door anyway. This one opened into an actual room, even if it was only someone's washing chamber, but there were no other doors leading from it, so Annabel closed it again. She made her way doggedly down the hall, opening and closing doors while Blackfoot followed along behind with a running commentary of: *A boot-black cupboard! and what's this? A laundry-room? Delightful! Perhaps when we're finished putting a shine on our rather useless plan, we can freshly launder it. It won't change the fact that it's threadbare, but at least it might smell a bit better. Dear me! Now a library! What giddy heights of excitement!*

"Oh, shut up," said Annabel mildly. The library seemed promising: there was even, she was sure, another door at the far end of it. "And stop dragging your feet. Oh! There *is* another door in here!"

Her fingers found the doorhandle and turned it, and Blackfoot said sharply: ***Not** that one, Nan!*

Annabel wrenched her foot back as a draft swept across the back of her neck, raising gooseflesh, and caught herself against the door-frame. Two hands mirrored hers on the other side of the doorway, and then Mordion was there, his blue eyes glowing.

"Careful," he said, and there was a delighted smile on his lips. "No, don't step back, darling, or you'll fall over your cat. He does seem to get in the way quite a lot, doesn't he?"

Annabel, catching her breath, threw a quick look behind her and saw that another tunnel had opened, this one in the floor. It was vast, yawning, and far too close for comfort. "Don't stand behind me like that, Blackfoot," she said. "I could have fallen in."

Nan, Blackfoot said, *Nan, I really protest–*

"I know. But I can't help it."

Mordion said: "Do you know, I always find it rather difficult to know when you're speaking to me and when you're speaking to the cat. It could be construed as rude."

"What a shame," said Annabel.

One of Mordion's brows went up, but he only said: "You're a little earlier than I expected. No trouble with doorways like your little friend?"

"Not with doorways," Annabel said, and felt a curious prickling sensation all the way up her neck to her ears. The heavy weight that had been resting on her since she woke that morning vanished away entirely, and left in its place a sensation of dizzying lightness. "Tunnels, mostly."

"I thought you might have." Mordion's smile had grown.

"Now who can have been putting out tunnels in the castle, I wonder? Now, who can that have reminded me of, I wonder?"

"Do you know what's interesting?" Annabel said slowly. "I don't know if I noticed it days ago without really seeing it, or if I only realised it now. Your feet don't touch the ground. Did you know?"

Mordion's face very carefully didn't change. When it had done with not changing, he looked at her with a slightly pitying amusement. "You have a fertile imagination, little cow," he said. "Or have you been drawing in low light for so long that you strained your eyes?"

Nan? What–

"Be quiet," Annabel said.

How rude, said Blackfoot, but he sounded more cheerful than otherwise, so Annabel didn't bother to tell him that she'd been addressing Mordion, who was looking very surprised. The sensation of lightness within her had grown until it was almost intoxicating.

"You should very carefully consider the next thing that comes out of your mouth," Mordion said, and his mouth was slightly thinner. That pleased Annabel. Mordion was always so smiling and debonair that she enjoyed seeing him jolted out of his easy superiority. "If you want your friend back–"

"I do," Annabel said. "But you don't have him, do you?"

One of Mordion's eyebrows rose. "Now this is curious. You came to me, if I recall correctly. You were certain that I had your friend: I told you I didn't."

"You said that at first," said Annabel. She wanted to giggle, but just as there wasn't time for crying today, nor was there time for laughter. "I thought you were being difficult, but you really don't have him."

"Of course I have him," Mordion said. "Who else would have him?"

Annabel settled herself into the blank, stubborn façade that irritated Peter so much when she did it to him. "Don't know. But I know it's not you. You your feet don't touch the ground and you can't even get through doorways. You're not exactly *here*, are you?"

"I'm enough here to influence the growth of the castle," retorted Mordion. "Enough to move about and meet with you– enough to tempt your young friend through a doorway and into my kind of *here*. And every day my *here* becomes bigger, while your *here* grows a little smaller."

"Yes. That's the thing I remembered," Annabel said, in quiet triumph. "Peter disappeared with an entire section of hallway. How could you trick Peter through a doorway when there wasn't a doorway in that hall?"

"Ah." Mordion sighed. "It was a sound guess, after all. I don't suppose I can persuade you that it will easier upon all parties if you simply step through the doorway right now?"

"No," said Annabel. "That'll only be easier for you."

"You remind me of someone I knew once," said Mordion, in a reflective kind of way. "She caused me a lot of trouble: I certainly hope you don't do the same."

Annabel heard Blackfoot chuckle. *There is a resemblance, now that I think about it. That's right, Nan, keep looking at him like that. Let him know that you can't be charmed.*

"Ew!" Annabel said indignantly. "Blackfoot!"

I'm so sorry to have turned your stomach, said Blackfoot, and there was a burgeoning amusement hiding just behind the words. *If it helps, I don't think he can help it: his default method of interaction with any female is charm.*

Annabel threw another disgusted look at Mordion that

made his brows rise again. "Then he should do a better job of it."

Mordion, looking very surprised, only managed to say: "What–" before Annabel shut the door in his face.

Blackfoot, who was doing the odd little *hui hui hui!* at the back of Annabel's mind again, said: *Oh, that was **immensely** satisfying! What now, Nan?*

"Now," said Annabel, leaning against the wall because her legs didn't seem to want to hold her up, "now we go back to trying Peter by ourselves. But first I want to eat something. And I need to think."

Back to the kitchen?

Annabel nodded. "Yes." She wasn't hungry, exactly, but she felt the need to eat something slowly and methodically while her mind plodded along just as slowly and methodically. "I think I almost understand something, but I don't know what it is. I need to eat grape-nuts."

Thinking was somewhat addictive, she had discovered. From her earliest memories with Grenna, Annabel had been too busy trying to find enough food to live on and trying to avoid the more unpleasant magic to have time for more than survival. Later, she had found her first papers and the pencil stub, and that had kept her busy enough not to think about the unpleasantness of her surroundings. The not-thinking had become something of a habit, a defence against life with Grenna, and it hadn't occurred to Annabel that there was any need to change this state of affairs until she was running for her life with Peter and Blackfoot.

Now that she had begun to think, however, it was difficult to turn those thoughts off. At first, sketching a quick likeness of Blackfoot at the kitchen table as she systematically ate grape-nut after grape-nut, Annabel followed her thoughts in a confused pattern of wondering where Peter could possibly be if Mordion didn't have him. She was half-way through that sketch when it occurred to her that she had stopped thinking about Peter, and that her pencil had begun to circle very slowly on the page.

Annabel looked down, frowning, and found that she had drawn in the wall rose that was part of the stonework mantelpiece behind Blackfoot. It was curiously familiar, and stuck in her mind tenaciously enough to make her page through her other drawings until she found the reason why: she had already drawn it.

"Oh, that's odd," Annabel said, tapping her pencil nub against her knee. "This is the one I drew on our first night in the castle."

What of it? asked Blackfoot, padding across the table to nose at the grape-nuts. *It's a good one: very detailed.*

"That's the thing," she said. "This rose wasn't in the kitchen when we got here. The kitchen was old and dusty and broken down when we arrived: the mantelpiece was mostly sheared away. I drew this picture the way I *wanted* it to look, not the way it was."

I see, said Blackfoot. *Then, Nan? What of it?*

"I don't know. It's– oh! I know!" Annabel paged feverishly through her sketchbook, and there was the first drawing she had done of the throne-room. It had been dusty, covered with raspberries and full of so much rubble that they hadn't been able to get through the doorway at the end of the throne-room. Then Annabel had drawn it as she wished it was: clear of rubbish and cobwebs, free from spiders and debris. "And that's what it was like the next day," she said slowly.

Blackfoot, peering at the drawing from the other side, said, *Well now. That's something.*

"Ye-es," Annabel agreed doubtfully. There was a slightly panicked feeling of dread spreading through her. The next few drawings after the one of the cleared throne room were the Caliphan and the other stranger that she had never quite been able to draw properly, and she could see the improvement in each drawing. The Caliphan became steadily more like the real one she saw in the reflections—who, by some law of equal reactions, daily seemed closer and clearer in the reflections—and even her attempts of the unknown strangers were more cohesive.

That, as far as Annabel was concerned, was fully as terrifying as having Mordion running about the castle freely. Because what if– what if, by drawing them– what if, by drawing *him*, Annabel was bringing him back into the castle? She thought about the Caliphan with his sharp eyes and lanky limbs: he looked friendly enough, but Mordion was quite beautiful, and in light of her meetings with Mordion, she was as little inclined to trust a face that seemed friendly as she was to trust a beautiful one.

She tore out all the sketches of the Caliphan and the other stranger with shaking hands, and stuffed them at the back of the sketchbook. It wouldn't do to be mindlessly working on details of those particular drawings.

It was impossible, of course. She couldn't do magic. It was one very certain constant of life, such as constancies went; just as sure as Peter's insufferable self-certainty and the feel of Blackfoot's voice in her mind. But as she thought about it, Annabel seemed to remember drawing in the diamond-shape of the castle wizard's quarters before ever it appeared; even those walls around the black squishy centre of the castle– she had drawn those, for sure.

Annabel found that she'd dropped her pencil nub and was

eating grape-nut after grape-nut, the sweet, dry, grapey taste and flesh of the nuts filling her mouth until it was almost too full to chew. Carefully, she pushed the nearly-empty bowl away, and wiped her hands on her red satin skirt, staining it with fat.

Then, picking up her pencil nub again with hands that still seemed to shake, Annabel drew.

<h1 style="text-align:center">TEN</h1>

Annabel woke with one thought in her mind. She'd gone to sleep with it there, too. More importantly, she'd gone to sleep with a drawing clutched in her hand, and that drawing depicted the castle wizard's quarters with rather more in them than they had had yesterday. It was a quick sketch that didn't go quite all the way to the edges of the paper, but Annabel had been very careful about what she added to the sketch itself. There were three very specific items she had included, in fact: a bowl of grape-nuts, a satchel that was small enough to be comfortably worn yet big enough to hold her pencil and notebook, and a pair of fluffy, knitted socks.

I see you've been busy. Blackfoot sat up and yawned, then stretched. He threw a cursory glance at her sketch and said: *We'll be off to the wizard quarters, I take it?*

Annabel nodded. "Is the black squishy stuff still pushed toward the centre of the castle, do you think?"

I would imagine so, said Blackfoot. *I won't be sure until we're a bit closer. We'll need to be more careful about going through doorways, Nan.*

Annabel sighed gustily. "You'll have to tell me which ones are safe."

Yes, it's a dreadful burden to bear, but one must do what one must do.

"Pft," said Annabel. "That wasn't what I meant, actually. I meant that it's a shame I can't tell these things for myself."

So long as you have me, you don't need to do it for yourself.

"I thought that was the kind of thinking you wanted me to get out of?"

You're a snide little thing this morning, aren't you?

"Pft," Annabel said again. "You're just being aloof because you like to be the one being snide."

I do such a wonderful job of it, you see. Shall we go, Nan?

"All right," said Annabel. "But if we run into trouble this time, it's your fault. And we're stopping at the kitchen for breakfast."

Annabel wasn't sure if that was because the castle was shifting about even more that morning, or if it was the stiff way Blackfoot was stalking around her, but everything felt slightly out of order, like a shoe that was just a little bit too small. Even if she couldn't sense or see the magic involved, she could feel the difference. Or perhaps it was simply because she was afraid that she had, in a small but irrevocable way, become a part of it when she had always been merely an onlooker.

Adding to the sense of oddness was the fact that the castle wizard's quarters seemed a little more complete from the outside when they finally found their way there. The door was just a bit more solid: the walls just a bit more well-defined. Or, thought Annabel dubiously, she could simply be imagining things.

Well, Nan? Are you going to go in, or will you continue to stare at the door?

Annabel took in a deep breath, let it out, and opened the door. She saw the new furniture before the door was quite open, and that made her heart jump, but she muttered: "Could've just come back overnight. It's not proof."

With the door fully open it was obvious that there was a great deal of change: the room was still far from complete, but there was an easy chair, a desk and attendant chair, and one cupboard that was overflowing onto the floorboards. Annabel was very familiar with each piece of furniture. She had drawn them in last night, exactly as she now saw them.

"It's still not proof," she said to Blackfoot. "The castle was bound to fill in this room some time or other."

Mmm, Blackfoot said, and began to prowl around the room. *There's something odd here. Perhaps we shouldn't have come. I wonder, Nan, exactly what it was you did last night with your drawing.*

Annabel, who had just spied a small bowl of grape-nuts on the desk, amidst the clutter, shivered. "It's *all* odd. But it's not all exactly the same, either. There's more stuff than I drew. Oh!"

The satchel she'd drawn last night was hanging by its strap over the chair back: she hadn't seen it at first because of the throw rug that was also draped there.

"Socks," said Annabel faintly, as Blackfoot stopped stalking around the room and began to wash himself. She had drawn them on the easy chair that was by the window, and at first she'd thought they were missing altogether, but once she moved past the desk and chair, there they were on the floor, as if they'd rolled off the plump seat cushion. She crossed the room and picked them up, a fluffy ball of wool that felt oddly heavy in her hand, and turned to look perplexedly at Blackfoot.

He was still washing himself languidly, but there was such a feeling of tightly wound expectancy to him that she expected him to leap sideways when she said: "Blackfoot."

Instead, as if he'd been waiting for her to speak, he said: *Well, Nan?*

"I don't have any magic."

So we've established.

"I can't *do* magic."

Even so.

"But somehow I *am* doing it."

Quite the puzzle, isn't it?

"Are you teasing me?"

With Mordion skulking around the castle and your young friend mysteriously vanished? Of course I'm teasing you. You should know me better by now, Nan.

Annabel was betrayed into a giggle. "It's obviously not me doing it," she said. "But it's being done. So is it the pencil or the notebook that's doing it?"

I really wonder why you're asking me.

"I'm not asking you, I'm thinking aloud. I'm an independent person who can think for herself."

Dear me, you really are taking all that to heart, aren't you? There is a vast difference between being able to think for oneself and ignoring all advice and help offered.

"You aren't offering help. You're being deliberately difficult."

That's true. There's also a difference between being able to think for oneself and asking for help when necessary. Even the most difficult people sometimes have something important to add.

"*Do* you have something important to add?"

No. I was just reminding you, since you seem to be inclined to take my words to heart lately. I thought I'd take advantage of that.

"I was thinking," Annabel told him repressively. "Now I have to start from the start again. I'm trying to figure out if it's the notebook or the pencil that's magical. Can't you tell?"

Blackfoot licked one of his paws and passed it over his face. *Don't you think Peter would have told you already if either of them were magical? More importantly, do you really think he would have given you that notebook if he thought it had even the slightest suspicion of magic about it?*

"That's a good point," said Annabel, sitting down cross-legged beside Blackfoot. After some thought, she added: "Well, if he was trying to look after me he might have given me something with a spell in it. He remembers to try and look after me sometimes."

That must be a great comfort to you. There's no need to be so hopeful about it: the notebook has absolutely no magic in it. It's a notebook, nothing more.

"It must be the pencil, then," Annabel said. "Are you *sure* you can't see anything different about it?"

If the boy didn't see anything different about it, why would I?

"That's not an answer—" began Annabel crossly, but a flicker in the window across the room caught her eye. The Caliphan was in the window again, pretending not to look at them. Even more crossly, she called across the room: "It's no use looking at me! I'm not going to draw you any more, so might as well stop looking through the windows!"

I'm sure he's abashed, said Blackfoot. *Or I'm sure he would be if he could hear you. What are you planning on doing now, Nan?*

"I–" began Annabel, and stopped. Lately, Blackfoot had been asking her what to do instead of telling her what to do, and that feeling was just as uncomfortable and unfamiliar as the feeling of being a part of the magic instead of an onlooker. "Well, I suppose I'd better try and find out which one of my things is making the castle come back when I draw. Then I'll probably want some lunch."

Worthy goals. I do wonder how you're planning on doing it, however.

"I suppose I'll draw something on a piece of paper with my pencil. Then I'll find another pencil and draw something into my sketchbook. Whichever one comes through overnight is the one that's doing it."

What if they both come through overnight?

"Then I'll just worry about lunch, clever clogs."

Annabel climbed to her feet, ignoring the Caliphan, who was still moving about in the window, and sorted through the things on the desk. There were quite a few loose papers there, all of them scribbled on at least one side, so she took the least-scribbled one and found another pencil that was still sharp enough to use.

"This will do," she said. She took the small satchel from the chair-back as well, and slipped it over her shoulders. She had been right when she drew it: it was just the right size to hold her sketchbook, pencil, and a sandwich or two. "What should I draw, then?"

I find myself wondering if it's wise to take things from the castle wizard's quarters, said Blackfoot, watching her with his tail flicking.

"Why? He's not coming back."

Ah. Well. But who knows, after all?

Annabel thought that he glanced slightly toward the window that still showed a shallow reflection of the Caliphan. "What? Him? You think he might be the castle wizard? Is that why he's still hanging around the castle like a ghost?"

Yet again I find myself wondering why it is that you imagine I'm likely to know?

"Then you shouldn't always act like you know everything," Annabel said pettishly. "I drew this satchel in *particularly*. I thought it would be useful."

I see, Blackfoot said mildly. *Although, no, I don't! In that case, whose is the satchel? Was it originally part of the castle? Or is it simply something you've created?*

Annabel shrugged. "Don't know. Actually, I don't care because I'm tired of having to hold things. Why didn't they put pockets in this dress?"

They possibly couldn't fit any on there between the frills and tucks, Blackfoot suggested. *I'm sure there are other frocks with pockets. Frocks that aren't quite as...red...as that one.*

"I don't want other frocks. I want this one."

Blackfoot sighed. *Of course you do. One day, Nan, you and I will have a discussion about the concept of elegant simplicity.*

"Yes," agreed Annabel, with a distinct lack of enthusiasm, "but right now I want to know what I should draw. It'll take all night to come in, but at least it'll be something to go by. I know! I'll draw you in a little cat friend!"

That was at the same time incredibly condescending and utterly terrifying, said Blackfoot. *In other words: please don't! I can only imagine that it will work, given this morning's events, and I wouldn't like to know what happens when a living thing is drawn into the castle by you or anyone else.*

Annabel, who was already sketching out skerry-fleece arm warmers for the easy chair in her sketchbook, stopped to think about that. "Well, it would depend, wouldn't it?"

On what would it depend? Blackfoot's voice was curious, which was somewhat gratifying. Annabel had expected him to be his usual sarcastic and dismissive self: she hadn't expected him to sound quite so...interested. Or so alert, for that matter.

She gestured vaguely with the borrowed pencil. "Won't it depend on whether or not I'm drawing back real things? I mean, if I'm just drawing them into existence from *nothing*, then maybe I wouldn't like to draw an animal. What if its mind didn't come with the drawing, or if it came through with a tiger mind instead? But if I'm drawing things back here that were already part of the castle or *in* the castle, it doesn't matter much, does it? So long as I draw them back properly, that is."

That, said Blackfoot slowly, *is something I would very much like to know the answer to.*

"Oh," Annabel said, taken aback. "I thought you'd know. All right, all right!" she added hastily, as she saw the gleam in his eyes, "I know: why should you know?"

On the contrary, Nan, said Blackfoot, with a wealth of rueful laughter to his voice, *it is undoubtedly something that I should know, and I very much regret that I don't know it.*

Annabel closed her sketchbook and put down the borrowed pencil. As pencils went, it was perfectly normal, but she was so used to the feeling of her own little nubby pencil that she found working with it to be oddly unsatisfying. "Anyway, I'm sure we can find out."

Are you? It must be pleasant to be so certain.

"It is," Annabel said serenely, well aware that he was teasing her. She made a swift outline on the pilfered paper: a small, ornate cup that should sit on the narrow mantelpiece, always teetering within an inch of falling. "Tomorrow, when we're sure how it works, we can try other things."

Very well, Blackfoot agreed, his ears pricking up in interest as she finished the last strokes of the drawing. *Then what now? If we have to wait until tomorrow for one or both of these things to show up–*

"Both?" said Annabel in dismay. "What do you mean, *both*? They won't both show up, will they?"

I suppose it depends upon whether or not your theory is correct, said Blackfoot. *Don't look so horrified, Nan! I'm only teasing. I'm certain that only one of them will turn up: after all, we've already established that you've no magic of your own, now haven't we?*

"Yes," Annabel agreed, glaring at him. She packed the two pencils and her sketchbook into her satchel with the scrap of paper, still glaring at him, but Blackfoot only twitched his gaze away and looked back toward the door into the hallway.

Well, then, how will we spend the rest of the day?

"Trying to find Peter again, I suppose."

A very worthy cause, I'm sure, Nan, but that boy knows how to look after himself. I'm also quite certain that if anyone can get themselves out of a sticky situation, Peter can. His ability to land on his feet is only slightly less certain than Mordion's. Or a cat's.

"I don't care," said Annabel obstinately. She was as well aware as Blackfoot that Peter had a way of turning up safe and sound when he was least expected to do so. She was also quite well aware that Peter had an overweening sense of his own cleverness, and she had had to rescue him more than once from the consequences of the same.

The castle is more dangerous now, Nan. We'll have to be careful where we go.

"So long as Mordion hasn't taken over the kitchen, it's all

right," Annabel said. "Well, I want lunch, so he'd better *not* have."

Despite the lightness of her retort, she was feeling more than slightly uneasy: the Caliphan was showing up far more often than he had to begin with—though how much of that was her own fault for having drawn him, she couldn't say—and she'd seen him often enough in her nightmares and in the window glass to make her uneasy about his presence. He may not be the direct, sharp fear that Mordion was, but there was a subtle, creeping *suggestion* of fear to his presence. As if, thought Annabel, as if it wasn't so much the Caliphan himself that was dangerous, as the fact that he was *here.*

She said as much to Blackfoot as she stood and brushed the dust off her skirts, and added reflectively: "I still want to know why that Caliphan is here. Actually, I want to know *who* he is, if he's not the castle wizard. I want to know both."

Worthy goals, agreed Blackfoot. *Very well, Nan: if we're going to look for Peter, where shall we start?*

"Well, that's the problem," Annabel said, her voice troubled. As they discussed her unexpected ability for drawing things into the castle, she had come to the conclusion that Blackfoot was right: it really was important to know what sort of things she could draw back into the castle. Because if Peter was still somewhere into the castle, technically, she *could* draw him back. At least, she was quite sure she could. "I think...well, I'm sure I could draw him back into one of the rooms, no matter how he disappeared. I've drawn him so often, and I know him so well. But what if I drew him back without his mind, or without the *Peter* bit of him?"

There was a pause long enough to suggest that Blackfoot had considered, and rejected, several sarcastic and uncomplimentary things to say about Peter's *Peter*-ness, before he said, *It*

*might be a good idea to experiment by drawing back an animal,
after all.*

"Yes," Annabel said. "I mean, *he's* come back all right–" she
pointed at the shadowy reflection of the Caliphan, "At least, I
think so– he hasn't come back all the way, but I haven't been
able to get his eyes right, yet. And it's Peter. I don't want to
make any mistakes."

Then we'll think on it, said Blackfoot, and his voice was
gentle. *After lunch.*

Annabel nodded, feeling a little bit better. "After lunch."

After you, Nan, Blackfoot said politely, making her giggle,
because he couldn't open the door for himself, after all.

She opened the door for him and said, "Oh," in a very
small voice. "Blackfoot, I don't think it should be like that."

Up to the doorframe, everything was as it had been when
they first entered the room. Beyond the doorframe...

"It's like a moat," Annabel said in fascination. Beyond the
threshold there was a ragged gap that wasn't quite space but
wasn't quite solid, either. It fluctuated from block to empty
space, then to floorboards, too quickly to keep track of, and
never quite solidly enough *anything* to risk stepping on. "The
floor is quicksand!"

Nan, do you really think that now is the time to be giggling?

Annabel giggled again, but said: "Sorry. It's just that it
reminds me of a game Peter and I used to play when we were
younger."

Blackfoot made a *pft* kind of noise in her mind. *I saw you
playing that game two weeks ago. Younger indeed!*

Annabel wasn't sure what made her look around. It could
have been the feeling of someone staring, but if so, there was no
one staring at *her*: the Caliphan was right at the forefront of
the window, his hands pressed against the window-frame and

gazing at the floor outside in horror. She nudged Blackfoot gently with her toe and said, "Look. He *can* see us."

It would appear so, agreed Blackfoot. *All very interesting, of course, but the Caliphan being able to see us is neither here nor there: the important thing is how we're going to get out of this little mess.*

"Oh, that."

Yes, Nan, that.

"Do you know," said Annabel, who was still looking at the Caliphan, "I think he's pointing at something."

Nan–

"You should stop saying *Nan* at me all the time. I've been right a lot of times lately."

There was a brief silence. *That's a fair point,* said Blackfoot. *But then, whose fault is that, Nan? I'm not used to you being so proactive and thoughtful. And there **is** a rather more current problem literally at our feet.*

Annabel rolled her eyes. "You always have to– wait, he's pointing at that cup."

Ah, Blackfoot purred, his gaze darting around. *Oh, now **that** is very useful to know.*

"How can it be here already?" demanded Annabel, staring at the decorative cup she had drawn barely half an hour ago. "It always took longer than this before! The rooms– everything came back overnight. Didn't it?"

Perhaps. Or perhaps we simply weren't around to see it happening. Perhaps we didn't notice it. Or–

"Or–?" prompted Annabel.

Or, now that you know about it, the effect is swifter. Magic does like an audience, after all. I must say, Nan, that you seem to be remarkably unconcerned for a girl surrounded by a floor shifting through time phases.

"Oh, is that what it is?" Annabel said, looking vaguely down at the shifting reality beyond the threshold. "I wondered about that. It's not as bad as the squishy stuff, though."

I'm not sure whether to deplore or commend your ignorance, remarked Blackfoot. *Naturally, I'm glad that you're not having hysterics, but I do think the situation merits a little more concern.*

"Actually," said Annabel, plumping herself back down on the floor and crossing her legs again, "I know what to do about this: it makes perfect sense. I think it's because I didn't draw right to the edges of the paper. It's the only castle drawing that I didn't finish right to the edges. Mordion must have found out somehow, and he's trying to cut us away from the castle through the blankness around the edges."

That... Blackfoot's voice trailed away and came back sounding a little more strained. *That is **not** an improvement. If Mordion has as much control as that over the castle, we're in a very sticky position, even if we do manage to escape the room.*

"I don't know about that," Annabel said, flipping through the pages of her sketchbook, "but I do know that I can fix this. Especially now that it's happening at once. We'll figure out the rest later. After lunch, probably."

Nan, I can't help but feel that you're not taking this situation seriously enough.

Annabel found her sketch of the wizard's quarters and fished out her pencil nub. "Ha! That's rich!"

This time, it was Blackfoot who laughed. *Very well, Nan! Well said. I would like to point out, however, that we **could** simply try to leap the gap.*

"*You* could," she murmured, solidifying her shadowy lines into certain, blockwork uniformity and shading them right to the edges of the page. "There's no way I'd make it."

Hmm. Well, there's something to that, after all: it's not some-

thing I'd like to leave to chance. Perhaps we'll be lucky enough to find another tunnel.

Annabel looked up in interest. "Perhaps we will. Will it be able to get through that...*stuff*, though? The tunnels that went through the squishy bit were squashed and kept turning on themselves."

Yes, said Blackfoot broodingly. *Rather annoying, that. And we can't forget that the walls you drew almost stopped them completely.*

"So I should keep drawing," nodded Annabel.

Blackfoot's tail twitched from side to side as he sat beside her. *Oh, undoubtedly. And yet, I have the desire to see which of them would win in this case.*

"I wouldn't bother, actually."

What do you mean, 'bother'?

"Well, I've finished," Annabel said. "Look, the floor is going back to blockwork again."

Bother, said Blackfoot. *I suppose we have our answer, then, Nan. It's certainly your pencil that does the magic.*

"Yes." Annabel looked down at the stubby little pencil that was still pinched in her fingers. She had the distinct desire to pitch the tiny thing through the nearest window, and hope that she never saw it again. On the other hand, her desire to stay alive was suggesting that it was best if she kept a rather tight grip on it. With Mordion gaining enough strength to affect the castle as much as he was doing, they would need every advantage just to stay alive.

She looked uncertainly at the now-steady floor and said: "Should we– I mean, is it safe to go now?"

Goodness knows, said Blackfoot cheerfully, but he stepped out into the corridor without hesitation. The blockwork stood up to his weight, and Annabel shuffled after him, feeling a little more confident. It held up beneath her more significant weight, too. *Shall we have lunch, Nan?*

Annabel, who had instinctively turned in quite another direction, said: "Oh. I suppose so."

What else, then?

"Well...Peter."

I see. I hate to mention it, Nan, but you seem to have lost weight over the last few days. It might be just as well to make sure you eat.

"It doesn't matter," Annabel said, though she felt touched. Her stomach was doing odd little sparks and swirls, and she was quite certain that she wouldn't be able to eat in any case. "I'll eat after we get Peter back."

Very well, said Blackfoot, though he sounded dissatisfied. *Just don't make a habit of it.*

"I have enough fat to live on, anyway. Maybe I'll get a waist after this."

Blackfoot made an impatient noise. *You shouldn't listen to that dreadful boy. There's nothing wrong with how you look.*

"He doesn't mean anything by it," Annabel said. "He just doesn't think about things before he says them. It's why he's always getting into fights at school."

Just because you don't mind, Nan– oh, never mind. I trust you know where you're going?

Annabel said cautiously, "Sort of. Things are still moving around, but bits of it are in the same order as yesterday: it's big chunks that are moving instead of little bits, now. And this part is just below the hallway we want. We just need to go up the next stairway we come to."

Well done, Nan! said Blackfoot. He sounded mildly surprised, which would have annoyed Annabel if she wasn't feeling just the tiniest bit smug. *We'll take this stairway, in that case.*

"It's as if two people are moving bits and pieces in the castle," Annabel said, climbing stairs more energetically than was normal. "Someone was moving little bits and pieces yesterday, and now someone else is moving big segments. It all makes a puzzly kind of sense."

I'm glad you think so.

"Hah!" said Annabel in satisfaction, as they reached the top step of the stone stairway. "See?"

I see a corridor. There's no indication that it's the corridor we want.

"Pft!" Annabel said at him, and continued on around the corner. There she stopped, her breath catching in her throat. She'd already known what she would see, but it was still something of a shock to see it again, after so long looking for it.

The whole corridor was still gone: gone as if it had never appeared again, or as if it was never there to begin with. Almost as if...almost as if the *castle itself* had taken Peter away to that *when* in the past, that *when* where there was still a whole castle.

Annabel clutched at the satchel strap with hands that were slightly damp. She had already suspected something of this, and she was really quite certain that she could draw Peter back in if that was the case. But was *really quite certain* enough when it came to Peter's safety?

"What if it's the castle that's taken him away?"

What if it is?

"Well," Annabel said, surprised, "why? Why would it take him away?"

I can perfectly understand wanting to be rid of the boy, remarked Blackfoot. *In fact, I should imagine it's a pretty common reaction when it comes to Peter. I'm constantly wondering at your staunch determination to have him back, in fact.*

Annabel made a face at him, but she was feeling very much more cheerful, despite her damp hands. The castle– no, she would think about the castle and its machinations later. For now, it was Peter she needed to think about.

"I started drawing Peter a couple of days ago," she said slowly, despite that. The same thought had been teasing her all morning, behind everything else. "But Blackfoot, if I'm drawing the castle back, and things back, how? I mean, I know the pencil is doing it, but where do the ideas come from? Is the pencil putting them in my head? I don't want something else in my head!"

Nan, breathe. I don't know how it works any more than you do. Consider this: do you want to rescue Peter?

"Of course I do!"

Then, for the moment, does it really matter where the ideas come from?

"No," said Annabel, sniffing. She had just told herself the same thing, after all. "But once we have Peter back, I don't want this thing in my head any more."

We'll talk about that once you've drawn him back here, promised Blackfoot.

"All right," said Annabel, and sat down by the ragged gap in the floor. She flicked through the pages until she found the sketch of Peter that she'd begun but never finished. It was just as she'd left it, a small, incomplete thing that showed Peter with his head bent over a desk cluttered with tickerbox parts, and she'd only sketched in a bit of the room. Now she finished it, right up to the walls, with careful, painstaking lines: here a little perspective to the walls, there the outside hall that had disappeared. She saw the hall as it appeared in front of her, a blurry certainty ahead of her that she couldn't concentrate on just now. Instead, she concentrated on the drawing, making shadows and lines on the paper version of Peter as definite and correct as she could manage. She covered every bit of the paper, shading here and there, and when that was done, and Blackfoot said critically in the back of her mind: *You haven't drawn in a door*, she said: "I know. That's the last bit. Just in case."

Annabel sat and scanned her drawing for far longer than she'd spent sketching it, her eyes stinging and watering as she searched for any tiny mistake that could ruin the inexplicable magic. And then, at last, she took up her pencil nub one last time, and drew in a door.

ELEVEN

She had known it would work. She had been almost certain. Well, she had been *reasonably* sure of it.

But it was one thing to be quite sure of it: it was quite another to see the door appearing in the wall as she drew it. At first it was all rough lines and flatness, then she shaded in the depth to it and it became, quite suddenly, solid. Still, it wasn't until Annabel's fingers were around the doorknob and it was turning, that she was able to feel that she had known it would work, despite the hallway that had reappeared before her.

The door opened quietly; almost anticlimactically. There was the boarded floor, just as she'd drawn it, and there were the books on the shelves. There was the table, littered with cogs and pieces of metal, there– *there* was Peter, his sleeves rolled up above the elbow but still stained with grease, and there was the preoccupied frown she had drawn much earlier.

Something that had been tightly wrapped around Annabel's heart loosened. She let the doorknob slip from her fingers without realising it, and the door slowly came to rest against the wall with a soft noise. At the sound, Peter looked up briefly. "Oh. Hallo, Ann. Hold this, please."

"Peter? Are you all right?"

"Of course I'm all right," Peter said irritably. "No, *hold* it, Ann!"

"But–"

"And this bit as well."

Annabel, bewildered, found herself holding a thin piece of metal in one hand and a metal plate in the other. From the thin piece of metal, a wire ran, joining it to the metal plate, and the metal plate was attached to a rather more scattered version of one of Peter's tickerboxes. It was open to the light, its insides ticking and whirring, and when Annabel moved unwarily, snapping the wire that joined the metal rod to the metal plate, it slowed, stopped, and then started up again, this time faster.

She froze, expecting Peter to expostulate, but he only said: "Oh, well. Now that you're here I don't really need that wire, anyway. Don't break the other bit, will you?"

"Peter–"

"Shh!" Peter said, watching his disemboweled ticker-box with bright interest. "Oh, just *look* at how fast its going now! Keep holding it, Ann!"

"Why did it stop? Why is it going faster? Why is it doing that?"

"It stopped because you broke the live connection," said Peter. "And then it started up again because you *are* the connection, now."

"I don't want to be the connection!"

"Too late. Don't move."

"Peter!" Annabel released the metal plate and threw the rod down on the table. "I've been looking for you and I thought that you were dead, or that Mordion got you, and that I'd never see you again!"

Peter, blinking, stared at her for a rather long time. Then he said: "Yes, but is that any reason to throw my things on the ground? We could have gone back in time by a whole minute!"

"What? I thought you didn't believe in time travel! What do you mean, go back in time? You should tell me before you do big magic like that!"

"Yes, but Ann! It's *not* magic! Not really: it's clockwork, and energy, and I think there might be a bit of *not*-magic stuff in there, too. It doesn't exist, but it's *there*, and I need to find someone who understands about not-magic stuff that doesn't exist. And when you get everything just right and the clock-work counts down properly, it keeps running in the back-ground for as long as the tickerbox keeps running."

Annabel, her mouth open, found her voice again. "Have you been figuring this out the entire time you've been missing? You haven't been trying to get back?"

"Not *all* the time," protested Peter. "I had a bit of a look around when I first got here, but I got sent back in time, Ann! What would you have done?"

"Did you even leave this level?"

"Why should I?" Peter demanded. "There were people out there! I didn't want them to see me: they'd know I didn't belong straight away. I stayed here and put a Don't See spell on the door while I worked on the new tickerbox. Besides, I *did* leave: I went down to the kitchen and took some pies after everyone else left. Oh, and I found the pieces for this tickerbox in the court wizard's rooms."

"Were you trying to get back at *all*?"

"What? No! Why should I? I knew you'd find your way to me sooner or later: I just wanted to get some work done in peace and quiet. I did think about trying to send you a message, but then I got caught up with altering the tickerbox."

"I should just leave you here!" Annabel said, bad-temperedly. "You can find your way back when you figure out your stupid little tickerbox!"

Peter caught at her arm. "Don't be like that, Ann! I would have come back, but there was so much to see here! Do you know, I saw the start of the Great Battle from this window? Someone moved it– *moved* it, Ann! They picked up the whole battlefield and just moved it."

"You've never cared about history anyway," grumbled Annabel.

"Yes, but it's different when it's happening right around you! And it's different when there's big magic going on just within reach, too. Oh! Where's your cat?"

"He's back in the hallway," said Annabel. "I told him to stay there, just in case we couldn't get back, or something went wrong. Wait! *You* were the one who took the pies! *You* took them out before, so they didn't make it to the now!"

"Technically speaking, the pies were never there in the first place," said Peter, his voice just slightly lecturing. "*Technically* speaking, your memories of them are simply a hiccough in the reordering of time."

"Technically speaking!" muttered Annabel in disgust. "There *is* no technically speaking! Nobody knows about the technical side of time-travel. You didn't even believe in–"

"All right, all right," Peter said. "Maybe I didn't. And maybe it's time that someone *did* know about the technical side of time-travel, and why shouldn't it be me?"

"Then find out about it back in your own time," Annabel grumbled. "Blackfoot and I have been looking for you for *ages.*"

"But it's so messy back there. At least Mordion isn't causing trouble here."

"I wouldn't be too sure about that." Annabel looked gloomily around the room. "Blackfoot has told me a few things about him. If there's big magic going on out there, I bet he's involved, somehow."

Peter stared at her. "You shouldn't listen to that cat of yours, Ann. That would mean he's–"

"Hundreds of years old. Yes. That's what Blackfoot says. Anyway, the castle is getting dangerous, and a lot of the doorways don't go where they should go. I need you back in our now so that I don't walk through any of the wrong ones."

"Wait up, Mordion is *in* the castle?" Peter said sharply. "How did that happen?"

"He gave proof of value, too," Annabel said. "He showed the castle how to move itself around, and now that he's in he keeps shifting things to trick us into going the wrong way. Actually, I think the castle might be doing some of this itself: I just haven't figured out why."

Peter laughed rudely. "I bet you haven't! You don't pay attention, Ann!"

"At least I'm *trying*. You've been sitting in here without doing anything."

"I was working! I've been breaking the secrets of clockwork assisted time-travel!"

"Nobody cares about that!"

"I care about it!"

I suppose, said Blackfoot's voice, *I suppose it would be too much to expect that you could continue your quarrel back in your own present?*

"Now Blackfoot is being snide again," Annabel said in annoyance. She looked around at the open door and saw Blackfoot sitting there, very carefully on his own side of the doorway. "He says we should go back now."

Peter shrugged, but began to pack his things. "What's the difference? I thought you said he was always snide."

"Yes, but he's usually being snide about you. No! I'm not going to carry your stupid tickerbox! Stop getting grease all over me!"

"Fine!" Peter said, stuffing random cogs and wheels into his pockets and pinching tiny metal spindles between his lips. He made a series of muffled noises through the metal in his lips that made Annabel giggle despite herself, and wrapped even more grease-smeared metal into a piece of cloth that she strongly suspected had been torn from one of his sleeves. Once that was done, he took the pins and spindles out of his mouth and thrust the cloth-wrapped bundle at her. "Then hold this!"

Annabel took it from him and led the way out of the room, still giggling, because even if Peter was just as annoying and frustrating as usual, at least he was *there* to be annoying and frustrating.

"You're in a silly mood today," Peter said disapprovingly, but he sounded less cross than he had before, and he followed her without wasting any more time.

That took far too long, Blackfoot said, when they were both out. *However, interestingly enough, you seem to have drawn the room and the hall back into the castle properly. I **was** afraid that you might have only drawn yourself into the past, but as far as I can see, the whole section has stabilised.*

"Good," Annabel said, in satisfaction. "I thought I'd only drawn myself into the past, too."

Peter shot her a narrow look. "What do you mean, draw yourself? What are you talking about."

"Nothing," said Annabel loftily. "I just rescued you by

drawing you back from the past, that's all! Just sat there and drew you, and the room, and brought you back. Nothing at all."

"*Drew* me–" Peter stared at her. "You *drew* me back from the past? We're back in the present? Why didn't I feel anything? And how on earth did *you* do it? You can't do magic– you don't even have magic!"

"That's right!" Annabel said happily. "But I did, actually. Look out the window."

Peter gave her one last, incredulous stare, and rushed over to the nearest window while Blackfoot made his little *hui hui hui* in the recesses of Annabel's mind.

Annabel hugged herself, grinning, and said: "This is more fun than I thought it would be."

"How, Ann?" demanded Peter, leaning dangerously far out of the window and then back in like a jack-in-the-box. "How did you do it? I can't even see the orangey glow from the Frozen Battlefield anymore."

"It's not me, exactly," Annabel admitted reluctantly. "It's this pencil. I didn't realise it until last night, but every time I drew something from the castle, it was bringing whatever I drew back to the castle."

"Oh." Peter thought about that for a little while, and said at last: "Well, I suppose that makes sense. You did find the pencil in the ruins, after all. My question would be why it didn't start working until now, but I probably know the answer to that as well."

"What answer?" demanded Annabel.

"Never you mind!" Peter said impressively, and though she pestered him for answers all the way back down to the throne room, he refused to answer in any other way than: "Don't think I'm supposed to tell you, actually."

At last Annabel stopped asking him, muttering to Blackfoot: "He probably doesn't know anything. He just wants to sound clever because he wasn't the one who got himself out of the past."

I warned you that it was a bad idea to rescue him, said Blackfoot. *You can take the consequences.*

Peter merely smirked at her and went back to his tickerbox, which was annoying, since it meant that he really *did* know something. Annabel, pretending that she didn't care, wondered aloud what she should try to draw back next, by way of trying to annoy Peter with the remembrance that she and not he had effected the changes upon the castle. It was a fortunate change of subject: Peter took it up with great enthusiasm and chivvied Annabel and Blackfoot outside the castle again to look up at the structure as a whole.

"There," he said, pointing. "There are still bits missing. Draw those back. I want to see it happen."

It won't do him any good, Blackfoot said, with amusement colouring his voice. *There's nothing to see, magically speaking. It's possibly the strongest magic I've ever **not** seen working. Do go ahead, though, by all means. I'm looking forward to seeing the crestfallen expression on his face.*

Annabel grinned, which made Peter look rather more narrowly at her, and took her pencil and sketchbook out of her new satchel. She could already see what she was going to draw, which would have been worrisome if it wasn't exactly what she was used to feeling when she went to draw something, since before this particular pencil and this particular time.

"I still want to know," she said, to the world in general rather than to Peter or Blackfoot specifically, "how I get the ideas. It doesn't feel like there's someone else in my head like when Blackfoot speaks, so is the pencil speaking to me, or is it just working with whatever I do?"

"I suppose it depends on whether it's actually a pencil or not," said Peter. "Hurry up and draw something, Ann!"

Annabel looked at him in surprise, the point of her pencil nub just touching the paper. "Well, what else would it be? Blackfoot says he can't see anything unusual about it."

"It's not that it's unusual, as such," Peter said slowly. "It's just that it's a very pencilly sort of pencil. There's no doubt about it."

"Isn't that just what I said?"

"Don't be silly, Ann. Anything made of wood is tricky: there's always a bit of magic running through it, not to mention the remnants of sap. Between the magic and the sap, and the fact that you can carve wood to be something else altogether, most wooden things think they should be something else instead. It's why wizards use wooden wands when they can't do magic without a conduit."

"What's that got to do with my pencil?" demanded Annabel irritably. "If it's a pencil, it should be allowed to be sure about it!"

"Yes, but it's awfully suspicious for a pencil to be so sure that it *is* a pencil."

"Then why didn't you mention anything earlier? If it's so awfully suspicious, shouldn't you have noticed?"

"I can't notice everything, Ann."

"You mean that it wasn't suspicious at all, and it's only suspicious now because you know," scoffed Annabel. "Stop trying to be so clever all the time."

Peter grinned suddenly. "Oh, well, maybe it wasn't so suspicious, but now that I know something's up, it *is* suspicious, Ann!"

He's not wrong, Blackfoot chimed in. *For a pleasant change. For pity's sake draw something, Nan, or you'll have him lecturing us again.*

Annabel, making swift, sure strokes of the pencil, said, "Is it suspicious because it could be magic so strong you can't see it?"

"Mostly," Peter agreed, craning his neck first to peer over Annabel's shoulder, and then to gaze up at the castle. "Wait, why can't I see anything happening?"

"It might take a little while to start. It usually takes a minute or two before what I draw comes to be."

"I don't mean that!" Peter said in disgust. "That's already happening: look!"

Very much surprised, Annabel followed his pointing finger and saw that the tower top she'd been sketching onto the castle was appearing as swiftly as she drew it. "Oh!" she said. "It's getting quicker! What are you complaining about, then?"

"But it's– it can't– why can't I see anything happening *here*?" complained Peter. He sounded vaguely insulted, as if Annabel had done it to spite him.

Didn't I tell you, Nan? said Blackfoot irrepressibly.

"Why would I know?" Annabel pointed out, going back to her drawing. "I couldn't see anything happening even if it was happening."

"That's very annoying, Ann."

Annabel cheerfully shaded the last of her drawing and made sure the paper was covered right to the edges. "I suppose it is."

"And tell your cat to stop smirking at me."

Oh heavens. How dreadful. My face has betrayed me.

"He's getting better at reading your expressions," remarked Annabel. "You'll have to be more careful."

Wonders will never cease, Blackfoot said. *Although, since he refuses to believe I'm capable of thought and speech, I suppose that's about all he'll ever have.*

"Oh heavens," said Annabel. "How awful for you."

There's no need for sarcasm, Nan.

"I can't even tell which one of us you're talking to any more," Peter said. "I hope you know that you're absolutely bonkers."

"Absolutely bonkers and able to draw back the royal castle at will," said Annabel irrepressibly. She was feeling more cheerful than she had felt for several days. "You're sane, but what can you do?"

"I can go back in time a minu– oh, never mind! You just wait, Ann!"

"I will," said Annabel. "I'll wait a minute, and you wait a minute, too: then you'll be right back where you started. What use is going back in time by one minute?"

Instead of being annoyed, Peter laughed. "All right, all right. But when I'm travelling through time, you'll be stuck in the same boring old time. I won't take you with me!"

"Pft," said Annabel. "I don't want to go. One time is hard enough without having to wade through all of time. Do you want me to draw more, or have you seen enough?"

"Enough?" spluttered Peter. "I haven't seen anything! Fine, just draw a bit more over there, where it still looks a bit spindly, and if I still can't see anything we might as well stop and eat."

"All right," Annabel agreed. "But I don't think there's much left to draw."

That should be the last of it. To Annabel's mild curiosity, Blackfoot sounded almost anticipatory. *Then things should get more interesting. I wonder if Mordion knows how close the castle is to being complete?*

Annabel made a face at the drawing she was working on. "Probably. What happens when the castle is complete? Mordion is already shifting things around, and he's taken some of the doors, too."

That depends, Blackfoot said. *I suspect that things will either get very much better or very much worse for us.*

"You said that before," Peter said. "About Mordion, I mean. What do you mean that he's taken some of the doors?"

"Well, it's like the Caliphan–" began Annabel, and added: "Wait, you don't even believe I've seen someone in the reflections, so why should I tell you?"

"Oh, that. No, I've seen him: I beg your pardon, Ann. He's been watching us in the windows all around the castle. Did you draw him back in, too?"

"Not exactly. I think I drew him in *partly*."

"I see," said Peter. "So you think he's in the castle but not quite in *this* time yet. And Mordion is–"

Annabel nodded. "Yes. I think he's in the castle but not quite in this version of it. Or something. I don't really understand, but I know he still can't get through some of the doorways. He's been shifting the castle around to try and get us to walk through the ones that lead to him. Blackfoot can tell which are which, but I can't."

This time it was Peter who said: "Pft." At Annabel's nose-wrinkle, he said: "You and your mental constructs! All right, we'll have to be more careful about going through the castle, then."

"Yes." Annabel drew in a rather surprised-looking bird on top of the roof she'd just finished, and went back to shading roof tiles. "We also have to watch out for tunnels."

"*Tunnels?*"

"Tunnels. They're all over the castle."

"Wait, there weren't tunnels all over the castle when I left!"

How would you know? Blackfoot retorted. *You don't even see what's under your own nose.*

"Blackfoot says you probably just didn't see them."

"I don't care what the cat says! I would have noticed tunnels all over the place. Are you sure that Mordion isn't doing that too?"

"Pretty sure," Annabel said. "One of them was there just in time to get us away from him the first time he appeared in the castle.

Peter grinned. "Was it, though? Now that's interesting!"

"Don't go getting all mysterious again," sighed Annabel. "And if you didn't already notice, there's also a lot of squishy black stuff in the middle of the castle, too."

"I saw that. It's not squishy black stuff, though, Ann: I think it might be shifted temporal remnant."

Look what you've done, Blackfoot said accusingly. *You've set him off again.*

"It looks squishy and black to me," Annabel said obstinately.

"Yes, but– oh, never mind. All right, if Mordion is making things difficult you'd better not go wandering around the castle without me. And you'd better not go around without that pencil of yours, either."

"I always have my pencil with me," retorted Annabel, adding the last few patches of cross-hatching to create some texture. She looked at the drawing for another thoughtful moment, then put both pencil and sketchbook back in her satchel. "It must be time for lunch. I don't want to draw any more. Mordion will only move it around anyway."

"All right," Peter said reluctantly, "but we should really see what else you can do with that thing this afternoon."

Our time would perhaps be better spent in trying to get away from the castle before Mordion takes over more of its functions.

"Blackfoot says we should be trying to get away instead."

"Well, maybe we can do that with the pencil, too. We'll try that this afternoon, too."

"All right, but lunch first," Annabel said.

Blackfoot was gone when Annabel woke the next morning. She would have been worried if it wasn't for the fact that she could still feel that peculiar Blackfoot-ness at the edges of her mind that meant he was still nearby. Blackfoot was inclined to be secretive and non-communicative, and Annabel was inclined, from long acquaintance, to trust him, so she only scrabbled quietly to her feet without wondering too much where he had gone. It was probably easier if Blackfoot wasn't there, if it came to that: he had a habit lately of warning her not to do dangerous things that always seemed to be necessary, and Annabel had an idea that she was about to do something that he would warn her very strenuously about.

She could have taken Peter with her, but she'd only just rescued him from the past, and as annoying as he was being lately, she didn't think that she'd like for him to disappear again. Besides, Peter was knowing things and not telling them, and Annabel didn't want him standing smugly in the background while she tried to find out a few bits of knowing by herself. So she left him sleeping and stepped carefully through the throne-room entrance and into the main castle. As much as the outside of the castle was nearly complete, was the inside nearly complete: it was now possible to travel straight from the throne room and into the main castle without having to take the roundabout route through the kitchen. They had discovered as much yesterday afternoon, when Peter had dragged Annabel all over the castle, demanding that she draw this and that, and nodding every so often with a "thought as much!" that became steadily more annoying as the afternoon wore on.

The only trouble was, thought Annabel, peering carefully at each archway and doorway as she passed through it, that she wasn't likely to notice if a doorway was suspect, no matter *how* carefully she looked at it. Peter had recognised them straight away, and whatever he saw was enough to sober him completely from his heady, secret knowledge. Annabel, without any such knowledge or sight, still looked suspiciously at each of them as she passed, and it wasn't until she was outside the castle wizard's quarters that she felt as safe as it was possible for her to feel.

"Inside or outside?" she wondered aloud. She would feel better about drawing the Caliphan back into a room that she could enter and exit easily, but she didn't like the idea of the Caliphan being able to exit so easily. Annabel bit her lip anxiously, and muttered: "Inside."

Once she was in the room, she sat herself on the floor with her back to the wall, and opened her sketchbook to a blank page. She didn't dare to try and draw the Caliphan into the sketch she'd already made of the wizardly quarters, and since she wasn't sure what would happen if she erased some of the drawing, Annabel also preferred to try and draw the room again without a door. It was easier to draw the room now that she knew what it should look like from sight and not from a nebulous idea in her mind, but she kept the drawing as simple as possible, anyway. Nor, after some thought, did she draw all the way to the edges of the paper.

When the room was fully drawn, with just a carefully blank space left for where she would draw the Caliphan back,

Annabel stopped and looked around the room. She hadn't drawn a door, and so there *wasn't* a door any longer, but she had the feeling that for herself at least, the door was still there. Curious to test her theory, she crossed the room and felt the wall where the door should have been. It was exactly where it had always been, and as Annabel found first the doorknob and then the door panels with her questing hands, it occurred to her that if the sense of satisfaction at being right was anything like Peter habitually felt, then it was no wonder that he loved to be right so often. She hugged herself as much in delight as in nervousness, and sat down again, this time with her back to the wall, to draw in the Caliphan. Now that she was sitting by the door with her face to the window, she could the reflection version of the Caliphan there: he was watching her without pretending otherwise, his eyes bright and interested.

"Just you wait," Annabel said, taking in the curve and brilliance of those eyes. "I'll see you in a minute."

TWELVE

It took a little longer than a minute. In fact, it took several minutes, and by then, Annabel was so caught up in trying to make sure she exactly captured the expression of the Caliphan's eyes, that she wasn't sure exactly when she noticed that he was in the room.

No, that wasn't quite right. She first noticed because she heard a snore, and she was quite certain that it hadn't come from her. Annabel looked up, and found that the Caliphan was there. Unlike the sketch she had made of him, he was sitting in the wooden chair by the desk with his feet on the desk, his eyes closed and his mouth open to the ceiling above. That struck Annabel as quite dangerous, considering the amount of dirt and cobwebs coating the rafters above him. She hadn't drawn those in, either: neither in the first drawing nor this second one. She climbed carefully to her feet and crept closer, placing each foot carefully on the floorboards and wondering what else wouldn't be quite as she'd drawn it. From further away, through the windows, he had looked quite young, but when she got closer Annabel saw that she'd been misled by his lankiness and the youthfully prominent adam's apple: there were deep lines beside his eyes and his hair was more salt than pepper, something that also hadn't shown through the reflections. He was quite a bit older than she'd thought at first.

He still didn't look *dangerous*, as such, and Annabel didn't think to have her pencil back at the ready until the Caliphan, without either moving or even seeming to wake, said: "If you're going to keep drawing the castle back bit by bit, do you think you could draw me some socks? Being drawn back into existence gives you a bit of a shiver. There were some here, but someone took them."

Annabel froze into her habitual, blobby facade of stupidity just as the Caliphan opened his eyes a crack and sat up. He stared at her for quite a while, his head twitching from side to side.

"Oh, that's good," he said at last. "I can do an impression of a stork. Want to see?"

"All right," said Annabel, letting her eyes glaze a little bit. Perhaps the Caliphan had seen too much of her in the reflection. It was very rarely that her facade didn't work: the eyes were usually the clincher.

The Caliphan lunged forward in his seat to peer at her. "You're really scaring me. How do you do that with your eyes?"

"You said you were going to do an impression of a stork," said Annabel sulkily. Most of it was just for show, but she did feel a little bit aggrieved: the Caliphan was acting as if he didn't believe her.

He lunged to his feet just as quickly and awkwardly as he'd sat forward, one leg drawn up high, almost to his chin, and both arms extended in hooked wings to the side. "It's the nose that really makes it," he said, thrusting forward with his nose as if it were a beak.

"No, it's not," said Annabel, looking at those stick-like legs with fascination.

He gave her a narrow-eyed look and then said quite calmly, "It's all a matter of perspective. Compared with a sparrow, my legs are elephantine: compared with an elephant, now..."

"Have you been here long?" asked Annabel, looking around again at the general slobbiness of the room. None of the other rooms she'd drawn back looked like this: they looked as though they'd just been cleaned. But then, she had very carefully not drawn in too much. Was it possible that the Caliphan had been living in this version of the room all the time, and that she had merely made it accessible to herself by drawing it?

"The mess, you mean?" said the man, still in his stork position. He added conversationally: "I have a brilliant mind, you see. It means I'm fated to live in squalor. And if squalor is not to be had, it must be created."

Annabel stared at him, quite forgetting to hold her blank expression. "You *made* it like this?"

"In a manner of speaking," he said. "You didn't draw this in."

"I know. How did it get here?"

"That's too hard," said the Caliphan. "My name is Rorkin. What's yours?"

"Then explain slowly," Annabel said coldly. "I'm sure you'll manage."

Rorkin looked slightly offended. "Not too hard for me: too hard for you."

"Then explain slowly," said Annabel again. "Use small words."

"You're quite a touchy little thing, aren't you?"

"Yes," said Annabel. "Actually, I'm very touchy right now. The castle has been playing games with us, and now

Mordion is playing games with us, and I'd like to know who you are and why you keep looking at me through the windows."

"Well, you didn't specify, did you? You just drew me, and the room, and left the edges empty. Probably didn't even draw right to the edges of the paper."

"Do you mean that you used the space to draw in things that you wanted?"

"I told you that you wouldn't understand," said Rorkin, with a faint air of triumph.

"Well, I do! Mordion did the same thing to Blackfoot and me when we were in one of the rooms."

"Then I should think you would have known better by now."

"I do," Annabel said. "That's why I did it. I wanted to make sure I'd left a buffer around this room."

Rorkin gave her another of those brilliant, narrow looks. "A lot cleverer than you look, aren't you?"

Annabel said simply: "Yes. Why have you been watching me through the windows? Don't think I didn't notice that you didn't answer the question."

"It wasn't just you. You're not as important as you think you are."

"I'm not important at all. That's why I want to know, and you *still* haven't answered."

"You're a very difficult person to talk to," said Rorkin. "Why do you suppose that is?"

"That? That's because I've lived with Peter and Blackfoot for so many years." Annabel sat herself cautiously on the easy chair, which was a lot dustier than she had originally drawn it, and crossed her legs. "And it's why I'm going to keep asking you why you've been watching me through the windows. I'm not clever enough to get distracted by other important things, so you might as well answer straight away."

"Hah!" Rorkin said, unexpectedly. "I knew you were the right one! All right then, you blobby little thing: I was watching you because I was trying to make sure you didn't die. And also because I'm grading your performance. It isn't just you, though: I've been watching everything that's been happening in the castle ever since your young friend gave proof of value to the castle."

"You were *grading* me? Grading me on *what*?"

"Very handy, that proof of use," continued Rorkin. "I'll have to remember to thank him. Will I meet him today?"

"No," Annabel said. "What were you grading me on?"

"How well you respond to things. I want to meet the not-cat, too."

"How well *do* I respond to things?" Annabel asked.

"It ranges from 'quite well really' to 'horrifically badly'," said Rorkin.

"Oh. Well, that's not surprising. I'm not used to responding to much, actually. Mostly I respond to Peter, and he's more annoying than anything, so I usually try to ignore him."

"No response is still a response," Rorkin said. "It's all in the eyes."

"Did I draw you back, or were you already here?"

"Yes."

Annabel stared at him. "Yes to what?"

"Yes to both."

"It *can't* be both."

Rorkin shrugged. "That's not my problem."

"All right then," said Annabel, used to Peter's deliberate unhelpfulness, "how is it possible?"

"I was already here, but you drew me back, just the same. And while we're on the subject, why did it take you so long to draw me back properly?"

"I didn't know you were safe to draw back," Annabel protested, because there was something of a reproachful tone to Rorkin's voice. "If it comes to that, I still don't know it's safe. Besides, I couldn't get your eyes to come out exactly right, and I didn't want to draw you back wrong."

Rorkin's eyes went rather wide and round. "I hadn't considered the effects of an artistic mind," he muttered, but when Annabel said: "What?" he only added: "Anyway, if you're being so cautious, you should have been more careful about who you let into my castle."

"*Your* castle?"

"Well, it was until you let Mordion in, anyway."

"I didn't let him in!"

"Well, someone did, and it wasn't me. I wasn't even here."

"You said you were here all along," muttered Annabel. "You should make up your mind."

"It's not my mind you should be worried about making up," Rorkin said. "It's the castle's."

"The castle's *mind*?"

Without regarding that, Rorkin added: "Ever since Mordion got in, the castle hasn't been able to make up its mind about which one of us is really Rorkin. If I wasn't drawn back a bit, I'd probably be confused, too."

"Why does it matter who the castle thinks is Rorkin?" Annabel asked, passing over the rest of his speech as incomprehensible.

Rorkin's bright eyes rested on her face in a particularly disquieting look. "Because the castle will only follow Rorkin's commands."

"But *you're* Rorkin."

"Yes, exactly. You'd think the castle would know me better by now. It's very confusing, and it shouldn't be happening." Rorkin's eyes flitted away from her face, and he wandered across the room to his window.

Annabel, who had been dazed almost into speechlessness by the first, inevitable idea that had occurred to her at Rorkin's words, said: "Wait." She thought about it again, and came to the same stunned, outraged conclusion that had first seared through her mind. "Have *you* been playing with us all this time? Switching the castle around, hiding my friend Peter, and letting Mordion in?"

"Of course!" Rorkin said. "Well, sort of. Not really. And yet, I really have been. I haven't been here for all of it, though, so you'll have to excuse my confusion."

"You said before that you didn't let Mordion in."

"Neither I did," said Rorkin with perfect cordiality, as if he hadn't just agreed to the direct opposite. "Wasn't even here."

"But you *said*–"

"Oh, that's really a bit irritating," Rorkin said. "I don't suppose you could *not* quote me to myself, could you?"

With the vague idea that she had perhaps met her match in sheer obstinacy, Annabel muttered: "Then you shouldn't contradict yourself."

"I told you it would be hard to understand."

Annabel blinked. "I suppose you did. All right. I'm Annabel, by the way."

"I know that," Rorkin said, then tipped his head. "Or did I? I probably did. It's the castle and the drawing back: it makes things confusing."

"Do you mean," Annabel said cautiously, with the dim

thought that she might, just possibly, understand, "that you were part of the castle before I drew you back in?"

"That's really very close to being not entirely wrong. Well done, you!"

"What part of it wasn't right?"

"Almost all of it. I wasn't part of the castle– well, the castle wasn't part of the castle, so how could I be a part of it?"

"All right," Annabel said. "Let's go back to the part where you said you'd been moving the castle around and hiding Peter."

Rorkin, very accurately, said: "I didn't say that. *You* said that."

"Yes, but you agreed!"

"I did, didn't I? Well, and it's not entirely wrong, either. It was the castle that hid Peter away, but it was only doing what it was supposed to do."

"What is the castle supposed to do?"

"It's a playground. No, it's more of a testing-ground."

"A *testing*-ground? What for? Were you testing Peter's magic– wait, didn't you say that you were observing my reactions?"

"Ha!" said Rorkin loudly. "There's no need to test *his* magic! No, no, much more interesting watching you run about the castle. You're quite the determined little blob once you get going, aren't you?"

"You were testing me? What for?"

"It didn't *have* to be you, you understand," Rorkin said conversationally. "It just happened to be you. I probably would have picked you anyway, but the castle picked you first, so *all's well that starts with a happy surprise*, as they say."

"They don't say that."

Rorkin peered at her. "Are you sure? It sounds awfully familiar. I'm sure I've heard it somewhere."

"It's *the man who goes to bed with his boots on starts the day with a happy surprise.*"

"That makes no sense at all."

Annabel, who had had to shake spiders and even the occasional toad out of her shoes before she put them on in the morning, muttered: "Well, maybe if he hadn't worn his boots his surprise wouldn't have been a happy one. Look, what do you mean by *it didn't have to be* me?"

"That? Well, it could have been any girl about your age. It alternates between male and female, and this time it just happened to be female."

"That doesn't make sense."

"Should've drawn me back better, then, shouldn't you? I might have made more sense."

There was no point in continuing that particular rabbit-trail, Annabel thought. She stared at Rorkin with her best expressionless face and said: "If I drew you *back*, where were you?"

"I wasn't," Rorkin said simply.

Dimly, Annabel thought she might understand. Besides, she had been used often enough in Grenna's spells to recognise that people could sometimes be *things* and not people when it came to magic. She said: "Were you part of a spell to make the castle the way it is?"

Rorkin beamed. "You clever little blobby thing! No, don't do that with your face, it's off-putting. I'm more of a power-source, actually. I built the scenarios into the castle to play out in certain ways depending on who came into the ruins, then I built myself into the magic to make sure it went on for long enough."

"Does that mean you can influence the castle?"

"Supposedly. On a sub-dungeon level."

Annabel felt the spark of kindling hope. "Does that mean you can help us?"

"That depends on what you need help with."

"Can you get us out of the castle?"

"Well," said Rorkin apologetically, "not exactly. Lately, the castle has been a bit standoffish. And when I say standoffish, I mean that it seems to think Mordion is me, and now it's following his commands instead of the directives I input into it when I first designed the possibility of it coming back."

"Do you mean," Annabel asked, rather dazed, "that the whole castle is under Mordion's control now?"

"Not the *whole* castle. Well, a fair bit of it, I suppose. He's having trouble with doorways, though. You'll have to be more careful about those: don't think I didn't see you skipping through them merrily this morning. If it hadn't been for Mordion, I would have been able to come back straight away when you drew me part-way back."

"So you're stuck here just as much as we are?"

"Of course not. You're free to leave if you can only find a way out through the changes Mordion has made. I can't possibly leave, no matter what I do." Rorkin sat on his chair again, and tilted it back on its back legs. Quite cheerfully, he added: "I'm afraid it's death and nothingness for me once Mordion has the whole castle."

Annabel very much wanted to tell him that it served him right. He'd allowed the castle to play with her and Peter and Blackfoot as if they were a chess pieces, and now that Mordion was in the picture, the game was running away from him more quickly than he could grasp it.

She wanted very badly to tell him that, but she found she couldn't.

"I know what you're thinking," said Rorkin, his brown eyes sharp. Annabel sank into her blank-faced fortress and didn't answer. "You're thinking that it serves me right. And you're right, of course: I'm sorry about all the tests. I had to be sure that you were the right one, you see."

"You said that before. The right one to what?"

"Be the queen, of course," Rorkin said, in surprise. "And as much as it serves me right, it probably doesn't serve *you* right. Or that terrifyingly clever boy or the not-cat."

Annabel, dazed, faltered out: "What?"

"I said, it doesn't serve any of *you* right. Making a play for sympathy, you understand."

"No, the other thing!"

Rorkin's long brown face stared at her. "What other thing?"

"The– didn't you say that you thought I'm the– well, the queen?"

"I don't *think* it, I *know* it," said Rorkin. "But that's not the important thing–"

"I'm not the queen," insisted Annabel, shaken entirely out of her comfortably safe expression of stupidity. "There *is* no queen. There's no king, either."

"Well, that's true enough. There isn't any king. But you are the queen."

"I'm not!"

"Rubbish," said Rorkin. "You must be. The castle chose you. More importantly, the staff chose you."

"What staff?"

"The one in your pocket. The one you've been drawing with."

"It's a pencil."

"Here," said Rorkin, dropping the chair legs back to the ground and making an expansive gesture with his long arms. "Have a lesson. Are you ready? What you think you see is more important than what you actually see. No, that's not right. What you actually see isn't what you necessarily think you see. No, that's not right, either. Anyway, people get so caught up with what they can see. It's a limiting sort of attitude to have."

Annabel gave him one of her particularly flat looks, but decided that this rabbit trail wasn't worth following, either. Instead, she said: "So from the time we got into the ruins until now, the castle has been testing me to see if I'll be a good queen? What if I'd died? I nearly did die! Why would you make a test like that?"

"There were safeguards," objected Rorkin. "I made sure of that: testing is all very well, but if your future queen is killed, what's the use of it? Besides, it's wholly automated. I'm only here as a custodian while the castle does what it's meant to do, so it *had* to have proper safeguards."

"Your safeguards aren't working very well," Annabel said. "Actually."

Not at all offended, Rorkin smiled brightly at her. "That's because of Mordion taking over. Now that the castle thinks he's me, it's beginning to follow his orders, but it's still programmed with its original directive, which is to test potential heirs. So now Mordion is using the castle to get to you, and the castle is using Mordion to test you. Which means the tests will keep getting harder, and– well, I suppose you could possibly die, after all."

Annabel, who had been living from day to day since she entered the castle ruins with the idea that any day could be her last, found that she could still be angry at this.

"It also means that I could possibly die, which is more problematic."

"How is that more problematic?" demanded Annabel crossly.

"If I die, how can I help you?" Rorkin said, with perfect logic.

"You can't help us, anyway. You said that the castle doesn't think you're you anymore."

"Well, on and off. Every now and then it knows I'm me."

"Wait," Annabel said suddenly. "Isn't it cheating, telling me about the castle and me being queen? If I know they're tests, won't that invalidate the tests?"

"Stop wriggling," advised Rorkin, his eyes suddenly very sharp and understanding. "You can't get out of it, no matter how much you wriggle. The staff chose you, and the castle chose you, and I probably would have chosen you if I'd been aware enough to do it. I'm telling you now because all the original conditions are out: if Mordion gets control of the entire castle we'll all die. Anyway, the castle will still be testing you, and since all the safety measures are gone, that's about as good a test as you could hope for."

"*Hope* for!"

"Oh, that was a bad choice of words. Well, if you prefer–"

"Don't bother. It's too late now. Anyway, I don't want to be queen."

"Doesn't matter."

"It does," said Annabel flatly. "You can't make me be queen if I don't want to be queen."

"Sure about that?" Rorkin's eyes still had that kindly and rather understanding look that was somehow more frightening than the brilliant kind of madness she'd seen in them earlier.

"Are you *really* sure about what the castle can and can't do right now?"

Annabel fidgeted with the clasp on her satchel. "No."

"Neither am I," Rorkin said unexpectedly. "But the staff and the castle both chose you, so there's about half of no chance at all that you'll be able to wriggle out of it."

"What if I get out of the castle?" asked Annabel. There was a heaviness somewhere around her middle that could have been either hunger or the weight of her heart. She was remembering just how long ago it was that she found her pencil: longer even than she'd known Blackfoot. It hadn't ever grown shorter, nor had the eraser end ever grown any smaller. Nor, despite her carelessness and thoughtlessness, had she ever managed to lose it, even when she thought she had. "What if I get rid of the pencil?"

"It's a staff." Rorkin wagged a long, knobbly finger at her. "Don't confuse the two, or you'll come unstuck."

"The staff then," Annabel said impatiently. "I'll get out of the castle. I'll leave the staff for someone else to find."

She knew as she said it that she never would: it had been in her life, almost directing her life, for far too long for her to be able to escape it so easily. Annabel had the awful feeling that as much as the castle had been a test for her to chosen as queen, so she could never have gone any other way than to have entered it at that particular moment. That led to other, more unpleasant surmises, that Annabel wasn't prepared to think about at the moment.

"Really? I bet you won't."

Annabel hugged herself defensively. "Why? There are tunnels all around the castle. We nearly got once, thanks to them. You shouldn't have put them out if you didn't want us to use them."

Rorkin peered at her. "I didn't put them out."

"The castle, then."

"The castle didn't put them out." Rorkin peered a little more closely at her. "Are you laughing at me? Run a warren of tunnels through my perfectly nice castle! Who else would do it?"

"I don't know! Why would I know? It wasn't me!"

"Never said it was. I really thought you knew. That's all very interesting and explains a few things I wondered about. When are you going to draw the other one back, by the way?"

"The other one?" Annabel stared at him, bewildered by the sudden change of subject.

"Your cat. The one you've been drawing into your little book: the one without a mouth. You must have known it was him."

"Well, I didn't," Annabel said sulkily. That wasn't quite true, of course: it was one of those thoughts she had just tried to push away, preferring not to think it was so. If it was so, it was too complicated to bear thinking about. "And it's not true! Blackfoot is a *cat*. I don't know who that other person is."

Rorkin's bright eyes peered at her. "Really? Now me, my left eyebrow starts twitching when I try to tell a lie, but you're such a solid little thing: it's hard to get a read on you. If you hadn't noticed, why have you stopped drawing him back?"

"Back? What do you mean, back?"

"Fibber, fibber, lily-liver!" shouted Rorkin, at once. "You *do* know what I'm talking about! I saw you drawing him back and then stopping just before you finished the drawing. Why don't you want him back?"

"Blackfoot is a *cat*," Annabel said defensively. "I don't know what you mean about *back*. And stop yelling at me! I don't like it."

"Fibber, fibber, lily-liver," Rorkin said again, this time more quietly. "He's a man, *that's* a staff, and you're the queen. It's no use pretending it's not true, and it's no use trying to run away from it."

Annabel, who in all her running away had never found it useful, said: "I know that. That's why I do it. It's no use, but if it's no use, and if I can never get away or get a choice, I'm going to make it as difficult for everyone as possible."

Rorkin blinked a little and sat back. "Ah. I see. Would it help if I told you that you have a choice?"

"No," said Annabel. "I can see your eyebrow twitching already. I'd know it was a lie."

"Knew I shouldn't have told you that," muttered Rorkin. "Well, what are you going to do?"

"I'm going to sit here," Annabel said. "And I'm not going to move."

"Well, that's novel, anyway," said Rorkin. "What will that do, by the way?"

"I'll sit here," said Annabel, "and I'll just start erasing."

Rorkin blinked once, and then twice. "You probably shouldn't do that," he said. "If you start erasing things, I'll vanish, too."

"Why would *you* vanish? I'd be erasing the castle! Shouldn't everything go back to the way it was before?"

"Perhaps it would if I wasn't so much connected to the castle," said Rorkin sadly. "It seemed like a good idea at the time. Back then people were dying and Parras was being over-run, and it was obvious that we would eventually need to start again. I programmed the castle to recognise and test the heirs, but there wasn't any way of powering it: it's why I had to program myself into the castle. I'm afraid it's a bit too late to be crying about it now."

"Oh," said Annabel slowly. "So that's what you meant when you said that you were here all along, but I drew you back."

"That's what I like about you," Rorkin said, in a friendly sort of a way. "You go away and think about things and then add up all the little bits you know into one big whole. You don't always get it right, but it's a sound system as far as it goes."

Her mind buzzing with too much information, Annabel said: "Blackfoot doesn't always get it right, either. Neither do you."

"Yes, there's a lesson there, too."

"Of course there is," muttered Annabel. She uncrossed her legs and put her feet back on the floor before she was aware of what she was doing. Once they were there, she gazed blankly at them for a few moments before she said: "I'm going now. I have to think about all this."

She went unerringly to the door she'd found earlier, an invisible commodity only for her, and heard Rorkin's chair legs thump back down on the floor.

"Hey!" he said. "You haven't given me a door!"

"No," Annabel said seriously. "And I'm not going to give you one. Not yet, anyway. I don't want you running about the castle when still I don't know exactly what you're up to."

"Don't want to run about the castle anyway," muttered Rorkin. "It's a bit late for that sort of thing when Mordion has taken over nearly the whole castle."

"Then why are you whining?"

"I like to have the option. Also, it's very insulting of you not to trust me. What if I need to escape in a hurry?"

"Then you should be more open," Annabel said. "You've talked and talked and you haven't really said very much."

"Said a lot more than I meant to," Rorkin offered, "if that helps."

"It doesn't," Annabel said, but there was a slight warmth to the words, anyway. "I'll come back and see you later, when I've sorted out a few things."

"Don't forget to let me out. You don't know what I'll do to the furniture if I'm cooped up in here for too long."

"We'll see."

Rorkin, his eyes bright and inquisitive, asked: "Are you going to tell the boy and the not-cat about me?"

"I don't know," said Annabel, with her hand around the knob. The truth was that she did know: she wouldn't tell the others about Rorkin. There was too much that she wasn't sure of at the moment. She didn't know how much Blackfoot had known when he chivvied her into the castle—or how much he'd known when he wriggled his way into her life, for that matter—and she didn't know how Peter would react to a stimulus like Rorkin. For the first, she was quite sure she wanted answers before she told Blackfoot *anything*, and for the second, Annabel was just as sure that she wanted to know a little more about Rorkin before she let Peter and his rather reckless love for anything twistily magical have access to Rorkin.

"I see," said Rorkin, and Annabel had the feeling that he did see. "Don't waste too much time, will you? I don't think there's too much of it left now."

Thirteen

"There you are!"

Annabel jumped guiltily. Peter was leaning against the middle one of three archways just ahead of her: if he'd been just a little further on, in the one she just passed through, he would have seen her exit Rorkin's quarters. That left her feeling more than slightly startled, and she said hastily: "What are you doing wandering around the castle by yourself?"

One of Peter's brows rose. "Really?"

"*I'm* not the one who disappeared without a trace," said Annabel. "*I'm* not the one who had to be rescued."

"I can tell which archways are dangerous and which ones aren't," Peter said. "Come along. You'd better stay with me."

Annabel gave him a hard look. "You first."

"What are you talking about?"

"Come through the archway."

Impatiently, Peter said: "Why should I? I'll only have to walk back through it again."

"That sounded a bit more like Peter," Annabel told him.

"But you're doing the wrong things with your face, and Peter would have been much ruder. He's fond of me, but he doesn't like to say so aloud."

"Is that so? I don't suppose you'd like to mention what it was about my face that gave it away?"

"No," said Annabel, who had seen that eyebrow lift several times on Mordion. Peter could wriggle his ears, but he couldn't lift one brow without the other. "Why should I help you?"

"Very well," said Mordion, the Peter-façade fading away into his own lean, beautiful figure. "Your friend may yet be sorry that you were so perspicacious."

"Peter? Why should Peter be sorry? What do you mean?"

"Why should I help you?" Mordion flashed her a dazzling smile and turned elegantly, disappearing from sight long before it was logically possible. Annabel was left staring through an archway to the empty hall beyond, hesitant to travel on any further now that a previously safe hall was now Mordion's.

She might have taken her pencil out of the satchel and tried to draw herself a new door if she hadn't heard Peter's voice the next moment, coming from another of the halls.

"I don't see why I should be chivvied out into the castle," it said crossly. "I'm busy trying to make sure that my mother is all right without me, and I have things to prepare. Ow! If you bite me just *one* more time, I'm going to kick you through the window, Ann or no Ann!"

"Peter!" called Annabel joyfully.

There was a brief silence before Peter's voice said: "Ann?"

"I'm over here! I can't go through the archways because I don't know which one is safe and Mordion was already wearing your face."

A streak of black darted through the archway to the right

of the one Mordion had disappeared down, and sprang to Annabel's shoulder.

Nan, you dreadful child! Why must you be wandering the castle when Mordion is looking for you?

"Why not?" Annabel said coolly. "You were. Besides, there are that many tunnels around the castle that I could have escaped into one of them if I ran into trouble."

*There aren't as many as **that** around,* said Blackfoot in annoyance.

At the same time, Peter said: "He was wearing my face? What does that mean?"

"It means he looked just like you. What are you doing out here?"

"Your cat wouldn't leave me alone until we came and found you. Oh well, I wanted to see some of the tunnels anyway. You'll have to tell me more about them, though, Ann: I haven't seen a single one around the castle. I had a look around while we were searching for you, and the only thing in the castle that isn't actual *castle* is the shifted temporal remnant that you've shut in behind those walls."

"Funny," Annabel said. "There's always one around when it's convenient."

"Maybe your pencil is doing that, too."

"It's not. Blackfoot, you're scratching me."

"Oh, and that reminds me!" Peter said, his voice injured. "Tell your cat not to bite me! I could catch anything from his teeth!"

Tell your irritating little friend that if he leaves you to wander the castle by yourself again, I'll do worse than bite him.

"Blackfoot thinks you're lacking in chivalry."

"Well, I like that!" Peter said indignantly. "I rescued you, didn't I?"

"No," Annabel retorted. "You didn't, actually. I rescued myself, and I sent Mordion packing just before you got here, too. He didn't get your face quite right. Oh, and he threatened to do something to you."

"Really? What?"

Annabel shrugged. "Don't know. He was smiling, though, so be careful."

"I'm always careful," said Peter, with greater confidence than accuracy. "I'd like to see someone like Mordion get the better of me! Anyway, I'm going to be busy today, so I won't be wandering the castle at all."

Nan, please tell this young idiot that he shouldn't be trying to piggyback his spells on the castle again while Mordion has so much control.

"Are you going to run a Look-See spell again?"

Peter tried to look airily unconcerned, and failed. "Don't be so serious, Ann! I know what I'm doing. I just want to make sure mum's safe, and let her know we're safe. I've spent the whole morning setting it up while you and your cat were off in the castle, and I think I've got it pretty much right."

"You shouldn't do that. What if Mordion sees it and goes back to get her so that he can use her to bring us through to his bit of the castle?"

"Do we know if he can still get out? He seems pretty connected to the castle."

Annabel looked at Blackfoot, and Blackfoot looked at Annabel. She was quite sure, after talking with Rorkin, that Mordion couldn't get back out of the castle: but that wasn't something that Blackfoot would expect her to know. While she could blame Blackfoot for extra knowledge to Peter, she couldn't do the same about Peter to Blackfoot.

I've no idea, said Blackfoot. *I was convinced that it wasn't possible for him to be in the castle at all, so I shouldn't speculate.*

"Yes, yes," interrupted Annabel, "but I know you want to speculate anyway, so what do you think?"

However, Blackfoot continued, **however**, *considering the amount of control that Mordion now has over the castle, it seems likely that he has bound himself to it. He always was a particularly sticky leech, so I can only assume that he has managed to convince it that he's its master, and that he's now availing himself of its not inconsiderable power.*

"Blackfoot thinks Mordion has sort of wired himself into the castle," said Annabel to Peter, who had been waiting impatiently through the exchange. She found herself wondering again just how much Blackfoot knew, and how much he was genuinely guessing. "He thinks that Mordion has tricked it into thinking he's its master."

Peter nodded thoughtfully. "That makes sense. If he's bound himself to the castle, he probably can't get out. Good! I don't want to give Mordion any ideas, but it's nice to know he couldn't act on 'em even if he did get them."

It's not just that it's a bad idea, Blackfoot said, kneading Annabel's shoulder with his claws. *It's that it's a ridiculously bad idea based on the hopelessly conceited notion that he's Mordion's equal. I should be surprised if he thinks he's Mordion's better, if it comes to that.*

"Don't run spells through the castle, Peter," Annabel said wearily. "You always think you're *so* clever– well, you are, but you're not as clever as you think you are."

"I want to see my mother," objected Peter. "Why shouldn't I? I just want to know that she's safe."

"Blackfoot doesn't think it's a good idea."

"Ann, if you don't think it's a good idea, *tell* me so instead of blaming it on the cat! You're too old to be still blaming things on your imaginary friend!"

"Blackfoot isn't imaginary!" Annabel said, in exasperation. "And if it comes to that, I just *told* you I don't think it's a good idea! Mordion has a lot more control of the castle than he had even yesterday, and he's powerful enough to look exactly like you, so I suppose he can do a lot more than he could before, too. He doesn't seem to be able to get to our part yet, but he's got more of the doorways now."

"Yes, but I won't be *using* the doorways!" Peter complained. "I'll be using the windows! And if it comes to that, I'm quite sneaky enough to be sliding targeted spells in underneath his notice!"

"But–"

"Besides, it's already ready, so it'd be a waste not to use it," finished Peter triumphantly. "Don't go through that hallway, Ann: it's one of his."

Annabel stopped short. "How do you know?"

"Don't know: it's sort of obvious," said Peter, marching away to a corridor of his own choice. Over his shoulder, he called airily: "It's hard to explain to someone who doesn't have magic."

What he means by that, Nan, is that he obviously knows better than you, and that he'll do his spell regardless of either you or me. It's not quite so complicated as that: the ones that Mordion has control of smell like him.

"They *smell* like him?"

Look like him. Feel like him. It's the same way I can look at a drawing and tell if it was drawn by yourself or Peter.

Annabel sniffed. "That's *easy*."

Exactly. We should catch up with this young idiot before he comes to grief.

By the time they caught up with Peter, he was already in the side courtyard by the kitchen, polishing the glass of a free-standing mirror. Before Annabel could remonstrate with him again, he said: "Of course, it won't have the depth of a window, but I only want a quick peek, so it shouldn't matter if the image is a bit flat."

Annabel glared at him. "That wasn't what I was going to say."

"I don't see why you're getting so precious about it. You're always doing things your cat doesn't want you to do."

"You don't even think he–"

"Anyway, it's too late," said Peter, with a rather guilty grin. "I started it when I got down here, so it's looking for her at the moment."

"Peter!"

"I *am* sorry, Ann. But I didn't get to make sure she was safe that night, and I don't know how long it'll be before I see her again. She must be half-mad with worry by now."

I doubt she'll return the favour by being glad to see him, Blackfoot said rather sourly. *She was probably glad to be rid of him.*

"No, she's very patient," Annabel said, just as the mirror began to come into focus.

"Mother!" said Peter in surprise. Annabel recognised the plump figure that was framed by sparkling glass: it was the right figure, but it was on the wrong background. There was a castle wall behind her instead of the gently floral walls of Peter's house. "This– did I do it wrong? I'm sure I didn't. Ann, did your cat do something?"

I have no part in this, said Blackfoot. *Don't blame me if the castle has been taking liberties with your spells.*

"Peter," said Annabel, her voice very small, because she had noticed something else that wasn't quite right: "why is your mother tied up?"

"Tied– what are you talking about?" Peter took a step closer to the window, and Annabel was sure he saw the same stiffness to his mother's position as she had just seen. He said uncertainly: "She's just– she's just sitting down."

"Then why is she sitting down in the castle!"

Nan, tell him to stop the spell, said Blackfoot sharply. *Now!*

"Oh, I'm afraid not," said a pleasant voice, and Mordion strolled into the frame of the mirror. "She's not tied up," said Mordion, still in that pleasant voice. "Not exactly. Allow me to adjust your spell slightly. I'm certain you can't see very well. There! You should be able to see much better now: I wouldn't want you to miss a moment."

The view twitched and scoped inward, closer to Peter's mother. Her eyes were wide and afraid, and she sat very still. Beside her was Peter's stepfather, Brannen, who sat just as still as she did. Neither of them spoke a word, and Annabel wondered fleetingly if they could even see Peter and herself.

"I would like you both," Mordion said, smiling, "to be quite aware of the seriousness of this situation. I would also like for you both to be quite certain that I mean what I say."

Annabel, who had already seen what Mordion was capable of, and who had a rather horrible idea of what he meant, swallowed, and said: "What do you mean?"

"This," said Mordion, and carelessly shoved in the centre of Brannen's forehead with two fingers. Brannen's head snapped back, the whites of his eyes showing, then dropped and didn't move again.

Peter's mother, her eyes steadfastly forward, began to cry without a sound. Annabel gripped her pencil so tightly that it would have snapped if it had been a normal pencil, but there was a swirling kind of roar in her mind. It was one thing to draw Peter back and draw Rorkin into a room: what was she supposed to do here? What could she do? It was already too late for Peter's stepfather.

"Leave my mother alone," said Peter. His voice still held all its usual command, but Annabel heard the raw edge beneath it, and as much as she worried for Peter did she worry about what his tone would egg Mordion on to do.

She said quietly: "You didn't have to kill him."

"Now, darling, I *did* warn you. I don't like this kind of unpleasantness, but sometimes I find it necessary."

"What do you want?"

"I should have thought that was quite obvious. Unless you're both through the closest doorway in the next two minutes, I'm going to kill Peter's mother."

"If you *touch* my mother–"

"If I touch her, she'll die," said Mordion. "You saw what happened to *him*: the castle is a wonderful power source for me. You really should have thought better before trying to run a spell off my power source. I don't particularly like sharing, Peter Carlisle."

Annabel curled her fingers even more tightly around the pencil. "What do you want Peter for? You only need me."

Nan. Nan, **please** *don't start acting out your unthinking altruism again.*

"I believe you're confusing the utensil with the food, darling," Mordion said gently. "I need both. You're a very useful little siphon, but one must siphon *something*, after all."

"I see," said Annabel, and her eyes met Mordion's for a cold, bright moment.

The mirror went blank. It was only for the slightest moment, but in that moment, Annabel heard Peter sob.

When it came back, Mordion was smiling pleasantly at them both.

"Time's up," he said. "Are you coming through?"

"I'm coming," said Peter hurriedly. "I'm coming, I'm coming!"

Annabel didn't recognise her own voice when it said: "No, you're not."

Peter looked at her rather wildly. "Ann? What– we have to go."

"No," said Annabel again. Was that really her voice, so cold and authoritative? "He'll drain you and kill you, and he'll do it by using me."

"I don't *care!*"

"I do. Your mother would." The problem with the castle being so very finished now, thought Annabel, her ideas bright and sharp-edged, was that there was nothing to pick up and throw. So instead of throwing something at it, Annabel kicked the mirror, shattering the glass and the spell at once.

Peter's eyes, wide and horrified, fixed on her face. "What did you do? Ann, *what did you do?*"

"You can't go through to him," Annabel said. "I'm sorry."

"That's rather unfortunate," Mordion's voice said. He was there in the kitchen window, a strained and almost transparent vision, and Peter's mother was there, too. "What shall I do, I wonder? Perhaps I shall be merciful. I've made a door here: it's unstable and I don't think it will last very long, so you'd best go through it before it closes. Do that, and I won't harm your mother."

"I'm coming," Peter said again, and this time Annabel didn't waste time contradicting him. She simply seized the collar of his shirt in both hands and hauled him backwards with her, away from that door that smelled, or looked, or felt like Mordion, but looked no different to her. Peter struggled and yelled and cried, but she grasped his collar just the same, resisting his surges forward until they fell over in a tangle of scraped arms and legs.

"What a shame!" sighed Mordion. Annabel couldn't see it, but she heard Peter sob, and she was dimly aware that the doorway must have closed again.

"Please," said Peter, and he didn't try to stop the tears. "Please don't."

"If I did that, now," said Mordion gently, "I'd lose something of my credibility, wouldn't I? I don't like to lose face any more than you like to lose face, Peter Carlisle."

This time it was just his index finger that touched Peter's mother: lightly, in the centre of her forehead. Her head dropped just as Brannen's had, but not before Annabel saw her eyes roll back. Then the window glittered once, and became just a window again, slightly reflective and not so clean as it had looked a moment before.

Peter was screaming hoarsely, tears streaming from his eyes, and Annabel, who didn't dare to let him go just yet, thought he was shouting: "Why wouldn't you let go, Ann! You should have let me go! She's dead! *Dead*!"

"I know," Annabel said, still clinging grimly to the back of Peter's collar. She settled into her familiarly fat and oblivious other self, impervious to Peter's struggling and bawled commands alike. Like a doughy sort of anchor, she stuck to the ground, and to him. "And you're not going to be if I can help it."

"Then why did you let the cat in?" howled Peter. "Why—why didn't you and Grenna keep all the mess down at the cottage? Why didn't you die instead?"

"Don't know," said Annabel, her face blank and stupid.

She let herself sink so deeply into that blobby imperviousness that her neck almost disappeared into her shoulders. "Sorry."

"Get off!" snarled Peter, his face flushed and streaked with tears. "Get *off*, Ann!"

"All right," said Annabel, without moving. Peter was like a wounded animal when he was hurt: he would bite and snarl and scratch, but so long as she held on for long enough and didn't mind the blood, and so long as her skin was thick enough, nothing would penetrate it deeply enough to really hurt. Like Grenna's kicks on her well-padded body, Peter's sharp hurt would only go surface-deep.

She held on to Peter until he stopped sobbing and until the only sound he made was a snuffling of breath in and out. Then she let go of his collar, and Peter flung himself away from her, scrambling to his feet. He didn't look at her, just stood where he was with his back to her, trembling, then started across the courtyard for the kitchen door.

Annabel caught up with him at the door, more because he had stopped there than because she had been very swift to move.

"It's no good going in there," she said. "She's– she's already dead."

"I know."

"And it's no good going after Mordion, either."

"I know."

"Because he's a lot stronger than you now."

"I *know*. I saw."

"But we might be able to get out." An idea had stuck fast in her mind: an idea that said if the tunnels weren't the doing of the castle, or of Mordion, or Rorkin, perhaps they were a different thing altogether. And perhaps a different thing altogether was what they needed to get out of the castle. "We need to find another one of those tunnels. Now that I know about the pencil, maybe I can make sure we get all the way out."

Annabel almost felt the gust of relief that came with the exhale in Blackfoot's inaudible voice. *At last,* he said. *Drag him with you if you must, Nan: we'll find a tunnel and be done with this place.*

"Not yet," said Peter, rousing himself. His face was still red and wet, and he wasn't quite steady on his feet, but he kept walking anyway. To Annabel's dismay, he was walking back into the castle.

"Peter."

Peter, his back stiff, didn't stop walking.

"*Peter.*"

Let him go, Nan.

Used to ceding to Blackfoot's better authority, or blindly following her own preferences without thought, Annabel found herself, for the first time, consciously considering both decisions. She considered them, then went with her own decision. To Blackfoot, she said: "We need to follow him. He's just upset because of his mother."

Of course he is. That's natural.

"No, I mean he's upset because he thinks it's his fault: you know, for not listening to us before. But he doesn't want to believe that, so he's just going to keep pushing and doing things this way because it has to be the right way to do things, or it's all his fault."

There are other ways of looking after the child than following him willy-nilly into danger, protested Blackfoot.

"I can't stop him if I'm not there," panted Annabel, stomping heavily up the stairs after Peter.

Peter's shoulders stiffened when she caught up with him on

the stairway that led to the lower rooms. "Leave me alone, Ann."

Annabel, trotting faster than was comfortable, gasped, "If you keep walking, I'm going to throw something at you."

"Leave me *alone*, Ann! My mother is *dead*."

"That's why," Annabel said. "That's why you have to stop and think about what you're doing. Because Mordion killed your mother, and how else are you going to do something about it? How are you going to stop him like this?"

"How?" Peter stopped at last. "I'll go through one of his doorways. We'll see who wins when it's me against him, face to face."

"Yes, we will," said Annabel, hauling on her girdle. She could feel the burn of her lungs. "And then Blackfoot and I will have to fight off Mordion while he uses your magic to come after us."

"What–" Peter's tone was a mix of incredulity and outrage. "What do you mean, when he comes after you? Why would he win?"

Because Mordion has made stealing magic a way of life, said Blackfoot. *And because he's roughly three hundred years older than either of you.*

"That's right," Annabel agreed. "He's older and sneakier, and nastier."

"All *right*, I won't!"

"Good, because you wouldn't w–"

"I said I won't! We'll just run away, then!"

Running away is a very sensible option, said Blackfoot. *And I would like you to consider, Nan, with your newfound maturity, that the feeling you're indulging toward Peter—the one that's telling you to get him out of the castle at all costs—is the same one*

I would very much like to indulge toward you. Unfortunately, it seems that I can't do so without your permission.

Annabel pulled in one, big breath, and let it out. "All right," she said.

I would be relived if I thought that was directed at myself, Blackfoot said, rather grittily.

"I'm *sorry*," Annabel said. It was strange how different it made her feel, being told that she was the Queen heir. As much as she didn't want to be the heir, for a range of reasons that were as varied as some of them were ridiculous, she could already feel the weight of it. It was a weight that told her Peter and Blackfoot were no longer just friends, but subjects to be protected– from themselves if necessary, and from all other comers at any cost. "I'm sorry, Peter. I'm sorry I couldn't protect your mother as well."

"You can't protect anyone," Peter said. "You don't have magic, and you can't even climb a flight of stairs without losing your breath."

"I know," said Annabel. "But I can kill Mordion."

Peter stopped in his tracks, so suddenly that Annabel walked into him. He hunched away from her, still too hurt and angry to react in any other way, and Annabel backed away.

"You can kill him? How?"

"Never you mind," said Annabel, who had the smallest sprouting of an idea that needed much more time to grow before it withstood the scorching light of Peter's scorn. "You have to promise that you're not going to go after him by yourself, though. Not at least until tomorrow."

"You can really kill him?"

"Yes. Promise me."

"All right, all right! I promise. I won't try to go after him until tomorrow. But what are you–"

"Never you mind," Annabel said again.

Peter, more suspiciously, said: "If you can kill him, why not draw him back now?"

"Can't," Annabel said. "Not yet, anyway."

"Why not?" argued Peter. "You did it with me."

"Yes, but it's *different*. There are things that I need to have ready before we try anything. He's dangerous, and if I draw him back into the here and now without being ready for him–"

"*I'll* look after him. You just stay behind me."

"What rubbish," said Annabel, well aware that Peter needed to be shoved out of his unthinking misery. "You're just annoyed that you can't do the drawing back. There's need to pretend you can out-magic anyone and everyone."

"I'm not pretending!"

"Then there's something wrong with your head. Mordion has the power of the whole castle behind him now: do you really think that's not going to be a match for you?"

If it came to that, Annabel knew it wasn't just the power of the castle that Mordion had going for him: it was Rorkin's power as well. If Rorkin was bound to the castle and Mordion was feeding off the castle, then he would also be feeding off Rorkin.

"Well," Peter muttered, "we don't know, do we?"

"You *promised*, Peter."

"All right, all right! I won't do anything until tomorrow! I don't expect you to be here, Ann. I'll make sure you're safe. I won't make the same mistake again, I promise you. I'll be ready for him this time."

FOURTEEN

It was sometimes difficult to remember how young Peter was. He was always so sure of himself, always so solid and unshakeable, that Annabel quite often forgot he was younger than she was. There were very few times during their friendship that Peter had been anything less than bossy and self-assured: in fact, Annabel could only distinctly remember two of them. The first had been when one of his spells went horribly wrong and his dog died. Annabel had stayed out of the cottage for the first time in her life, while Peter cried, clung around her neck, and bitterly repulsed any attempts she made to talk to or reason with him. She didn't leave him until he'd reasoned himself out of his instinctive clinging, and although Grenna beat her for staying out in those days, Annabel was well-padded enough to bear the hits. She knew that she would have gone through worse to stay there with Peter.

The second time was that night: the night after Peter saw his mother die. He cried bitterly at first, but worried Annabel more by the silent sleeplessness that came upon him afterward.

His eyes, wide and red-rimmed, were luminous with tears in the moonlight, and Annabel wasn't sure that she saw him blink. In this mood, he was very capable of getting up and going in search of Mordion. It wasn't until Annabel, made restless by that thought, tried to get up and draw all of the exits shut, that Peter threw his arms around her neck and said: "Don't go, Ann! You can't– you can't die."

"All right," said Annabel soothingly, settling back down again. "It's all right, I'm not going anywhere. I was just going to make sure all the doors were safe."

"Don't go, Ann."

"I'm not. I'm not going."

"If you die too–"

"I won't."

"You can't leave."

"I won't."

But it wasn't until Annabel said, very carefully, "I promise I won't go through any of these door without you," that Peter closed his eyes and went to sleep.

The morning came slowly, stifling and heavy in its sense of menace. Peter was still clinging tightly around Annabel's neck when she woke from a short, shallow sleep, and though she couldn't sense or see magic, the castle was feeling especially perilous around her. Annabel stared at the grand ceiling of the throne room for some time, almost determined on drawing Rorkin back into the castle properly, but found that she couldn't do it. Not when Mordion was doing so much harm around the castle. If Rorkin was lying, two wizards running around the castle would be far more dangerous than one: if he was telling the truth, it was very likely that Mordion would kill him. Annabel was quite sure that as much as the walls she had drawn around Rorkin prevented him from escaping, just so much did they stop Mordion from getting to Rorkin.

Peter was sleeping deeply still, but when she tried to get up he held her tighter and complained in a sleep-fogged voice: "No! You promised!"

"I know," Annabel murmured, extricating herself as gently as possible. "I promised. I won't go through those doors without you."

Peter's face crumpled in his sleep, but although he whimpered and curled around Blackfoot instead of Annabel, he didn't wake up. Much to Annabel's relief, neither did Blackfoot.

"You're getting old," she told him softly, gathering her skirts around her so that she wouldn't rustle too much. "You've been sleeping in the warmth for so long that you've gotten soft."

True to her word, Annabel didn't try to leave by any of the doors in the throne room. Instead, she drew a quick sketch of the throne room and added a small, faint door behind one of the decorative pillars. She had to flip between that sketch and her original sketch of Rorkin's quarters to make sure she'd drawn it correctly with all its cheerful patterns, but when it was done she was quite certain that it would lead exactly where she meant it to lead.

When it was done, Annabel closed her fat, scribbled-over sketchbook and put it carefully in her satchel with the pencil. Then she threw one last look over at Blackfoot and Peter and opened her newly-drawn door right into Rorkin's quarters.

"Oh, hallo," said Rorkin's voice listlessly.

"Hallo," Annabel said, looking around the room with a frown. "What happened here?"

If the room had been ridiculously cluttered yesterday with

knick-knacks and odds and ends on every surface, and cobwebs and dust on *those*, it was now conspicuously bare. The easy-chair, desk, and chair were still there, but everything else was gone, and even the furniture had a scrubbed look about it, as if it had been drawn with single, bare strokes of the pencil.

Rorkin, who was sitting in a depressed sort of heap on the floorboards instead of in one of the chairs, looked up fiercely. "What happened? Calamity! Infringement on my personal space! *I have no socks.*"

"You mean Mordion has siphoned off a bit more power from you?"

"They were nice socks, too," Rorkin said sadly. "Now when my toes wriggle, I feel a draft."

Annabel sighed. "I can draw more socks for you. That's not important."

"It's not important until you've got a draft around the toes. Then you understand."

"How much more of the castle does Mordion have today?"

"Everything but the windows and a few doors," said Rorkin, pleasingly prompt. "What are you going to do about it?"

"I don't know yet," Annabel said. "I have a little bit of an idea, but it's too small to be any good at the moment. And if Mordion is going to be taking over the castle so quickly, I won't have enough time to make it any bigger."

"You need time? I could probably get you some, but it wouldn't do you much good, and it's awfully hard to get out of your hair if you get it stuck."

Annabel, ignoring this as incomprehensible, asked: "How long will it be before Mordion has control of the whole castle?"

"A day or two, I expect," said Rorkin.

"What will happen then?"

"Then he'll have access to everything and everyone."

"So if we haven't found a way to stop him within a day or two, there's no hope?"

"There's a way," said Rorkin. His eyebrow wasn't twitching, which was a good sign, but Annabel didn't like the apologetic way he was looking at her.

"What way?"

"Your pencil—the staff—it can draw a door out of the castle."

Annabel scrabbled for her pencil. "Why didn't you tell me this before? I could have taken us all out of the castle before Mordion killed Peter's mother!"

"Killed his mother? Nonsense. Even Mordion can't interfere with certain threads in the time-line. He should know: he's tried often enough."

"I saw it!"

"*Told* you about seeing things," pointed out Rorkin. "You're going to have to learn to listen, your highness."

Wavering between two questions that had to be asked, Annabel finally chose the less confusing option, and asked: "What do you mean, I can draw a door out? We could have been out of the castle a long time ago?"

"You could," Rorkin said. "That's the problem. You can draw a door, but it will only work for you."

"*Only* for me?"

"You alone. Singly. With no other."

"Why?"

Rorkin shrugged. "It's one of the castle's failsafes. The point is that you could get out by yourself. Safe. Whole. In one piece. From there, you could try to find a way to help your friends."

"What if I didn't find a way? What good would it do to

have me on the outside?"

"You wouldn't be dead. That's an advantage."

"Don't be stupid," Annabel said angrily. "I couldn't leave Blackfoot and Peter in here by themselves!"

"*Wouldn't*, not couldn't," said Rorkin. "All right. No need to be shrill about it. Then what will you do?"

"Something," said Annabel. "But not yet, because I have to make sure they're safe, first. Is Mordion really connected to the castle?"

"Like a limpet to a log!" Rorkin said promptly.

"Limpets don't cling to logs."

"Him to the castle, the castle to him: there isn't a lot of difference any more. You couldn't get him free if you were to poke him with a prybar."

"Good," said Annabel.

Rorkin looked doubtful. "I suppose you know what you're talking about, but it seems like the opposite of good to me."

"Yes, that's why I wasn't sure at first. I'll have to think about it again, just to be certain."

"Thinking is a good habit to get into," agreed Rorkin. "Oh, are you going now?"

"Yes," said Annabel again. "I just wanted to be certain of a few things. Look, I've drawn you some more socks: they're on the table. Don't let Mordion get them."

She left Rorkin chuckling contentedly to himself with his new socks, and carefully let herself back into the throne room. Peter and Blackfoot were both still asleep, so Annabel sat down on the throne by way of a change, and thought.

By the time Blackfoot began to stir, waking Peter with him, Annabel's backside was sore and there was a warm red mark beneath her chin where she had leaned it on her fists.

"We'll have to get a cushion for this," she muttered.

"Ann," mumbled Peter, looking around a little wildly as he woke. When he saw her, his face lost something of its wildness and grew almost vulnerable for the briefest moment. It was only for a moment: the next it was as hard as Annabel had ever seen it. "There you are," he said. "I hope you've got your plan sorted out."

"Mostly," Annabel said. "Do you still want to kill Mordion?"

"If you won't do it, I will."

"All right," she said. "You promised–"

"I promised not to do anything until today. What are you going to do?"

"I need you to start up a spell for me in one of the lower rooms."

Peter's eyes regarded her coldly. "What spell? And why the lower rooms?"

"It's closer to the black squishy stuff," Annabel said, and tried to look mysterious.

"Why does that– oh, never mind. All right, let's get started, then."

Nan, said Blackfoot curiously, *what exactly are you up to?*

"We're going to get rid of Mordion," said Annabel. "Peter, you'll have to lead the way so we don't walk through any wrong doors. Take us as low as we can safely go: somewhere that was already here before I started drawing."

*I understand that. How are you **planning** on getting rid of him?*

"You'll see," Annabel told him, grateful for the first time that Peter and Blackfoot couldn't communicate. Peter could be just as sharp and short with her as it pleased him to pretend to be: she wasn't taken in. He was fully as determined to make sure that Annabel didn't die as Annabel was to make sure *he* didn't die. She was quite certain that he was planning on a spell of some sort to keep her out of the way while he went looking for Mordion, and if he and Blackfoot had been able to talk, she was likewise sure that they would have been planning together.

The thing was, thought Annabel, her fingers wrapping tightly around her pencil, to make sure she was just a little bit quicker than Peter. Blackfoot was another matter entirely.

Nan, I won't be put off. How exactly do you plan on getting rid of Mordion? It may seem like a simple thing to you, but I assure you that Mordion has been the end of many a better prepared and stronger opponent than yourself.

Without answering him, Annabel said to Peter: "Make sure you don't get us to any rooms with snake-locks, this time."

"I won't," Peter said, and though his voice only sounded irritated, Annabel couldn't feel comfortable about him. He was holding together rather better than she'd expected, but she didn't dare to tell him that she thought his mother might be alive, even if she thought so. Peter had a tendency to look and speak as though he were perfectly fine, right up until the moment that he collapsed. Like his sharp tongue, it was a mechanism that kept people as far away from him as Annabel's blank face did from her.

NAN.

"Ow," Annabel said, rubbing her ears.

Blackfoot hissed. *I refuse to be ignored!*

"Stop shouting," she muttered at him.

Peter, for once ignoring her asides to Blackfoot, led them through a doorway and down a spiral stairway that hadn't been there the first time they travelled this way. There were three archways at the bottom of it, and after a brief glance at all three, he took the left-hand archway.

"Don't touch the edges," he said over his shoulder. "I think

Mordion's trying to get to it, and he'll probably know where we are if you do."

"Ugh," said Annabel, and huddled her arms around herself. "Ow! Blackfoot! Don't bite me!"

"What's wrong with your cat this morning, Ann?"

"He doesn't like being ignored."

"Oh. Look, will this do?"

"Where are we?"

"Beneath the throne room, I expect," said Peter, shrugging. "I wasn't paying much attention. Why can't you pay more attention? I shouldn't have to do everything for you."

"Is the doorway safe?"

"I should think so," Peter said, looking critically at it. "Unless it falls down from old age. I thought you drew all this back?"

"I did, but I think it was already old. Can you make sure you check that there's no other magic in the room? This room will only work if there's nothing magical about it."

That makes no sense, Blackfoot said in annoyance, stalking into the room after Peter. Annabel felt a small smile curl the edges of her mouth: he had obviously decided that if she wasn't going to tell him anything, he was going to figure it out for himself.

"Nothing that I can see," said Peter, making a quick circuit of the room. "It's safe to come in, Ann."

But Annabel, her pencil in hand and her sketchbook open, was already erasing the door from the inside of the room, and drawing the wall back smoothly where it had been. For a moment she looked at the blank wall in front of her, and there was silence.

"Ann?" That was Peter's voice, sharp and cracking. "Ann, what have you done?"

Annabel sat by the door that no longer opened on the inside and wrapped her arms around her knees. "I've drawn you in."

"You can't– Ann, you can't *do* that! We were going to– we have to get to Mordion!"

"I'll look after Mordion. It's just that it's not very safe."

Nan, let us out at once!

"You can't do that!"

"Blackfoot," called Annabel, "what spell has Peter been running for the last few minutes?"

"Ann–"

Something quiet and sleepy, came Blackfoot's voice. *Something that would have put you to sleep very nicely.*

"Blackfoot says you were trying to put me to sleep."

"Ann, you can't go up there by yourself! What if you go through the wrong doorway?"

"I'll go back the way we came down. Don't worry, Peter."

For the second time in as many days, Annabel heard Peter sob. This one, she was rather sure, was as angry as it was forlorn.

"Ann, don't you dare leave me in here with your cat!"

"I promise," said Annabel, "I promise I won't die."

"You can't promise that!"

"Neither can you, and I've got a better chance than you."

That's no reason to go after Mordion by yourself, Nan!

"It's not the only reason," Annabel said, but she said it quietly.

"Just let us out, Ann. We'll go after Mordion together: open one of the doors into the place where he's hiding. I won't go after him alone, I promise!"

"It's no use your doing that, anyway," said Annabel. "You

can't beat Mordion like that. Actually, you can't beat him at all. You can't–"

His voice thick with grief and frustration, Peter snarled: "I know, I know! you're the only one who can beat him!"

"That's right," said Annabel. "So you need to stay here, nice and safe."

"I don't want to be safe, Ann! You can't run off to fight Mordion without magic, you know!"

"I can, actually. Well, I won't be without magic: I have the pencil."

"You don't even know how it works!"

"No," agreed Annabel, "but I've got a good idea, and I can't look after you both if you're there, so you have to stay here."

Nan, let me go at once!

"No," said Annabel. "I told you: you can't come with me. I don't know how to look after you."

There was a wordless howl around the edges of her mind that sounded like *Not again!* before Blackfoot said icily: *If even the boy thinks it's a bad idea for you to go alone, it's time to rethink your opinion.*

"I've already rethought it," said Annabel. "And every time I think about it, it comes out the same way. I know—I *think* I know—how to beat Mordion, but I don't know how to keep you safe, and if he takes you and your magic as well–"

That's not your decision to make, Blackfoot hissed.

"It is my decision, you know," Annabel said.

"Your decision?" Peter spluttered. "What rubbish!"

Blackfoot, more sedately, said coldly, *How so?*

"Oh, that." Annabel cleared her throat. Awkwardly, she added: "I'm the heir. You know, the one the castle is looking for?"

There was a very distinct silence from Blackfoot, but Peter gave a rude snort of laughter. "As if we didn't know that!"

"What? How did you know?"

"How do you *not* know?" Peter said in disgust. "Ann, do you even pay attention at school? The castle has been coming back ever since we got here, and it never occurred to you?"

"Anyway, that's why," Annabel said. "It's my decision, and I'm not going to let you out, so you might as well stop trying to get out."

There was another brief silence before Peter said cautiously: "How did you know I'm trying to get out?"

It doesn't take a great deal of mental ability to know that.

"What else would you be doing?" Annabel said, more kindly. She had expected Peter to use his formidable powers of magic to get out of the room: it was why she was now drawing walls around it just as she'd done to the black squishy stuff, and leaving the edges of the paper blank. Mordion was going to be just a little bit too busy to be sniffing around the room, after all.

"Yes, but why should you go alone, Ann? I know it's not much good my going by myself, but won't it be better if we all go? I might not be able to beat Mordion, but I'll be able to singe his eyebrows a bit, after all."

"Maybe, but he'd probably do more than singe your eyebrows after that. It's no good arguing, Peter. I'm not going to let you out. And– and I'm going away now, so it's no use arguing. I won't be able to hear you."

She left them both behind, Peter yelling at the wall and Blackfoot howling in the back of her mind, and went back through the castle alone. Peter's shouts faded from earshot first, and her footsteps echo more loudly against the castle walls than she was used to hearing. When Blackfoot's voice also began to wane, the silence in her mind echoed even more loudly than her footsteps, and Annabel was glad to come out into the sunny courtyard through the throne room. When she reached it, she sat in the sun for a little while with her pencil and notebook still clutched to her chest. It was no good starting just now: she would have to wait until tomorrow, when Rorkin had said that Mordion would have control of the entire castle. So Annabel sat in the courtyard, plump and silent and sturdy, and waited.

The next morning broke early and cold. Annabel didn't mind: it meant that she had a reason for the shivers that wouldn't stop, although she was quite certain of her plan. It was an odd feeling, being so absolutely certain of herself. Spending so much time with Peter, Annabel had naturally grown used to being often contradicted, and almost as often, proved wrong. It hadn't made her any less sure of her opinions than she had been by nature, but it had made her less precious about them.

Peter couldn't argue this time, of course, but even if he had been able to argue until he was blue in the face, Annabel knew she wouldn't have faltered. If Rorkin had made himself so much a part of the castle that anything affecting it affected him, then Mordion, in taking over the castle, had made the same mistake. Rorkin had given her the answer, even if he'd done it accidentally: erasing the castle was the only way that Mordion could be defeated. Like Rorkin, Mordion had committed too much of himself to the castle, and while it gave him a great deal of power, it was also his weakness.

Annabel didn't eat breakfast that morning. She was too busy thinking about what she had to do, and what the consequences of it would be. The biggest consequence of erasing the castle was Rorkin, and that consequence was a hard one to swallow. She'd been meaning to draw him back in properly eventually, erasing away the safe space of doorless walls that she'd drawn around him, and now she was glad that she hadn't. That was a rather horrible feeling, being glad that Rorkin was trapped like soap in a box, unable to do anything to help himself, unable to slide away like the slippery thing he was.

She could have simply left him there while she did what she had to do, erasing all traces of the castle without having to look at his face any other way than in her sketches. But that didn't seem right, and Annabel used the stable wall to reluctantly draw herself into the room again.

"Hallo," said Rorkin's voice as the door went from a sketchy kind of existence into a solidly realistic one beneath her fingers. His voice sounded sad, and Annabel felt her throat close up.

"Your window's gone," she said scratchily, clearing her throat.

"That? Yes." Rorkin smiled at her, and that was sad, too. "The castle isn't responding to me any more."

"No. I think Mordion is controlling every bit of it except this room and the one Blackfoot and Peter are in."

"Did you draw them in?"

"Yes," said Annabel. "They wouldn't go in there by themselves, so I had to draw them in. They wanted to come with me."

"Good, good, good," said Rorkin. His brown eyes were very bright, and very understanding. Annabel knew that she didn't really have to explain it all to him—he already knew what she was planning—but that would have been the easy way out. "Then this is goodbye?"

Annabel nodded with a tightly knotted throat. "Yes."

"What will you do?"

"Erase it all," Annabel said. "You said– well, you said you're connected with the castle."

"That's right: erase the castle, and I'll vanish too. Are you– this is the only way, I suppose?"

"Yes." Annabel felt the tight hotness of tears at the corners of her eyes, and cleared her throat. She said: "Blackfoot and Peter– they're mine, you see, and with Mordion out there it's either them or you. And then, if he gets out of the castle..."

"I'm so sorry," said Rorkin, and this time Annabel was quite sure he was sorry. "I didn't think you'd have to start being queen quite so early. I'll be all right, you know. Someone will come along later and start the whole thing up again."

Annabel nodded. "That's what I thought. But I'm sorry anyway, because I don't know how long it will be. I'd try to draw you back, but Mordion will still be in here somewhere."

"Yes," agreed Rorkin. "Bit of a puzzle, isn't it? I really am sorry."

"Aren't you afraid I'll turn into a ruler like the Red Queen? She must have started somewhere, after all."

"No," said Rorkin. "I can see your hand shaking, and your face has gone all red. So long as you can still cry about the awful decisions that have to be made, you'll be all right."

"I don't want to be queen," said Annabel.

Rorkin, meditatively, said: "I didn't want to be a wizard, if it comes to that. Nearly killed my little brother when I was a child. Power doesn't strengthen family ties at all, I find."

"So there's really no choice?"

"There's always a choice. Some of them are bad choices, and some of them are hard choices, but they're there."

Annabel stared at him. "That's not what you said before. You said there was no choice."

"Didn't, you know," said Rorkin. "I said it was no use running *away* from it. You could try running *to* something."

"Maybe I will," Annabel said. As with rather a lot of what Rorkin said, she felt that she hadn't quite understood what he meant by it. "Maybe I won't, though. You keep talking as though there are only two choices: what if I don't want either of them?"

Rorkin smiled at her brightly. "Oh, that's the easy bit. Make yourself a third choice."

Annabel sat in the courtyard for rather a long time after she left Rorkin's quarters. She knew what she had to do, and she even knew how to start doing it: Peter and Blackfoot were safe, and Mordion wasn't anywhere in sight. The problem, Annabel knew, was Rorkin. She could tell herself that he had brought everything on himself—and perhaps he had—but he had only been trying to set the kingdom in order, after all. And now she was going to erase him as thoroughly as she planned to erase Mordion, without even the certainty that she'd be able to bring him back. She would try, of course: even if she hadn't promised Rorkin, she would have tried. But she couldn't even risk drawing back the castle if Mordion was still in there, and Annabel very much doubted that Rorkin would be able to come back without the castle: he was too much a part of it, or it of him, if it came to that.

So Annabel sat where she was, her eyes just a little bit glazed and her pencil nub that was really a staff pinched between her fingers. The smell of bread had faded over the days that they spent in the castle, but she could smell the cinnamon that had appeared on the table yesterday. It was a comforting smell: more comforting, however, was the fact that little things were still appearing all over the castle. If Annabel had drawn in the basic framework of the castle, then it could be said that the castle was doing a very good job of bringing itself the rest of the way back. That gave her a little bit of hope that no matter how much she erased, the castle might one day come back, bringing Rorkin with it, and that by then, there would be someone who could deal with Mordion, too.

At last, Annabel sucked in a deep breath and opened her sketchbook. The drawings of Rorkin and the mouthless man, she carefully removed and put neatly beside her on the table. She didn't want to accidentally erase any of them: for all she knew, having pictures of Rorkin there might help him to come back. Then Annabel started at the back of the book, where all the higher rooms and outer architecture was drawn, and methodically began to erase.

She didn't notice a difference at first; and despite Peter, and Rorkin, and any number of bricks that had built up into that one, solid certainty, Annabel felt a breath of insecurity. She ignored it and started erasing the lower levels. Skirting around Rorkin's quarters as if, hoping against hope, she might be able to avoid erasing him in the end. That was even more ridiculous than the faint fear, Annabel knew, but she did it anyway.

It wasn't until she began erasing the level directly above her that Annabel began to notice the difference: beams in the kitchen roof grew transparent and vague, and the small changes she had unwittingly made to the kitchen when they first arrived, vanished. She stopped to rotate her aching wrist, drew in a deep breath, and started to erase the ceiling.

If she had been previously unaware of the extent of the changes she had made, Annabel was now only too well aware of them: beyond the roofless kitchen there was only empty, blue sky. Around the edges of that too-bright blue were teetering spires of brick, block, and mortar that had once been as familiar to Annabel as the completed castle now was. If she craned her neck—and she did—she could even see the unstable remnants of Rorkin's apartments, perched atop a few pylons that were too thin to bear their weight but bore it anyway.

She gave vent to one last, gusty sigh, and searched among the scattered papers around her—now so rumpled and blank— for the one that still contained the sketch of Rorkin in his doorless apartment. And then, because it still didn't feel right, she said "Sorry," again, even though Rorkin couldn't possibly hear her.

Annabel didn't stop erasing until all but the last few scraps of paper were bare of any pencilled version of the castle, and until the ruins were levelled around her as they had been when she first came to the castle. With each drawing that she erased without a sight of Mordion, there was both a lightening of her heart and a tightening of her throat. And as she continued to erase without a sign of him, the lightness grew greater, until there were only three sketches left to erase. By now, there was a hollow kind of feeling somewhere in her stomach, or maybe her heart: Mordion might be gone, but so was Rorkin, and she wasn't sure what she could do about that.

It was something of a surprise when, at last, she found herself looking down at the drawing of the room where she had trapped Blackfoot and Peter: once she erased it, they would begin to scramble themselves out of the rubble and into the throne room again. That would take a little while, and they were both likely to be quite cross when they saw her. Still, it had been worth it to make sure that Mordion couldn't get to them while she was erasing the castle. Annabel, resting her aching hand, left that drawing for last, and gazed down at the other two sketches until a shadow flitted past the edges of her sight and made her jump.

"Where are the others?"

Annabel froze. That was Mordion's voice. She didn't look up: she reached out for the next drawing and began to erase with a hand that shook slightly.

"Where," said Mordion's voice again, in an ice-laced parody of friendliness, "are the others?"

"None of your business," said Annabel, shuffling her right foot over the drawing of the room in which she had shut Peter and Blackfoot. "They're safe, and that's all you need to know."

Mordion smiled at her. "Is that so, darling? How long will they stay safe, do you suppose?"

"Longer than you will, actually," Annabel said, still busily erasing. There was a horrible sinking in the pit of her stomach: she only had two more drawings to be erased now, and the castle was almost exactly as it had been when she entered it with Blackfoot and Peter. She had expected, by now, that Mordion would have either disappeared with the castle, or that he would have died from the same kind of magical asphyxiation by which he had caused Grenna to die. "You shouldn't have come here."

She brushed the last crumbs of peeling eraser from the second-last drawing, leaving another rumpled sheet to throw down with the others, and puffed an automatic breath of air at the eraser end of the pencil, even though she was quite well aware that the eraser wouldn't have lost any of its surface.

"Oh, this is very interesting!" said Mordion, and if his tone wasn't quite as light as he pretended, and if his face was very carefully smiling, he still wasn't disappearing.

Annabel dashed at the last of the drawings, scrubbing out the lines and shadows of the room she'd drawn around Peter and Blackfoot with a desperation that she hadn't had when she first began, and heard Mordion's soft laugh on the morning air as the very last scratching of pencil disappeared from the page.

"What now?" Mordion was smiling at her again. His expression was almost delighted now, with none of the stiffness it had had just a moment ago. Annabel had the distinctly uncomfortable feeling that he was exulting, not so much in his own cleverness, as in the fact that Annabel had been clever and he had been cleverer. He had expected something like this, and he had made preparations against it. "You've gotten rid of all those troublesome doorways for me, but I don't see how that benefits *you*. You've never drawn me, have you? Then how will you erase me?"

In the swirling sickness of failure, Annabel found that she could still think, and so she thought. What was it that Rorkin had said about the staff? *What you think you see is more important than what you actually see. No, that's not right. What you actually see isn't what you necessarily think you see. No, that's not right, either. People get so caught up with what they can see. It's a limiting sort of attitude to have.*

"That," she said rather slowly, "is a limiting sort of attitude to have."

Mordion's eyes narrowed at her. "You've been spending too much time with that half-mad wizard," he said. "Or perhaps not enough. Do you really think he'll help you now?"

"No." Annabel arranged her face in its blankest, most cowlike expression, and blinked at him. "He can't. I've erased him."

Mordion gave a short laugh. "Really? That was rather stupid of you! He's the only thing that's been keeping me from taking over the whole castle: there's always just a tiny little bit of him hanging on when you think you've got rid of it all. Even with the castle thinking that I was him, he was still a sticky-burr in my ear."

"He is a bit like that, isn't he?" Annabel said. "Even when he's not really *there*, he has a way of making things happen."

"Not for you, I'm afraid," Mordion said pleasantly. "You've reached the end of your tests, and it seems that you've failed."

"That's just what a sticky-burr does, isn't it? It makes you think that you've got all the pieces, then you try to move and it pricks you again. Well, something has been pricking me for the last couple of minutes."

Mordion smiled that delighted smile again. "Is that so, darling? No, do please, enlighten me!"

"All right," said Annabel. "But I don't think you're going to like it. What you think you see is more important than what you actually see: that's what Rorkin says, anyway."

"It sounds just like him." Mordion smiled gently at her. "But I'm not sure how that applies in this case, darling. You're still in a bad situation: you have no drawing of me to erase, and you have no magic to harm me in any other way. I may not have much magic left, but I can assure you that I have just enough to peg you out in a power-letting spell and drain both of your little friends right through your prone body."

"You keep saying I have no drawing of you," Annabel said, swallowing down the sick feeling that his words had brought up, "but that doesn't matter. Maybe it would matter if the drawing was the thing doing the magic, but it's not. It's the staff. It's only because I don't really know about magic that it's been communicating with me by drawings. It's the only way I would understand."

Mordion's smile vanished entirely. "What are you talking about?"

"You already know, or you wouldn't be so pale." Annabel

lifted her pencil from the paper and reversed it, closing one eye so that the eraser bit at the end had a Mordion-head on the end of a pencil body. "You're a lot cleverer than me: you got it straight away. The drawings are how I consciously affect the castle with the staff, but it's not magic itself. Actually, I don't think I need to do *this*, but it makes it easier for me to visualise what I'm doing."

"Stop!" said Mordion, but it was too late. As she said '*this*', Annabel was already twitching the eraser end of the pencil that was a staff, swirling it in the air where she could see his feet. "You stupid child, stop playing– *stop*–!"

"You have no feet," Annabel said. And Mordion *didn't* have any feet: they had vanished as completely as the castle had vanished. The black, squishy place that was still at the centre of the castle now that she knew where to see it, grew just a little more. This time it didn't leave Annabel with the horrible, creeping feeling that she usually got from it. Instead, she felt the bright, light knowing that in yet one more thing, Rorkin had been, in his own peculiarly round-about way, entirely accurate. "And pretty soon you'll have no legs. Everything has its own shape, but some things are meant to be less shapey than other things. There's no need to worry about it."

"You stupid child!" snarled Mordion. He was writhing impossibly in the air, his legs entirely gone from the knee down and that lack of substance growing slowly but surely. "How do you think I'll grow the castle if I'm a part of that shapeless powerhouse at the centre of the castle?"

"You won't," Annabel said. "That bit isn't about making the castle anything: it's just where the *possibility* of the castle comes from. Rorkin is the powerhouse, and the Staff does all the forming that needs to be done."

"I suppose Rorkin told you that, too!"

"No, I think I figured that bit out for myself. I didn't know that's where you'd go if I erased you, though. Oh! Your legs are gone!"

Mordion howled, thrashing helplessly until she could see the whites of his eyes, then stopped, panting, and glared at Annabel. By now he was only a torso, suspended in the air at just the right height, supported by an idea and nothing more.

"Want to know what's funny?" Annabel asked that horrified torso. She was feeling more than slightly sick, and she was afraid that if she stopped talking, she would start to throw up. "If you hadn't tricked your way into the castle, if you hadn't tricked it into thinking that you were Rorkin, and if you hadn't bound yourself to it, I wouldn't be able to do this. You bound yourself to the wrong power. I mean, the castle is strong, but the staff can still un-do it. And now that you're bound to the castle, you're losing power: you probably forgot about it because you were so excited to find me at last."

Mordion's mouth opened and closed, but didn't make a sound. His eyes, wide with panic and fear, said everything that was necessary.

"Or maybe you thought that it would only affect Rorkin," Annabel said. "I don't know. There's still a lot I don't know, actually. But if you hadn't joined yourself to the castle and made yourself dependent on its strength, I wouldn't be able to erase you now."

"It doesn't matter," panted Mordion. His eyes were ablaze now with hatred and a manic kind of laughter that frightened Annabel even though he no longer had legs with which to approach her. "Do you think you'll ever be safe? You won't, I promise you! You'll never be able to bring back the castle, or Rorkin, or rule New Civet, for that matter! Because every time you think about bringing all of this back, you'll wonder just how soon you'll see me again. And I promise you, I'll only have grown in strength with the years! I always do."

"Oh, that?" Annabel found that she was rocking back and forth slightly, but didn't seem to be able to stop herself. "That's funny, too. If you'd disappeared with the castle, I wouldn't ever have been sure: I wouldn't have been able to draw it back, or let anyone else draw it back, just in case you came back. But now that I've seen you like this, now that I know how powerless you really are, I'm not afraid any more. You remember that squishy stuff, and the walls that went up around it?"

"It is *shifted temporal remnant*, you ignorant little *cow*!"

Annabel, rather quietly, said: "I *am* ignorant. That doesn't matter, though. Maybe it would have mattered if I didn't have Blackfoot to snip at me, and Peter to laugh at me, or if I couldn't do anything about being ignorant. You might grow with strength through the years, but you never actually change, do you? I can change. That's how I managed to beat you, even though you're much cleverer than I am. You couldn't shift the walls that went up around the– the shifted temporal remnant, could you? That's because I drew them with the staff. You'll never get through them. I don't think you'll even want to. Actually, I don't know that you'll have thoughts and wants at all."

"Then I'll make the most of those I have now," said Mordion, with a twisted half-smile, and Annabel saw his hand rise. She couldn't see the magic, but she knew it was there. She also knew that she couldn't draw quickly enough to stop whatever he might throw at her. "If I'm to lose all my wants and thoughts, you can lose them with me."

His other hand lifted, and although it was shaking, Annabel ducked instinctively.

Mordion laughed bitterly. "I've not started yet, darling. But

I'm curious: do you really think you can avoid this by ducking?"

"Probably not," Annabel said. "But I'll do it anyway. Can't help it, actually."

"You always did have good self-preservation instincts, didn't you? They won't save you this time."

Annabel didn't have time to duck. Mordion's hands were shaking with effort, or fear, but they swept to the front more quickly than his torso could be erased, and something should have happened.

Something did happen: the ground fell away beneath Annabel, and she tumbled head over heels into a darkness that was forgiving and familiar, and didn't hurt too much when she hit the far side of it. She could hear screaming above her head, but she was safe in the tunnel that had opened just for her. And as the reserve of shifted temporal remnant grew little by little, and Mordion screamed above her head, Annabel curled safely at the bottom of her short tunnel, out of range of the storm above her.

She stayed where she was, in fact, until Peter's voice called from somewhere above her: "It's all right, Ann, you can come out now. He's stopped throwing magic. Actually, he's stopped throwing anything because he's not here any more."

"Peter?"

"Of course. Think I was going to stay in that room you drew around us? Do you know that the cat is the one who's been making tunnels around the castle?"

Annabel sat up, cautiously making sure that she still had both arms and legs, and that they were each where they should be. Then she said: "I guessed. Can you get me out of here?"

"Don't know," said Peter. His face appeared at the top of the tunnel, rather paler than it usually was. "It's probably something you should ask your cat. He's not particularly strong, but he's pretty tricky, and I think he's a bit cross with you at the moment."

"Oh," said Annabel. "Are you cross, too?"

"Don't know," Peter said again. "Did you get hurt? I saw Mordion chucking that bit of magic, but I wasn't quick enough to stop it. That's what took us so long: I had to stop it running around before we could get to you. Lucky your cat dropped you down there when he did, or you'd be running around in bits and pieces, too."

"I'm not hurt."

"All right. I'm not cross, then."

"Where's Blackfoot?"

I'm here, Nan.

"He looks pretty fierce."

If you expect me, Nan, to let you off as easily as your gullible little friend did–

"I don't," Annabel said. "But do you think you could let me out?"

Blackfoot didn't say anything, but she felt the tunnel contract beneath her, and the ground seemed to rise beneath her. The twin faces of Blackfoot and Peter drew rapidly closer, and as the tunnel spat her back out onto flat ground, Annabel stumbled in her now rather ragged skirts.

"Is it all gone?" she asked urgently. "The wall around the castle?"

"That? No, it's still there."

"But I erased it all!" wailed Annabel. "It should be gone!"

It won't be gone until you draw the castle back, said Blackfoot, and there was the unconscious certainty that she had become used to in his voice when he talked about the castle. *Nan, I have a few very important things I want to say to you!*

"You might as well," Annabel said. "You can start by telling me how you know so much about the castle, and why you tried to run a tunnel out of here without Peter that day."

Ah, said Blackfoot. *Then perhaps we might defer our discussion until the castle is drawn back?*

Annabel stuffed her notebook and pencil into her satchel rather grimly. "I thought you might say that."

FIFTEEN

Annabel went to sleep with the unsettling feeling that all things had become new, and woke bitterly clinging to the hope that nothing essential had really changed. There was the furry warmth of Blackfoot around her neck—if she pushed away the thought that it was very likely Blackfoot was more than a cat—and there was the regular, almost-snore of Peter's breathing—if she refused to acknowledge the fact that he was now subject as well as friend—so what was really new apart from the castle she had drawn back in yesterday?

The castle that, even now, had as its core a formless, black squishiness that had once been a person called Mordion.

Annabel gave up trying not to think, and unobtrusively got up.

Despite that, Blackfoot stirred. *Nan?*

"Go back to sleep," Annabel said quietly. Much as she had expected, they had *not* discussed anything yesterday. She didn't really mind: there was an anger that had been growing at the back of her mind that she didn't want to think about too much. "I'll bring breakfast with me when I come back."

There was a contemplative silence from Blackfoot as he evidently considered any dangers and remembered that Mordion was no more, then he curled around himself again, and his voice muttered: *Sausages*, in a sleepy kind of way.

Annabel didn't go to the kitchen. Instead, she climbed up through the castle again, following the familiar way that now no longer shifted at either Mordion's or its own will, and knocked at the door of Rorkin's quarters.

"Don't have to knock, you know," came Rorkin's voice through the door. Annabel felt her stomach unclench, though she hadn't been aware that it was knotted. She had drawn him back with the castle, so why was she so relieved that he was indeed back? "You're the Queen heir. You can go wherever you like without knocking."

"I know," said Annabel, opening the door. "But I don't think I was quite sure you were back."

Rorkin was sitting back as he had been when she first met him, his feet up on his desk and his chair tipped on its back legs. This morning, however, his eyes were open, and they were watching her unblinkingly. "That's because you still think that you're the one doing everything. You're not. You just hold the Thing that does everything."

"I know," said Annabel. "Maybe my mind doesn't know it yet."

"Your mind knows it," Rorkin said. "It's your heart that doesn't know it yet. You're still trying to do it all by yourself and being worried that you won't be able to do it properly because you're not strong enough. You're going to have to start remembering that it's the Staff that does everything, and that its magic is more than enough to look after things. It chose you, and it'll make sure you stay safe."

"Now that it thinks I'm *worthy*," said Annabel, and there was something of a sour taste in her mouth.

Rorkin grinned at her suddenly, surprising her. "I think you're worthy, too, if it helps."

Annabel made a *pft* sound. "Not really."

"You're blushing."

"Oh, shut up." There was a momentary silence before Annabel added: "I drew you some more socks."

Rorkin lifted one huge foot and waggled the woolly member at her. "Yes. Found 'em."

"I need to know something."

"Bribe, was it?"

"Yes," said Annabel. "Rorkin, it's *important*. Peter's mother–"

"Told you that. I don't know what you saw, but she's not dead. I told you the castle would get more savage with its tests."

"How do you know she's not dead?"

Rorkin looked at her for a very long time, his eyes sharp and mirrored. At last he said, "You'll find that out later. Or maybe you won't: I'm not very sure about that bit. But I know she's not dead."

"I want to be sure," said Annabel. "Because if I tell Peter that she's alive, and she's not–"

"If you don't believe me, ask that cat of yours," Rorkin said mildly. "He'll– why are you glaring at me?"

"I'm not glaring at you."

"Who *are* you glaring at, then?"

"Never mind."

Silence fell again. Rorkin picked at his woolly socks, and

Annabel hugged her satchel to her chest, trying to think of a way to say what she wanted to say.

"Yesterday," she said slowly, at last. "Where I erased things, and you disappeared, and I– and Mordion– and Mordion was erased– was that part of the tests?"

"Yes," Rorkin said, and if his eyebrow twitched, and he hesitated just a little bit too long before he said it, at least he tried. He looked up, then away, then back down at his socks. "All part of the tests. You passed with flying colours: well done, well done!"

Annabel looked at Rorkin, and he looked at her. Then she threw her arms around him and hugged him, and although Rorkin made muttering, dissenting noises, he still hugged her back.

At last he pushed her away in series of gentle shoving motions with his big hands, and said: "That's enough of that. You can't go hugging people you meet around the castle. Your subjects will think you're odd."

"I am odd," said Annabel. "If I'm the queen, I'm *allowed* to be odd. I'll make it a decree or something."

"Can't do that," Rorkin said. "It'd never pass parliament. What are you sniffling for? That's not hygienic."

"You have cobwebs again."

"Make a nice ambience, don't they?"

"They're not hygienic."

"Clean little things, spiders. Don't leave carcasses around the place when they kill."

Annabel ran her finger over the woodgrain on the desk. "Rorkin."

"No."

"No, what?" Annabel said, very much surprised. "You don't even know what I want to ask!"

"Ask him yourself. And turn him back into a person while you're at it."

"How did you know–?"

"I'm not going to get between you and your cat," continued Rorkin. "If you want to know how much he knew —or knows—in advance, you'll have to ask him yourself."

"It was a *lot*," muttered Annabel. "I know that much. I just don't know where to start asking."

"I'm not going to get between you and your cat–"

"Yes, you *said* that–"

"–but you might want to think about asking him for the *full* story of the Sleeping Princess. He may have mentioned a spy that went along with Mordion and the others at the time of the Great Cat Incident. Start there: ask him about that spy."

"You mean that Blackfoot was the spy?"

"I'm not–"

"I know, I know. You're not going to get between me and my cat," huffed Annabel. She turned to leave, but there was a lingering sense of transience to Rorkin that made her ask uneasily: "You won't go, will you?"

"Not just yet, I should think," Rorkin said.

"Good," said Annabel, and closed the door behind her. At the moment things were still too confused in her mind, but she was really quite certain that there were other questions she would want to ask Rorkin later, too.

She meant to go back to the throne room—ridiculous to think that they were still sleeping there, with a whole castle of beds to choose from—but somehow she found herself climbing up through the castle instead. Annabel climbed through floors and stairwells, up towers and across connecting walkways, until she ran out of stairs to climb. Then she stood at one of the ramparts and looked out over the countryside below, her pencil stub still clutched in her hand. That was ridiculous, too. Ridiculous to think that she hadn't known there was something odd about it from the start: she'd had it since she could remember—or at least, since she could remember drawing—and it had never grown any shorter despite constant use. Nor had it ever required sharpening.

"You probably enchanted me so I wouldn't notice," she said to it. She didn't think she was quite as unnoticing as that, and Peter certainly wasn't. "That's not fair. So I hope you don't mind, but I don't want to be queen, and I'd rather not keep you. It's no good thinking of this like another test, either. It's not that I don't want the power, or that I think I'm unworthy, or any of that stuff that's supposed to make a good queen. I just *don't want to do it*. I want to live with Blackfoot and eat nice things and not have to bother with the whole kingdom. Pick someone else."

That seemed too little to say. Annabel sighed, and added: "Please understand." Then she pinched her fingers just a little tighter around the pencil nub, brought her hand back, and threw it as far as she could. It vanished in a moment, too small to follow as it flew through the morning air, but Annabel stood where she was for quite some time despite that. It wasn't until quite some time later that she muttered: "It's just me and Blackfoot now," and stumped away downstairs, feeling at the same time a little freer and a little more guilty.

She meant to go to the kitchen, but somehow she found herself turning down the particular combination of stairs and corridors that led to the room where she'd first found her red dress. She hadn't expected it to change very much, so it was a surprise to find that it was even more full of clothes than it had been the first time she visited. She wandered through the racks of clothing in her torn red satin, wistfully touching similarly rich frocks but quite well aware now of how useless they would be.

"Pockets," she said to herself, and passed by the richer frocks completely. After all, there were some quite lovely ones that were in sensible materials like cotton, and a few of them were even colourful. Annabel picked the most colourful of them, a bright yellow dress with a waist that looked just a little too narrow, and two big, decorative pockets at the sides.

Much to her delight, the waist proved to be just the right size—had she lost weight, or had she always been just a bit smaller than she thought she was?—and the pockets were even more spacious than needed. Annabel slipped her sketchbook into one of them and patted it contentedly. It made a tiny clicking noise that was so familiar to her that she didn't really notice it until it occurred to her that she had thrown away the staff pencil. So then, *why was something in her pocket clicking against the front board of her sketchbook?*

Fatalistically, Annabel slipped her hand back into the pocket and felt around the sketchbook. Her fingers met with a small, familiar shape, and when she brought her hand out, she found herself looking at her same old pencil nub...

Peter found her in the kitchen later. He was pale and tight about the mouth, but he was still making an effort to pretend that nothing was wrong, and he whistled at her new dress. "Ann! You look half decent! Maybe you won't be so ugly when you grow up, after all."

Annabel, hunched over a new sketch that was complete but for the mouth, only made a half-hearted face at him and kept drawing.

"Thought you'd be getting breakfast by now," he said,

leaning over her shoulder with his hands in his pockets. He nodded at the sketch. "That's better than usual. Thought you could never finish that one?"

"I know how to finish it now, that's all," said Annabel listlessly. And she did know how to finish it: she'd left Rorkin's room with a very clear idea of what that face looked like. It was a big part of the reason she'd tried to get rid of the pencil.

"Why aren't you finishing it, then?"

"Don't know," Annabel said, and threw her book down on the table. "Let's have breakfast."

"Aren't you going to get your cat?"

"No. Let him sleep. I'll get him later."

I'm here, Nan, said Blackfoot, nosing his way through the open kitchen door. *I thought you were bringing breakfast?*

"Why does everybody want breakfast so much this morning?" Annabel said irritably.

"More importantly, why don't *you*?" Peter demanded. "Are you sick? Here, let me check—"

Annabel batted his hand away. "I'm not sick."

I see that you've been busy, remarked Blackfoot. He had leapt to the table top while Annabel was fending off Peter, and now he was crouched over her drawing with his tail softly lashing from side to side.

Annabel snatched it away from him and stuffed it back into her pocket with the pencil nub. "I'm hungry," she said. "Don't eat all of the apricot pies, Peter! I want some!"

Finish the drawing first, Nan, said Blackfoot. *You can't tell me you haven't already eaten.*

"Well, I haven't," Annabel said defiantly. "And I'm hungry. I'll finish it after."

Very well, Blackfoot said, though there was a tightly-wound feel to him that suggested it cost him a little to say so. *I expect sausages, in that case.*

"I got some for you already." Annabel pushed the dish across the table and whisked the cover off. "Peter, if you eat all the pies– oh."

Peter had already put down one of the pies in front of her. "All right, Ann," he said. "I was just getting one for you. You're in a mood this morning, aren't you? Are you still cross about your red dress?"

Annabel blinked. She hadn't thought about her red dress since she put on the yellow one: she had been unwilling to admit it at the time, but the long satin skirt had been dreadfully inconvenient. The yellow one, on the other hand, fell just short of her ankles and was held out a little by a fluffy petticoat that meant it didn't tangle in her legs. "No," she said. "I like this one now."

Since I daren't hope that your taste has improved, I'm going to assume that you picked it based on its vibrant colour, Black-foot remarked.

"Don't talk with your mouth full," Annabel told him sourly. Blackfoot shot her a bright look across the table that held a great deal of amused understanding in it, and she went back to her pie with cheeks that were awkwardly tight and hot. Almost without realising it, she found her pencil nub back in her hand and the sketchbook out in front of her, the remains of her pie uneaten and unappetising beside it.

Across the table, Blackfoot had finished with his sausages. He leapt from the table and padded over to sit very precisely at her feet.

Finish the drawing, he said. His voice was quite pleasant, but Annabel caught the hint of steel to it.

"Don't tell me what to do," she said, retreating to the safety of stubborn stupidity. "The mouth isn't coming out right. What if I draw it wrong?"

Annabel knew perfectly well what mouth was meant to go there: it was a thin, sarcastic and not entirely kind mouth. She didn't like it much. It made her think of the Blackfoot who was sharp and impatient, not the one who curled up warmly on her pillow and talked to her through the worst times.

"Ann? What's going on?"

"Nothing."

"It's not nothing, there's something really big stirring up—are you drawing someone *else* back? Should you be doing that?"

Nan, said Blackfoot, and this time his voice was soft and cajoling.

"Shut up," said Annabel, hunching her shoulders against his plea.

Peter, very much annoyed, went back to his breakfast. "I was just *asking*."

Nan, please. I've been this way for so long. I'm more than this.

"You're big enough already," Annabel said. There was a vast hotness to the edges of her eyes that seemed to fill her head. The little nub of pencil was in her fingers and she was drawing human Blackfoot's mouth even as she said: "I don't want you to go away."

I won't go away, Nan. I promise.

"You're already going away," she said sadly. There was a kind of blurring to Blackfoot's form that she recognised. She wanted to dash at the drawing but that would have spoiled it, so she kept drawing surely, rhythmically, stopping every now and then to smudge a shadow with her finger. Beside her, Blackfoot continued to blur and then seemed to expand.

When the drawing was complete, with human Blackfoot's sarcastic mouth slightly curved and mocking, Annabel tossed her sketchbook to the floor. The movement turned her away from Blackfoot and sent her pencil tinkling across stone. Annabel ignored both, and stared with her hot, tight eyes at one of the new, old mantelpiece roses that she'd also drawn into existence.

There was a flutter of movement in her peripheral– Peter cleaning his glasses in awestruck silence, Annabel thought. When there were two, solid male figures in the corner of her eye instead of just one Peter-sized one, she heard Peter say: "*What* did that? You can't tell me it was Ann! She's not got a lick of magic in her!"

The other figure, long and lean, stretched and became longer and leaner. "I wouldn't dream of telling you anything," said Blackfoot, his voice smooth and familiar, and utterly alien. "You already know everything, after all."

Annabel turned in time to see Peter flush a deep red, and caught the curl of Blackfoot's lip. Peter caught it, too, and flushed even deeper red. Annabel didn't think it would hurt Peter to be a little bit squashed, so she ignored his angry embarrassment in a combination of kindness and satisfaction, and studied Blackfoot instead. He didn't look too many years older than herself: perhaps only eighteen or nineteen, and he was very elegant, with a tracery of silver vines all over his sleek waistcoat, and impeccably creased trousers. His coat was unbuttoned, but fit so perfectly that he could have stepped from the gilded frame of a fashion-plate.

He smiled at her, slight creases at the edges of his eyes softening the sarcastic curl to his mouth, and said: "Well, here I am, Nan."

"You look ridiculous," said Annabel. She stomped over to her sketch book and pocketed the pencil nub that was also a staff, ignoring the smile that deepened on Blackfoot's face. She knew it wasn't reasonable, but somewhere in the back of her mind—perhaps that place where she had always heard Blackfoot's voice—floated the idea that Blackfoot the cat was her friend, always present, always wise, while Blackfoot the man, with his thin, sarcastic lips, was the one who had lied to her, tricked her, and kept things from her. "What are you dressed for, an evening party?"

"Council session, as it happens," murmured Blackfoot. "If I'd known it would meet with such disdain I would have taken the trouble to change, but there was rather a lot happening at the time. Council members being turned into cats, the love of my life kissing another man– it was a busy day, all in all."

"Wait, *you* were there when the Great Cat Incident happened?" said Peter, forgetting his annoyance and embarrassment. "That was the work of the Enchanter Luck, wasn't it?"

"Indirectly," said Blackfoot. "Actually, it was his dog that did the mischief."

"And you were what, collateral damage?"

"More of a spy in the midst," Blackfoot temporised. "Magic was flying, cats were getting away, and you know how slippery Mordion can be. I wanted to make sure he didn't get up to any more mischief."

"Well, he did," muttered Annabel. There were still a lot of things she meant to discuss with Blackfoot, not the least of which was how much he'd known when he chivvied her and Peter into the castle. "Didn't do a very good job, did you?"

"Thank you, Nan: no. It's very kind of you to mention it."

Annabel folded her arms. "What's your real name, then? Blackfoot's the name I gave you."

He hesitated. "You can still call me Blackfoot, Nan."

"No," said Annabel, with finality. "Blackfoot was my cat. You– you're something else. What's your real name?"

"Melchior," he said. "That's the name I had until five years ago, at least. I've gotten used to Blackfoot."

"All right," Annabel said. "Melchior, then: I want you to answer some questions."

Melchior swiftly curled in a semi-circle and sat down, as she had seen Blackfoot do so many times. "That's not like you, Nan."

Annabel felt a poniard of painful familiarity pierce her chest. "Don't do that!"

He looked up at her in surprise. "Nan? Do what?"

"Don't sit like that!"

Peter frowned. "What's wrong with you, Ann? Why are you picking fights with the– with Bl– with Melchior?"

"Yes, Nan," Melchior said, looking at her curiously, "why *are* you picking fights with me?"

"Well, why did you lie to me?"

Melchior froze for an instant, but relaxed again in his off-puttingly catlike way so quickly that she wasn't sure it had really happened. "What's this, Nan?"

Peter laughed rudely. "Oh, so you've only just figured that out, have you?"

"No!" flashed Annabel. "I knew about it a while ago. I've just been waiting for him to tell me the truth. He's been lying to you, too."

"Don't be silly," said Peter, but he sounded uncertain. "What do you mean, lying to me?"

"Your mother and stepfather aren't dead."

Peter went very white. "What are you talking about, Ann? I saw them die– *you* saw them die! They– they have to be dead, or why would–"

Annabel glared at Melchior. He'd gone almost as white as Peter, which only made her angrier: what did he have to be pale about? "It was a test, wasn't it?"

"Yes," said Melchior. "They all were."

"A tes– testing *what*? Why would Blackf– Melchior be testing me?"

"It wasn't Blackfoot," Annabel said, plunging on through. Peter would have had to be told at some stage, and she was too angry to stop and give him a chance to process it all. "He just knew it and lied about it. It was the castle. And it wasn't a test for you, either: it was a test for me."

Peter, alternately white and flushed, said in a suffocated voice: "The *castle* was doing it?"

"Well, not exactly: I'll explain that later. The important thing is that your mother isn't dead: it was just a test to see how I'd react to your– to your–"

"Grief and anger," choked out Peter, more red than white now. He took in a deep breath and said, more clearly: "They're really not dead?"

"Yes."

"Are you sure?"

"Yes," Annabel said again.

Peter kicked at a rock, almost visibly swallowing several things he wanted to say. "All right, Ann. I see why you're angry. What's the cat got to do with it, though?"

"He found out I'm the heir," Annabel said. "I don't know how, but he did. And then–"

"I can explain that," Melchior said, and his voice was less smooth than it had been at first. "My original directives were to find the Sleeping Princess, then the Queen, then to reinstitute the monarchy."

Peter huffed again. "Didn't want much, did they?"

"They, who?" demanded Annabel. "*Who* was giving you orders? And why you? Why are you so special?"

"They," began Melchior, and stopped. "Come to think of it, there are two different *they*s. The first ones, I can't tell you about. The second are Black Velvet."

Annabel felt another surge of anger. "*Spiders*! There never were any spiders, were there?"

"Not as such, no," said Melchior. "And I'll have you know that I'm not afraid of them, either, Nan. That was a ruse."

"I don't care about your stupid ruse," snapped Annabel. "It wasn't clever of you, it was deceitful!"

"Well, yes," said Melchior. "But it hurts my pride to have you thinking I'm afraid of spiders."

"I don't care about your stupid pride, either," Annabel said. "Who are Black Velvet?"

Melchior looked distinctly rueful. "That's another thing I can't really tell you."

"All right," said Annabel. She didn't mind not being told things if she *knew* she was not being told them. "So what about the Sleeping Princess?"

"You remember I told you a curtailed version of the story? The Sleeping Princess, rescued from her sleep, Mordion's part in her curse, and the Great Cat Incident?"

"I remember." Annabel folded her arms across her chest. Just as she had thought: Melchior, in telling her the truth, had only told her part of the truth.

"What I didn't tell you was my part in that story. I found her," Melchior continued, and his sarcastic lips quirked in a particularly thin half-smile, "but unfortunately, someone else had already found her. Things got a little messy, as I mentioned —magic flying, love of my life kissing someone else, cats, the spy that followed Mordion, etcetera—and at the end of it all, there you were. The Queen heir. Mordion got wind of you somehow: I'm not sure how. I was following him, trying to keep him out of mischief. As soon as he narrowed it down to this general area of New Civet, I separated from him to try and find you first."

"And so you did," Annabel said, her voice particularly flat. "Or was that just part of all the tests? Try and teach me first, then test me? Must have been a bit of a shock to find me, then."

"It wasn't a test, Nan," said Melchior. "I was desperately trying to keep you out of his sight. I didn't realise how dangerous you were until I met you."

"Yes, Rorkin explained about that," said Annabel. "He took off Grenna's bit of magic, too. He said the staff will be enough to keep me safe and stop me from being used now that it's accepted me as the heir."

Melchior sat back again, slightly dazed. "Ah. You've met Rorkin, have you?"

"What?" said Annabel, rather nastily. "Worried about all the other lies you've told? You could have told us about the tests this *whole time.*"

"I suppose it seems like that," Melchior said. "And technically, it really is like that; but if I'd told you, the tests would have been null and void, and you would have been disqualified as the Queen Heir."

"I don't want to be the Queen Heir!"

"Unfortunately, Nan, there's not really a great deal you can do about that."

"Rorkin says there are always choices."

"Oh, does he?"

"Yes. It's just that this is one of the bad ones."

"Regardless, I would like you to know that I wasn't the one testing you: the blame for that lies squarely on the castle itself. It's how Rorkin set it up when he arranged the magic and made the staff."

"Yes," said Annabel, who was beginning to wonder a little about that as well. There were one or two things about it that didn't quite add up, and that was something else she needed to think more about. "I knew you weren't the one testing me."

"I see," Melchior said, and his hazel eyes were very narrow. "Then, Nan–"

Turning her back on him, Annabel said to Peter: "It was Rorkin who told me your mother isn't dead. He's very clever, and he knows things. Rorkin says–"

"Since I don't suppose Rorkin mentioned anything about what to do or where to go next," said Melchior, his lips particularly thin, "do you think we could discuss what is going to happen now that the castle is back and you've been recognised by both the castle and the staff as the Queen heir?"

"Rorkin says–"

"Nan, I'm growing a little tired of hearing what Rorkin says."

"Well, I'm getting tired of hearing what you say," Annabel said, losing her temper. She left the room despite Melchior's calling, and went away, leaving Peter and Melchior to get along together as best they could.

Annabel went back to see Rorkin that night after dinner. Peter wouldn't have missed her: he was running a Look-See spell again when she briefly saw him in the kitchen, but Annabel didn't tell Melchior where she was going, either. Wandering the castle alone, she'd had more time to think about things, and if she'd grown angrier at Melchior the more she thought about some of those things, she'd grown steadily more astonished at Rorkin the more she thought about others.

She had been right when she told Mordion that he had bound himself to the wrong power. She'd been thinking of the staff, but the staff hadn't ever been the greater power, either. The greater power, that power that had formed the staff, bound the castle, and set Annabel, Peter, and Blackfoot up against Mordion in a deadly game– that power was Rorkin himself. Clever, tricky, lying Rorkin, who had made her believe through her own deductions, everything that she was meant to believe in order to make sure that the test was as effective as it could possibly be.

And so Annabel went back to see Rorkin.

"Rorkin," she said as soon as she was in the room, giving him her flattest look. "You've been lying to me, haven't you?"

Guiltily, Rorkin said: "Told you that already."

"Yes, but I mean that you've been lying to me about lying."

"Who could keep that straight in their head?" protested Rorkin. "No, no: far too devious!"

Annabel gazed at him without blinking. She was quite certain of what she knew: it was only after she had erased Rorkin, after all, that the castle had lost its power. The castle had never been the controlling power behind the tests. Nor, now that she came to think about it, had she been in absolutely mortal peril at any time, unless she counted the time when Rorkin had been deleted, and she wasn't even sure about that. To Rorkin, she said: "You're a very devious person."

"Don't look at me like that: it gives me the shivers."

"Good," Annabel said. "You said– well, you didn't *say*,

exactly. You did that thing with your eyebrow so that I'd think that Mordion almost managed to take over the castle. You made me think that it wasn't all part of the plan, or test, or whatever it is you were doing here. But that's not true, is it? You were in control the whole time. Even me erasing you, and Mordion, and the whole castle: that was part of your plan, wasn't it?"

Rorkin blinked. "After all, what's control? Is it in the grasping, or the letting go?"

"That's what's so hard to pin down about you," Annabel said accusingly. "You answer questions without answering them, and change the subject without changing it. *And* you say things that can be taken more than one way. It's very slippery of you."

"Mother always said I'd come to no good," Rorkin said sadly. "Wouldn't she happy if she knew how bad!"

Annabel, ignoring this aside, demanded: "How am I supposed to know what the truth is, then?"

"I suppose you'll never know," said Rorkin. He sounded faintly smug, but Annabel was aware in an almost amused, wondering way, that she couldn't even be sure of that. He was too good at discreetly leading people to see what they were prepared to see.

"I suppose I won't," she said.

"Shall I tell you?"

Annabel surprised herself by giggling. "Don't bother. I wouldn't know whether or not to believe you."

"And thus my last lesson," Rorkin said impressively, wriggling his eyebrows at her. "Even if you're the wisest queen the Two Monarchies have ever seen, there are some things you'll never be sure of. Sometimes you'll just have to make the best guess you can make. And sometimes you'll be wrong. Actually, you'll probably be wrong at least as often as you're right: that's just the law of averages."

"There never was another choice, was there? I've always been the heir. The rumours of heirs and the castle coming back: you did that, didn't you?"

"Well, it adds such an air of mysteriousness to the whole thing! And it wasn't me that spread the rumours, if it comes to that. I have two little minions to do that for me."

"I remember," said Annabel, "when I was born."

"So do I," Rorkin said unexpectedly, and entirely without hedging. "Ugly little thing, you were! And you were pulling in every bit of magic around: your poor parents didn't know what to do with you."

"I knew it!"

"If you'd known it, things would have been very different."

"I sort of knew it, then! And the tests– I was the heir all along, by blood, wasn't I?"

"In a manner of speaking," hedged Rorkin. "There were one or two other choices, but they weren't particularly good ones."

"Wait, though! If you were part of the castle, how could you get away to me when I was born?"

"That?" Rorkin's eyebrow twitched.

"Don't do that!"

"Let it be a lesson to you," Rorkin said impressively.

"A lesson in what?" muttered Annabel. "How to lie by implication?"

Rorkin, agreeably, said: "If you like. Or it can be a lesson on not taking a slip of the tongue at face value. Take it any way you want."

"Thanks."

"Don't do that with your face. It's frightening."

"I can do what I want with my face. I'll make that a law, too."

Much to Annabel's surprise, Rorkin giggled. "Don't be like that. Don't you want to know how you did in the tests?"

"No," said Annabel. "Why should I? You just played games with me and prodded me until I did the things you needed me to do."

"What are you talking about?" said Rorkin, in surprise. "Did you a *world* of good! You don't think you'd have pushed yourself to do things if I hadn't held that boy hostage, do you?"

"How would I know?" Annabel said angrily. "Maybe I *would* have! You don't know, because you made me do it!"

"Ah," said Rorkin carefully. "I can see why you feel that way, but I didn't make you do anything. I just gave you the opportunity to do it. You could have done nothing, after all."

"No, I *couldn't*," said Annabel coldly. "It was Peter! How could I leave him with Mordion?"

"He wasn't with Mordion, was he?"

"No, clever clogs, and I couldn't leave him stuck in the past, either!"

"Why not? He's bound to get to us— well, well, never mind that."

"What?" Annabel gave him her flattest look. "Laying another trail? Or did you say something you weren't meant to?"

"Wouldn't you like to know!"

"Actually," Annabel said, "I want to know if me figuring out that Mordion didn't have Peter was part of the tests, or if it was just what made you think of the idea of pulling Mordion into the tests."

"Oh, that. Yes, of course it was part of the tests. What else?

He was already there as an unexpected element, and it would have been a shame not to use him, so–"

"Yes, but *how* unexpected, I'd like to know," complained Annabel. "You're just lucky I remembered about Mordion and doorways."

"Did, though, didn't you?"

"But what if I *hadn't*?" demanded Annabel. "Would you have said I couldn't be queen because I did badly then? Because that's not fair–"

Rorkin looked startled. "Not fair? But you passed that bit!"

"That's what I mean. You were just lucky that day: it could have easily gone the other way if I hadn't remembered. So that's not really what I'm like. For all you know, I'll be an awful queen."

"The whole test didn't hinge on that one little thing," Rorkin said. He sounded vaguely insulted. "The castle uses a sliding scale to determine the final results. And if you *must* know, I was looking for patterns of repeated behaviour: if you'd shown a habit of determined stupidity, there would have been something to worry about."

"Patterns?" Annabel thought about that. "Wait, what about my pattern of not doing anything unless I have to do it? Why didn't you notice that? That's not a very queenly trait."

Rorkin gave her a rather more narrow look than usual. "I'd stop wriggling, if I were you," he advised. "You're not getting out of it that easily."

Annabel made a face at him and plopped her chin into her palms.

"You really shouldn't do that," Rorkin said. "Your subjects will think you're odd."

"You're the only one around, and you're odder than I am."

"That's rude and more than slightly true."

"Wait, does that mean you thought I was being noble when I went to offer myself to Mordion in exchange for Peter?"

"Oh, no," said Rorkin. "You failed that bit. The impact of your capture would have been far greater than the impact of one person's death: the Two Monarchies wouldn't have suffered alone. The repercussions would have been felt all the way to Lacuna and Calipha. You were supposed to consider how the outcome would affect the whole country, not you personally. But it was close enough, so I let it slide."

"Are you allowed to do that?" Annabel said doubtfully.

"Why not? I made the rules, after all."

"Who put you in charge, anyway?"

"Oh, that. I did that. Well, it was me and– enough of that. You passed! Aren't you happy?"

"Happy? Why? I don't care about your stupid tests! I don't want to be the Queen Heir!"

"A sense of a satisfaction is a great thing," said Rorkin. "Don't go sniffing at it."

"You– wait, what was that?"

"What?"

Annabel, who was quite certain that she had heard something drop, and someone swear, looked accusingly at Rorkin. "There's someone in your cupboard."

"Can't be," said Rorkin promptly. "I don't keep people in that cupboard."

Distinctly, from the cupboard, came the sound of something being hit, and another voice.

Annabel's eyes narrowed on Rorkin. "There's someone in there."

"Can't be." Rorkin's eyes looked away and back at her again.

Annabel let her face go blank and slack again, by way of unsettling him, and saw him twitch. "Are you lying to me?"

"Maybe."

"Did I draw them back in, too?"

"What, them?" Rorkin giggled. "No one draws *them* anywhere! They just show up and make a space for themselves. All through the length and breadth of history, there they are, making changes and leaving clues. You can be sure that whenever they turn up, something is going to happen. Even in their younger incarnations, they tend to pull the timeline out of skew. Well, look at how quickly the castle came back! You don't think you did that *all* by you– well, now, look at the time! It's past your bedtime."

Annabel took in a slow, meditative breath through her nose, considering whether or not it was worth pushing him on the subject. She looked up to find that Rorkin was watching her with bright eyes, entirely unapologetic, and decided that in this, as in quite a few other things, she would simply wait and find out what he meant by it.

"Thanks," she said, surprising herself again because she found that she *was* thankful. She leaned up and kissed Rorkin's cheek, and he went as dark red as it was possible for someone of his skin colour to go. "I'll remember that."

"Are you quite finished, Nan?" said Melchior's voice. He was leaning elegantly in the open doorway of Rorkin's room— and since when had it been open? She was sure she had closed it—and it was impossible to tell how long he'd been there. "We'll have to leave tomorrow, as soon as the warding comes down. You should be sleeping."

Rorkin, eyes bright and a little mad, gurgled with laughter. "Heard about you! Wondered what you looked like!"

"Is that so?" Melchior's gaze wandered over Rorkin, as if

he, too, had been curious to know what Rorkin looked like, and Annabel had the sense that there was another thing that she would learn about in due course.

"I'll come down soon," she said. "You don't have to wait for me."

"It's no trouble," Melchior said, with an insincere smile. "I'll be in the hall."

"Think he wants you to go with him," pointed out Rorkin, as the door closed behind Melchior.

"I suppose so." Annabel looked around the room one last time, and having done so, understood something else. The cobwebs and the general mess might be back in Rorkin's quarters, but it wasn't quite as messy as it had been. That, she was quite certain, was because several things were missing: she was also quite certain that those things were in the small, bumpy bag that was sitting next to the cupboard. "Are you leaving? Is that why there are people in the cupboard?"

"Got to," Rorkin said. "I'm not supposed to be here yet."

"Yet?"

"And your little friend can't go home just yet. Make sure you tell him. Mind you, he might not need to be told, if it comes to that."

"What do you mean?"

"And you– stop wriggling. You can't go home, either."

"But you said–"

Rorkin put his fingers in his ears. "Told you before about quoting me to me. It gives me a nasty shiver."

"That's because you lie so much."

"Probably."

"Will I see you again?"

Rorkin looked a little surprised. "Hm. Don't actually know that. I know what I'm meant to do, but I don't know if

I'll be able to do it. Think I've come to the end of my knowing. Mind the gap when you leave the castle, won't you? It won't be quite so big when you get back."

He pushed her toward the door as he spoke, and Annabel, who wanted to ask about quite a few more things, was expelled from the room, still protesting.

"I need my beauty rest, too," said Rorkin.

Sixteen

Annabel woke to the disrupting motion of Peter bouncing on her bed. Last night, it had made sense for them all to find rooms to sleep in: now, with Peter's energetic bouncing, she wasn't so sure.

"Ann, get up! The wall has gone down! We can leave whenever we're ready!"

Annabel groaned and rolled over, wrapping her arms around her head to block out Peter's exuberance and the bright light of morning alike. "Go away!"

She didn't have any hope that he actually would go away. With Peter, bouncing ignored usually turned to being pinned beneath the covers while he merrily poked fingers in her ears and cold cogs down the neck of her night-dress. So when there was a brief scuffle and Peter's weight abruptly lifted from the covers above her, Annabel sat up, fuzzily confused.

"All right, all right, I'm off!" said Peter's voice, rather annoyed. Annabel rubbed her eyes and found that he was now standing by the doorway with his collar pulled up at one side, flustered and untidy. Melchior, beside him, was fresh and neat, with a distinctly sardonic gleam to his hazel eyes.

"Come along, Nan," he said. "The triad is well up and the barrier is indeed gone. We should be getting along now."

"Getting *along*?" Annabel spluttered. She hadn't meant to speak to him at all—she was still furious with him—but despite what both he and Rorkin said, she had thought, somehow, that now everything was all over, she would simply go home with Peter. If she had thought any further, it would only have been to decide that she might like to clean out Grenna's cottage and see if she wanted to live there by herself. "Where are we going?"

"You'll recall, Nan, that I told you about my missions?"

"I remember," said Annabel, rather grimly. "What about them?"

"There are a lot of people in the Capital who will be very happy to meet you. If it comes to that, there are quite a few people you'll need to meet before you can even think about being officially named the heir, Rorkin or no Rorkin. On the bright side, you have the staff, so that should smooth most things over."

Annabel hunched her shoulders. "I don't want to meet anyone. I don't want to go to the Capital. I want to go back with Peter and live with him."

"Who invited you?" demanded Peter. "If we're going to have emissaries and couriers knocking at the gate all the time, wanting to speak with the heir–"

"You won't!" Annabel flashed. "Because I'm not going to be the queen!"

Peter snorted rudely with laughter. "I bet a few people will have something to say about that!"

"More than a few, if I know anything about it," Melchior

said. "Nan, it's no use staying here: when it gets out that the queen heir is staying at a country estate near the castle, there'll be a veritable stampede to curry favour. What else will you do?"

"There's the cottage," Annabel muttered, but couldn't bring herself to voice the nebulous idea she'd had of turning Grenna's cottage into her own quiet, comfortable little world.

"We'd best be going soon," said Melchior, as if she hadn't spoken. To Peter, he said: "You'll go home now, I suppose?"

"What?" Peter sounded as taken-aback as Annabel had been at the thought of leaving. "Home– well– I suppose– No, of course not! I should go with Ann."

Melchior raised one brow, his lips particularly sarcastic. "Should you, though? I suppose we'd best begin, then."

Peter hesitated. "What about the castle?"

"What about it?"

"Well, can we leave it empty like this? Won't people notice it?"

"I should hope so," said Melchior. "It *is* rather large, after all. I'd be disappointed in Mr. Pennicott if he didn't notice."

"But is it all right just to leave it there?"

"We can't pick it up and take it with us," said Annabel snidely. "Of course we're just going to leave it there!"

"Actually," said Peter, willing for an argument, "I bet if we asked Rorkin, he could do it."

"We can't ask him," Annabel said. "He's gone."

"*What*?" said Peter and Melchior together.

Annabel, pleased to know something they didn't, said: "He went last night, while you were sleeping."

"You–"

"Why didn't you *tell* me, Nan?"

"Why should I?" demanded Annabel. "You lied to me this whole time. I just didn't tell you all the truth. Anyway, he has other things he needs to do: he told me. He said he's finished what he was meant to do here."

"I'll say," muttered Peter. "Bother! I wanted him to teach me magic!"

"Maybe that's why he left without telling you," said Annabel, even more snidely. "Go away, both of you. I need to get dressed."

"I don't see why you're worried about that now," Peter said, much disgruntled. "It's not as though we haven't gone swimming and run about in our underwear together for the last– ow! All right! I'm going! Don't tear my collar out!"

Still protesting about the misuse of his collar, he was dragged out by Melchior, who closed the door behind him. Annabel made a face at the closed door, refusing to feel grateful to Melchior, and took a leisurely half hour dressing as a quiet sort of rebellion. It was a wasted effort: Peter had already gone down to the courtyard by the time she emerged, and Melchior, who was waiting for her, only pushed away from the wall he'd been leaning against and enquired affably if she was quite ready to go down now.

Annabel murmured something that could have been yes, and followed him down through the castle silently. Melchior didn't comment, but his eyes were thoughtful and maybe a little bit sorry. Annabel saw that, and, hardening her heart, stomped out into the courtyard ahead of him.

Peter rolled his eyes at her. "Took you long enough, didn't it? What were you doing, sewing a whole new frock? *All* of the suns are up now, and it's going to be hotter, so it's your own fault if you get too hot walking."

"I won't be walking very far," Annabel said grimly, and went on ahead of them through the courtyard gate.

Rorkin had said to mind the gap, but although she was

very careful about how she stepped over the stone-paved gateway, Annabel didn't notice anything particularly dangerous. It wasn't until she turned around and saw that Peter and Melchior were gazing around in wonder, with the ruins of the castle behind them that she felt the first stirrings of discomfort.

"What–" she said. "What happened? It's all in ruins again!"

Peter blinked a little and woke from his trance. "Ann," he said. "I think you might have done something a bit odd when you drew the castle back in."

Melchior, who had been gazing around in the same, stupefied sort of way, smiled a slow smile. "A very good job, Nan," he said. "At my guess, we've gone back by about three years. No, don't go that way: it's not a good idea to meet yourself face to face."

"What do you know about meeting your younger self face to face?" Peter demanded, his eyes bright.

"It's more what I know about meeting someone else's younger self face to face," said Melchior. "And don't ask me any more about it, because I won't tell you."

"But–"

There was a nasty sinking feeling in the pit of Annabel's stomach. "What do you mean, we've gone back by three years? How can we have gone back three years? I drew– I drew the castle back the same way the second time!"

"You can't have," Peter said. "I felt the change as soon as we got past the gate. Actually, I should have noticed that the triad was in a different place, but I didn't even think about it."

"We'll get Rorkin to fix it," Annabel said, rather blindly. It was only now that she knew there was nothing she could do about it that she realised how very badly she had wanted to be able to slip away and go back to Grenna's cottage by herself.

"He'll help me to erase it all and bring it back into the right time."

"Rorkin's gone, remember? And really, Ann, I don't think he'd be able to do much about it, not without worrying that Mordion was going to come back."

"Well, what about your tickerbox, then?"

"I don't see why *you're* so upset," remarked Peter. "If I'm right—and I *am*—I can't go back to see my mother for another three years. *And* I'll have to find somewhere to live in the meantime."

"I would be very much surprised if Rorkin didn't have a hand in this somewhere, Nan. That being the case, I very much doubt there's anything you or I can do about it."

"That wizard!" muttered Annabel. The more she thought about it, the more certain she was that Melchior was right. Not content with causing her to run around and take tests that were as varied as they were dangerous, Rorkin had, for reasons entirely his own, plumped Annabel, the castle, and all those it contained, squarely back in time by three years. "It probably didn't have anything to do with me at all! I'm sure I drew the castle back the same way the second time. He must have put a spell on the gate. What is he up to now?"

Peter shrugged. "Maybe there's something you need to do in the next three years. Maybe there's someone you need to meet. *Don't* I wish I could have asked him a bit about time-travel!"

"He should have asked us!"

"I don't think Rorkin makes a habit of asking, Nan. I've found that wizards who are more than two hundred years old very rarely ask permission to do the things they do."

"I suppose you're more than two hundred years old, then," Annabel said. "You don't ask permission to do things, either."

"There's no use complaining about it," Melchior said gently. "We'll just have to go on to the Capital and keep things very, very quiet until three years have passed."

"Where *exactly* are we going?" Annabel demanded, since there was no point in refusing to go with Melchior now that she couldn't go back to the cottage. She still felt decidedly off-balance with human Blackfoot: his voice was familiar but everything else was completely alien. Worse, she had become used to hearing his voice at the back of her mind. Now that she couldn't hear it there, it left an uncomfortable space that was horribly similar to the core of blackness that still remained at the centre of the castle.

"I told you that, Nan," said Melchior's familiarly unfamiliar voice. "There are people who will want to meet you."

Annabel stared up at his face, searching for anything recognisable as Blackfoot, and felt a sharp pain in her chest when she couldn't find it. "Yes, but that doesn't actually *tell* me anything. *Who* wants to meet me? Where are they?"

Melchior sighed. "A great many people, Nan. But most importantly, Mr. Pennicott will need to see you. His office is... well, it's in the Capital, but not quite. He'll want to talk to you and set things in order in a legal sort of a way. He'll also be very useful when it comes to making arrangements to keep you out of sight for the next three years. Then, of course, you'll need to be taught how to act and speak, and you'll need to take more lessons than you've ever imagined in your worst nightmares."

"That'll take longer than three years!" Peter said brutally. "And don't expect me to stay around for all that, either, Ann! I don't want to be in the same classroom as you. It's embarrassing."

"You," said Melchior, "are welcome to go away whenever it

seems good to you. I'm not remotely interested in making sure that you get lessons."

"Hey!" Peter protested. "You shouldn't talk to me like that! I'm just a kid: you can't tell me to go away when I haven't got anywhere to go! I might starve!"

Melchior muttered something that sounded like: "One can only hope," and added more loudly: "It's no use wasting time here, at any rate."

Since he reinforced these words by opening a tunnel without warning in the biggest available piece of castle wall, Annabel jumped and scuttled away from the swirling darkness.

"Sure that's a good idea?" enquired Peter. "What with the castle being stuffed full of shifted temporal remnant and the time shift?"

"Let's put it this way," Melchior told him, with an entirely sardonic twist to his lips, "with the castle in ruins again, I'm certain at least that it won't enable Mordion to take over so that he can kill us all. Shall we go, children?"

He didn't give them a chance to respond: he simply caught Peter by the much-misused collar, Annabel by the wrist, and pulled them after him through silent darkness that opened into light, bright bustle.

They were on the sidewalk of a paved street that positively *seethed* with wheeled traffic, and around them was the push and pull of so many pedestrians that it didn't really surprise Annabel that no one seemed to notice them arrive, even though they made a brief, black patch in the wall that ran alongside the road.

Peter looked around him in growing excitement. "We really are in the Capital! That didn't take anywhere near as long as I thought it would! Is it because you used the castle? It must be. Ann, there are street vendors here!"

"Go get yourself some food, then," said Melchior, with a weary, avuncular air. He patted his pocket and produced a few thin, folded pieces of paper. Annabel, who was only used to seeing the older, coin-style money, took a little while to realise that it was paper money. Peter obviously had no difficulty in recognising it: he took it with alacrity.

"There was food in the castle," Annabel mumbled. "It's probably going to go bad, now."

"I don't see why you're so cross, Ann. Look, I'll buy us all something nice to eat: you'll like that. Where are we supposed to meet, anyway?"

Melchior pointed to a small office-front across the busy road. "We'll be in there. Don't bother to buy breakfast for us: Mr Pennicott will feed Annabel as soon as he knows who she is, and I won't be around for long enough to eat. Mr. Pennicott will find a place for you both to stay for the time being, too, so there's no need to worry that you'll starve."

Peter grinned. "I was only larking around about that. I didn't really think you'd let me starve. Where are you going to go, then?"

"There's someone I want to see," said Melchior. Then, pulling a reluctant Annabel with him into the terrifying throng of horses, carts and pedestrians, he hove them both through the door he had pointed at. It was a small, orderly office with white-painted windows that let in the light and small, orderly, white-painted furniture. It looked entirely ordinary. The little clerk looked ordinary, too; neither fat nor thin, with no particular features worth remembering.

Annabel looked at him in dislike and mumbled, "S'prised they didn't paint *you* white, too."

She didn't think she'd spoken loud enough for him to hear,

but he looked first surprised and then perhaps amused. "Can I help you, sir, miss?"

"Yes," said Melchior, treading on Annabel's foot as a warning.

"Ow," said Annabel, not quietly. "You stood on my foot!"

This time the clerk was definitely amused.

Melchior gave a pained sigh. "I did. It was a vain attempt at subtlety."

Annabel sank into the most sullen, blank-faced look she could manage, and stared him down. Somewhere during the transition from castle to outside, or perhaps from outside to Capital, the sticky, burning ball of anger that sat at the back of her throat had turned to an even hotter, stickier misery. She could have dealt with the anger, but the longer that sticky misery sat at the back of her throat, the closer she could feel herself to tears. If she could hide behind her most solidly stupid face for just long enough, perhaps she didn't need to cry.

"Don't give me that," said Melchior. He gave her the nice smile—the one that reminded her of Blackfoot's purr—but Annabel was now well caught up in her own misery and only stared him down. The smile vanished, and Melchior opened his mouth just as Peter crashed into the tiny office, making it far too small simply with the force of his entry.

"All set?" He looked from Annabel to Melchior, and his brows rose. "No? What's wrong?"

"That's what I was just trying to find out," said Melchior, as Annabel said shortly: "Nothing."

She turned her back on them both and sat down on one of the white chairs, clutching her fingers together in her lap and staring straight ahead. She could feel scalding tears piling up at the back of her eyes. They made her cheeks too hot, and she could see her reflection in the glass pane across the office;

sullen, red and silent. It was useless to try and stop them now, but she could try to hold onto them just a little longer until Peter and Melchior left.

"Hurry up and go away," she said to them, watching as her window-double did the same. "You said you were going to go see someone."

"We want to see Mr. Pennicott," Melchior said quietly to the clerk.

"Mr. Pennicott?" said the clerk, faintly puzzled. "The name is not familiar, sir."

"Tell him it's Melchior," said Melchior. "I'm sure that will be enough to jog memories." He left Peter standing by the desk and sauntered over to Annabel. "What's wrong, Nan?"

The tears had already started, gliding swiftly in a hot stream down her cheeks. Annabel said in a tight little voice: "There's nothing wrong. Go *away*."

"You've done it now," said Peter. "She's not going to stop now."

His hazel eyes just a little narrower, Melchior asked again: "What's wrong, Nan?"

"Go away! You're going to go away anyway! Leave me alone!"

"I'm only going for an hour or two," Melchior said, in surprise, "not going away entirely. Not just yet, at any rate. There's quite a lot to do before you become Queen, of course, so naturally you won't see as much of me once we're at the Capital, but I'll be there just the same."

"I don't want to be queen!" sobbed Annabel, abandoning all hope of pretending nothing was wrong. "I don't want to be in the Capital! I don't want Mr. Pennicott and I don't want lessons and I don't want you! *I want Blackfoot!*"

Melchior kneeled by the chair, one hand on his leg and the other hovering uncertainly in the air. "Nan–"

"*Go away!*"

"There's no need to shout, Nan."

"Yes, there *is*! Why did you have to come back? Why couldn't I keep Blackfoot?"

"You silly chump, he *is* Blackfoot!" protested Peter.

"You," said Melchior, very quietly and chillingly, "Out!"

"But you are!"

"If I have to repeat myself just once more–!"

"All right, all right, I'm going!" Peter backed away with his hands up placatingly, and exited by the front door to the tinkle of the bell and a protest from the vanilla clerk that all parties should remain in the waiting room and not lollygag in the street.

Melchior, crouched at Annabel's feet in an achingly familiar way, said to her sobs: "Nan, it's still me. I was me when I was in that body just as much as I am now."

"No, you're not!" wailed Annabel, unable even to speak quietly now. "Blackfoot wouldn't have made me be queen! He wouldn't have lied to me and tricked me and left me in the Capital like a parcel of clothes someone ordered!"

"I'm not going to leave you, Nan."

"You will," Annabel hiccoughed. "You'll get your next directive and then you'll go away and find someone else to lie to."

Melchior made a small huffing noise that was almost a laugh. "I suppose that's a not-too-inaccurate description of my life thus far, after all. There's something you haven't yet grasped, however: finding the heir was my last directive– my *last*. There will be no more directives."

Annabel, who knew much better than that, said: "Hah.

They'll offer you something interesting and twisty and devious, and you won't be able to say no. And I'll be stuck in the Capital, or at the castle, being the queen while you're being sneaky without me."

"What do you want me to do, Nan?"

"I wanted you to ask me that this morning," said Annabel. "But you didn't. You just brought me here without asking, and looked all top-lofty and wise about knowing what was best for me."

Melchior gazed at her for rather a long time, his face impossible to read. At last he said: "I see."

Annabel wiped her wet face in the crook of her arm, blotting her swollen face. It felt scratchy and sore, and the tears began leaking again straight away. She would have liked to ask Melchior exactly what it was that he saw, but Peter set the bell on the front door ringing again as he ducked back in.

"Thought you might like to know," he said. "Something really quiet is going on at the back of the office."

Annabel stared at him in swollen, wet-faced incomprehension, but Melchior rose swiftly.

"Quiet, you say?"

Peter nodded. "It's not strong magic or anything like that, but everything else, all the magic things around it– they're getting out of the way."

"Then we'd better go."

"Go?" Annabel looked up at him in sudden hope.

"Too late now," said Peter gloomily. "Whoever it is, they're coming out."

"We'll see about that," said Melchior, seizing Annabel by her grimy, tear-wet hand, and Peter by the equally grimy collar. At the clerk, he said: "Tell Mr. Pennicott that Mordion is disposed of."

Then the wall beside them seemed to open, or soften, or perhaps *twist*, and Annabel found herself looking into the welcome blackness of one of Melchior's tricky little tunnels...

"Dear me," said Mr. Pennicott, blinking at the empty front office. He turned to look at the clerk, who was still gazing bemusedly at the empty space in front of him, and the now whole wall. "I'm quite sure someone sent for me to tell me that Melchior was back. I'm also quite sure I gave instructions to seal up the office until I could get here."

"Sir," said the clerk, "the wall– it– well, it *wasn't* there, and now it's back again."

Mr. Pennicott sighed. "That's a shame. Did he say when he'd be back? I can't help feeling that it would be a distinct relief to be able to debrief him."

"No, sir. But, sir–"

"Yes, Campion?"

"That was really *Melchior*? The *real* Melchior?"

"Well, Campion, since he was gone before I got here–"

"Yes sir. Sorry sir. Oh! Before he went, he said to tell you that Mordion was disposed of."

Mr. Pennicott's mild eyebrows rose just a little. "How interesting," he said thoughtfully. "There are a lot of people who will be very glad to hear that. Was that why you sent for me?"

"No sir," said Campion. "I'd heard about the Council debacle, of course, but anyone could have said that if they were trying to wriggle in to see you. It's just that when he was asking me to get you, he used the code word for the Crown–"

"I see," said Mr. Pennicott. "Did he, perhaps, have anyone with him?"

"A sulky little girl and a grubby little boy, sir."

"There wasn't a Caliphan with them, by any chance? Tall, with shifty eyes?"

"No, sir."

"Well, well," said Mr. Pennicott. "So Melchior has completed all of his directives at last. I wonder when he'll come back?"

"Do you want me to put someone onto finding him, sir?"

"I shouldn't bother," Mr. Pennicott said. "If he's gone where I think he's gone, it won't do any good. He'll come back when he's ready."

"But isn't he one of ours, sir?"

Mr. Pennicott smiled primly. "In a manner of speaking, Campion; in a manner of speaking. Let me know when he comes back, won't you?"

SEVENTEEN

In the darkness, Annabel heard her tear-snubbed voice mutter: "I can walk by *myself*."

"Of course!" came Melchior's voice, with great affability. "But perhaps I should point out that one of the last people who ran through one of these without me ended up in two pieces?"

"Oh."

"Stop sulking, Ann," said Peter's voice. "I don't know what you're making a fuss about. What's wrong with being queen?"

"*You* be queen, then!" flashed Annabel. "I don't want to be! I didn't ask for a stupid pencil to pick me!"

"It's not a pencil, it's–"

"I know what it is! Where are you taking us *now*?"

"Somewhere pleasant," said Melchior. "I thought you didn't want to be in the Capital? Well, you're not. Aren't I nice?"

"You're a *liar*."

"That's rude, Nan."

"It's true, though," said Peter. "Actually. You lied to us the whole time."

"You didn't even believe I could talk," said Melchior coolly. "I couldn't have lied to you if I'd tried."

"You–"

Melchior, sighing, said: "Do try not to be tedious, Peter. Nan, if you *will* tug away from me like that, I'm going to have to end the tunnel spell."

Annabel, ignoring him, continued to drag herself determinedly ahead, despite his fingers grasped just as determinedly around her wrist.

"Very well," Melchior said, and they stumbled into bright light as the triad blinked startlingly into existence. "We'll walk the rest of the way. Are you satisfied?"

This time, when Annabel tugged ferociously at the grasp around her wrist, Melchior let her go. Rather more annoyed but no less biting than usual, he said: "I would like to know, Nan, if you're planning on ignoring me for the rest of the day?"

"Yes," said Annabel, and continued to stomp ahead.

There was a stifled giggle from Peter. "You can't *tell* him you're not talking to him, Ann!"

"Yes, I can," said Annabel. "I can do anything I want to do. I'm the queen. *And* I didn't give you permission to speak."

"Any more of that and I'll rub your face in the dirt," retorted Peter. "You're not too old to fight, you know!"

Melchior interrupted Annabel's heated reply to say even more bitingly: "If you imagine that I'll stand by while you rub Nan's face in the dirt, you're even more ignorant than I'd come to expect."

"There's no need to be so annoyed about it," muttered

Peter, flushing red. "We'd been rubbing each others' faces in the dirt long before she met you, you know."

Annabel, surprising herself as much as the others, cut in on both of them to say coldly: "I didn't give you permission to speak, either! And you can call me your majesty, if it comes to that!"

"Nan–" began Melchior, and then said in some wrath: "*I'll* rub your face in the dirt. What do you mean by telling me how to address you?"

Annabel turned and glared at them. Then she scraped up two handfuls of dirt and, quite deliberately, smeared them on her own cheeks. "There!" she said. "I've done it myself! Happy? Shut up and leave me alone!"

She stomped away again, trying to ignore Peter, who was giggling helplessly behind her as he followed. She was quite sure that Melchior was laughing, too, so she was gloomily unsurprised when he said a little later, in a voice that was suspiciously even: "You're not *your majesty* until you're officially crowned, Nan: *your highness* is the correct terminology."

This time, Annabel didn't try to reply. Years with both Peter and Blackfoot had taught her that she wasn't capable of beating them when it came to a war of words: her time in the castle had taught her that she didn't have to engage to win without words. And if Rorkin had taught her many things, he had also taught her that silence was a weapon.

So she was silent when Melchior asked loudly enough to be overheard, if Annabel had always given the silent treatment to those who angered her, and Peter said, both coolly and amusedly: "I don't know. I've never annoyed her this much." She was silent when Melchior wondered, also pointedly aloud, if she had any idea of where she was going; silent when he resorted to his old trick of calling: "Nan. Nan. Oh, Nan!" after her, as he had done as Blackfoot.

Before long, Melchior ceased to tease, and a silence grew behind Annabel that felt fully as dangerous as her own. She had begun to feel, in fact, that her choice of weapon was as unfortunate as if she *had* chosen words, when Melchior overtook her on his long legs and stood in her way.

"I'm curious, Nan," he said, and Annabel was taken aback at the anger she heard in his voice. Very little of it showed in his face, unless she counted the thinning of his already thin lips, and that was rather off-putting. "Rorkin imprisoned you in the castle ruins and ran rings around you—kidnapped your best friend, let the castle be taken over bit by bit, allowed you to run into very real danger in pursuance of his plans for you—and you've forgiven him with the sunniest of attitudes. May I ask why the same consideration doesn't extend to me?"

Annabel stared at him for quite some time. At last, she said: "Your *feelings* are hurt?"

"A little, yes. You parted from Rorkin on the best of terms: as a matter of fact, I've never seen you kiss someone before. What did I do to you that he didn't do, worse?"

"He didn't comfort me when I was lonely, and look after me when there was no one else to look after me," said Annabel. "He didn't make fun of me, or shame me into doing things I should do. He didn't sleep on my pillow for five years and never stop talking at the back of my mind so that– anyway, he did what he did when he didn't know me. I *trusted* you. And it's no good," she added, when she saw his mouth open, "it's no good talking to me about it. I'm angry and there's nothing you can say, anyway."

"I see," said Melchior again. She couldn't read the expression on his face, and she wasn't sure about the tone of his voice, either: but Rorkin had said that sometimes she wouldn't know, so that was all right. "Well, I certainly hope you won't give up talking to me altogether. It will be rather difficult to set up your household staff and parliament if you're refusing to talk to me the entire time."

"I'm not going to be queen, either," Annabel said. Rorkin had said there were always choices, and Annabel herself had made a third choice where only two were given to her: she hadn't given up hope that somewhere in all this, she could make another one of those third choices.

"Hang on, Ann!" protested Peter. "You can't just say you won't be queen! The staff chose you."

Melchior said, quite amiably, "Be quiet, Peter," and to Annabel's surprise, Peter *was* quiet. To Annabel, Melchior said once more: "I see. Then do you have any objections if we make a stop somewhere along the way?"

"Somewhere along the way to what?" Annabel asked suspiciously.

"Along the way to being Queen. You don't have to make a decision right now: that's why I took you away from the office. There's somewhere safe—well, moderately safe—that you can spend these three years before making any important decisions."

Annabel looked at him even more suspiciously. "What if you don't like the decision I make?"

"Then I suppose I'll try to change your mind," said Melchior. "And unless you have the faintest idea where you're walking, may I suggest that we use my tunnel spell again?"

That made Annabel stop and take stock of where the first tunnel spell had brought them. They were walking in an open field with the first sun of the triad quite high in the sky, and for the first time, it occurred to her that it was quite a nice day. "Why did you bring us here, then?" she demanded.

"That was *your* fault, Nan!" protested Peter. "You can't blame Melchior for that!"

"Yes, I can!" instantly replied Annabel. "Whose fault is it that I'm so angry I didn't want to hold his hand? Whose fault is it that–"

"Undoubtedly mine," Melchior agreed. "Nan, do you think you can bear to hold my hand for another few minutes? You're quite free, of course, to keep walking for another two weeks to get to the same place that will take us only a minute or two by tunnel spell: no doubt you have your reasons."

Annabel glared at him but took the hand he offered, and on Melchior's other side, Peter did the same.

"How are you going to do a tunnel spell without a wall to burrow into?" he asked. "That other one– I haven't seen anything like that before. Well, besides that one in the castle."

"I don't need a wall," said Melchior. "My tunnel spell is somewhat different to the traditional model. I'll explain it to you later when I can do justice to my cleverness. For now, all you need to know is that I can tunnel through anything and almost any spell."

"Through the castle wards, as well," Annabel said pointedly. "I know."

Melchior cleared his throat. "Are we quarrelling again, Nan? Do mind your step: you might find yourself a little dizzy, but it's nothing to worry about. Here we go–"

The ground before them swirled and turned to darkness as Annabel, all unsuspecting, took her next step. She gasped and grasped Melchior's hand with both of hers, the world tilting around her and realigning as she found her feet in the tunnel spell.

"Brilliant!" crowed Peter, gurgling with laughter. "Never seen anything like it! Even that one in the castle didn't do this!"

"I should think not!" said Melchior. "Nan, this is all very affecting, but do you need to hold my hand *quite* so tightly?"

Annabel muttered and released her death-hold on his hand, forcing one of her hands to drop away altogether and the other to curl loosely within his fingers. "You're not as clever as all *that*," she said aloud.

"Of course I am," Melchior said. "I'm the only person in the whole of the Two Monarchies who can do that spell."

"Only until I find out how to do it," said Peter, with relish. "You'll have to teach me how."

"I'll do nothing of the sort!" Melchior said. "What, give up my notoriety?"

"Notoriety?" spluttered Annabel. "Hah! The little man in the office didn't even know who you were!"

"That's hurtful, Nan. I'll have you know that–"

"Anyway," interrupted Annabel, who didn't care to be chivvied into a conversation with Melchior again, "where exactly are we going?"

"That's what I'd like to know, too," said another voice. It sounded quite inoffensive and curious, but Annabel felt Melchior's fingers suddenly grip hers, and on his other side, Peter's breath hissed through his teeth. "It's not that I'm nosy, but it *is* my house, after all."

They emerged, blinking, into the light interior of a decidedly odd room, and Annabel, edging slightly behind Melchior, saw three people through the gap between his waist and his arm. There was an older man with green—or were they gold?—eyes, and a lady whose dark hair was intermingled with beads, colourful glass, and feathers. That dark hair was also, if Annabel wasn't wrong, moving of its own accord.

When she saw them the lady's face grew bright, and Annabel thought there was the slight sparkle of tears to her eyes. "Melchior!"

"It's good to see you again, Poly," said Melchior, smiling at her in a way that made the wizard step between them.

"I won't have you flirting with her," said the wizard. "There was enough of that sort of thing last time."

"Don't worry," Melchior said. "I'm here for another reason."

"Good grief!" said Peter, who had been staring around at the room. "The floor is grass!"

Poly looked at him in the same bright way that she had looked at Melchior, much to Annabel's interest. There might even have been the slightest suggestion of a laugh in her voice when she said: "Peter! It's good to see you, too."

The wizard muttered something under his breath that might have been: "Huh. I thought it was too quiet to last," and went back to what he had been doing before Melchior's tunnel spell opened the wall in his home. It must have been something distinctly strong, because Peter, who had been staring narrowly at Poly, turned his head instantly to see what it was.

"Is that why the floor is grass?" he asked, pointing at the tangle of root and brick that the wizard seemed to be weaving together.

"The floor is grass because the dog likes it," said the wizard.

Since the only other occupant of the room was a young boy, this confused Annabel. Annoyed at that, and at life in general, she muttered: "That's just silly. How do you sweep up, anyway?"

The wizard looked at her with bright eyes. "That's the joy of it," he said. "You don't."

Annabel tore her gaze away from his compelling green one, and found that the lady was now looking at her thoughtfully. "You're the heir," she said. "So you completed your last directive, Melchior! What's your name, darling?"

"Annabel," said Annabel. Her hand was still in Melchior's, and she tugged it away in annoyance. "I'm not going to be queen."

"I see," said Poly, her grey eyes flicking up at Melchior and then back to Annabel. "You can come into the kitchen with me, if you like: it's time for Onepiece's lunch, so we might as well eat. You'll probably want to wash your face as well, I expect. They'll be busy talking about politics and confidential informants for hours, anyway."

Annabel straightened a little, hopefully, and shot Peter a narrow look when he snickered aloud.

Melchior said: "There is still a lot to discuss, Poly–"

"I'm not going to discuss *anything*," said Annabel. "You don't tell the truth anyway. I'm going to *eat*. You can talk all you want."

Melchior started after them. "Nan–"

"Not you," said Poly, quite firmly. "Talk out here with Luck, if you're going to talk. Annabel and I want to eat."

"I will also have eating," said the young boy, who had been watching Annabel intently. "There is never enough eating. This girl has dirt on her face. I like dirt."

Peter, grinning, said: "You've found a kindred spirit, Ann!"

"You go and eat as well," Melchior said to him, as Annabel was tugged away into the kitchen by the little boy. He called after her: "Nan, we'll talk later."

"But I wanted to ask about the not-magic thing!" protested Peter's fading voice.

"That, *much* later!"

Peter stomped out into the kitchen a moment later, his face sulky. "Your cat's getting a bit much, isn't he, Ann?"

Poly, who was watching them both from the other side of the table, dusted the table with a little flour and said: "I hope you both like scones. Luck likes them, so I learnt how to cook them, but it's about all I *can* make."

"I am liking scones," said the young boy. "I'm like scones?"

"*I like scones*, darling," Poly said. "Or *I'm fond of scones*."

"Because *contractions*," said the boy. To Annabel, seriously, he said: "I'm fond of contractions. I'm Onepiece. What are you? My magic likes you."

"I'm Annabel," said Annabel cautiously.

Reprovingly, Onepiece said: "*Heard* that. But what *thing* are you?"

"She's not a thing, she's a girl," said Poly. More pointedly still, she said: "People are not things, and you need to ask permission if you want to play with her."

"Oh," said Onepiece. "Can't do just a little bit of magic?"

"Not without asking."

"Oh," said Onepiece again. "I'm stopping spell?"

"Unless you want me to tie up your magic for a day," agreed Poly.

Annabel, very much confused, asked: "Was he doing a spell?"

"Yes," said Poly. "Sorry about that. We're still learning about asking permission first. Luck has a habit of forgetting things like that, so I'm trying to make sure Onepiece remembers. You're such a bright little beacon that he forgot his manners."

"I'm a *beacon*?"

Poly nodded, kneading her dough while Onepiece wriggled his fingers at the flour that floated in the air and turned it into different shapes. "Even my magic is trying to get closer to you, and I've usually got it under pretty good control these days. Do you see how my hair is wafting toward you?"

"I *thought* it was moving!" said Peter in triumph. "That's– I haven't ever seen anything like that! I can't even tell what sort of magic yours is: it's got too many different facets."

"Ah yes. Remind me to show you my anti-magic arm later."

Peter, sitting up very straight, said excitedly: "Is *that* what that is? I didn't know it could be found in people."

"It can't," said Poly. "Technically, that is. Annabel, if you want to wash your face, there's a basin over there. It fills and empties itself, so don't be alarmed. I usually use it for washing peas."

Annabel left her seat and inspected the basin with some caution, but it wasn't so very frightening, after all: it filled itself in a smooth flow from a small, pumpless faucet, and then seemed to wait patiently for her to begin.

"Baths," said Onepiece, who had followed her over to the sink, "is necessary and evil."

"A *necessary evil*, darling," said Poly, as Annabel dipped the fingers of one hand in the basin. "Now, I quite understand *you*, Annabel, but why are you travelling with Peter?"

"That's Rorkin's fault," Annabel said grumpily, splashing water over her dirty, swollen face. It was pleasantly cool without being too cold.

"Rorkin," said Poly thoughtfully. "How interesting."

"Ann's just annoyed because he put the castle back three years into the past. Well, three years into *our* past, anyway."

"Thought I felt something odd this morning," said Luck's

voice, from the doorway. "Poly, I was promised scones, and there are no scones."

"If you're in that much of a hurry, you can magic them yourself."

"Can't," Luck said sadly. "They taste wrong. Yours are the best scones, Poly."

Annabel was wiping her face, but she saw the pleased flush that rose in Poly's face. Poly said: "It's no good buttering me up. They still have to cook. Ten minutes."

"We'll come back in ten minutes, then," said Luck, but Melchior was already pushing into the room to inspect Annabel's face.

"Much better," he said. "You don't look like a snotty little girl any more."

"You can find a couple of rooms for Annabel and Peter to stay in, then," Poly told Luck. "Not ones that will wander off again, either."

"*I* don't mind!" said Peter at once, looking very much interested. "Oh! You mean Ann! Oh well, I can go and find her if she goes missing, after all."

"Wait," said Annabel uncertainly. "I'm to live– I don't want to live here! I'm going to live with Blackfoot. With Melchior, that is."

"I thought you were still cross with him," said Peter impatiently. "Make up your mind, Ann!"

"I am," Annabel said. "But at least I know he's a liar now. I know not to trust him. And if I have to be queen, I'm going to make sure he's got to do something nasty, as well."

"Well," said Melchior, grinning, "then that's settled. Annabel's my ward. I'll keep her at my place in– what?"

Poly, shaking her head, dusted off her floury hands and said: "You can't, Melchior. What would people think?"

"What would they– I'm old enough to be her father!"

"You're not, you know," said Luck. "What is she, fourteen, fifteen? Even if you count five years of being a cat—you *can't*, by the way, because your human self hasn't aged and some idiot thought it was a good idea to involve you in a three year time shift—you're still only...wait, how old is he, Poly?"

"Twenty-four, at my count," said Poly. "And my count won't matter, anyway, because people will think you've only been gone two years. You can't, Melchior. You don't look a day over twenty."

"Exactly," said Luck, who didn't look much older than Melchior himself.

"If we're going to talk about human selves not aging," said Melchior, his sarcastic mouth particularly thin, "we might consider this instance a particularly egregious example of the nose telling the feet they smell."

Annabel coughed a laugh into her collar in spite of herself, and Peter grinned.

"Besides," said Luck, ignoring both the jibe and Annabel and Peter's laughter, "she'll have to go to school eventually. It's no good trying to learn to be a queen here. She'll have to go to Trenthams, I should think."

"*I* want to stay here," said Peter unexpectedly. "I can't go back just yet, anyway. Ann, you can come back to visit on holidays. I want to learn about magic here."

"I want to see *Blackfoot* on holidays," Annabel said, rather more loudly.

"Well, that shouldn't be a problem," Poly said thoughtfully. "There's no need to start at Trenthams until you're sixteen or seventeen, anyway. If you're going to visit your guardian during holidays, with a friend, there shouldn't be too many raised brows. You'll have to clear out your house and get a housekeeper, though, Melchior."

"And a maid for Nan," agreed Melchior.

Luck tilted his head and stared at Annabel until she wanted to squirm out of sight. "All right, but what do we do with her until then?"

"I'm *here*," she said. "I'm not '*her*'."

Luck only stared at her for a little longer before he said: "I can't teach her anything about magic, you know. She won't understand. What will she do here?"

"I'll give her lessons," said Melchior. "I'll be gone for a while to visit Mr. Pennicott, but after that, we'll begin lessons on foreign policy, statecraft, and how to say things nicely."

"Yes," said Annabel, not nicely. "You can teach me how to lie. It'll probably be very useful."

"Nan, I'm *sorry*."

"No, you're not," Annabel said. She knew he was sorry, to a certain extent; she was also quite well aware that he was, to a large degree, *not* sorry. "You'd do the exact same thing again."

"Yes," said Melchior. "That's why you have to forgive me. I'm not sorry, Nan: forgive me."

"All right," Annabel said. She saw that he was looking slightly speculative, and added: "Don't go giving me another cat."

Melchior choked, and Poly chuckled.

"Nan–"

"I don't like cats."

"All right, all right, Nan. I won't give you another cat. It simply occurred to me that you might like–"

"Well, I wouldn't, so don't."

"She has *dog* now," said Onepiece, leaning his head

worshipfully against Annabel's hip and grabbing her hand with both of his. "Dogs are *better*."

Melchior eyed him with disfavour, but only said: "Very well. I'll bring you something back from the Capital instead."

Annabel huffed out a breath. "I suppose I'll stay here until I have to go to Trenthams, then."

"That's very good of you, Nan. I'm sure Poly feels adequately thanked for her hospitality."

Annabel, who had never learned the niceties of behaviour with Grenna, turned her eyes on Poly, and saw that she was looking very much amused. "Oh, sorry. I didn't mean to be rude."

"That's quite all right," Poly said. "Luck still hasn't learned to be polite yet, and he's rather older than you."

Luck gave Annabel a glassy look that she returned with one of her flat, blank looks. It made Melchior choke with laughter, and Poly's low little chuckle curled through the air again.

"Oh, I'm looking forward to this!" she said. "I would have been glad to see you again anyway, Melchior, but this is just wonderful. And now that Isabella has gone to Trenthams for her first year, it'll be nice to have some company for Onepiece around the house."

"The little firebrand is grown up, is she?"

"Sixteen," agreed Poly. "And she's so stylish, Melchior!"

"When was she anything else?" enquired Melchior, his hazel eyes nearly as fond as Annabel had ever seen them.

Frowning, she asked: "Who is grown up?"

"Isabella Farrah," Poly said. "She's the daughter of our ambassador. Goodness, that will be fun, too! We'll have to arrange a meeting for you– I don't suppose you particularly love clothes, do you? There's no need to choke, Melchior.

Never mind, Isabella has an adaptive sort of mind: you'll get along very well, I think."

"Who knows, Ann?" said Peter, grinning, "Maybe that's why Rorkin put the castle back in the wrong time. He probably thought it's the only way you'd make friends."

"*You* should talk," Annabel told him. "I'm the only one who can put up with you, at school."

"I'm constantly astonished at your forbearance," agreed Melchior. "And speaking of forbearance, Poly, I suppose you know that Luck's already eaten all the scones...?"

————

If you enjoyed *Blackfoot*, please consider leaving a review on Amazon, Goodreads, or your blog/social media. Sharing the love helps me sell more books, and selling more books helps me write more books!

You can keep up with all the latest news and book releases by joining the WR(ite) newsletter.

————